THE EXHIBITION

Book Three in the Executive Decisions trilogy

An erotic novel

Grace Marshall

Published by Xcite Books Ltd – 2013
ISBN 9781908917843

The story contained within this book is a work of fiction. Names and characters are the product of the author's imagination and any resemblance to actual persons, living or dead, is entirely coincidental.

The Exhibition is dedicated to the wild and wonderful world we live in, love in, and are inspired by and to the deep connection we have to it. May we never take that precious connection for granted.

Thank you, with all of my heart to:

Renee and Jo and all of the lovely Ladiez at Sh! Thanks for all of your inspiration, wisdom and encouragement. You are truly my heroes! Hugs and kisses and my deepest gratitude.

Hazel Cushion, and Liz Coldwell and all the fabulous people at Xcite Books for making my dream of the *Executive Decision Trilogy* a reality.

Lucy Felthouse, for boundless PR expertise and even more boundless patience when it comes to staving off more than a few panic attacks and encouraging this neurotic writer to soldier on. Thanks for all that you do. I couldn't have done it without you, EP!

Kay Jaybee, for being my partner in crime, my "terrible twin", and for just being your fabulous, beautiful self. The journey has been so much more fun because we've shared it. You're amazing!

Raymond, for putting up with all my neurotic craziness and loving me anyway. Thank you for believing in me and being proud of me and easing the journey. There's no one I would rather have by my side for the ride. Volim te mnogo!

Prologue

What she was about to ask was a terrible thing to ask of a friend. Stacie Emerson had ridden MAX in from Gresham, which had taken forever, but the long ride on public transport gave her time to think about it, to back out and turn the whole event into just two friends meeting for coffee. And then what? Where else could she turn? The two met in Pioneer Square just before the deluge began.

Kendra Davis gave her a fierce hug, and they hurried the few blocks to the coffee shop that looked up on to Portlandia, Raymond Kaskey's colossal sculpture, which graced the third story of the Portland Building. Just as the downpour got serious, they shoved their way into the cafe and settled at a table near the window with a good view of the sculpture. It had always been one of Stacie's favorite things about Portland. She never grew tired of it, no matter how many times she looked up at Portlandia with her hair caught up in the artist's imagined breeze, with her strong Amazon body leaning down from on high, trident in one hand while the other arm reached out to the world below. Stacie never got over the urge to lift her arms up to the sculpture in hopes of being drawn into her magnanimous, muscular embrace.

When both women had given Portlandia the

homage she so richly deserved, they turned their attention to each other.

'How's Garrett?' Stacie asked.

'Recovering nicely, thanks. He's a horrible patient, though. I practically have to tie him to the bed to get him to rest.'

Stacie offered her a wicked smile. 'Somehow I can't picture him really minding that too much – you tying him to the bed, I mean.' Was she mistaken, or did Kendra actually blush? 'And what about you? How are you doing? I mean recovering from what you've been through can't be an easy task.' Stacie shivered at the thought of Kendra's ordeal at the hands of a stalker and what might have happened if her friend hadn't been made of sterner stuff than just about anyone she'd ever met.

Kendra looked down at her hands folded around her cup and the smile she offered, though genuine, clearly took some effort. 'I'm all right. The dreams are coming less and less often, and I'm seeing a psychologist. We both are. I won't lie; sometimes it's rough, but we have each other and …' This time her face broke into a broad, easy smile. 'God, I can't get used to saying that … We have each other. It sounds so presumptuous, yet I love it.'

'It sounds just perfect,' Stacie said, giving her arm a squeeze. 'And you two deserve to be very, very happy together.'

Kendra reached up and patted her hand. 'You should stop by for dinner some night. I don't cook, but I've learned Garrett makes a mean bolognaise.'

Stacie offered her a knowing smile. 'He certainly does. Who do you think taught him how to make it?'

She waved a dismissive hand. 'But honestly, to see the two of you so happy, I'd come for peanut butter sandwiches.'

'That I think I could almost manage,' Kendra said. Then the smile slipped from her face, and she held Stacie in a gaze that was all business. 'Now that you know how Garrett and I are, I imagine it's K. Ryde you really need to talk to, or you would have met me at Garrett's or invited me for a look-see at the progress you're making at the gallery.'

Kendra was dressed in a white T-shirt, faded jeans, and a pair of black ankle boots. Her hair, once again golden-blond, was pulled back in a ponytail and she wore no make-up. No one would have ever imagined her to be the best in her field. Only a small handful of people knew anything about the mysterious PR guru, K. Ryde, and if they did, they'd certainly never met the legend in person. K. Ryde had worked for Stacie all this time, and it had only been during the horrible incident with Kendra's stalker, when K. Ryde was working for Garrett, that she'd actually discovered Ryde's true identity.

'When I hired the Ryde Agency,' Stacie began, 'it was a long-term project, and then – well, then it was all so nebulous. I mean, I had no idea who K. Ryde really was, and it didn't matter. But now –' She scooted closer to the table and leaned over it. 'Now it does.'

Kendra laid down the spoon she'd just used to scoop a mound of cinnamon-dusted foam from her cappuccino into her mouth. 'Then you're ready for the next phase.'

Stacie nodded, feeling the tremor of nerves in her belly as she thought about what the next phase would mean. To both of them. 'And I need to know if I've been handed over to the agency or if you're still in charge. I assume you were in charge.'

Kendra offered her a half-smile in response. 'I was always in charge, and your … request intrigued me a lot so I took a personal interest. You're one of the few clients I kept after I sold the agency, one of the few that I could continue working for on my own without anyone being the wiser for it. And I only did that because it interested me so much.'

'Even after everything with Dee and Ellis? I mean, I know you blamed me, and rightfully so,' Stacie said.

Kendra studied her for a moment, then nodded slowly. 'K. Ryde's business is business, Stacie. My personal feelings didn't figure into it. K. Ryde never got involved personally … not until Garrett came into the picture, and that was … well, that was something I could have never foreseen.'

Love was like that, Stacie thought. She released a shaky breath and wiped sweaty palms on her trousers. 'I guess I need to know if I'll be continuing to work with you, now I'm ready to move forward with … my project, or if I'll be working with someone I don't know.'

Again Kendra studied her. 'Do you want someone to take over?'

Stacie shook her head and stared down into her cup, trying to gather her thoughts. 'It's just that – well, what happens next … you probably won't like, and now that our situation has changed, I'm not sure I like having my friend involved. In fact, what I'm about to ask is a pretty terrible thing to do to a friend, if you want the truth.'

'Stacie, if you want me to hand you over to the agency, all you have to do is ask. But …'

'But no one else could handle it like you could, if they could handle it at all, right?'

Kendra didn't answer. She only held Stacie's gaze.

'I know that, and yet I also know what it'll mean.' Stacie looked out at the sculpture with its outstretched hand as though somehow it would offer her an easy answer for what she knew was ahead of her. But there were no easy answers. There could be none. She knew that. 'It's just that I … Well, it's complicated.'

'Most of what K. Ryde deals with is complicated, Stacie. That's why K. Ryde deals with it.'

There was a sudden flash of sunshine through the rainclouds, bathing the sculpture in bright light, and Stacie blinked back the after-image, then turned her gaze back to Kendra, who sat for a second with Portlandia's features superimposed onto her own. Then Stacie blinked again and it was Kendra who sat across from her, offering a sympathetic smile.

She knew how tough Kendra was, how much fire there was in that slender frame. But she also knew what the woman had already been through, and what she was about to ask her seemed cruel.

'After everything that's happened … to you, to Garrett, I don't know …'

'Stacie, Garrett and I are both struggling to put what happened with Edge behind us and move on. For me, that means finally being able to have my life back. Oh, I'm not moving back to California.' She nodded up at the sculpture. 'Portland is my home and I want to stay here – especially the way things are with Garrett and me now. But I have no intention of not working and, frankly, you know me well enough to know how bored I'd be with anything that wasn't up to K. Ryde's usual clientele.'

'What about Garrett?'

Kendra raised a golden eyebrow. 'What about Garrett? My love life most definitely doesn't involve breaking client confidentiality. If you want me to finish what we started, I will. In fact, I've always had every intention to.'

Stacie gripped her hands in her lap to keep them from shaking. 'You won't like it.'

'Tell me, and let me decide,' Kendra said.

Forty-five minutes and two more lattes and a Diet Pepsi later, Kendra blew out a sharp breath and scrubbed a hand over her face. 'You're right. I don't like it.'

Stacie felt her stomach drop and the fear that all of her efforts, everything she had done so far, had been for nothing threatened to overwhelm her. 'Then I need to find someone else?'

Kendra shook her head slowly. 'I didn't say that. I just said I didn't like it. Besides, you wouldn't find anyone else who'd do this for you, even if they could.'

'I don't want to … I never wanted to put you at risk.'

Kendra reached across the table and took Stacie's hand in a strong grip. 'Some things are worth the risk, sweetie. But this is the last time we meet like this. From now on you only see Kendra Davis in person. K. Ryde will be in touch and inform you of what comes next.' She squeezed her hand hard. 'I mean it, Stacie. From this moment on, you've never met K. Ryde, and you won't ever meet him again. Are we clear?'

Stacie squared her shoulders and nodded, unable to speak around the claw of nerves in her chest.

Kendra's face softened to a warm smile, and she released Stacie's hand with a gentle pat. 'Good. Now the sun's out and I'm dying for a walk along the river so that I can bore you beyond words with the latest about Garrett and me.'

And really, there was nothing in the whole world Stacie needed more at that moment.

Chapter One

Stacie nearly fell off the chair behind her desk as she jerked to wakefulness. It took her a second to realize she was in her office at the gallery. A quick glance at her watch told her she had maybe a half-hour before the workmen arrived. She yawned and stretched, then shoved to her feet to open the utilitarian mini-blinds. They would soon be replaced with lush spring green drapes at windows that would be flanked by plants from the same nursery that had furnished the greenery for Ellis when he'd opened the Pneuma Building.

Even unfinished as it was, she loved the feel of the place and what she was building it into. Stacie already owned a thriving gallery, and she had every intention of making the West Coast gallery as successful as the one in New York. Two trips to Japan in as many months and the constant yo-yoing back and forth to New York until she could get her manager there trained and up to speed had pretty much guaranteed that she wasn't getting enough rest. She was jetlagged as hell, so she tried to make the best of it and get some work done when she couldn't sleep. That was to be expected. It was a challenging time. It wouldn't last forever. But the stress of opening the new gallery meant the nightmare she had lived through in the early days of the New York gallery was bound to bubble up and kick her unconscious in the butt. It had been a bad dream that had woken her in the wee hours this morning. Even the pep talk she had given herself – that this time was different, that this time she was going in with her eyes open, that this time she knew what she was doing – didn't lull her back to sleep, so here she was.

She glanced round her makeshift office with its folding chair and battered pine desk buried beneath shipping documents for the Japanese part of the exhibition and plans for the completion of the interior of the gallery. In her office, the walls were already painted, the floor was laid. The furniture would be delivered next week, and that included a comfy chair and a sofa for her to doze on when she was jetlagged. It was coming together, she thought. It was coming together.

Just then her BlackBerry buzzed. She scrabbled to find it beneath the stack of papers, nearly dropping it in the trash can when she finally unburied it and read the reminder to call Harris Walker. Again. She'd already rescheduled the call three times in the past 24 hours because she knew the drill. Either she'd get his voicemail and he wouldn't return her call or he'd tell her he couldn't talk right now, but he'd get back to her, and then he wouldn't. But Harris Walker had no idea just how tenacious she was and how badly she wanted his work for the gallery's opening exhibition. He'd have to personally tell her to fuck off and die before she would even begin to take the hint. And though Harris Walker didn't much like her, she knew he was way too nice to tell her to fuck off and die.

The sunshine was just beginning to make a golden

path onto the newly laid wood floor, and she had it on good authority that Harris would be up. In fact, she had it on good authority that he'd spent the past night in a hide photographing great horned owls. Owls slept in the daytime so she figured he'd be finishing up, but not yet have had time to tuck up in his jammies for a nap. She'd invite him to breakfast. Surely he must be starving after spending the night in the woods. Of course, even if he were, he'd still tell her no. Then she'd invite him for coffee and work her way down from there. Maybe they could compromise on a glass of tepid water in her disaster of an office.

She really didn't need to refresh her memory on Harris Walker's work. She'd studied his photographs in detail long before she knew him in person, back when she'd had no reason to believe that when they actually met he wouldn't like her. But as she pulled up the website of *Wilderness Vanguard*, she told herself it was to give him time to get back to civilization before she became the unpleasant point in his morning. He was the editor of the *Vanguard*, and some of his work was in almost every issue.

After she'd looked through the latest edition, she brought up Harris' own website and flipped through the photo galleries. She flipped past the photos of pristine Cascade scenery, past the photos of birds preening and elk rutting, past the photos of sunsets over the Pacific Ocean and sea lions lolling in the sand near Lincoln City. She even flipped past the gripping photo-diary he had done of his trip to the forests of Valderia with Ellis a few months ago. She flipped instead to the images of mining run-off and erosion-ravaged landscapes, to the photos of landfills, oil-slickened waterways and clear-cuts, to the photos of small, dying communities that'd lost their livelihood when the lumber industry went belly-up. As she studied them for the hundredth time, she wondered how he did it; how he could revel in such beauty as the Northwest was famous for, then immerse himself in landscapes from hell without somehow damaging his soul. She'd like to ask him if he'd ever consent to at least meet her for coffee.

She really thought that, of Dee Henning's two best friends, Harris would be the easiest to win over. Stacie knew what men saw when they looked at her, and she seldom had to do much more than smile at a man to get his attention. Socially, she wasn't even close to desperate. She was used to being able to date anyone she wanted whenever she wanted.

Though Harris Walker was definitely the stuff of sex dreams, with his broad shoulders and outdoorsy good looks, all she wanted was the man's photos. It was strictly business. At first, she thought he simply couldn't forgive her for her inadvertent role in her and Garrett's bumbling attempt to get Dee and Ellis together, the attempt that had nearly had the opposite result. But Garrett he seemed to have forgiven, so she suspected his less than warm feelings toward her had as much to do with her past relationship with Garrett and Ellis as anything. Ex fiancée to one, ex-wife to the other. OK, it wasn't a shining resume, but she had only been 18, for fuck sake, and that horrible mistake had cost her way more than she could have ever imagined.

Anyway, it wasn't like she was asking Harris to marry her, or even to like her. Could he possibly think she'd try to seduce him? There were at least five other wildlife photographers who were practically begging to be a part of her opening exhibition, but it was Harris she wanted. She flipped back through the pictures of devastation one last time, then grabbed the BlackBerry and pulled up his number.

It rang until it went to voicemail. She rolled her eyes, then put on her sweetest voice and asked him, for the hundredth time, if they could get together to talk about the exhibition. When she hung up, she left a text as well, all the while having visions of the man slapping a restraining order on her. Well, that's what he'd have to do if he wanted her to give up. She'd beg, bargain and grovel if she had to. She'd try again a little later.

While she made herself coffee in the kitchenette next to her office, she went down the mental list of questions she'd ask him, just in case today was the day when he actually gave in and returned her call.

Still thinking about the stubbornly uncooperative Harris Walker, she started a second pot of coffee. The workmen would be here soon and the bakery around the corner would be delivering shortly. She had made special arrangements for a delivery daily as long as the workers were finishing up the gallery. She needed them happy and pleased to do things exactly the way she wanted, and nothing said *do it my way* quite as nicely as fresh pastries and quality French roast coffee.

That done, she took her own coffee back to her desk. She glanced through Harris's photo galleries again, studying the horrendous detail of some of the scenes of destruction and environmental damage. She took a pen and a small pad of paper and scribbled notes about the ones she hoped to include in her exhibition. While she was at it, she made a note to call the young reporter, Carla Flannery, for more details about the illegal landfill she had uncovered in the John Day area. There was a whole series of photos on Harris' site from that unfortunate incident.

While jotting down notes, she tried Harris' number again. Still no answer. She left another message and decided to let it go for the day. She could only do so much harassing before she had to give the poor guy a break. She had dinner plans with Dee and Ellis this evening before she took the red-eye to New York, and if he hadn't gotten back to her by then, she would exercise her option to manipulate and get the two of them to talk to him. He'd probably like her less for it, but since she didn't know him well enough to know how much less he was still capable of liking her, she supposed she could live with that. The man was just being stubborn. He'd exhibited his work all over the Northwest and beyond. She'd made it clear the proceeds from the exhibition would go to fund the Vigilant Trust, which *Wilderness Vanguard* and Ellis and his company had been instrumental in starting between them. The Vigilant Trust was money for reclaiming land that had been damaged and for helping the communities that had suffered from job losses. Stacie was proud that her gallery would begin its life supporting such a good cause.

Into her silent reverie, her BlackBerry buzzed the arrival of a text, causing her to jump and drop the notepad onto the floor. Maybe this was it. Maybe Harris Walker was finally getting back to her. Her mind was already racing as she grabbed for it. She had no doubt she could convince him to allow her to exhibit his work if he'd just listen to her. She was sure he'd be intrigued.

When she opened the text, all thoughts of the exhibition, all thoughts of Harris Walker, all thoughts of the workmen she could now hear arriving, went out of her head. Her stomach rebelled, and for a second, she thought she would vomit her coffee. But she forced herself to breathe deeply, forced herself to calm and focus. After all, this was not unexpected. She had lived in the shadow of this moment for ten years, and she would never be more ready to face it than she was now. She took another breath, squared her shoulders and read it.

Welcome to the West Coast, Stacie. It's such a pleasure to have you close once again. Feels like old times. We must meet for drinks and dinner. I'm dying to catch up on all your news. I do hope the gallery renovations are going without a snag. So many unexpected, and expensive, glitches can happen when you're on a tight deadline.

Yours always,

TJ

The BlackBerry slipped from her hands, and disappeared in the mound of papers on her desk as she shoved back the chair and ran for the stairs.

'What the fuck?' she heard one of the workmen exclaim, and she nearly ran into Ted, the foreman who was racing up the stairs toward her. He caught her before she could lose her balance. His expression was hard; his voice tightly controlled. 'Ms. Emerson, you'd better come look at this.'

He kept a protective hand under her elbow as he

led her into the main exhibition hall. It was probably a good thing he did. The red paint was splashed over the newly laid floor and onto the freshly painted wall where it dried in thick spatters. Oxygen rushed from her lungs and everything else disappeared as the past forced its way into the void. 'Zoe!' Stacie could never remember if she had actually called out her friend's name or if it were only in her head. She was no longer in the vandalized gallery. She was transported back to Zoe's flat, back to the gunshot that shattered her world, back to the blood on the walls.

'Everything was locked up just like we left it last night, just like always,' Ted was saying, but the rest of his words were drowned out by the ringing in her ears and the present fell further away.

When she allowed herself to think about that horrible time, it was always with thoughts of what might have been if she could have gotten Zoe away from him, if they could have gone somewhere he couldn't find them. Strangely, it was his scent that permeated all of her memories of him. Every time she had ever been with him it had surrounded her, practically drowned her; when he held her, when he stroked her hair, when he caressed her. He always smelled like the desert, with everything that was dangerous about it. Everything that was poisonous or desolate or sharp-angled and deadly seemed to seep through his pores in a way that was both dark and compelling. How was it that something as simple as the way someone smelled could elicit such desire, such hope, such terror, such rage? How was it that the scent of the man was the first thing she remembered about him and the last thing that haunted her in her dreams?

When she came back to herself she was seated on a folding chair and Ted was offering her a glass of water. This is how it all begins, she reminded herself. And this was not the time to be squeamish. It wasn't as though she hadn't expected to hear from Terrance Jamison. That was inevitable. It was just that she hadn't expected to hear from him quite so soon, and she had at least expected a little grace period before the harassing began.

'Shall I call the police?' Ted was saying.

She shook her head. 'No.' There was a shuffling and a mumble of surprise among the workmen. She drank the water down and stood. 'I know what this is all about, and I don't have time to go through a police investigation, which will turn up nothing, not if this gallery's going to open on schedule. How soon can you fix it?' she asked Ted. Before he could respond, she added, 'I don't care how much it costs. I don't care what it takes. I need it fixed immediately if not sooner.'

The foreman looked around at his crew. 'All right, I can call in some extra workers, we can arrange for an extra shift, work into the night if we have to. But are you sure you don't want the police to check this out? This is vandalism, ma'am, and no doubt –'

She cut him off. 'I know what it is, and I'm sure. Just do whatever it takes. I'll be in my office if you need me.' She turned on shaky legs and walked carefully back to the stairs. Already Ted was barking orders and the place erupted into action. Back in her office, she forced herself to read the text through one more time and then again. She forced herself to remember, to remember all of it, all she knew and all that she couldn't prove, but she knew with a certainty that was unshakeable. She forced herself to remember every detail, every nuance, every injury suffered, and when it felt like a cold, hard stone in the pit of her stomach, she closed the text without answering it.

Chapter Two

Harris Walker shifted in the branches of the beech tree just enough to allow the feeling to flow back into his numb legs and instantly regretted it as the pins and needles of returning circulation shot down to his toes. He gritted his teeth and forced himself to hold still. He'd never photographed a family of great horned owls as up close and personal as this before, and he was determined to get just a few more shots into the neighboring tree before he was forced to call it a night. The sun had been up nearly an hour, and the birds should have settled down to sleep by now, but an unexpected bedtime snack had delayed the normal routine.

The female was divvying up bits of a freshly killed skunk among the three fairly mature branchers. Skunk was one of the favorite foods of great horned owls who, blessedly, had no sense of smell. Harris, however, did, and even olfactory fatigue wasn't quite enough to keep his eyes from watering at the barbed scent of skunk musk, which didn't exactly make for good photos. That really irritated him because this was a view into the life of these birds only days, he would guess, before the adults sent their progeny out to fend for themselves and find their own territories. The golds and bronzes of early morning light, with the dappled shadows of the foliage, would make for interesting shots.

He was in an uncomfortable position, halfway up a good-sized beech tree looking over into the branches of the neighboring oak where the owl family had settled. He knew he shouldn't be. He knew it was risky, especially being out here on his own. But after the previous night's less than satisfactory shoot in the hide, he'd opted for the tree this time and was rewarded with some truly intimate shots of the birds. But he was tired now. His body ached from his vigil, and the smell of skunk was becoming nearly unbearable. Just a few more shots, then, when the adults settled in to rest, he'd scramble down and be home in time for breakfast.

Gradually, the pins and needles subsided in his leg. He blinked his watering eyes and kept shooting. Just a few more shots … He leaned out precariously onto the branch, wrapping his legs around its girth and securing his position with his feet, ankles turned, the soles of his hiking boots pressing hard into the wood. He was just focusing in for a close-up of the largest brancher, who was doing its best to swallow the huge piece of skunk, when, into the silence, his Blackberry rang, and both the adult owls were instantly hyper-vigilant. Shit! Had he really forgotten to turn the stupid thing off? He never forgot. Ever!

Hanging on for dear life with his legs, he contorted himself to reach it in his pocket before he realized the offending device was still in his backpack, which he had left at the bottom of the tree. It was a damn good thing he had. Immediately, the owls' necks swiveled *Exorcist*-style, and those wild yellow eyes honed in on the bag, instead of him. The female rose up silently, the tips of her wing feathers nearly slapping Harris in the face, before both she and the male attacked his pack, talons first, with a terrifying force. He figured the female, who was the larger of the two, weighed in somewhere around five pounds. That might not sound like much, but it was five pounds of super-charged predator on wings that spanned well over a meter, and most of that weight was muscle, sharp beak and talons – talons strong enough to sever the spinal cord of its prey and do severe damage to a human, even one the size of Harris. As the device kept mindlessly ringing they kept attacking. And it wasn't difficult to see that the backpack was losing the battle. They continued to shred it even after the BlackBerry went silent.

Harris stayed very still, holding his breath, goose flesh rising on his neck. Jesus! It could have been him. Whatever had possessed him to leave the phone in his backpack could very well have saved his bacon. Great horned owls were known for being aggressive, especially close to their nest or their young. He held tight and watched the destruction below. And when the backpack was truly destroyed, and the owls seemed to consider it no longer a threat, they decided to find a more peaceful place to finish their snack.

Once they'd flown, he waited a full five minutes before he moved, straining to hear owl sounds or see the returning flutter of wings. There was neither. He eased his aching body down the tree and surveyed the pathetic remains of his pack, which was not only well-shredded but liberally dotted in owl poop.

He found the offending phone and shoved it into his pocket; he stuffed everything he could salvage into one of the waterproof bags he always carried in the pack for kayaking trips, then stuck the remains of the backpack in on top and sealed the bag. He'd no sooner finished than the BlackBerry began to ring again. But it was quickly drowned out by the squawks of the owls, who returned with a vengeance. With the phone tinkling away merrily and the two adult birds dive-bombing him, Harris half ran, half belly-flopped beneath the partially upturned stump. Fuck! Why hadn't he remembered to turn the damn thing off, and who the hell would call him at this hour anyway?

From the safety of his hidey-hole, he pulled out the offending device and frantically clicked it into silent mode, but not before he noticed that it was Stacie Emerson who'd been trying to call him. Damn it, he thought to himself as he listened to the squawks and barks of the angry owls, why couldn't she just leave him alone? He really didn't want to work with her. Maybe Ellis and Dee and even Kendra could forgive and forget, but he didn't find it that easy. How could someone be all sweetness and light and do the things she'd done? And how could everyone just pretend that none of it had ever happened?

Other than the text that told him he had two missed calls, there was a text from Stacie as well.

Hi Harris,

Ellis told me you spent the night with the owls and that I might be able to catch you when you'd finished the photo shoot. Would love to treat you to breakfast and talk about the exhibition. I really think you'll like my ideas.

Stacie

Harris shut down the device with a stern punch of

the keys and shoved it back in his pocket. Who the hell did she think she was to pretend like all was well and wonderful, to act like they were best buds? They weren't! He didn't want to be her buddy, and he didn't want to work with the woman.

He tried not to think about the way she'd draped her arm over his and acted as though they were all but in the sack together at that press conference, back when Kendra was pretending to be the hotshot romance novelist Tess Delaney. Well, at least Garrett Thorne had grown a pair and come clean. Everyone knew now that Tess Delaney was really Garrett. And everyone knew that he was head over heels in love with Harris' friend, Kendra Davis. Harris still wasn't sure he liked that idea, but even he had to admit he loved seeing that silly grin that lit up Kendra's face every time she talked about Garrett.

That was fine, that was fair enough. And Garrett was Ellison Thorne's brother, after all. There wasn't anyone Harris respected more than he respected Ellis. And if Garrett was Ellis' brother, and he did right by Kendra, Harris supposed he could learn to tolerate him. But in all honesty, he couldn't see why his benevolence should extend to Stacie Emerson. Stacie had been engaged to one Thorne brother and had eloped with the other. Surely that was not the mark of someone who could be trusted. And no matter how many excuses everyone made for her, well, in his opinion they were just excuses.

And damned if he didn't find himself sporting wood, thinking about her! That really pissed him off. OK, so she was beautiful. No one could argue with that. She had all the right curves in all the right places, and when they were pressed up close in his personal space, well, he was a man, wasn't he? And in his weakest moments, his very weakest moments, when he was tired from spending the night in a hide taking pictures, when he'd spent the day with the board of directors of *Wilderness Vanguard*, he had, on the very rare occasion, fantasized about what it might be like to have her no doubt substantial charms turned in his direction. But those were weak moments and they didn't happen very often. Well, not all *that* often.

The sun was properly up now, and sweat trickled down his back and under his armpits as he eased his way out from under the tree stump, secure in the fact that the offending BlackBerry would not betray his presence to the owls again. He shuffled down the slope toward the Jeep, muscles aching from the night in the tree, and, as he settled into the driver's seat, he resisted the urge to check back and see if there was another message from Stacie. Kendra had told him the woman made incredible blueberry pancakes, and wow, did that sound good right now. His stomach rumbled. His mind conjured an exquisite image of Stacie, that pale hair of hers all bedroom mussed, making him blueberry pancakes, clad in nothing but a loosely tied silk bathrobe barely long enough to cover her luscious bottom. Now he was hungry, *and* he had a hard-on. Damn the woman! He started the engine and headed down the canyon. He'd stop at a drive-through and grab something. He was anxious to see the photos he'd taken, and not at all anxious to talk to Stacie Emerson, even if it were just business. Even if she bribed him with blueberry pancakes.

Chapter Three

'You're early,' Dee said, giving Harris a bear hug that threatened to crunch his ribs. 'It's just as well; we're running a little late. Ellis is just now home and in the shower. The cooking's done. It's Galina's evening off with her sister – a girls' night out to celebrate her niece's engagement – so I told her I'd take care of the salad. Even I can't mess up a salad. You can wash the lettuce.' She returned to chopping cucumbers.

The boardroom was Dee's forte, not the kitchen, but of the Three Musketeers, Dee, Kendra and Harris, she was best at cooking real food in a pinch. Now that she spent as much of her time at Ellis' house as at her own, she had the benefit of a real cook at least some of the time, and Galina was amazing. Still, Dee could have served up stale cheese sandwiches and Harris wouldn't have minded. As well as the chance to spend time with his friends, it was the view from Ellis' balcony and the lovely woodlands beyond that he loved, and that's what he'd come early for.

Dee didn't miss his quick glances out the kitchen window, and she offered a knowing smile. 'Put the lettuce there to drain and go for a walk. I know you want to. You probably have 30 minutes before Ellis is ready and we can get dinner on the table. I'll give you a shout on your BlackBerry when it's time to eat.'

He shoved the lettuce into the draining rack and wiped his wet hands on his jeans, already heading for the door. 'Thanks Dee, I won't be long.'

'Oh one more thing,' she called over her shoulder as he headed out of the kitchen, 'Stacie ...'

That's all he heard as he closed the door behind him and hurried toward the woodland. He turned his BlackBerry on as he went so Dee could call him. He'd had it off since his morning run-in with the owls, just in case Stacie tried him again and, in all honesty, he'd forgotten about it. He didn't turn back to catch what Dee said. He figured a part of tonight's dinner plan was to try and convince him to talk to Stacie. To be fair, he had all but invited himself when he heard the menu, so he supposed he could endure the two of them regaling him with what a nice person Stacie was and how he ought to consider working with her. He could endure that if it got him a walk in Ellis' wilderness and the chance to sink his teeth into some of Galina's famous chicken parmigiana. Plus he had it on good authority that her even more famous red velvet cake was on the dessert menu, so if they had to talk about Stacie, well, he'd endure it and be rewarded with some nice woodland shots and a delicious meal for his sufferings.

In spite of the warm, welcoming feeling Ellis' home always gave Harris, he couldn't fight back a little shiver as he remembered the stalker who had sneaked onto the property a few weeks ago to watch Kendra and Garrett while they lay stargazing in Ellis' meadow. He felt a little queasy every time he thought about how close he came to losing his friend. The stalker had used night vision goggles, the police said.

Frederick Parks was his real name, though he'd called himself Edge. He had been watching them from just inside the woods, and before the dust finally cleared, before the whole horrifying event was over, Kendra had been kidnaped and Garrett shot. Jesus, their lives had all been so banal until the past few months. He lifted his camera and got a shot of a robin on the edge of the lawn wrestling with a very large worm.

Garrett was well on the road to recovery now and love was in the air. Again. And though Harris never felt left out, there were times when, no matter how much Ellis, his brother, and Stacie shoved into their lives and no matter how happy he was for both Dee and Kendra, nothing else would do but a few hours spent with his friends. Still, as much as he respected and liked Ellis and, all right, Garrett was definitely growing on him, it felt strange to have the dynamic of their friendship in flux in a way he never would have imagined. There were times too when he sort of suspected that he was getting the push toward Stacie just so he wouldn't be the odd man out. But then, he told himself, neither Dee nor Kendra would ever do that deliberately. Sure, they would both love to see him happily matched, but they also knew how he felt about Stacie. And whether he liked her or not, Stacie was still friends with everyone else, and he could be polite and tolerate her if he had to. But that didn't include doing an exhibition for her, even though he knew it would be good publicity for him, even though he knew she had a reputation for being the best in her field. It was the principle of the thing, he told himself

Harris shot a couple more photos of the wrestling match between the robin and the worm then slipped into the cool of the woods. As always was the case, he quickly became fascinated by the living snapshot that was nature. He took several photos of a brightly colored slime mold growing near the remains of a decayed stump and a few shots of the soft-needled branches of a larch tree just beginning to turn golden with the approach of autumn. He'd just gotten a nice close-up of the thick blanket of moss on a rotting tree trunk and the microcosm living there when his phone rang. He answered, still studying the moss that, up close, looked like a miniature jungle.

'Did you see Stacie?' Dee spoke. 'If you do, drag her on back with you. Dinner's about to be served.'

'See Stacie?' His attention was still focused on the moss. 'Why should I have seen Stacie?'

Her exasperated sigh from the BlackBerry sounded like a gust of wind. 'Harris, I told you she was out walking too, but you were so anxious to get into the woods, I didn't figure you'd heard me. Besides, I emailed you that she'd be here. Don't you ever read your emails?'

'I had the BlackBerry turned off, ever since her call this morning nearly resulted in death by owls,' he replied, trying not to grind his teeth. 'I just now turned it back on.'

'Oh? Then you've talked to her. Death by owl? Didn't you have your device turned off? Harris, you know how dangerous great horned owls can be. What were you thinking?'

'I forgot.'

'What do you mean, you forgot? You never forget. That's not the kind of thing you would dare forget.'

'Fortunately I'd left it in my backpack on the

ground, so it was all right, no damage done. At least, none to me, though the pack's a goner, and if Stacie hadn't called –'

'Hold it, Harris. If the pack was on the ground, where the hell were you? Weren't you in the hide?'

He found himself wishing he'd kept his mouth shut. 'It doesn't matter where I was; the point is who the hell calls someone at seven in the morning?'

'Oh for fuck sake, Harris, you're always up before God, everybody knows that, and you still haven't answered my question.'

'I was up a tree, all right? I was up a tree, and I got some fantastic photos for it. And never mind that, you know how I feel about Stacie. I'd say it's pretty damn manipulative of her to arrange for you to invite the two of us together and –'

There was a soft chuckle behind him. 'I'm very glad to hear you got fantastic photos, Mr. Walker, but you could have gotten yourself killed.'

He nearly dropped his device as he spun around to find Stacie Emerson standing right behind him. And no one, especially someone he didn't like, should look that good wearing faded jeans and a T-shirt. But the jeans hugged her curves just right, and made it difficult for him to remember what the hell he and Dee were talking about. Her arms were folded across her very nice front, which even the modest-fitting T-shirt couldn't disguise as anything other than lush, and the black of the shirt made her hair look almost white in the sharp-angled light filtering through the trees. The sight of her made him breathless, and damn if a good deal of the blood supply that he really needed in his brain right now wasn't being hijacked to regions farther south.

Wishing desperately the forest floor would open and swallow him up, he forced his voice to sound normal. 'Dee,' he spoke into the device, struggling to act as though he hadn't made a total ass of himself, struggling to keep his eyes locked on Stacie's, which sparkled like she'd just heard the best joke ever. 'She's here. We're on our way.' He shoved the BlackBerry back into his pocket without taking his eyes off Stacie. 'How long have you been listening?'

'I wasn't listening, but you weren't exactly being quiet, so I heard enough to know that I'm not your favorite person at the moment. No surprise there, really. I already knew that.' She gestured toward the house. 'Shall we? Don't want that delicious chicken getting cold, do we? I must get the recipe. The red velvet cake recipe is actually mine. I gave it to Galina way back when Ellis first moved into this house.' She shot him another amused glance. 'And no, I'm not trying to win my way to your heart through your stomach. I figure you're way too sophisticated for that. Though it is a damn good recipe.'

It was frustrating as hell that she could make what was for dinner sound like polite, witty conversation and he couldn't think of two words to rub together now that she was here next to him, now that he'd already made a fool of himself in front of her. The last of the evening sunlight filtered through the trees like thick golden syrup as the two slipped out into the open of the meadow. 'I didn't hear you,' Harris said, feeling embarrassed that he'd been caught in the truth and pissed off that it embarrassed him.

'Obviously, though I am surprised, I'm a bit like a moose in a crystal shop when I get out in the woods.

Honestly, I stumble about like an accident waiting to happen. But then you were pretty distracted.'

'I'm sorry,' he said.

'What? Sorry that you said it or sorry that I heard it? Nothing to be sorry about, but really, even I know you shouldn't have been up in the tree near a nest of great horned owls.'

'It would have been a lot less dangerous if you hadn't chosen that time to call me,' he said.

She deliberately shuffled her feet in the high grass, making a *swish, swish* sound as she walked. 'I never imagined you'd have left your phone on while you were communing with the great outdoors.'

'Usually, I don't.' He tried to think of an excuse, but the truth was he'd simply gotten careless. He couldn't blame Stacie for that, no matter how badly he'd like to.

'Glad it's not a habit then,' she said. 'I figured that it probably wasn't or, judging by some of the amazing shots you've got on your website, you wouldn't have survived this long.'

Jesus, the woman wasn't even going to give him the chance to be indignant and tell her it was none of her business. Did she have to go and compliment him like that?

'I especially loved the mountain lion shots, up on the Crooked River, weren't they? I can't even begin to imagine how you managed those safely.'

'By making sure my BlackBerry was turned off,' he replied, feeling a little more at ease. The mountain lion shots were some of his favorites, and it had been one of the most adrenalin-laced shoots he'd ever done. He hadn't dared tell Dee or Kendra just what had been involved in getting those shots. They would definitely not have approved, and it was almost a sacred experience for him. He didn't want anyone's disapproval tainting it.

'I think I read somewhere that the best way to keep a mountain lion from attacking you is to make sure your cell phone is turned off,' Stacie said.

She understood, then! The thought flashed through his head before he could stop it, before he could remind himself she was trying to get him to exhibit his work in her gallery, that she had manipulated his friends into arranging this meeting; of course she'd say flattering things.

Ellis met them at the door and folded Stacie into a quick hug, lifting her off her feet. Then he gave Harris a friendly slap on the back. 'Come on in, both of you. Dinner's on the table, and it's warm enough to eat on the patio so you won't have to completely give up the great outdoors just yet.'

'I see you two found each other,' Dee called over her shoulder as she brought the chicken from the kitchen and nodded everyone to follow.

'You could say that,' Stacie said with a smile that might have passed for naughty if Harris hadn't known she was really having a laugh at his expense. To her credit, she only commented about the autumn colors beginning to work their way into the woodland's always stunning décor. Harris was surprised at her eye for detail, but then he shouldn't have been. She was a successful gallery owner, after all. He'd get back to Dee later about allowing the woman to manipulate her into getting the two of them together, but for the moment, he'd be polite and not ruin anyone's dinner. He knew how hard Dee and Ellis worked and how little free time the CEO of Pneuma Inc. and his second in command got these days.

'So then, are you an artist? Is that what got you into the gallery business?' Harris asked as the chicken was served up with a seasonal veg mix that he figured came from Galina's garden.

'No. I just enjoy looking at beautiful things,' she replied around a mouthful of green beans.

'Plus she has a head for business,' Ellis added. 'The gallery was a money pit, in debt to the hilt when Stacie took over. She made it work when anyone else would have ran away screaming.'

Harris understood humility at such a compliment coming from a business wizard like Ellison Thorne, and he would have expected a modest blush. Instead, the look on Stacie's face was more like he'd just told her that her best friend had died. She caught herself quickly enough and offered a demurring smile, but not before Harris knew it wasn't a topic she wanted to discuss. That certainly surprised him, since he figured she'd want him to know just how good she was at her job.

'I ended up there by default,' she said, matter-of-factly. 'And it was probably more dumb luck than any gift I had in that direction.'

'But you are tenacious.' The words were out before Harris could stop them.

She offered him a half-smile that, he hated to admit, got his cock's attention. Then she lifted her wine glass in salute. 'I am that.'

He was certain that this was the opening she was looking for, and he figured he'd offer it, then cut her off at the pass so they could all relax and enjoy the rest of their dinner. But she surprised him again by ignoring him completely and turning her attention to Dee. 'I had a call from Al Marston this morning. He certainly can't say enough nice things about you now he knows what a badass business woman you are. He said you'd been yo-yoing to New York and back almost as much as I have recently. Sounds like the deal with Scribal is coming together.'

'It's been exciting,' Dee replied. 'I'm off to Paris on Monday to meet with Trouvères one last time before we start production. I hope to be in Atlanta when the new plant opens.'

Strangely, Harris felt disappointed, and that made him angry. He didn't want Stacie's attention on him, he reminded himself.

'Is Al coming for the opening of the gallery?' Ellis asked.

OK, Harris thought, it was a team effort, then. This was where they'd bring it all back around to the exhibition, casual like, and then he'd be cornered by the three of them.

'Says he wouldn't miss it,' Stacie said. 'Al and I've been friends for a long time. It would mean a lot to me if he could be there. Speaking of big events, have you two set a date yet?'

Wrong-footed again, Harris thought.

'Next May,' Ellis said. 'We can take some time off then, and I want us to have a real honeymoon.'

'You're such a romantic,' Stacie said.

The rest of the main course passed with talk that had nothing to do with the exhibition, nor were any propositions aimed at Harris other than to ask if he'd like red velvet cake, a question for which there was really no need. By then, he just figured Stacie was saving the propositions for dessert and coffee. But she properly surprised him by refusing the offer of cake.

'As much as I'd love to, I've got a plane to catch, and if I miss this one it'll make it tight for me to be sure everything's ready for the art auction tomorrow night. My new East Coast manager's still a little overwhelmed by it all, but she's getting there.'

'Art auction?' Harris repeated.

'In New York, yes,' she replied. 'I do one every year. The country's most promising artists auction off their work to some of the world's richest art lovers, and the money all goes to Americans for the Arts and several other charities aimed at funding art education in public schools. It's one of the big events of the gallery year for us, as well as for new artists. Several have had their careers launched from the event. This is my last year to orchestrate the East Coast event. I'm hoping next year I'll have one in New World Gallery West as well.'

And still she didn't proposition him. Harris would have thought such an event would be the perfect set-up. It was very impressive.

'I've sent Lynn with express instructions to buy something nice and earthy and pay lots of money for it,' Ellis said, then he addressed Harris. 'Lynn's quite a talented artist in her own right, you know?' Harris had only met Ellis' executive secretary once, but he would have never guessed the woman to possess any artistic talent.

Then Ellis turned his attention back to Stacie. 'I'll have Jeffries meet you around front with the limo.'

He pulled out his phone and called the chauffeur.

The whole entourage headed down to the front door. Harris went along because it was polite and he certainly hadn't been very polite earlier.

At the door, Ellis' butler, Harold, appeared with Stacie's bag just as Ellis' phone buzzed. He glanced at it, then back at Stacie. 'It's Blankenship. I've got to take this. I'm sorry. Have a safe trip and good luck with the auction.' He gave Stacie a quick hug and headed back into the house.

'Wait a minute, why don't you at least let me send a piece of cake with you?' Dee said. 'You can eat it in the limo. Believe me, Jeffries has had to clean up worse than cake crumbs.'

'I'd like that,' Stacie said. 'Though I'll probably hold out for a midnight snack in the gallery flat when I get there. I doubt there'll be anything else to eat. I forgot to ask Maggie to stock the fridge.'

'I'll get it. Won't be a minute, Jeffries,' Dee called over her shoulder to the driver as she disappeared back into the house.

Stacie handed Jeffries her computer bag, which he stowed in the trunk. 'Sorry it's so heavy,' she called after him. 'I travel light clothing-wise, but books – well, I still like the real thing.' Still talking to the chauffeur, she headed toward the limo and missed the last step off the porch. With a startled yelp, she fell heavily against Harris, who was standing just below her, still looking after the retreating Dee. Combined with the forward momentum of someone who had someplace important to go, the woman would have done a complete nosedive onto the driveway if Harris hadn't caught her.

'Oh God, I'm sorry! I'm so sorry.' She tried to pull away, but even that move was none too stable, so Harris did the only thing he could. He held her there, pressed to his chest. 'I told you I'm clumsy. I'm so sorry I wasn't paying attention, and –'

'And it was a good thing I was here to catch you. The sidewalk's not nearly as forgiving.'

'I'm not entirely certain of that, Mr. Walker.' Her voice was breathless and her words unsure. Was she actually nervous, the woman who never was anything but sure of herself?

'Perhaps not then, but I'm definitely less painful.'

'I'm really sorry,' she repeated in a half-whisper. 'I'm not very safe to be around sometimes.'

'I don't doubt that,' he said. And then he did the dumbest thing ever – something he would have never imagined himself doing. He lifted her in his arms and felt her little gasp of surprise, felt her arms circle his neck as he carried her to the open door of the limo and deposited her on the seat way more gracefully than he would have imagined himself capable. In his head, he gave himself a high five just before he gave himself a mental kick in the ass for doing something so stupid. 'You don't want to go to your big auction tomorrow night with a concussion or a broken ankle, so at least this guarantees your safe arrival at the limo.' God, could he sound any more lame?

She smiled up at him and found her voice. 'Harris, I need to ask you something.'

Jesus, was she really going to choose now to ask him about the exhibition? His shoulders stiffened, but if she noticed, she didn't say anything. Instead, she slid a hand down to rest against the breast pocket of his shirt where he'd absently stuffed the offending BlackBerry after she interrupted his conversation with Dee earlier in the woods. 'Please remember to turn off your BlackBerry next time you're in the woods with the owls or the mountain lions. How could I live with myself if I were the cause of serious injuries to a man who takes such wonderful photos?'

Dee chose that moment to return with a goody bag Harris figured contained a lot more than cake. The two women hugged and giggled their goodbyes while he stood back, wondering what the hell just happened and why he was the one who now felt unsteady on his feet.

As the limo pulled away, Dee grabbed his hand and guided him back into the house, where cake had been served in the den in front of the big stone fireplace, and Ellis, who had finished his phone call, was pouring coffee.

She waited until they were all settled with coffee and huge wedges of cake before she offered him a wicked smile. 'I don't know if Stacie was impressed with your show of manly strength, but I certainly was.'

Ellis raised a questioning eyebrow. Harris blushed. 'The woman's dangerous,' he said. 'She tripped.'

Ellis nodded. 'She does that a lot. She's not the most coordinated person in the world. Though you'd never know that when you put her in a room full of wealthy people she thinks can contribute to a good cause. Then she's the picture of grace and charm.'

'Well, I'm so glad you were there to catch her and carry her safely to the limo so she'll have the chance to charm that room full of rich folks out of their money,' Dee said.

‘Carried her to the limo?’ Ellis asked.

‘The woman’s dangerous,’ Harris grumped, ‘and personally I think it was pretty manipulative of her to get you to invite *her* for dinner too.’

Ellis and Dee looked at each other and shrugged, so he continued. ‘And then she didn’t even have the nerve to confront me about why she was here.’

‘She was here because we invited her,’ Dee said. ‘And there was no manipulation. She was invited first. It gave us a chance for a little catch-up and made her trip to the airport easier with the limo. You’re the one who invited yourself along, Harris. And if you’d read your emails, you’d have known she was going to be here.’ She sat her coffee cup down, folded her arms across her chest and glared at him. ‘Were you rude to her?’

‘Not deliberately.’

‘What do you mean not deliberately? How can you be rude to somebody not deliberately?’

‘She accidentally overheard our conversation on the BlackBerry before dinner.’

‘Jesus, Harris!’

‘I’m sorry. I wasn’t expecting her to sneak up on me.’

‘Did you apologize?’

‘Of course I apologized. Kind of.’

‘Well she didn’t seem too upset by whatever it was you said,’ Ellis commented.

‘Then the woman’s a saint, I’d say.’ Dee returned to sipping her coffee. ‘Because you weren’t very nice at all.’

‘Dee –’ Ellis laid a kiss against her temple and slid an arm around her. ‘It’s all right. Stacie can fight her own battles, and if she were really bothered by what Harris said, believe me, she'd have let him know.'

'Dee's right,' Harris said. 'I was rude. I'll make sure I apologize properly.' Even as he said it – and he meant it, he really did – he braced himself for what he figured would be a suggestion that he might apologize to her by listening to her proposal to have him exhibit his work for the opening of her gallery. But it didn't come.

They finished their cake in more companionable conversation. When they were done, Harris excused himself. He'd been up all night the night before and hadn't slept much that day, so he was ready for a rest, and he knew Dee and Ellis had limited time together with their busy schedules, so he said his goodbyes.

At the door, Dee gave him her usual bear hug and a kiss that almost missed his ear, and Ellis gave him a nod.

'We still kayaking Sunday morning?' Ellis asked.

'Wouldn't miss it,' Harris replied. 'And since Dee can't make it, how about we grill some steaks after when she's free to join us, and maybe invite that no-account brother of yours, and Kendra.' Then, as an afterthought, he added sheepishly, 'And we can invite Stacie too if she's back.'

'She won't be,' Dee said. 'She won't be back till Monday, but knowing there are steaks waiting and an icy bottle of Mirror Pond would make me feel a little less sorry for myself for having to work Sunday.' Dee had a meeting with a client in Eugene she'd been trying to get with for several months, so when he'd offered her Sunday morning, she had taken it.

‘Kayaking in the morning then steaks in the afternoon,’ Harris said. ‘It’s a deal.’

Before he could leave, Dee handed him a huge slice of the red velvet cake in a plastic container and offered him a wicked smile. ‘Breakfast.’

Chapter Four

The red-eye to New York was definitely not Stacie's favorite flight, but she was way more familiar with it than she wished she was. Though she always slept well on planes, these days, with the opening of the new gallery and the big auction coming up, she had designated the fight between Portland and New York as office time. It was like having an extra five hours added to the work day. The attendants knew her fairly well by now, and kept the caffeine coming. Tonight, she broke protocol and indulged in one of the three hefty pieces of red velvet cake Dee had sent with her. Her quick search through Dee's care package showed she'd stuck a couple of Galina's homemade cinnamon rolls in as well. Breakfast was sorted.

It was especially good to be busy after her earlier dealings with Jamison. He hadn't texted again, but then she hadn't expected him to. Not just yet. He would give her just enough time to think everything was all right, just enough time to doubt herself, before he escalated things. When she'd left for Ellis' in the evening, the workmen had made major progress on cleaning up the paint damage to the main exhibition hall. The gallery would open on time no matter what she had to do to make it happen. That was essential.

Having the lovely time with Ellis and Dee, and

even a sexily uncooperative, but very intriguing, Harris Walker had helped ease the angst. Still, even with the heavy workload, even with all the tasks demanding her attention, it was the middle of the night and she was 36,000 feet in the air. Everyone around her slept; it was impossible to keep her thoughts from drifting. When she was alone and tired and heading back to New York, back to where it had all begun, it was impossible not to let memories skulk in and rise from the places in her unconscious where she'd buried them. Who could have ever imagined that anything with such a promising beginning could turn into such a nightmare?

That first night had literally sparkled. Stacie had sparkled. Never mind everything she wore came from charity shops. Only she knew that, and she knew how to make the best of what she had. She'd always known that. But it wasn't the chic black dress and expensive-looking fake pearls that made her sparkle; it was the fact that this was her second big exhibition for New World Gallery since Zoe had turned over the running of events to her. Both events had been highly lucrative for the gallery and the artists, drawing the attention of the powers-that-be among the art world; something that New World Gallery had never quite managed to do until Stacie took over. Zoe was beside herself with excitement, and Stacie was the toast of the evening. She was just wrapping up an interview with a reporter from the *New York Times* for a series on small galleries in the city worth checking out, when Zoe motioned her over.

There'd been a million exciting things on Stacie's

mind that night. She was riding the adrenaline high of success, enjoying the feeling of having possibly found her niche. At the time, all she knew about Terrance Jamison was that he'd helped Zoe out financially with the gallery when things were lean. Stacie suspected that Zoe's admiration of the man ran in directions that had little to do with business, but Zoe had never said anything. Stacie was still thinking about the reporter from the *New York Times* when she found herself face to face with a man who took her breath away. It wasn't so much that he was handsome, though he was that in a strange way. It was that he was powerful and just being in his presence was all that was necessary for one to be completely certain of that. He'd already taken her palm into his strong, well-manicured hand before Zoe was able to say, 'Stacie, this is Terrance Jamison, and he's been wanting to meet you.'

The man's short hair was that shade of blond that would never show grey, or perhaps it was already grey. At any rate, his age was impossible to determine from the strong lines of a face that might have been handsomely nondescript had it not been for the startling icy blue of his eyes. And it wasn't even the color of his eyes that made Stacie's heart race in an adrenaline spike, but something about the way the broad smile he offered her and the geniality of his greeting never quite reached those eyes.

She noticed all that, along with his desert heat scent, before she managed to focus on his words. He was saying something about how delighted he was to meet her and what a wonderful job she was doing. She realized she had only been smiling and nodding dumbly until he raised her fingers to his lips and brushed them with a kiss that was cooler than his desert scent would have suggested, more in line with his icy eyes, and yet she felt it as though he had brushed her pulse points, her throat, the tips of her nipples, her inner thighs.

'Thank you, Mr. Jamison,' she managed as he stood there, still holding her hand, and she stood there, looking into his eyes, wanting to run away even as she felt her own lips tingle and tense and wonder what it would feel like to taste that mouth that smiled so handsomely for the rest of his face.

Zoe was talking about Jamison Holdings and about Omega Trust, the organization Jamison ran that had been of so much help to New World Gallery during its difficult times. Stacie could tell then that Zoe had been drinking a bit more than she should, but it was a celebration, after all, and the night had certainly been something to celebrate. But Jamison totally ignored Zoe; his complete attention was on Stacie.

'You're the toast of the town, Ms. Emerson. In New York City, that's no small task.' He stepped closer, still holding her hand in his. 'I've been dying to meet you ever since I heard about Zoe's wonderful new assistant. It seems like you're very much up to the task. In fact –' he stepped still closer '– I think Zoe could just turn the shop over to you and take that long overdue holiday she's so much in need of.' His fingers were massaging hers in tight, circular motions that she was definitely feeling in places beyond her fingers. It was disconcerting to both be frightened for some irrational reason and, at the same time, want to drag the man to the back room and throw herself on him. Stacie was used to men ogling her. She had her mother's good looks and her father's height. She could handle just about any advance and had handled more than a few, but this man wasn't putting the move on her. It felt more like he was hypnotizing her with his eyes, with his touch, with his scent.

'Do you dance, Stacie?' he was asking. 'It is all right if I call you Stacie, isn't it?'

'Yes, Stacie's fine, and I do dance, yes.'

'Wonderful, that's wonderful! Perhaps I could interest you in –'

'Excuse me, but I think you've commandeered this little lady long enough, Jamison, and she and I have some unfinished business.' It was that irritating Alan Marston with his loudmouth southern accent who shoved his way in, front and center, and took Stacie by the arm. Jamison only nodded politely to Marston, with just a twitch at one corner of his smile, but even then, whatever passed between the two men gave Stacie a chill.

'Very well. I won't deny you the pleasure of Ms. Emerson's company, Marston.' By that time, Zoe had taken Jamison's arm. His winter gaze lit once again on Stacie, and for some reason she felt strangely exposed. 'We'll talk later, my dear, I'm sure.' Again he brushed a kiss across her knuckles and her insides fluttered like so much down caught in the wind. 'Until then, Stacie.'

Marston had written a huge check to the gallery, and in exchange for just enough of her time that when they were finished, Zoe and Terrance Jamison were nowhere to be found. And, even mingled with her disappointment, she felt his absence almost like the absence of pain.

That night, she had masturbated to thoughts of Jamison, to what it would feel like to be in his arms, and the edge of danger she had felt in his presence sent her into shudders of orgasm in the safety of her own bed. Back then, she hadn't yet known how fleeting a thing safety could be.

It was a relief when the pilot announced their descent into LaGuardia. Strolls down memory lane involving Terrance Jamison were not her favorite pastime on a night flight. The descent was fairly fast, and they were on the ground almost before she knew it. With only carry-on luggage, she was swiftly in the taxi and on the way to the flat above the gallery. She'd already sold her own apartment for a very hefty profit and was renting a small place in Portland until she had time to look for a house. She was looking forward to having a place with a garden, some flowers, maybe a place outside the city, where she could see if she still remembered how to use a telescope to view the night sky. Maggie was quite capable of running the New York gallery and Stacie was looking forward to being home on the West Coast after so long away.

When things had gone to hell between her and the Thorne brothers, she and Garrett had fled to different parts of the country. Garrett had never been anywhere longer than a few months. That's why everyone thought he was unemployed, living off Ellis' money. Truth was, he just couldn't settle with the guilt he bore, the guilt they both bore.

She had fled to New York. There she had finished university, shifted around from one boring job to another, then got hired on by her friend, Zoe Hanson, who owned a gallery that was barely keeping its head above water financially. The rest was history.

She checked down through her emails. Mostly the usual stuff. A few from Maggie, just letting her know that all was on track for the auction. Maggie had learned that Stacie really liked to be reassured. There were emails from Dee and Kendra and both Thorne brothers wishing her the best with the auction. She knew there would be a hefty check of a donation from Garrett, who contributed as Tess Delaney. Tucked in unobtrusively amid the emails from contributors, the workers on the gallery renovations in Portland, and even one from Al Marston, was an email from Harris Walker.

She opened it with a smile and a little eruption of butterflies as she remembered him lifting her as if she weighed nothing and carrying her to the limo. Nice arms, she thought, and a nice, hard chest. But then the man did climb trees to photograph owls and mountain lions. She opened the email.

Stacie,

I owe you a huge apology for being so rude. I've been properly enlightened by Dee that you did not *manipulate to get me to dinner at Ellis' (which was delicious and would have been worth attending even if you had, by the way.) In truth, it was actually I who invited myself along for the food and the views. You were far better behaved than I was. I'll try to be more civilized in the future.*

Harris

She tapped in a quick answer.

Apology accepted, Mr. Walker. And it was indeed a delightful dinner.

She thought about using his goodwill to ask him again to meet with her, but she decided not to. Not just yet. She decided just to bask in Harris Walker's rather stingily given goodwill. Just for a little while. And when this insane weekend was over and the auction behind her, she'd scheme another way to get him to relent and exhibit his photos with her.

Stacie paid the cab driver, who dropped her off outside the closed gallery only a little while before sunrise. She made her way up the stairs in the back to the flat that belonged to the gallery, the flat that used to be her home before she was able to turn the gallery around. She let herself in, pulled down the Murphy bed, and stripped. She slid under the covers and within minutes she was sound asleep.

Chapter Five

The day had been busier than she had planned, and that was saying a lot. It wasn't that Maggie hadn't taken care of everything as far as the auction was concerned. Unexpected events on the West Coast took a huge chunk of Stacie's time, including repairs of the damage from the vandalism. She'd finally been contacted by a photographer who was famous for shots of urban decay and renewal. His main stomping ground was the Northwest and Stacie wanted him in her exhibition. His work would complement Harris' and be a part of the overall story she wanted to tell. Kyle Waters had been shooting in South America. His timing for getting in touch with Stacie hadn't been the best, but after a two-hour Skype session, she was pretty sure he was on board. She'd meet him to watch a shoot in Portland after she got back.

That all happened just after she returned from the emergency room. Not her clumsiness this time. One of the artists had sprained an ankle in a freak accident on the steps of the subway, and Stacie had ended up holding his hand in the emergency room while the doctor reassured him it wasn't a bad sprain and he wouldn't have to miss the auction.

It was always this way. There had never been an auction in the ten years she'd been doing them that had run smoothly and by the book. There had always been at least one major disaster, and often it looked as though the event would have to be cancelled at the last minute. One year the basement flooded when a pipe burst. Another year there was a partial brown-out in the area. And yet the event had always happened, each year with more glitz, more charm, more panache than the year before. And more contributions. This year was relatively easy, she thought, as she made one last pass through the exhibition of paintings and sculptures waiting to be auctioned off. They'd been on display in the gallery for the past month leading up to the event so everyone could enjoy them before they were auctioned off to grace the homes of the wealthy. The whole place glistened with vintage champagne, designer gowns, and jewelry that Stacie had no doubt was heavily insured and spent more time in vaults than it did displayed on women's throats and fingers.

Stacie's dress was deep cherry red, showing only a hint of cleavage but plenty of décolletage. She wore her hair up so her neck was also bare other than the simple string of pearls Alan Marston had given her just before her first big exhibition, the one that had gotten the gallery out of debt forever. Those pearls had a value to her way beyond the monetary, though, knowing Al, she figured that was substantial too. Stacie knew how to turn heads, and she knew how to appear the epitome of grace and polish when there was money at stake. She dressed to attract attention and yet at the same time to send out the message that she was above it all, that she was untouchable by even the rich and possessive.

She looked out over the sparkling scene with the

same champagne flute held delicately between her fingers that she'd been sipping at for the last hour and a half. The early pieces had already been auctioned off to a crowd that was clearly more than pleased to part with lots of money. The break gave everyone a chance to move around, grab a drink and a canapé, and return to their seats fresh, energized. Stacie didn't want them tired. She wanted them happy, exhilarated, and ready to bid the night away.

She knew the first half of the bidding had gone very well. Ellis' secretary, Lynn, had outbid everyone for a gorgeous sculpture of Diana at the Hunt that Stacie could very easily imagine fitting into either the Pneuma Building or Ellis' home. Lynn was sipping champagne and talking to the artist of a woodland scene that looked as though it might have been painted from one of Harris Walker's photos. Stacie figured that was next on the woman's "must have" list. Ellis had always been extravagant at the auction, though he never attended, and his home and the Pneuma Building were the lovelier for it. It was also well-noted that Tess Delaney, AKA Garrett Thorne, had taken away a few choice pieces as well, though this year he was at home, recovering from his injuries from the horrible kidnapping attempt on Kendra. He'd still sent a whopping check, and so had Kendra or, rather, K. Ryde. If she didn't like the woman already, she certainly did when she saw the size of the check.

Al Marston was inspecting a cityscape he'd just purchased before it was taken away to be packed up and delivered. His extravagance was renowned, and she loved him for it. When he realized she was watching him, he smiled and gave her the thumbs-up sign. It was all shaping up to be a fine evening until Terrance Jamison walked through the door. Stacie felt his presence like a gut punch. The room spun and the sounds of the party going on around her were drowned out by the ringing in her ears as Jamison took in the room with a single glance. His gaze came immediately to rest on her, like he knew exactly where she would be in the throng, like he could sense her above everyone else. And she held his gaze even as she felt herself struggling to stand under her own power.

'Come on, Stacie, I can't make heads or tails out of this painting and I can't find the artist. Thought maybe you could help me out.' She felt the reassuring girth of Alan Marston close to her, his arm encircling her waist gently but firmly as he turned her away. 'What the hell's that bastard doing here? Trying to convince the world there's a human being under that snake skin?' He chuckled softly. 'Gonna take a damn sight more than a charity auction or two to prove that, lemme tell you.'

The gentle ringing of a bell informed everyone the auction was about to resume. After a reassuring hug from Al, Stacie took her position next to Maggie, who didn't seem to notice anything unusual about her boss. And neither would anyone else, Stacie promised herself, forcing her anger at what Jamison had done in Portland away from her. This was not the time to deal with it. This had been bound to happen – running into Jamison – and it was best to get it over with and get used to it. The man had a luxury apartment in Manhattan, though he most often stayed at the Plaza, and he owned a ranch in Oregon, but he seldom stayed there. She knew that, and she'd never expected for one minute that the two of them wouldn't run into each other, that he wouldn't make a point of it.

It didn't surprise her at all that, when the auction resumed, Jamison bid on the most extravagant piece of sculpture done by a first-time exhibitor who looked to be barely in her 20s. She was dressed in black and gold lace, with equally black hair flowing wildly around her shoulders. Stacie knew immediately that Jamison wasn't the least bit interested in the woman's art, and ultimately he wasn't interested in the woman either, but she was young and very pretty and the perfect way to send a message to Stacie. If it had been anyone else, she could have blown it off as jealousy, but she wasn't jealous. Dear God, she wasn't jealous! If she'd had that kind of money, she would have bid against Jamison, but she knew she couldn't win. Oh, Marston and several of the gallery's other wealthy supporters gave him a run for his money, but he would not be denied. She knew how he was. In his mind's eye, he was not only purchasing the sculpture, modern and abstract but wonderfully intriguing, he was also purchasing the artist who had created it, and he was doing it to remind Stacie that he could have whatever he wanted – have *whoever* he wanted.

Whatever he thought, he couldn't, she reassured herself. He couldn't. She watched as he planted a gentlemanly kiss across the knuckles of the young artist, who was over the moon with excitement, as anyone would have been in her shoes, anyone who didn't know.

But Stacie knew. And she remembered exactly how it felt to be the apple of Jamison's eye.

‘Are you serious? A partnership?’ Stacie needed to work on her poker face, but wow, she almost had to pinch herself for a reality check.

Zoe and Jamison, who had insisted by then that she call him Terrance, offered each other knowing smiles and nodded in unison.

‘Why shouldn’t you be a partner in the business you’ve single-handedly turned around?’ Zoe asked. The woman looked particularly stunning that night. The copper shimmer of the cocktail dress that Stacie was pretty sure was new and expensive made the pale of her skin and the russet of her hair look like she was bathed in candlelight. The blush on her cheeks had risen as the evening progressed from dinner to drinks back in Jamison’s suite at the Plaza. Jamison had already opened the second bottle of champagne and Zoe was partaking liberally. ‘I just can’t see the point of having you be a wage slave when you’re worth your weight in gold. Besides –’ she leaned over the table and gave Stacie’s hand a squeeze ‘– you’re so damn much fun to work with, Stacie.’ Zoe downed her champagne and held it out for a refill. ‘Of course, right now all you’re really getting half of is my debt, but the gallery has huge potential to earn and, with your business savvy and what you’ve got in mind for the gallery in your five-year plan, I think we’ll see that debt disappearing quickly.’

‘And the fact that the entire debt of New World Gallery has happily been taken on by Omega Trust –’ Jamison laid a hand against his chest as though he alone were Omega Trust, and that was pretty much the case from what Zoe had told Stacie ‘– means that the three of us will be working very closely together, and I have to admit, the only thing I like better than working with competent, talented people is working with competent, talented people who are also lovely members of the opposite sex.'

He raised his champagne glass in salute. They toasted and Stacie sipped cautiously.

'If I agree to this, what will be involved? I have no money. I can't buy half that debt.'

Jamison offered an easy shrug. 'Really, it's just a legality, a matter of signing papers, a matter of taking on half of everything Zoe owns, which will be yours now in debt as well as it will be when New World Gallery is financially sound and running in the black. I'll simply be the keeper of that debt – or, rather, Omega Trust will be. That'll insure that in order for the gallery to reach its full potential it'll be financially able to get exactly what it needs resource-wise.' He held Stacie's gaze. 'Simple, really.'

Of course, it wasn't. How could she have been so naïve? But once she'd agreed, Jamison had played something slow and sultry on the sound system, and he had offered her his hand. 'Now, Ms. Emerson, I believe you said you could dance.' He held her close and she lost track of time and space. For a little while, Zoe stumbled around the floor with them, her arms draped over both of them as they laughed and swayed to the music. But then she gave it up and fell asleep on the couch.

They danced and danced. The movements became less formal and slowed to a shuffle with her head resting on his shoulder, and both of his arms wrapped around her waist possessively. The slower they went, the harder it became to breathe. She hadn't drunk that much and yet she felt muzzy-headed, dizzy, as though wherever she was at, she wasn't supposed to be there. The slower they danced, the harder it became to think. At some point she became aware of the press of him. He'd lost his jacket and his tie and the tense insinuation of his nipples through the expensive shirt felt like brands against the plunge of her neckline. Her own nipples knotted to get closer to him. At some point she became aware that he was hard, that his hand had moved down to rest at the juncture between her lower back and her bottom. At that point, all he would have had to do was take her. And he could have taken her right there and then and she could have never said no, even though in the deepest part of her gut she knew she should. It seemed he possessed her soul for a moment, and she felt him move across her like a fast-moving storm cloud, leaving her in the deepest shadow of herself, in a place she had never strayed to before.

Then Zoe had made a mad dash to the bathroom to throw up. By the time they'd gotten her home to her flat she was running a fever and Stacie was unwilling to leave her friend alone, even though it clearly made Jamison unhappy, even though he clearly wanted her to go back with him.

There were so many omens Stacie should have seen, and she not nearly as young as the artist whose work Jamison had just bought, but still unprepared. So unprepared. Stacie forced her attention away from the dark descent of memories and back to the glitter and glam of the gallery.

Jamison was a showman's showman. He had timed his little display of generosity just right, chosen an extravagant piece of art created by a young and very attractive, if very naïve, artist in just the right part of the second half of the auction to guarantee his show of grandiosity would be the climax of the evening. It couldn't have been more obvious if he had thumbed his nose at Stacie. But then, she reminded herself, she knew him better than most.

There were only a few more pieces left to be auctioned after Jamison's little display, and though they were now rendered anti-climactic, they gave Stacie a chance to gather her thoughts for the closing statements and the presentation of the award for best new artist, which always went to the creator of the piece that had brought the most money. Jamison had guaranteed that would be Ingrid Watson, the lovely, dark-haired artist who now sat calmly looking down at her hands in her lap, but had to be ready to jump off her chair with excitement. She had to know that she had won. Everyone had to know.

This was Jamison's message to Stacie: that he still could control her; that he still could have whatever he wanted whenever he wanted, and there was nothing she could do about it. For a second, she fought back total panic. For a second, she fought back the urge to run, to just walk out of this room, pack a bag and go. She could do it. She could go anywhere she wanted and let the rest sort itself out. Let everything she had worked for just slip away. It had all been an accident anyway, hadn't it? This had certainly never been the path she had intended for herself, and did it really matter? What mattered was never having to look into those icy, controlling eyes again, never having to wonder what he would do next.

But there was Ingrid Watson, young and naïve. Hailing from rural Minnesota, Stacie recalled, where she helped her father run a dairy farm. Jesus! Jamison would chew her up and spit her out before she even knew what happened. And if that occurred, whose fault would it be but Stacie's?

From the middle of the crowd, Ellis' secretary raised a number. Stacie noticed that the woman held two numbers. Maybe one for Dee? She was bidding on a lovely Western-style painting of a mountain lion stretched on a ledge above a river, and it was clear she wasn't about to be outbid by anyone. Not far from her, Al Marston offered Stacie a reassuring nod and a hint of a smile.

She remembered that Jamison didn't always get his way. Ellis had been standing toe to toe with him for a long time now and holding his own. Jamison hated him for that. Al had given the man a run for his money a time or two, and she – well, she owned this gallery outright, and that was a testament to standing up to Terrance Jamison. She squared her shoulders and turned her attention to Jamison, who sat as cool as winter, unflinching, unmoving, his eyes locked on her. And she returned his gaze in spades. None of this was unexpected, she reminded herself. She knew when the time came, he wouldn't let it go. Well she wasn't a naïve young girl any more, and she wouldn't let it go either.

She returned her gaze to Ellis' secretary, who'd just given the winning bid for the mountain lion painting.

'Sold!' The auctioneer pounded his gavel on the

podium. In spite of herself, Stacie jumped. '*Sunset Vigil* by Andrea Vargas sold to Mr. Harris Walker.'

Stacie felt as though the sun had just come out. She hadn't seen that coming. A quick glance at her BlackBerry, and, sure enough, there was a message from Harris.

Stacie

Just my way of making it up to you for my bad behavior. It's a lovely painting, BTW. And I trust the artist had her BlackBerry turned off when she painted it. Best of luck tonight. I hope you rake in the dough.

Harris

She didn't know how he'd done it, some scheming with Ellis, no doubt, but she was more certain than ever that she would have Harris Walker's work in her exhibition. It was essential. And the timing couldn't have been better if he'd planned it. It was just the reminder that she needed that she had an exhibition to plan and a new gallery to bring on line with all the fireworks and excitement she could manage. And she planned to manage a lot. Quickly, she texted back.

My hero! Apology most definitely accepted, Mr. Walker.

Stacie

She'd barely gotten the text sent off before Maggie was introducing her and calling her to the podium. She stood and offered the whole room a broad smile, which she now definitely felt. Then she moved to stand next to the gallery's new manager. There was a round of applause and then silence as she took the podium. For a lingering second, she looked out over the room full of wealthy people, people making an effort to give something back, perhaps even making an effort to assuage their guilt for being "haves" in a "have-not" world or perhaps just putting on a good act. Her gaze came to rest first on Ingrid Watson, then on Jamison. Then she spoke.

'It's no secret, I've always loved being surrounded by beautiful things, and I've always had a deep respect and admiration for those who create them, for those who have studied and trained and sacrificed and put in long hours to create something breathtaking, something moving, something astounding. And I think there's no one in this room tonight who would deny that we've been surrounded, for the past month, here at New World Gallery, with some of the most powerful works of some of the most promising new artists of the day. I'd like to thank all of them for their contributions to this event, for the gift of their time and their talent to give back to future artists.'

There was a round of enthusiastic applause. Then Stacie continued.

'We need art maybe more than anything else because art is a reflection of ourselves, of our souls, of all the things within us that we can't see, but know are there. Art feeds us, nourishes us, strengthens us, encourages us and moves us beyond ourselves to act boldly and live bravely and openly, even when we're frightened, even when we're unsure. Art gives us that and so much more.

'Having said all that, having been surrounded with so much manifest creativity, it's my great pleasure to announce that tonight's award for Outstanding New Artist goes to Ingrid Watson for her work, *Inspiration in Stone*, purchased by Terrance Jamison for a cool million.'

The room erupted in applause as the young artist came to the podium to take the plaque that Stacie offered. The two women shook hands. Ingrid offered a few nervous words of thanks, her eyes continually returning to Terrance Jamison, who smiled up at her indulgently. Stacie fought back a wave of vertigo, remembering the first time she'd seen that look on his face. She grabbed onto the podium with both hands and forced the thought out of her mind. Then she shook Ingrid's hand once more and watched her return to the audience, this time to sit next to Jamison.

As the auction ended and while the champagne and canapés made another round, Stacie did her best to mingle and smile. It was what she was good at, especially for a worthy cause. And she was certain that no one had any idea of what a rough evening this had been for her. The crowd thinned and Maggie flitted about making sure final details were taken care of. Stacie had just finished talking with Lynn when she turned to find herself face to face with Jamison. Ingrid Watson's arm was folded over his and the young woman looked totally delighted.

Jamison leaned in and kissed Stacie on each cheek, taking his time to let a free hand slide onto the bare skin of her shoulder. 'A lovely evening, Stacie.' He brushed a loose strand of hair back behind her ear in a way that made her shiver, but she held herself, she held herself as though she was encased in glass and his touch meant nothing. 'You always did know how to make the money,' he whispered against her ear. Then he pulled back and straightened, patting Ingrid's hand. 'Ms. Watson and I are having a late dinner, and she's going to tell me all about her work, aren't you, my darling?'

Ingrid offered an adoring nod.

'We'd both love it if you'd join us.' The surprised look on Ingrid's face told Stacie that clearly wasn't the case.

'Thank you, Terrance –' Stacie was amazed she could speak to him without her voice trembling '– but it's traditional for the winner of the Outstanding New Artist award to join the VIP list for dinner.' He knew this, and Stacie knew that their conversation was making Ingrid Watson uncomfortable. Clearly she'd rather be with Jamison. But then she had no idea how dangerous being with Jamison could be. Stacie added, 'There are always reporters and gallery owners hoping for exhibitions with the artists.' She could see the dilemma in the woman's eyes. 'It's your chance to shine, Ingrid.'

'Come now, Stacie, don't be so stingy.' Jamison drew the woman possessively closer to him. 'I've just paid a million dollars to share this lovely woman's company, and you and I both know I have plenty of connections to make sure her work gets the attention it deserves.'

If Ingrid noticed Jamison's derogatory play on words, she didn't show it, and in all honesty, it was meant for Stacie, but Stacie could take care of herself. It was Ingrid she worried about.

Just then Al Marston lumbered over to her side. 'You ready to go, Stacie? The limos have arrived for the artists.'

Ingrid looked desperately from Jamison back to Stacie and Al. Jamison forced the issue. 'Come now, my darling. I'm sure Ms. Emerson knows better than most I'm the best thing that could possibly happen to your career.' He nodded to Stacie, his eyes never leaving hers while he completely ignored Al. Then he turned on his heels, still holding Ingrid Watson's arm in a possessive grip.

But before he could get completely away, Stacie grabbed Ingrid's other hand in a hard handshake. 'I just want to congratulate you again, Ms. Watson. Thank you for your contribution tonight. You clearly impressed everyone. Your heart shows through your work. That's where your power is.' She held the woman's gaze. 'And it's a lot of power. A lot of power. Remember that.'

Then she turned and moved on shaky legs toward the exit, thankful for Al's strong arm to lean on.

Chapter Six

Ingrid Watson woke alone amid a tangle of expensive linens in the middle of a huge bed. Through the thick haze of a champagne hangover it took her a few seconds to remember where she was and how she'd gotten there. And when it all came flooding back to her – the big win last night at the art auction; the evening with Terrance Jamison that had ended in the glorious suite at the Plaza Hotel – somehow her head hurt just a little less. She had won! Ingrid Watson from *Farmville,* Minnesota had won! She had won out over the sophisticated, polished locals and the graduates from expensive art schools. Her work had made an outrageous amount of money for the auction and got everyone's attention, hands-down. And then she'd left New World Gallery on the arm of the very sexy man who had just bought her sculpture for a million dollars. A million dollars!

She sat up in bed and looked around the room for Mr. Jamison, realizing with an embarrassed smile that even after all the naughty things they'd done in that big, expensive bed, they weren't even on a first name basis, but then what was in a name? When the man was nowhere to be found, she recalled that Terrance Jamison always rose before dawn. She had gleaned that fact in her frantic and less than thorough search for information about him on her iPhone while he was bidding for her sculpture. She hadn't even known who he was until he bought her sculpture for an obscene amount of money. The man had driven the price up in a dizzying competition with two other bidders, and then it was as if he had just gotten tired of the game, and simply bid a million. A nice round number, he'd said later as they rode to the Plaza together in his very swank limo. And that had been that. His generosity had left the room in an uproar and had left an excited Ingrid claiming the prize and frantically trying to figure out who this insane man was.

She eased herself out of bed, sore from way more sex than she'd had, well … ever. After a night with Jamison, she could hardly count the gropings and fumblings of her limited experience, not really. She looked around. Her clothes, which last night had been strewn carelessly across the floor from the sitting room to the bed, were nowhere to be found. But Mr. Jamison's white shirt was still draped neatly over the back of the chair where he had left it last night. She pulled the shirt to her face, taking in the smell of expensive cologne mixed with the dark, mysterious scent of the man himself. Then she slipped into it and wrapped it tightly around her. Instantly she felt her nipples peak against the fabric that had caressed his body just a few hours ago.

She smiled to think what a gentleman he had been. Perhaps that's the way it was with older men. She'd never been with one before. She'd never been with anyone who wasn't either as awkward and bumbling as she was or so full of themselves that they were barely aware of her being anything more than a hole for their cocks. But Terrance Jamison had even asked permission to kiss her, had even asked if she was sure she wanted him to make love to her. Of course, by the time he got around to asking, she was aching for it in every cell of her body, aching for it in a way she didn't even know she could. And my God! He hadn't disappointed. He was a bit rougher than she had expected, but not without her permission, and she figured, experienced as he no doubt was, he'd intuited that she would like it that way. That was something even she hadn't known about herself.

Then the silence of the present encroached on her thoughts, and she wondered if he had left her there alone. But the smell of fresh coffee was encouraging. Wrapped in his shirt, she tiptoed into the lounge in search of him, hungry for more of him.

He sat reading the *New York Times* at the table in front of the window. He was already showered and dressed for business, even though it was a Sunday. For a second, she stood in the doorway watching him, letting the wave of butterflies flutter over her. This man, this very powerful, very wealthy man, singled her work out from all the rest; this man believed her worthy of his attention. He sipped his coffee and sat the cup carefully back onto its saucer. She hadn't thought him even aware of her presence until he spoke. 'There's a robe in the closet,' he said without looking up from the paper. 'Go put it on.'

She obeyed, stripping off the shirt in full view of him before she walked slowly back into the bedroom. When he didn't look up, the champagne headache spiked in a wave of confusion. The man had been the best host ever last night. He had taken her to dine at

Per Se, putting out way more on one meal than she paid for her apartment for six months. Then he had brought her back to his penthouse suite in the Plaza Hotel. She'd never even been to Minneapolis until her senior trip, let alone New York City, so she reacted like a kid at Christmas – maybe a little embarrassing the morning after, but last night he seemed to relish her delight. This morning, he was miles away. Surely it couldn't be anything she'd done. She hadn't done anything that he hadn't suggested or recommended. Perhaps he was just distracted. An important man like Terrance Jamison had plenty of things other than art and artists on his mind.

She slipped into the robe and joined him at the table. He still didn't look up. 'Help yourself to coffee. I've ordered breakfast to be delivered –' he glanced down at his watch '– in twenty minutes.'

She poured herself coffee, then moved to admire the view out over Central Park. 'It's so beautiful,' she said, her voice breathless with nerves.

Still he said nothing. So she took matters into her own hands and leaned over his shoulder. 'What are you reading?'

'The write-up about last night's little soirée,' came the reply that sounded neither irritated nor warm. 'It seems Ms. Emerson has done it again. Even without our little contribution, Americans for the Arts has done very well from her efforts.'

She studied the picture of Stacie Emerson shaking *her* hand and offering her the plaque for Outstanding New Artist. Ingrid looked a bit shell-shocked, but Stacie looked polished, at ease, and gorgeous. Her insides somersaulted with a strange mix of envy and hero worship. She owed the woman big time. If Ms. Emerson hadn't given her the chance to display her work in the gallery for the charity auction, she'd still be just Jim Watson's little girl who dabbled in the arts in the old barn behind the cowshed, and Terrance Jamison would have taken no notice of her. And yet she couldn't help it. She would have liked it if the gallery owner had been a little less perfect, a little less comfortable in her own skin. There were several other posed shots with Stacie Emerson and people Ingrid would know if she ran in the same circles. Perhaps they were people she might have had the opportunity to meet if she had joined the other artists for dinner. The little niggle in the pit of her stomach made her wonder if she'd made a mistake by not going along last night, especially when her absence was noted in less than gracious terms in the article. But Terrance Jamison had said he could help her career at least as much as Ms. Emerson. And she had wholeheartedly believed him. Then. Right now she wasn't so sure.

'How long have you known her?' she asked, recalling the twinge of jealousy she'd felt at the way he looked at Stacie Emerson, the way he touched her when he'd asked her to join them for dinner.'

'Oh, Stacie and I go way back,' he said, still not showing any emotion. 'She's a very talented girl, our Ms. Emerson.' This time the corners of his mouth turned up into a smile. 'I doubt there's anything she couldn't do if she set her mind to it.'

Ingrid certainly wouldn't have called her a girl. Encouraged by the sudden shift in his humor, she settled onto the arm of his chair and leaned close. 'Were you lovers?'

He shrugged her off so quickly that she stood to keep from falling. Then he pushed back from the table and tossed the paper into the trash can next to the sofa.

'I'm sorry,' she whispered. Confusion escalated to something a little more alarming as he began to pace in front of the big window. 'That was none of my business. I'm sorry.'

He turned on her so quickly that she nearly tripped over the leg of the chair he'd just vacated trying to step away. But there was no need. There was a broad smile on his face, and he took her into his arms and smoothed her mussed hair. 'Stacie and I did some business together,' he said, one hand moving inside the robe to fondle her breasts while the other undid the sash. 'And certainly for me, that business did involve some … pleasure.' He pushed the robe off her shoulders and, in spite of all they'd done last night, she felt shy, but he only chuckled softly and gave her body the onceover the same way she'd seen him appraising the art at the gallery. 'You have nothing to be jealous of, my dear Ms. Watson. While Stacie Emerson likes to be surrounded by lovely things, I prefer to possess them.' He gave her nipple a pinch for emphasis and she flinched, feeling a flush of heat between her legs.

He pushed her back until her bottom pressed against the table, then he lifted her onto it, rattling the cups and spilling coffee on the white linen tablecloth. With one hand he opened her legs and stroked her down there until she trembled with something more edgy than just arousal. With the other hand he opened his fly, eased out his erection, and pushed into her with no warning, no foreplay. She couldn't help it, she cried out. It felt as if he had forced a battering ram up inside her. For a second, she couldn't breathe; for a second, her eyes watered; for a second, she felt fear tangle and knot with the beginnings of arousal. But just before she could get truly frightened, his efforts calmed and he held himself still inside her, catching his breath, studying her face, her breasts, her thighs, the place where their bodies joined. The pain gave way to an achy, prickly, almost panicky sort of pleasure. He stroked her breasts, examining them like they were one of her sculptures, thumbing her nipples until they were raw and hyper-sensitive. All the while his gaze took in her body as though he were judging it, as though it fascinated him in an abstract sort of way.

'But what's most interesting about lovely things, Ingrid, is that lovely things need to be possessed. I believe that's their sole purpose.' Then he began to thrust, both hands moving to grip her hips and pull her tighter against him. 'What do you think, darling?' He held her face so she couldn't look away. 'Do you think that might be the case?'

His thrusting grew harder and she wrapped her legs around his waist to steady herself. A coffee cup rattled off the edge of the table and shattered on the floor. He held her chin in a tight grip between his thumb and forefinger and kissed her with a kiss that threatened to smother even as it aroused her. When he pulled free, he still held her so that she couldn't look away from him. The tension in his body told her he was about to come. 'Not that it matters.' His words were now breathless and forced from his throat. 'I don't have to have permission to possess what I want,

Ingrid. I simply take it.' And then he came with a hard thrust that forced the breath from her lungs and felt as though it would split her in two.

Before he could bring her to orgasm – though she was already pretty sure that was not his priority – and before he could even fully recover himself, there was a soft knock on the door. He pulled out and wiped himself on one of the linen napkins. 'That'll be breakfast.' He tossed her the napkin. 'Clean yourself up.' Then, without so much as a backward glance , he went to the door, leaving her feeling nearly as shattered as the cup on the floor.

She hurried to wipe herself and retrieve the robe. She had just cinched it tight around her when he returned looking as though nothing at all out of the ordinary had happened.

She was mortified when the room service waiter followed, pushing the breakfast trolley in front of him. 'Leave it,' Mr. Jamison said without even looking at the waiter, who obeyed with a deferential bow of his head.

The man had barely shut the door behind him before Mr. Jamison gave a quick glance at his watch. 'I have a plane to catch, but you have the room for the rest of the day. There are clothes in the closet that should fit you. I've arranged for your gown to be dry-cleaned. It'll be returned to your hotel room by the time you get back.'

He picked up a small case from where it sat near the sofa and headed for the door, leaving her stunned and confused. Then he stopped, came back to her, and pulled her into a demanding kiss. He slipped a hand down between her legs, thrusting two fingers quickly up inside her and thumbing her clit until she came with a startled sob. Then he pulled away all business-like. ‘My secretary will be in touch with plans for furthering your career, and I’m sure the two of us will be entertaining each other again soon.’ He left without another word.

Chapter Seven

The light over the water was changing from hues of bronze and mauve to chrome and silver when Harris and Ellis slipped their kayaks from the river and settled on one of the sundrenched rocks for the breakfast they were both more than ready for. They'd been in the river for nearly two hours now and hunger had finally driven them to ground.

'Let's see – BLTs on Galina's homemade potato bread, cinnamon rolls, and some of the blackberries she picked last night. Doesn't get any better than this,' Ellis said, pulling breakfast for the two from one of the waterproof bags while Harris poured coffee from the Thermos.

'Well, it beats the hell out of the peanut butter and crackers I'd have packed,' Harris said, as Ellis handed him a sandwich. 'Say, does Galina have a boyfriend because I think I might be in love?'

'She'd got two, actually.' Ellis said. 'She doesn't think I know it, but I hear things.'

'I don't mind being a third.' Harris spoke around a huge mouthful of sandwich. 'Not if it gets me meals like this.'

'I'll give her your resume,' Ellis said.

The men ate in companionable silence, watching a pair of dippers, now fully into their molt and unable to fly until it was over. They flitted in and out of the river, as at home in the water as they were on the rocky banks. The woodland was alive with the sound of birds and the rustle of a breeze in the evergreens, all set against the gurgling backdrop of the water. It was on the second refill of coffee that Ellis spoke again. 'So, I hear Lynn was able to find a painting that suited you at Stacie's auction.'

'Yep. Mountain lion. For my front room above the fireplace.' He glanced over at Ellis. 'I hope it makes up for my rude behavior Friday evening.'

'I'm sure it didn't hurt,' Ellis said, stuffing the last of his sandwich in his mouth and washing it down with coffee. 'And Stacie was probably happy for a friendly gesture after Jamison showed up.'

'Jamison? What the hell was he doing there?' He found himself feeling way more sympathy for Stacie than he'd intended. 'Wouldn't wish that bastard on anyone. Is she all right?'

'He spent a million dollars on a sculpture by an artist no one heard of before. A very good-looking artist, apparently.'

'Jesus,' Harris said, spilling coffee onto the rocks in front of him. 'A million dollars? What the hell is he up to?'

'I suppose he could be thumbing his nose at me after the Valderian incident. We may have won this round, but if he can toss about a million dollars for an evening's entertainment, it's pretty clear the message is that it would be unwise to underestimate him. The man's not above using people I care about to get to me.'

Harris studied him for a minute, then bit a chunk out of his cinnamon roll. 'Stacie's your ex fiancée.'

OK, he sounded a bit tetchy, but if Ellis was going to marry his best friend, he just felt better stating the obvious.

'Stacie's a good friend. She's my friend and she's Dee's friend. If you've got problems with it, that's just too damn bad.'

'I don't have problems with it,' Harris said. 'But just so you know, the same rule still applies until I'm certain you'll make Dee deliriously happy for the next 50 years or so.'

'You mean the "rip my throat out" rule?'

'That would be the one,' Harris replied.

'Then you'd better find another outlet for your violent nature, Walker, because a deliriously happy Dee Henning is my new long-term business plan.'

'It better be,' Harris grumped. In all honesty, there really wasn't any doubt about Ellis' feelings for Dee. No one could be stupid enough to miss how the two adored each other.

'So, did Stacie tell you about her run-in with Jamison?' Harris asked.

'Nope. Lynn did. I haven't heard from Stacie and probably won't till she gets back to Portland. Maybe not then.' He raised an eyebrow at Harris' look of surprise. 'When are you going to get it through your head the three of us all have lives of our own now? Stacie doesn't run to me with all of her news any more than Garrett does.' Before Harris could respond, Ellis continued, 'Look, Walker, whether you like it or not Stacie is friends with both Garrett and me, and now she's friends with Dee and Kendra too.'

Silence returned as Harris thought about that fact. It still bothered him, though he wished it didn't.

'Stacie would never manipulate me or Garrett, nor Dee or Kendra, for that matter. Especially not where her business is concerned. She's the best in her field. She's the whiz kid who single-handedly arranged a major exhibition of rare works from the Hermitage in Saint Petersburg, an exhibition that saved the gallery from certain bankruptcy and closure. The woman knows what she's doing.'

'Look, I didn't mean to suggest that she isn't competent at her job, it's just that …'

'That she makes you a little nervous because of our history and because she's persistent?'

Harris didn't answer.

'Tell me, would she make you feel that way if she were older, uglier, male?'

'I'm not sure how to take that,' Harris said.

Ellis shrugged. 'I know you don't trust her, and I can't make you, though if you'd give her a chance, it wouldn't take her long to win that trust.'

There was more silence. Harris didn't know what to say.

Ellis drained his coffee cup and wiped his hands on his trousers. 'Harris, Stacie didn't need Jamison's million-dollar contribution to make her auction a huge success. It was a guaranteed done deal without his help. She's that good.'

Again Harris said nothing.

'This opening exhibition she's planning for New World Gallery West,' Ellis said, 'all the proceeds will go to the Vigilant Trust. Surely I don't need to remind you of that. And I can promise you right now it'll be a lot of money, a helluva lot of money, for a cause you and I both believe in. It feels to me like you're just being pigheaded. You can't not know this would be a good thing to be a part of.'

Harris took a deep breath. 'Are you asking me to do the exhibition?'

'I'm asking you to at least meet with her. Then, if you're not impressed – well, no one can really make you exhibit with her. Not if you don't want to. And I promise you it won't be difficult for her to find someone else willing to take your place. You're the one she wants, Walker, or the position would have already been very well filled.'

Harris resealed the remaining food into the waterproof bag and tucked away the flask. 'If I listen to her proposal, will you stop nagging me about it?'

Chapter Eight

Stacie sat at the dining table in the flat above the gallery, swaddled in an oversized pair of grey sweats and a ratty undershirt. They were Garrett's, from the days when they were still occasional friends with benefits, after they finally realized the divorce was the best thing that could have happened to them. She owned the gallery outright by then and things were looking up. Neither he nor Ellis knew about the hard years before, and she planned to keep it that way. She flipped through the press coverage of the auction on her laptop. The amount taken in had been colossal. Maggie was beside herself, since it was the first auction she'd presided over.

Even without Jamison's not-so-welcome million, the auction had been the gallery's most successful ever. Stacie was clearly leaving New World Gallery in good hands. Now she could concentrate on the West Coast gallery. And on getting Harris Walker to exhibit his photography. That was the next step on her agenda.

She'd just read the write-up in the *Boston Herald*, concerned that still another paper had made a critical mention of Ingrid Watson's absence at the after-party and dinner for the artists. Not a great start to the woman's career. Her BlackBerry rang, and she knew immediately who it was. 'Morning, Dina.'

'I've done what you asked. All the money for the gallery's expenses from the auction's officially been transferred from your savings.' Before Stacie could even offer a thank you, she added, 'I don't like it. I know I've already told you that.'

'Ad nauseam,' Stacie managed to put in before her accountant continued.

'But I'd be lax in my duty if I didn't tell you again. My job is to take care of your finances and advise you wisely. That's what you hired me to do. And I wish you'd let me do it. I'll remind you again that, under the circumstances, we could claim bankruptcy and you'd come out with at least something to live on, but like this, and with the opening of New World Gallery West – well, your savings won't last long, and then what?'

'You let me worry about that, Dina.'

'You keep saying that, Stacie, but I don't think you understand the gravity of what you're doing.'

Stacie rolled her eyes and sipped her coffee. 'I appreciate your concern, really I do, but I've already guaranteed you'll get paid no matter what happens.'

She could almost hear the woman bristle on the other end of the phone. 'You know that's not the issue. How long have I worked for you now?'

'Long enough to trust me, I hope.' Stacie didn't give her a chance for further nagging about using up her savings. 'And the other account?'

'It's set up just exactly as you requested. All you have to do is go in and sign for it when you get back to Portland.'

'Good. That's great. Now, tell me, Dina, why are you working on a Sunday morning?' She peeked out the window to check the weather. 'And a beautiful Sunday morning at that. You know this late in the season there won't be many more days like this. Take the girls out on the boat or go on a picnic, go to the zoo, do something other than worry about me. I'm all right, really I am.'

There was a long pause on the other end of the phone and Stacie could almost hear her accountant choosing her words carefully. At last she released a sigh as though she recognized the futility of arguing with her client and said, 'Stacie, if you need me … If there's anything I can do, you know you just have to call.'

'I know that, Dina, and I appreciate it. Believe me, I won't hesitate if I need your help. Now, go have fun with your girls. Pretty soon they'll be teenagers, and then they won't want to spend time with their boring old mom, so go. And Dina … Thanks. I don't know what I'd do without you.'

The line went dead, and Stacie realized, as she laid her BlackBerry back on the table, that her hand was shaking. Now she really was in over her head. It was sink or swim, and at this point, she was really keeping her fingers crossed that she could swim even half as well as she thought she could back before this whole thing began, back when she was only planning and scheming, back when it all seemed so doable.

She poured another cup of coffee and paced the small wood floor in the middle of the studio flat that had been her home for those first few years as she struggled to get the gallery back on its feet. No, this wasn't the first time she'd had to sink or swim. Not by a long shot. At least this time she was going in with her eyes open. Not like back then. She leaned against the kitchen counter and let the thick morning light bathe her face, her eyes open just enough to see the slight motion of the lace curtains on the soft breeze that felt more like spring than autumn.

When she let herself into the flat that day, he had been standing there, the halo of that heavy, lazy light surrounding him, making him look like an angel, or maybe an apparition. Her gasp of surprise caused him to turn just enough that his face was in shadow, and he could have been anyone for an instant, except for the scent, except for the power of his presence that always filled any space he entered so there was room for nothing else. Come to think of it, he could have never been mistaken for anyone else. She would have known the feel of him anywhere. Then he moved forward out of the shadow, offering her a reassuring smile.

'I'm sorry, Stacie. I didn't mean to startle you. Zoe gave me a key to the flat a long time ago, and I forgot that this is no longer gallery property. This is your home. Please forgive the intrusion.' He bowed his head in what, on anyone else, would have passed as an act of humility. Then he offered her a smile that made her feel things; the hammering in her chest that made her want to run away, the pulsing low in her belly that made her want to stay.

'On the other hand –' he stepped closer '– it is beginning to seem like if I want to see you I have to break into your flat to do it. If I didn't know just how busy you've been with the gallery, I'd think you were avoiding me.'

‘I’ve been busy.’ She repeated his words, sounding breathless and slightly idiotic. ‘Where’s Zoe?’ she asked, fighting back the urge to run and close the door behind her. She hung her jacket on the peg in the hall and glanced at her watch. ‘What’s going on? I told her I had lunch with the rep from Americans for the Arts before our meeting. Didn’t she tell you we’d meet in her office?’

‘She told me, Stacie.’ His gaze felt like it would bore right through her. It made her squirm; made her feel as though she’d somehow done something wrong and he was here to punish her. Or maybe it felt like she’d done something very right and he was here to reward her. She felt wrong-footed having him here in her private space uninvited, having him here in a space that reminded her how tenuous her life in New York really was, no matter who she rubbed shoulders with. She’d been to Jamison’s penthouse suite. The bathroom alone was bigger than her whole flat; and it wasn’t really her flat. It was the space she stayed in, the place for her meager possessions, the only place she could escape to. But then again, why shouldn’t he come in without asking permission? After all, at least for now, the place technically belonged to him.

‘Darling, Zoe won’t be at the meeting today, and I didn’t have the key to her office. That’s why I came here.’

‘I don’t understand,’ Stacie said.

‘Oh, I think you do.’ He moved into her personal space and smoothed a strand of hair away from her face. His touch felt electric against her skin, like it always did; slightly disturbing; intriguingly arousing. ‘I think we both do, dear. Zoe’s drunk. Very drunk.’

Before Stacie could protest, he placed a cool finger against her lips and shushed her as he might a child. 'I know, we've both made excuses for Zoe – Zoe's sick, Zoe's exhausted, Zoe's too busy to attend – but we both know, we've both known for a long time that Zoe's a drunk.'

Stacie's face burned with embarrassment for her friend, but when she started to speak, he shushed her again, still holding her in the ice blue of his gaze. 'I understand that Zoe's alcoholism is an illness, believe me I do, but no one can force her into recovery, can they? And honestly, darling –' he made a sweeping gesture to include the whole gallery '– we both know Zoe's the reason the gallery's in such bad financial straits. She's made poor, incompetent decisions that a sober person, a stable person, would never make. We all know how much she depends on you now.' He took her by the shoulders and gave her a gentle shake. 'You're the salvation of this gallery. She knows it, and I know it. Everyone knows it.'

Stacie stepped back, finding it strangely difficult to breathe. Trying to remain casual, she straightened her shirt and offered her best business smile. 'While it may be true that Zoe's going through a rough patch at the moment, the gallery's never done better. You've said it yourself, the last four exhibitions have all made money, and every one of them has gotten the right kind of attention it'll take to move the gallery into the limelight, to make it even stronger and better than it is. Whatever Zoe's problems are now, the gallery is here because of her, and I have a job because of her.'

'The gallery's her inheritance, Stacie, and don't tell me you don't know that. I know the two of you were childhood friends. The gallery's Zoe's because her parents left it to her.'

'Maybe so,' Stacie said. 'But she's kept the doors open through difficult times. Anyone can struggle, Terrance. You know that. I've seen the books. I've seen how things have improved in the last year. And I'll do what I have to do until Zoe's better.'

His look of pity took her totally by surprise as he tut-tutted her in the same condescending way he would a child. 'Stacie, come, sit down. The reason I'm here is to show you the real situation, to show you what your dear friend hasn't had the courage to.' He took her hand and guided her to sit at the dining table where there was a black leather portfolio with the Omega Trust logo embossed in small gold letters at the lower right-hand corner.

Once she was seated, he opened the portfolio and sat by quietly while she read, her world collapsing around her in a mountain of debt she could have scarcely imagined, a mountain of debt all owed to the Omega Trust. And now half of that debt officially belonged to her.

'This can't possibly be right,' she said when she was finally certain she could open her mouth without being sick. 'Zoe didn't show me this. She didn't show me any of this or I would have never … and you … you didn't say anything, even though you knew.'

Terrance looked deeply sympathetic, heartbroken almost. 'I thought you knew, darling. I really thought you did. And I confess, I had hopes, I had real hopes that you could help Zoe out of whatever funk she's in and that the two of you together could turn the gallery around, get out from under the debt. And then I realized she'd not been completely honest with you; that she hadn't told you what the real situation was or surely you would have never come on board.'

She tried to push away from the table, but he grabbed her hand and held her there with the damning pages in the portfolio staring back at her. How stupid could she have been to trust to the situation without checking it out in more detail? How stupid? But she had wanted it all so damned badly and … she had wanted to please Jamison. As much as she hated to admit it, she had wanted, even needed his approval.

'Listen to me, darling,' he was saying, stroking her fingers in that same way, that same disturbing way that made her feel like he was way more intimate with her than she'd given him permission to be and yet not nearly as intimate as she pictured in her wild dreams. 'Listen to me; don't you understand? Your debt, yours and Zoe's, is with the Omega Trust.' He laid a hand against his chest. '*I'm* Omega Trust, Stacie. I'm the one who can make it easier for you.' He lowered his gaze slightly; another attempt at humility for a man who'd never had to be humble. 'All you have to do is not make it harder on yourself.' He brought her hand to his lips and lingered there in a kiss that sent shivers up her spine. 'Oh, I know it won't be easy. Nothing worth doing ever is.' He scooted his chair closer to hers, so close that she could feel his breath against the bare skin where the buttons of her blouse came together, hunched as he was, almost as though he were a knight petitioning his lady. Almost.

'Stacie, if you'll just trust me, just work with me on this, I'll help you get through it.' He laid a hand on her thigh, again no more than a parent soothing an upset child. 'Together we can get through this and, in the process, maybe we can help Zoe too.' He gave her thigh the gentlest of strokes through the fabric of her black wool skirt. 'Obviously we can't count on her help at the moment. She's ill, darling, and we have to do our part to pick up the slack and to encourage her to seek thc help she needs.' He cupped her cheek, then ran a thumb along her bottom lip, and her insides felt as though they had been shocked into attention, knotted tight in anticipation. 'It's all right, darling,' he said as he scooted still closer, his knee exerting an almost negligible press between hers, where they rested against each other just below the hem of the skirt. 'I promise I'll help you through this.' His lips brushed hers, his fingers sliding down the side of her throat to the collar of her blouse and to the top button.

Stacie had no idea what might have happened if the phone hadn't rung just then. She bolted backward, screeching the legs of her chair across the wood floor, 'It might be Zoe,' she managed breathlessly.

It hadn't been Zoe. It had been Al Marston, and for the first time since she'd met the man, she was glad to hear his loud, jarring accent on the other end of the phone. The invitation he had extended for coffee she had managed to spin into an urgent meeting, and though it was clear Jamison wasn't pleased, he could hardly interfere with the doing of business by a firm that owed him money. That meeting with Al Marston had been the beginning of a long friendship at a time in her life when she desperately needed a friend.

As Stacie struggled to deal with Zoe's death and … everything else, she had meticulously paid off all the gallery's debts, but the debt of gratitude she owed to Al Marston was one she knew she could never repay. She wondered if the man had any idea just what a lifeline he'd been to her.

Those were hungry times, painful times, and she'd prayed that she'd never be put to the test like that again, but her conversation with Dina was the reality check, the wake-up call that said there would now be no turning back.

Settling again at the table, she pulled up the website of the *Washington Post*. It was Jamison's face that smiled back at her, accompanying the write-up about the auction. Jamison and his million dollar sculpture. Was he turning over a new leaf? the article asked. She was sure the reporter didn't believe that any more than she did, but there were a lot of naïve people in the world. On a whim, she punched in Ingrid Watson's number, but there was no answer. She left a message. It was just your basic *congratulations, sorry you couldn't join us last night; if you need me, I'm here* sort of message. She tried not to think how the young artist's evening with Jamison had gone. She tried to hope for better, but if that had been the case, the woman would have joined the party with the rest of the artists and the people in the art world who could have made a real difference for her. She would have chosen the legitimate path to success and not the quick fix Jamison offered her, the one with way too many strings attached, strings Ingrid Watson would only discover when it was far too late.

Stacie was still thinking about the young artist when her BlackBerry signaled a text into the silence of the flat. She jumped at the sound, then fumbled to check it.

Congratulations, my darling, on the stunning success of the auction last night. It certainly was an extravagant event and, as always, NWG spared no expense. I missed your company afterwards. Though Ms. Watson is truly delightful, she's just a little girl compared to you. We must catch up, Stacie. We have so much to talk about, and even more so as you face the challenges of opening New World Gallery West.

TJ

The chill that climbed her spine left her reaching for the hoodie hung carelessly over the back of her chair. She wrapped it tightly around her and moved again to stand in the sunshine, but still she felt like she had been touched by winter. She'd had a long grace period in which she'd stayed beneath his radar, but she always knew he hadn't forgotten what had happened between them. She always knew her return to Portland, her opening of the new gallery, couldn't help but catch his full attention. It had begun. And now she would have to play out the game to the bitter end.

Terrance Jamison was her past, and when she had left him in that place of dark, gut-knotting memory, her world had blossomed bright and warm and urgent. For ten years she had lived in the sunlight, lived free of the man's grasp. And now, he was about to come into her present. But this time he wouldn't be dealing with an innocent. This time she knew who he was, and this time she knew she would walk back into that darkness willingly and deliberately. Her choice, this time. Not his. That thought was meant to cheer her up. It didn't.

It was another incoming text that made her aware of the painfully tight grip she had on her BlackBerry. She yelped out loud and dropped the device as though it had bitten her. Her heart hammered in her chest. She closed her eyes tightly and breathed in and out, waiting for her pulse rate to steady. At some point, she'd have to text Jamison back. It was her move now, and they both knew it.

As her breathing slowed, and the tension left her stomach, she picked up the phone and opened her eyes to see that the text was not from Jamison after all. It was from Harris Walker.

Impress me. Tell me why I should exhibit my work in your gallery.

She nearly cried with relief. This was good news. This was something positive, and wow, did she need something positive right now. All right, he hadn't said he'd do it yet, but she'd cross that bridge when they got to it, and she'd win him over. She knew she would. With a smile on her face, she replied.

All right, I will. Meet me at the Boiling Point, Wednesday evening, at 7.

His reply was almost instant.

Urg! The Boiling Point is not the place to impress me, Ms. E!

Dee had told her about the little adventure she and Harris had had at the Boiling Point a few months ago, but there was a good reason she wanted to meet him there.

Not your fave place, I know, but I'm meeting Kyle Waters there. Sure you've heard of him – does photos of urban decay and renewal. Believe it or not, the BP is a fine example of both. I'm there to watch him work. We can talk after.

Again the response was almost immediate.

All right. I'm intrigued. But we leave before the police arrive and the raid begins!

She chuckled to herself as she replied.

Will do my best to keep us out of jail, Mr. W. See you there.

Can't wait :-/ came the reply.

And instantly Stacie was in a better mood than she had been since Jamison arrived at the auction last night. It would be a rough ride from here on out, so she would happily take whatever good cheer she could get. If that cheer came in the form of Harris Walker, surly, moody but totally hot photographer extraordinaire – well, so much the better.

Chapter Nine

The Boiling Point was as dark and shadowy as ever, though quieter than usual, since it was only seven in the evening. But even if the room had been crowded, Harris would have immediately picked out Stacie Emerson. The woman had a polish and shine about her that set her apart. Granted, there wasn't much competition here when it came to polish and shine, but still, he was pretty sure she would be eye-catching anywhere. She sat in a booth across from Kyle Waters wearing snug-fitting red trousers and a black tank top that wasn't risqué by any means, but on her, it didn't have to be. On her it said classy and sexy in a place where both were seriously lacking. Not that Harris minded a little biker bar smuttiness from time to time, but wow, it was highly overrated when Stacie was in the room.

She motioned him over with an enthusiastic wave.

'I hardly recognized the place without the long row of Harleys outside or the lovely smell of pot wafting through the air,' Harris said.

Stacie gave him a wicked smile. 'The night's still young.'

He slipped into the booth next to her and offered a handshake to Kyle Waters, who sat across from her looking like a cat who'd just eaten a very succulent can of tuna. 'Waters. Good to meet you.' It surprised Harris to realize that it really wasn't, that he really wasn't keen on sharing Stacie's time with a man who looked a little too much like someone had used an airbrush on him.

The man returned a hearty handshake. 'Love your work, Walker. Great to finally meet you in person.'

Harris was pleasantly surprised when Stacie kissed him warmly on the cheek. 'That is for the mountain lion,' she said, when he shot her an inquisitive look. 'And thanks for agreeing to talk with me here. I know you have tender feelings for the Boiling Point, but I wanted you to join us because I'm here to watch Kyle work. That's a part of the PR for the exhibition, which, if you agree to work with me, I'd want to do with you as well. I like to understand, as much as I possibly can, the artists who exhibit in my galleries and what inspires them. That also helps me plan the best, most effective way to display and promote your work.' She shoved her iPad across the table to him. 'These are some of the pictures Kyle took in Brazil.'

Harris glanced down at the iPad then back up at the photographer, who shrugged modestly. 'Those are just raw images. I haven't had time to work with them yet or to choose the best ones.'

'Everything of Kyle's work I'll be using – and of yours if you agree to the exhibition – will be from the Northwest only, of course,' Stacie said.

Harris had seen Waters' work before and, though he found urban photography a bit claustrophobic, he had to admit this was powerful and gritty in ways that captured the observer and drew him in.

With a quick flick of her fingers, Stacie brought up

another page. 'These are the images Kyle's taken of the Boiling Point so far this evening They'll be exhibited along with this set taken ten years ago, and these that were taken when the building was bought out and rebuilt by a local company hoping to make the place into a successful roadhouse-style restaurant. But there were problems,' she said, flipping through from the very modern, very quirky clean rebuild to its decay and fall into disuse, and then continuing on to the next incarnation, more similar to the squat cinder block build of the present. 'At this point,' Stacie said, 'the place was bought out by Core Invest.'

Harris stopped her hand with his palm. 'Wait a minute. Core Invest – isn't that one of Terrance Jamison's companies?'

She held his gaze. 'It is. Though they don't own the Boiling Point now. At least not technically.'

'Not technically?' Harris asked.

Her gaze didn't waver, but it was Waters who spoke up. 'The place has stayed open through some seriously nasty legal battles, which tend to magically disappear just when it looks like the doors are about to close for good.'

Almost by instinct, Harris glanced around to make sure no one was listening. There was no one else in the place but the bartender and a couple of slummers in designer smart casual who leaned against the bar. Across the cavernous interior that appeared much bigger inside than it did from the parking lot, a grungy-looking band was setting up. 'I thought this was photography, not investigative journalism.'

Waters gave him an impish grin. 'Come on, you're a fine one to talk about art, Walker, when you're the editor of one of the most trouble-making green rags on the West Coast. And the trip you made to the Valderia a few months ago with Ellison Thorne – well, that wasn't exactly about taking pretty pictures, now was it?'

Before Harris could respond to what he could only consider a compliment, Stacie cut in. 'I'm not looking for pretty pictures. I'm looking for stories, stories of the Northwest. I'm looking for histories and journeys and the things that make this place what it is.' She waved a hand to indicate the space around them. 'I don't mean just the Boiling Point, although its history goes way back to before Prohibition. I mean the whole Northwest. It's shaped by the people who live here. There's no place left you can go where that's not the case. In some areas, the evidence of human interaction is less than in others. But the evidence is there, and in some cases it's devastating. In others, the environment and humans have evolved to live in some kind of tenuous harmony.'

The band began to warm up, and Harris noticed that while they were talking, there had been a steady trickle of people coming through the front door past the bouncer, a trickle that was increasing rapidly.

'Here's my moment.' Waters grabbed his camera, practically bounced out of the booth, and began to snap photos, leaving Harris and Stacie sitting next to each other to observe.

For a little while they watched Kyle moving easily in and out among the new arrivals, who were a well-tattooed lot, mostly clad in leather and denim with a fair smattering of overworked spandex.

'There.' Stacie nodded to half a dozen suits at the

bar who Waters was now shooting. 'They know how to work the camera,' she said. 'I recognize their type; cocky, barely out of university, more money than brains, most of which they spend on hookers, blow and expensive cars. They're a big part of the problem here, if you ask me.' She spoke next to his ear. 'They never used to hang out here until about the time Core Invest sold the Boiling Point to a company out of Vegas, which magically appeared out of nowhere when it looked like Core Invest would have trouble holding the place legally. I don't know all the details, but all at once this was where all the testosterone-driven banker boys came to party.'

Harris felt his shoulders tighten as he watched the men preen for the camera and check out the asses of a couple of women in very short, very tight skirts. 'It bothers me a bit that you know all this stuff. Hardly a part of the typical gallery owner's education.'

She smiled without looking at him, and somehow it wasn't a smile that did anything to relax the tension in his shoulders. 'I'm nosey. You should know that by now, Harris. I want to know everything. All of it. Every last detail.'

'Sounds kind of dangerous,' he said.

She laughed, and this time the softening of her face was genuine, self-deprecating. 'As you've seen already, walking's dangerous for me.'

Waters had lost interest in the pretty boys, who were now chatting up the two women. He moved to the band, snapping shots of their set-up and of their interaction, managing to render himself so innocuous no one paid him any attention. This crowd seemed a lot more forgiving of photographers than Harris' great horned owls had been. Grudgingly, he had to admit that he admired Kyle Waters' ability to blend in and shoot without disturbing his subjects. But he couldn't hold Harris' attention for long when he was sitting next to Stacie Emerson, who was practically bursting with enthusiasm. He turned to her. 'So what exactly is it you want from me?'

'I want your worst, Harris. I want your worst.'

'What?'

A waitress delivered a pitcher of margaritas and three glasses, and the band began to play the Eagles' *Take it Easy*, certainly a bit more palatable than the heavy metal blasts Harris remembered from his last experience of the place.

Stacie leaned close to be heard. 'The beer here's crap, but the margaritas are drinkable. Plus, I paid the bartender extra in advance to actually add tequila.' She poured them both a glass, then nodded to where Waters was snapping away near the bar.

'Kyle's work will definitely compliment yours. He deals with urban settings. But your work shows the broader impact of how humans have affected the natural environment in the Northwest.' She took a sip of her margarita, then pulled up Harris' website on her iPad. 'I don't want pretty pictures. Those are easy to come by. I want the reality of how humans live in the world they've taken over.' She flipped to the most devastating of Harris' galleries – the clear-cuts, the oil spills, the illicit landfill near John Day – and slowly scanned through the photos of destruction. As always, his stomach churned and his palms felt damp when he revisited those photos and the memories of those shoots. None of them had been in the least bit pleasant. But at the same time, his respect for Stacie rose another notch. She appreciated more than just the pretty pictures; she understood what his art was really all about.

She continued. 'Oh, I don't want to just show the destruction. I know there've been some amazing reclamations of old mill sites, of eroded clear-cuts. Polluted streams have been cleaned up, the balance has been restored, even been restored to benefit both nature and humans. I want to see both sides of the story.' She nodded to Kyle. 'From both of you.

'And you, Harris, can give me what most people can't. You can give me the full story behind it all, both the devastation and the hope, as well as the legal implications, being a lawyer and all. Ultimately, hope is what the Vigilant Trust is all about, isn't it? What *Wilderness Vanguard* is all about, what everything you do is all about.'

He sipped at his margarita and stared at the dance floor now filling with goths and bikers and more than a few slummers here from their posh jobs in the city. 'You don't want mountain lions or owls, then.'

She offered him a smile that did things down below his navel. 'Not this time. No. I want you to tell a story that may not be so pretty, but that might still give us hope. I want you to *show* us a story that we absolutely need to see and know and understand.'

Harris had to admit the idea intrigued him more than just a little bit. He hadn't expected that from Stacie. He'd figured she'd want a few of his adorable baby wildlife shots, a few stunning sunsets over the Pacific and that would be it. But this was something that excited him, something that he'd thought of doing in *Wilderness Vanguard*, but never really had the scope – nor had he known exactly how he wanted to approach it, especially since it was very hard for him to spend time revisiting any of the photos from what he called his Armageddon Shoots.

'I don't think anyone could get the message across in a visual form quite like you can, Harris. And since the proceeds all go to Vigilant Trust, it seems to me this is the perfect exhibition for New World Gallery West's maiden voyage. Don't you think?'

On stage, the band cranked up a notch and blared an earsplitting version of REO Speedwagon's *Riding the Storm Out*. It was only then that Harris realized the place was nearly full. Kyle Waters returned to the booth. His shirt was partially unbuttoned, his chest was heaving, and the shit-eating grin plastered on his face made him look like he'd just gotten laid and was up for round two. He put his camera down and shot Stacie a wolfish glance. 'Care to dance?' he asked.

Harris would never know what came over him. He wondered if Stacie had paid the bartender to spike the margaritas with something other than tequila, but he slid from the booth. 'Sorry, Waters. You're too late. The lady's dance card's already full.'

He offered Stacie his hand before he gave any thought to the very real chance of her turning him down. Certainly after the way he'd behaved toward her, he deserved it. But he needn't have worried.

She smiled up at him and took his hand. 'How can I refuse the man who bought my mountain lion?'

They left Kyle Waters in the booth, looking a bit dazed as he poured himself a large margarita and drank thirstily.

After the tumble she'd taken into his arms Friday night, Harris was a little surprised to discover that Stacie was such a good dancer. But then just being comfortable with making a fool of oneself was pretty much all that was required in places like the Boiling Point. And though he wasn't really … comfortable with making a fool of himself, he was the one who asked her to dance, so he would do his best to act like he knew what he was doing.

'Are you hoping I won't fall on top of you and embarrass us both, Harris?' she asked, almost as if she had read his mind.

'I'm just a little surprised after Friday, I guess.' There was no way for him to approach the topic of her clumsiness gracefully, so he continued to move about the crowded dance floor in front of her, feeling very much like he was the one about to fall over his feet while she watched him with her usual inside-joke smile.

'I grew up with the Thorne brothers,' she said as she moved in close. He held his breath, half fearing half anticipating what would happen next. 'No one could spend any time with that family and not learn to dance. Dr. Thorne thought dance lessons might make me a little less clumsy. Did you know Emma Thorne was a certified ballroom dance instructor as well as a physics professor? It's the truth, I swear. She taught Ike Thorne to dance. Two fabulous sons later, and the rest is history. Garrett tells me his parents still never miss a chance to tango.'

'I didn't know,' Harris yelled back, admiring the way she shook her booty in the tight red trousers that made her stand out in the sea of leather and denim.

‘No one taught me to dance. Your bad luck, I guess.’

‘I don’t care if you can’t dance,’ she said, placing both hands on his shoulders and shimmying like she meant business. ‘Just as long as you’re here to catch me if I trip.’

‘So Dr. Thorne’s efforts didn’t work, then?’

‘Oh, they helped, but in my case, there was only so much the poor woman could do.’

As the music slowed and the band began to play Meatloaf’s *I Would Do Anything for Love*, Harris settled his hands onto her hips and found he rather liked the way moving with her made *him* feel less awkward. She slid her hands behind his neck, and he held his breath, preparing for the full frontal rub-up he both anticipated and feared. But she surprised him by talking business.

‘Look, I don’t expect you to make the decision to work with me right here and now. I know it’s a lot to take in, and I know … well, I know how you feel about me. But if you can put that aside and look at what I’m proposing objectively, I’m sure you’ll see that it could be good for everyone. If it’s OK with you, I’ve got a written proposal that should answer all of your questions and clarify anything you’re not sure of, and –’

They found their space invaded by Kyle Waters and his camera. He was dancing with some woman in very tight black spandex, who smiled and blew them a kiss.’

‘Just had to get a picture of this,’ Waters yelled, snapping shots as he moved way less awkwardly on the dance floor than Harris would have liked. ‘Never figured you for a dancer, Walker.’ Before he could respond, Kyle continued, 'I think these shots might be good for my portfolio even if they're a bit too gritty for your exhibition, Stacie.'

Harris wanted the man to go away, but all at once it was as though Stacie was on exhibition, draping herself over Harris and forcing him into a mock tango that had him laughing in spite of himself. It wasn't just that; it was the fact that he was now the plaything of clearly the most interesting woman on the dance floor, and people were staring at them, something he normally would have loathed. But he was first and foremost male, and he could almost guarantee that there were very few men in the room who weren't jealous of him. And Harris wasn't a total stick in the mud. He could certainly play along, letting her sway around him and dipping her dangerously close to the hard wood floor, only to hear her squeal of laughter as he pulled her back to him, with a little *Dirty Dancing* thrown in for good measure. All the while Kyle Waters snapped away.

He spun her in a dizzying ring-around-the-roses and she literally tripped and stumbled into his arms, laughing hysterically. 'Go away, Kyle,' Harris yelled. 'Photo shoot's over. Go dance!'

With his arms wrapped tightly around Stacie's waist, he half marched, half dragged her to the quieter edge of the dance floor, if there was a quieter spot.

Stacie was still giggling, still draped around him up close and personal. 'Did you just drag me away from the photographer I've been propositioning for the last three hours?' Her voice was breathless and close to his ear to be heard above the driving beat of the music, which had turned heavy metal, a song

Harris didn't recognize.

'Oh, I'm sorry,' he said, pulling her way closer to him than was polite. 'I thought you'd propositioned Waters already. I thought you were propositioning me now, and I'm the jealous type, prima donna, you know? Artsy fartsy and all.' He was just about to lose all propriety and kiss her when the police showed up.

Chapter Ten

The fact that cops were pouring through the door only half registered in Harris' Stacie-addled brain. Then some woman screamed raid, and people were running and shoving in all directions. Someone was shouting something in an authoritative voice into a blow horn. It all felt like a scene right out of a gangster movie.

Stacie grabbed him by the hand and dragged him back toward their table. She shoved her iPad in her bag, and shouted at Waters, who had rushed back to the booth with his dance partner hanging on for dear life and was now shooting pictures like crazy.

Every time the man had a camera in his hand, he looked like he was about to get well laid. Did his work really do that for him? The adrenaline rush that came from fear of losing life and limb was the best Harris ever managed.

'You all right?' Stacie yelled to Waters.

Nodding breathlessly, he handed Stacie something that Harris couldn't see. 'Need you to do me a favor.' His words were clipped, excited. 'Can you take care of this for me?' He nodded toward the ladies' room.

'Seriously? You brought that here?' For a second, Harris thought Stacie was going to belt the man.

Waters only shrugged, gave her a sheepish grin, and kept shooting. 'I didn't think.'

She said something that Harris couldn't hear over the chaos, something he figured wasn't very nice.

She grabbed Harris by the hand and headed toward the bathrooms, dragging him right into the women's room. 'What the –?'

She shoved her way into the first stall, dropped a tiny plastic bag with what looked like a couple of roll-your-owns into the commode, and flushed with her booted foot.

'Jesus! Are you kidding me?' He felt the tension ratchet up a notch in his shoulders as she watched the swirl of water in the toilet to make sure her efforts were effective. 'He brought pot here? Idiot.'

She placed a finger to her lips, then slammed the cubicle door shut once she was satisfied with the results. 'I'm sure that's not what they're looking for, but it's enough to land him at the police station.'

Outside someone shouted, 'Hastings, check the crappers.'

Before Harris knew what hit him, she pulled him into the cubicle at the other end of the row and locked the door behind him, talking in a fast whisper. 'Sorry about this. It's not very professional, I know, but I promised to do my best to keep us out of jail, and I'm thinking groping in the ladies' room's not what this raid's all about.'

The words were barely out of her mouth before she launched herself at him, lips first. Damn it; he wanted to be mad at her. They were about to go to jail, for fuck sake! But instead of giving her a piece of his mind, he kissed her right back, hard, and felt her yield and open, and his tongue was in heaven, sparring with hers, tasting, testing, thrusting. Harris found himself hoping that the inevitable arrest would wait until after he got his fill of Stacie Emerson, and that could take a while. She felt way better than she had even in his fantasies, and when his badly behaving hands moved down to cup her magnificent bottom and pull her closer, she returned the favor and gave his ass a good grope. As if that gave him permission to explore, he slid anxious fingers inside her trousers, wriggling down past a minuscule thong to cup an impossibly soft, impossibly firm buttock that gave a muscular clench in his hand, forcing her hips forward until she couldn't possibly miss the press of his appreciative hard-on straining his jeans to get closer to her.

In the hall the noise got louder and the door burst open.

She had just managed a good, firm stroke to the front of his trousers that had his full attention and then some when a heavy-handed knock on the door caused her to yelp, and he nearly fell back onto the commode.

'All right, you two, tuck it in, and come on out.'

Stacie opened the door before they could even attempt to disguise what they'd been up to. He cursed out loud just as the door swung wide and an unimpressed policewoman, who looked as though she could take them both in a wrestling match and not break a sweat, stood glaring at them without the least bit of surprise on her way-less-than-interested face. 'You two got any drugs?'

'I've got some aspirin.' Stacie held her gigantic shoulder bag open for the police officer's perusal.

The woman gave her a bored look. 'You?' She nodded to Harris.

Harris pulled his pockets inside out and a quarter and two pennies pinged against the edge of the toilet and went rolling across the floor.

The officer shook her head. 'Get outta here and get a room. I really don't need to see this kinda shit when I'm trying to work.'

As she herded them out of the bathroom and disappeared into the chaos, Stacie came to a stop and pointed to the crowd shoving toward the door. 'We're never gonna get out that way. I saw a couple of the wait staff taking a smoke break by the back door. Come on.' She grabbed his hand again, took a quick look around, and when it was clear no one was paying any attention, she pulled him behind the bar, around a tight maze of booze crates and boxes to where the back door was propped open with an empty keg. They pushed their way past the keg and immediately came to a halt in front of a brick wall that was forehead-high to Harris. On one side, the building joined the wall at a right angle; on the other, a police car was wedged in tight in an effort to prevent exactly what they were attempting. The car was deserted at that moment.

'Damn it,' Harris said. 'The park's just beyond the wall. If we can get over it, then we can come back around to the parking lot.

'Give me a boost.' She offered him her very sexily booted foot, and he made a stirrup from his hand. Once she was up, he had an enticing moment with her gorgeous butt right at eye level, then, with a little yelp, she disappeared over the wall.

'Stacie! Jesus! Stacie, are you all right?' He had visions of the woman breaking her neck, but at last she answered.

'I'm fine! I'm fine.' Her voice was breathless, and unless he was seriously mistaken, the woman was actually enjoying this! 'It's an easy landing. A grassy slope. Can you make it over?'

He had already backed up and was making a run for it. His feet hit the wall as though he planned to climb it, then he heaved himself up and over, lost his balance, and found himself in a breathless heap next to her on the grass.

'Are you all right?' She grabbed his hand and pulled him to his feet, and, to his surprise, she burst out laughing, then covered her mouth just in case whoever belonged with the cop car came back.

He wanted to ask her what the fuck was so funny, but her laughter was contagious, and he couldn't keep from laughing right along with her. 'Well, that wasn't the most graceful moment for either of us,' he finally managed. They could hear voices on the other side of the wall that sounded like they were getting closer.

'Come on. I know this park,' he said, easing down the dark slope with her hand still in his. 'Dee and Garrett live on the other side of it.' They were just at the bottom of the grassy slope when they heard voices and Harris shoved her behind a hawthorn hedge and pulled her close as a couple walking matching corgis passed in mid-conversation, lingering long enough for one of the dogs to lift his leg on the other side of the shrub, and Stacie was fighting back giggles again.

'It's maybe a good idea if we stay off the beaten path,' he said as the couple and their corgis passed.

'What? To avoid getting peed on?' She offered him a mischievous smile as he pulled her farther off the path to where the grass was a little less manicured and the surface was a little rougher.

'It's the barking I worry about more than the peeing,' he said.

She let out a little gasp, lost her footing, and her forward momentum pulled him off balance too. They rolled ass over elbows down a grassy hill, her huge bag whopping him up the side of the head before the strap broke and the bag gained speed and rolled on ahead of them. She gave up trying not to laugh and totally ignored his efforts to shush her.

The harder he shushed, the harder she laughed, until they came to an abrupt stop in a patch of high grass on the edge of a rhododendron thicket. Stacie landed on top of him, forcing the breath from his lungs with a heavy "hmph". It was dark, he couldn't see well, and she was still laughing helplessly. On top of him! He reached to cover her mouth with his hand, but instead he found his fingers in a tangle of her soft hair and felt her breath on his mouth and there was nothing for it. It was hopeless, and he knew it. He fisted his hand in her hair and pulled her mouth down to his, inhaling her laughter as his ability to breathe came back, inhaling her soft gasp of surprise, inhaling his name forced between her lips, startled, surprised, but not in an unpleasant way. Not in an unpleasant way at all.

Her hands found their way to his hair, using it to pull his face closer to hers, nipping at his beard with her teeth as her mouth took on any challenge his could offer, full and hard and soft and inquisitive, teasing and sweet all at the same time.

His hands were on autopilot as they strayed down her spine and slid into the waistband of her trousers, back to the mounded pillows of her buttocks. A sharp little sigh caught in her throat, and she wriggled her bottom against him. He rolled until he was on top of her and kneed her legs apart. With awkward yanks and tugs, he opened her fly. Her hips jerked and she caught her breath in a moan as he slid his hand down over soft pubic curls, anxious for what lay beneath.

'Harris … Harris, touch me there,' she managed, biting her lip and shifting to accommodate him as he wriggled his fingers down. With her hand on top of his, she guided him to open her, to stroke the soft warm wet of her, to feel the grip of her. And when he found the place where it was warmest, tightest, softest, she trembled and practically cried out loud. 'There, oh yes. There. That's the place. That's it.'

The ease with which she told him what she wanted made him blush into the darkness even as it made his cock jerk in his jeans. With his free hand he grabbed her trousers and tugged them down until he could see the shape of her, the rise and fall of her, the tremors low in her belly.

Though he couldn't imagine how he still had the higher brain function to manage it, he unzipped one of her boots and tugged it off, allowing her to free one leg from her trousers while she worked on his fly, releasing his erection into the grope and tug of her strong hands, which he slapped away to keep from coming too soon.

'Why, Mr. Walker,' she said with a half giggle. 'I'd have never figured you for a commando man.'

'World's full of surprises,' he said, slapping her hand away again. 'The condom, it's in my wallet.'

He tried to grab it from his back pocket, but this

time she slapped his hand away, pulled the wallet free, found the condom and tossed the rest on the grass. Somewhere in the back of his mind he thought he should be worried that their things were scattered all over the great outdoors in the middle of the night, but then she eased the condom onto him, rose above him and mounted him, sliding down so tight and so warm that any other thought that didn't involve him being inside Stacie Emerson went straight out of his head.

And then they were rolling, tumbling, scrabbling in the grass like two wrestlers. Him thrusting, her shoving, him feeling grass in his ass crack before she rode him down hard onto the cool earth, and he no longer cared. She ripped open his shirt to kiss and bite his nipples while he struggled awkwardly to return the favor, finding her bra a fortress to be assaulted until she reached behind her and undid it with a single flex of her fingers. Then she shoved up her top until he could feel her breasts against his chest, rising and falling and pressing hard with each labored breath, vying for the space they shared up close and personal.

In the tense darkness that practically crackled with the night's excitement, it couldn't last long, no matter how much he wanted it to. It was the heat of the moment. It was the fire at the core. It was the pure sensuality of the woman, of her laughter, of her ability to joke in the face of what could have been a disaster and turn it into … well, outrageous sex.

She came seconds before he did, and her spasms of release brought him to his own peak. Neither of them came quietly. Harris didn't know he could make so much noise during sex. And when they both lay back in the grass, laughing nervously and struggling for breath, it occurred to him that any efforts he had made earlier to stay quiet and unnoticed had surely been negated by their lovemaking. ‘Well, I guess if the cops are gonna find us, they’ll find us,’ he said. ‘But it was worth the risk.’

Chapter Eleven

It was possible they both dozed, but Harris wasn't completely sure. He wasn't too familiar with post-coital bliss – at least not when it involved sex with someone other than himself. It was Stacie's little yelp that brought them back to reality, as she shoved into a sitting position and rubbed her bottom.

'I think something just bit my ass.'

He could see her eyes in the sliver of moonlight. 'Lucky something,' he said.

She giggled. 'Maybe I'll let you kiss it better.' Her sentence ended in another yelp. 'Ouch, I'm serious, that hurt!' She jumped to her feet, rubbing her bare bottom.

'Let me see, let me see.' Harris pushed himself up to stand next to her.

In spite of her discomfort, Stacie offered him a throaty laugh as she turned her bottom to him. 'Oh, aren't you just so helpful?'

'I do what I can, ma'am,' he said in his best white-knight-to-the-rescue voice. 'I'm certified in first aid, you know.'

'Can you see anything?' she asked.

'Oh yes, can I ever.'

She punched his shoulder with a loose fist just as he gave her bottom a solicitous grope. 'Well, I'm not lying back down there.'

He pulled her to him, hands cupping her butt, then moving up her spine and around to her delicious, firm breasts, and she responded with a lazy kiss. 'There are lots of other places to lie down where the only thing biting your magnificent bottom will be me,' he said. Then he lowered his mouth to a pert, irresistible nipple.

'And so there are.' She gave his penis a rough stroke, stepped back out of reach, and began to dress. 'But I think we better get decent and see if we can round up our stray belongings first. Can you get us back to the parking lot?'

'Of course I can.' He found his wallet and stuffed it back in his pocket as he tugged his jeans up over his hips.

She was already examining the contents of her damaged bag by the time he was tucked and tidied. 'Would you look at that, the iPad's no worse for the tumble. That's good news.' She dug a little deeper. 'Got car keys, got BlackBerry, got wallet. All good.' She smiled up at him.

'And how's the bottom?' he said, giving her butt a good cupping as they turned to head back up the hill.

'Anxious for you to kiss it all better.'

It was a steeper climb to get back to the main path through the park than Harris had realized. They were lucky they hadn't broken more than the strap to Stacie's bag in their fall.

They stepped out into the clearing where they could at last see the parking lot of the Boiling Point, now empty of police. He was just about to invite her to his place, where the crescent moon reflecting off the lake would be gorgeous, when her BlackBerry rang. 'Leave it,' he said. But it was too late. She'd already answered.

'Kyle? Are you all right? What's going on?' She stopped mid-stride, and Harris could just make out Waters' voice over the device, but couldn't tell what he was saying. Finally, she replied, 'All right, listen. Call your lawyer and I'll be there as soon as I can.'

'What is it? What's going on?' Harris asked.

She shoved the BlackBerry back into her bag and picked up the pace. 'You know that chick Kyle was dancing with? Well, she was apparently well-supplied with blow and not smart enough to try and get rid of it. And Kyle was with her.'

'Shit,' Harris said. 'So the bastard ended up in jail anyway. Well it serves him right, shoving his mess on you to clean up and … Hey, where are you going?'

'To the police station.'

He grabbed her by the arm and turned her to face him. 'You're kidding, right?'

She blew out a breath and ran a hand through her hair, still deliciously mussed from their romp in the park. 'Look, he's scared. They've confiscated his camera and he's never been in jail before. He didn't know the woman had a stash. I'm sure everything'll come clean in the end. He hasn't done anything but still, he needs a ride back to his car once they release him.'

'Well, have him call a fucking cab, and chalk it up to a lesson learned.'

She offered him a look he'd seen parents give kids when they were trying to explain a difficult concept. 'Harris, he was here because of me, and OK, he was showing off a little bit, but how can I not feel at least a little bit responsible?'

She turned and kept walking and Harris followed her, mentally calling down curses on Waters' future offspring for his interruption of their night while at the same time feeling a sting of jealousy that he didn't like at all. 'Are you dating him?' The words were out before he could stop them.

'What?' She tripped over her feet in response, but when he grabbed her to steady her, she pushed him away, and nearly went over backwards with the momentum. 'What kind of stupid question is that? Of course I'm not dating him. He was here for me, so I'll go, just like I'd do if it were you.'

'Oh, so that explains what just happened in the park then? That was you being there for me? Well, I certainly got the better deal then, didn't I?'

Even in the streetlights he could see the fire in her eyes, see the fisting of her hands, and he braced himself for … for what didn't come. Instead, she turned fast and furious, none too steady on her feet, and stumbled to a blue Lexus parked by the curb, unlocked the door and nearly fell in.

He ran after her. 'Wait, Stacie. I'm sorry. I have a big mouth, and sometimes I speak before I think.' He grabbed for the door and held it so she couldn't close it, but she didn't look at him. He could tell by her breathing that she was angry, probably even hurt, but she said nothing.

'At least let me go with you. The police station's not a very nice place to go alone.'

When she turned to face him, her eyes were icy calm. Everything about her was calm in a way that made his blood chill. 'Believe me, I've been alone in far worse places.' Then she slammed the door and sped away, leaving him standing in the parking lot feeling mean-spirited and miserable.

He didn't know how long he stood there like an idiot, trying to figure out what had just happened, but he was certain he didn't want things to end this way. He found his Jeep where he'd parked it what seemed like ages ago and headed for the police station.

He probably would have caught her too if not for the highway patrol. Christ! It really wasn't his night where the authorities were concerned. He'd never had a speeding ticket. Well, he did now, and all because of Kyle fucking Waters. No! It was all because of Stacie Emerson. What the hell was he thinking? She was trouble. Hadn't he said all along she was trouble? And yet, even after the officer had issued the ticket, told him to slow down and given him the whole be-safe-out-there spiel, did he go home and pretend he'd never met the woman? No! He went straight on to the police station. No matter how hard he tried, he just couldn't get the look on her face out of his head. He had been rude. She had not. She had just shut down. He would have never expected that from someone as fiery and confident as Stacie Emerson.

He shoved his way through the door at the police station a full 30 minutes behind Stacie. Neither Stacie nor Waters were anywhere to be found. The desk sergeant gave him a bored look over the top of his glasses.

'I'm looking for Stacie Emerson.'

The man shook his head. 'She's not here. She left about ten minutes ago.'

'You're sure?' Harris said.

'Look, buddy, I forget most faces that pass this desk before they're even signed in, but not hers. Tall, blond, prettiest smile I've ever seen, and nice. Really nice. I don't get a lot of nice in here.'

Just then Kyle Waters came out of a door leading into the bowels of the station with a man dressed in smart casual who Harris guessed was probably his lawyer. Seeing Harris, he pushed forward toward him. 'Did you see Stacie?' Before Harris could answer he said, 'She got here just after my lawyer did. God, Walker, I was so, so stupid. I need to apologize to her big time.'

The desk sergeant handed him a sheet of paper. 'I'm not a secretary but, like I said, the woman was really nice. If you're Kyle Waters, this is for you.'

Harris didn't care how rude it seemed; he moved in close and read over Waters' shoulder.

Glad your lawyer's here, Kyle, and that everything will be fine. I'm really sorry, but something's come up and I have to go. We'll talk later.

Stacie

When the desk sergeant noticed both Waters and Harris looking at him, he shoved his glasses up the bridge of his nose with his middle finger and said, 'She got a text. That's all I know. And whatever was in that text didn't seem to make her real happy. Then she asked if she could leave a message, and she left.' He looked down at his watch. 'About ten minutes ago.'

I paid a million dollars for a sculpture by a woman I barely know, my darling. How much more do you suppose I would gladly pay to help support a woman

I respect so much and know so very, very well?

Yours most sincerely,

TJ

Stacie looked down at the text again as she paced the floor of her office, clutching her BlackBerry. She had gone to the gallery rather than going home to her apartment. The apartment was just a rented space. The gallery was hers. It represented a new beginning. It represented more of her soul than anyone would ever know, and even when the rooms were still bare, even when the workers were still coming and going, even after it had been violated and vandalized, the space was hers, really hers. Maybe that was why she found she could always think better there.

She looked down at her watch. It was almost two in the morning. The furniture would come the day after tomorrow; after that, she could truly occupy the space. She brought up the calendar on her BlackBerry and scrolled down. Martin Flannery was sending in a crew to start work on her security system that same day. There was a message concerning the progress of the Japanese exhibition. Everything was right on schedule, even slightly ahead. She stood and looked out the mezzanine window which overlooked the main exhibition hall. True to their word, the workmen had finished repairs on the damaged floor and walls and, in her mind's eye, she began mentally placing exhibits. In spite of the vandalism, everything was coming together. But she still wasn't sure if Harris Walker was in or not. Her insides felt like they were in freefall as she thought about him, as she thought about the way the evening had begun, so promising, and the way it ended with him still thinking the worst of her.

She moved back to the desk and settled in the uncomfortable metal chair. Opening her laptop, she found the proposal she planned to send Harris. She could kick herself for letting things get so out of hand with him. Granted, she had no way of knowing there would be a raid on the one night she chose to show up at the Boiling Point, on the one night she invited Harris Walker, who'd come even though she knew he hated the place. But that didn't excuse her thoroughly unprofessional behavior in the park after the raid. In one short evening, she had managed to destroy any chance she had of him believing her to be anything other than the bimbo who fucked the Thorne brothers. In less than 30 minutes she had done more to cement his opinion of her than she could ever possibly undo, and going to Kyle's aid only seemed to prove his point.

Quickly she typed up an email.

Dear Mr. Walker,

Please find attached the proposal of which I spoke when we met. Don't hesitate to get in touch if you have any questions. I look forward to working with you.

All the best,

Stacie Emerson

Then she added quickly:

PS. I'm sorry for tonight's mishaps. I apologize for my bad behavior and will do my best to conduct myself more appropriately in the future.

It sounded stilted and stuffy, but she was desperate to salvage the situation. He was still the one she wanted, the one she needed in her exhibition. He could do what no one else could, and as much as she hated it, she could live with him thinking badly of her if he would only agree to the exhibit. She sent the email. She'd call him at a decent hour and do her best to salvage the situation. In fact, it took all her control not to call him now. But it was hard to think about what happened and not be angry and hurt by his response. It was better that she wait.

She stood and paced again, then looked back at the text from Jamison. It had rattled her way more than it should have. It simply meant there was no room in her life for any kind of distraction now. Not even one as exciting as Harris Walker. Her insides did a little flip-flop as she recalled their breathless tumble in the park. Especially no room for a distraction as exciting as Harris Walker. Focus was paramount if she was to survive this. Everything was ready, checked and re-checked. She was ready, as ready as she would ever be. So why didn't she feel like it?

She spent another hour answering correspondence and doing busy work – anything to take her mind off the night's misadventures and the text from Jamison. When she could no longer function properly, and her body ached from the uncomfortable chair, she shut down and left the gallery, which had no bed. Until the comfy sofa arrived, she'd have to go to her apartment if she wanted to sleep, and she found she really did. In fact, she half-hoped she could wake up and find the whole incident had been nothing but a bad dream.

Stacie had deliberately rented close to the gallery, and that meant a tatty place in a faded but relatively safe apartment complex. Being frugal was still her default setting after everything that had happened with the New York gallery. It didn't matter what she could afford; for now all she needed was a bed and a shower, both of which she'd have at the gallery when the work on it was finished. The rest would come later, but, at the moment, *later* was a step too far to even contemplate.

Inside the entryway to her apartment block, she unlocked her mailbox, which was stuffed with mostly junk mail and a sales flyer for the local Fred Meyer. She sorted through it as she climbed the stairs and stuck the whole lot under her arm while she unlocked the door, an awkward act that resulted in her dropping her damaged bag on the floor. Contents skittered and rolled in all directions on the worn green carpet, the mail following suit in a flapping flurry of paper as she made a heroic, but ineffective, effort to grab the bag. Numb from a day that felt as though it had gone on forever, she dropped on all fours and shoved lipstick, BlackBerry, three pens, a compact, and an all but empty bottle of hand cream back into her bag before she came to the one letter in among all the junk mail. It lay upright in its clearly expensive handwritten envelope. The return address was Jamison Holdings. She sat down hard in the middle of the paper litter.

For a long time she just sat there, leaning against the wall, staring at the letter as though she could will it to go away. Then she fumbled in her bag for a nail file, picked up the envelope and opened it carefully. Folded in an expensive sheet of stationery was a check for two million dollars, made out as casually as if it had been only the money to pay for the dry cleaning. The little whimper that escaped her throat echoed in the empty hallway. She clasped her hand over her mouth and fought back tears. She wiped frantically at her eyes with the back of a hand so that she could read the note on the paper, then she took a deep breath.

You see, my darling Stacie, I know what you need. I've always known what you need even before you did. And now it's time to let me take care of those needs. It's time to let me ease the burden.

Very truly yours,

TJ

She stared down at the note, not really seeing it, the check held absently in one hand. Then she jolted into motion, scooping the rest of the contents of her bag back into the gaping maw and shoving the junk mail in on top of it. At the very top, she added the envelope from Jamison and its contents. Then she heaved herself to her feet and let herself into her apartment. Once she was safely locked inside, she shoved the bag onto the kitchen table and pulled out the letter and check. She read over it one more time. Then she pushed everything back into the envelope, scotch-taped it shut and wrote on the front in her most careful penmanship: *Return to Sender*.

Chapter Twelve

‘You look like you had a rough night in the hide,’ Garrett Thorne said as he handed Harris a cup of strong coffee and settled across from him at the picnic table on the patio behind his house. Harris was sure Kendra had encouraged more al fresco dining now that she lived with Garrett. She always did like a good picnic. But today Harris had deliberately timed his visit to talk to Garrett alone while Kendra was with her psychologist.

‘I was at the Boiling Point.’ He barely opened his mouth, half daring Garrett to tease him about it.

‘Right. With Stacie. How’d that go?’

‘Does no one ever mind their own business around here?’ Harris grumbled.

‘Nope, no one does, but as far as I was aware, that wasn’t a secret.’

When Harris said nothing, Garrett set down his coffee and offered him the look that said he was about to turn pit bull and have fun doing it. ‘So, what? Why do you look like you slept with the dogs and could bite the head off a rattlesnake?’

‘I don’t have a dog and there are no rattlesnakes in this part of Oregon.’

‘So?’ Garrett gave a shrug. ‘What, then?’

I … I didn’t behave very well.’

‘Oh, now that’s a shock,’ Garrett said, folding his arms across his chest. ‘What did you do?’

‘She really knows her stuff, doesn’t she?’

‘We already told you that she does. Now what did you do?’

Harris drummed his fingers on the table top and avoided Garrett’s gaze. ‘She doesn’t want to use my great wildlife shots. She wants to use my slash and burn photos – you know, clear-cuts, oil slicks, that sort of thing.’

‘And you didn’t want to do that? Garrett asked.

‘No! No, I wanted to. I think it’s a great idea. I was surprised she even knew about those photos.’

Garrett offered him a smirk. ‘Trust me, Harris, she probably knows about the photos you took with the first camera your parents bought you when you were a little boy.’

‘The woman does her research.’

‘She does. Yes. So what did you do?’

Harris looked down into his cup, still avoiding Garrett’s gaze. ‘The place got raided.’

Garrett threatened to choke on his coffee in a fit of laughter. ‘You’re shitting me. Sounds like an exciting night. So what happened?’

Harris offered a half-committed shrug. But Garrett was on a roll. ‘You two didn’t end up in jail, did you? I mean, I know Stacie doesn’t do drugs, and you – well, I’m always a bit surprised when you even have a beer.’

‘Fuck you,’ Harris growled.

Garrett gave an exasperated sigh, but even Harris could tell he was struggling to keep from smiling. ‘So what the hell happened? Why are you here when you knew full well Kendra wouldn’t be?’ He raised his arms as if to shove back any protest. 'Hey, don't get me wrong, I'm kind of getting used to you not hating me quite so much. But something major must have happened for you to seek out my company. Are you going to do the exhibition?'

'I'm not even sure she'll want me after last night.'

'Harris, what the fuck happened?'

'We … I … I mean, we didn't plan it, and I would have never … I mean, she's – well, you know what I mean. She's … We were dancing, and then the police came, and then we were hiding in the ladies' room and there was this wall and we climbed over it to get to the park and we –'

'You had sex with her.'

Harris' throat felt dry, and for the life of him he couldn't remember how to speak. He swallowed hard and stared dumbly at Garrett, figuring this was the point where the man would clean his clock, and he absolutely deserved it. He did! Not only had he had sex with Stacie Emerson, but then he'd followed it up by being really rude and … Before he could prepare himself for the punch he figured was coming, he realized Garrett was shaking, violently. It took him a second, and a couple of snorting gasps from the man, to comprehend that it wasn't anger that was making him shake. It was laughter! Fucking Garrett Thorne was laughing at him.

He squared his shoulders and sat up straight on the bench he'd been hunching over. 'I don't think it's funny at all.'

'I'm sorry, I'm sorry.' Garrett raised a hand like he was erasing a chalkboard in an effort to negate his unwelcome outburst, but then gave another snort and dissolved helplessly back into laughter, grabbing at his wounded side and groaning in the middle of a belly laugh.'

Harris only glared at him.

'I'm sorry, really I am.' Garrett wiped tears from his eyes with the tips of his fingers and swallowed down another snigger. 'But really, Walker, seriously. I could see that coming a mile away. We all could. I can't believe you didn't.'

'What? You expected she'd try to seduce me and you didn't say anything.'

'Hold it, buddy. Hold it right there.' His smile was completely gone, and the hard set of his jaw made him look like he could chew concrete. 'I seriously doubt if Stacie tried to seduce you.'

Harris felt a hot blush flood his cheeks. 'No. She didn't.'

'Didn't think so. Not the Stacie I know, anyway. I'd imagine she's as upset about the whole incident as you are right now. She wants you to do the exhibition for her really badly, and she'd never do anything to sabotage that, especially when –' he gave a snort and half a snigger '– you hate her so much.'

'I don't hate her,' Harris sputtered. 'It's just that –'

'I know.' Garrett was dead serious again. 'You still blame her for what nearly happened to Dee and Ellis, and since I'm with Kendra, and she's happy and safe, Stacie's the only one left you can openly blame.'

Harris felt like he'd been slapped. 'That's not fair.'

Garrett held his gaze. 'You're right. It isn't fair, but believe me, no one was happier about Dee and Ellis getting together than Stacie. It's true, she can sometimes behave like a bumbling idiot when she catches the scent of possible romance. Hell, so can I. But she never, ever wanted anything but the best for the two of them. And something else you need to know, Walker: you're not the only one around here capable of rendering serious bodily injury if someone hurts one of your friends.'

'She's your ex.' Harris struggled to find his voice.

'She's my friend first, foremost, and always. And if you knew her at all, knew anything about her, you'd understand why Ellis and I stayed friends with her even after everything that happened, and why Dee and Kendra like her too.'

There was frosty silence. Then Garrett downed the last of his coffee and folded his hands on the table, still holding Harris in a hard glare. 'Now, suppose you tell me exactly what happened, and I'll decide if bodily injury is necessary.'

Just as Harris finished telling Garrett how he'd missed Stacie at the police station and hadn't had the guts to call her, Kendra slipped through the French doors with a Diet Pepsi in hand. She gave Garrett an enthusiastic kiss on the mouth then offered Harris a bear hug that slopped her soft drink on the paving stones.

'Hey, sweetie! What brings you to our neck of the woods?' She gave his hair a mussing.

'Harris had sex with Stacie,' Garrett said.

Kendra gave a happy yelp followed by another bear hug and a near miss with her drink. 'How was it? Good, I bet.'

'You've got a big mouth, Thorne,' Harris growled. Then there was no choice but to recap events that he found extremely embarrassing as the two listened – rather politely, all things considered. He had to admit to a very persistent Kendra that, indeed, it had been good sex. Without a doubt the best sex he'd ever had, but he didn't tell her that.

At last Garrett spoke. 'Stacie's done her research, but it sounds to me like maybe you haven't done yours, Harris. If you had, you'd know Stacie Emerson is a goddess in the art world because she did the impossible with the money pit that's now New World Gallery, so much so she's now opening New World Gallery West. And believe me, she totally deserves her reputation.

'And just so you know; Stacie isn't likely to let your bad behavior change her mind about wanting you to exhibit your work. She's got to be used to your being rude to her by now, and she has a fairly thick skin. She has to have to be able to do what she does and do it so well.'

Harris didn't know what to say, so he said nothing. What could he say; that he was stupid for writing Stacie off as some relationship-breaking bimbo when everyone else respected her and liked her? Well, that pretty much went without saying, didn't it? And really, the one he needed to be talking to right now was Stacie, not Garrett and Kendra.

Before he could do more than let out a soft "wow", his Blackberry buzzed with an incoming text from his assistant over at *Wilderness Vanguard* wondering if he could approve her choice of photos for the article on migration they were running.

He texted her back to say any of the ones he'd left with her were fine. It was then he noticed an email from Stacie. Kendra and Garrett spoke practically in unison.

'It's a message from Stacie, isn't it?'

Harris white-knuckled the BlackBerry to his chest, where his heart was now jackhammering wildly as Kendra practically leapt over the table to look over his shoulder. 'Jesus, do you two take nosey lessons or is it just a natural talent?'

'Well, in my case it's a natural talent,' Kendra said. 'Don't know about Garrett. Go on, read it. What does it say?'

He skimmed through the stilted *Dear Mr. Walker* part all business-like, feeling as though Stacie had reached through the device and gave him a hard slap. But then this was business, he reminded himself, and if she were anything like Garrett and Ellis said, she wouldn't let last night's fuck-up put her off. He couldn't help noticing the email was sent in the wee hours. He could have called her then. He should have.

At a glance he could see the attachment. He'd give it some serious attention when he got home, and send her a proper response. Just when he thought she'd pretend nothing had happened he read her PS.

PS. I'm sorry for tonight's mishaps. I apologize for my bad behavior and will do my best to conduct myself more appropriately in the future.

He fired back a response, typing with awkward fingers, oblivious to Kendra and Garrett trying to wheedle out of him what the message said.

Thanks for this, Stacie. I'm very intrigued by your proposal. As for last night's bad behavior, you're not the one who needs to apologize. Don't know how many more mountain lions I can afford. Will try to behave myself in future.

Harris

‘Was it good news? It was, wasn’t it?’ Kendra said as Harris stuffed the device back into his pocket.

‘She sent a detailed proposal for the exhibition,’ he replied.

‘There, you see,’ Garrett said. ‘She doesn’t hate you and she still wants to work with you.’ Then he offered a crooked smile and a little shrug. ‘Well, at least she still wants to work with you.’

That fact alone made Harris way happier than he would have expected, when, only 24 hours ago, he just wanted the woman to leave him alone.

Chapter Thirteen

Stacie already regretted starting this little adventure so late in the day. She should have waited until tomorrow and started fresh. The weather was getting worse by the minute, and the road gradually muddier, but she was committed now. Really, Stacie knew better than to bring her leased Lexus up onto these logging roads. She was planning to get something a little more practical for off-road conditions, but she just hadn't had the time yet, and when the rain set in, she was too close to her goal to turn back. She pressed on, tense in the seat, foot gently easing on and off the gas pedal with as much finesse as she could manage. OK, it wasn't a lot, but it had been enough to keep her out of the ditch so far.

The knot in her stomach got bigger as she neared the site. She tried not to remember how it looked before. That would do nothing but make things more difficult, cloud her judgment with more anger, and there was already enough of that to deal with. She was seriously considering turning around without seeing what she'd come for when the wheels began to spin, and the car lurched sideways dangerously close to the embankment. An effort to gently reverse and ease around the slick, muddy patch resulted in a backward slide that left her crossways in the road and then nearly in the ditch. After that, no amount of effort would force the vehicle forward or back.

'Damn it!' She hammered her fist hard against the steering wheel and looked out the window into the deluge. Just as she turned off the engine to try and regroup, her BlackBerry signaled an incoming text. It was from Harris Walker and, in spite of herself, she smiled. He couldn't afford many more mountain lions, he said. So he'd have to behave himself in the future.

She had to fight the urge to write back that she really didn't mind him misbehaving. She liked that part, as long as he wasn't rude. His rudeness hurt her pride. That she could live with, but it was the nerves he had inadvertently touched with his rudeness that hurt much worse. Still, he didn't know that. She didn't want him to know that. Ever. She texted back.

No more mountain lions necessary. Your apology is accepted.

On a lark, she sent him her GPS coordinates. *BTW, do you know this clear-cut?*

She was immediately sorry she'd done it. This was not something she really wanted to share with him. His message came back almost instantly.

Yes. I know it's horrible. One of the worst. Why?

His response made her wish even more that she hadn't come. She replied.

I need to check it out. Not the best weather for it.

Now? he asked.

She kept her answer much lighter than she was actually feeling at the moment.

No time like the present. Ditching the Lexus (LOL, I know. Must get a Jeep) for the walking boots and waterproofs. Will send pics.

She promised herself she'd take pictures, no matter how hard it was. She was convinced that this was something she needed to do. Now she wasn't so sure. She stuffed the BlackBerry in the pocket of her Columbia and zipped it tight, then shoved her keys in the small rucksack. She pulled the hood of her jacket up and stepped out into the rain. This was the Northwest. She should have suspected what she might be getting into weather-wise when she headed out. No use dwelling on it. She was here now, and the Lexus wasn't going anywhere so she might as well get on with it. She'd deal with getting the car unstuck when she got back.

Stacie headed up the logging road, slipping and sliding as she went. Thankfully it wasn't windy or cold, which it easily could have been with fall rapidly bearing down on the Cascades. That meant she could concentrate on moving forward, one step at a time, which was about as much of an effort as she could manage in the mud. The rain let off slightly, then intensified again. The slope steepened, and inside the tight confines of the hood of her waterproof, she could hear the raspy in and out of her labored breath.

As she pressed one foot in front of the other it was impossible to hold back the flood of memories. The first time she read about the clear-cut, she had been researching Terrance Jamison, the man she and Zoe Hanson were in debt to, the man who was sometimes too good to be true and other times too frightening to even consider. She'd found the article in the archives of the *Oregonian*, and she had wept. She knew the place. She loved the place. She had watched the night sky there with the telescope she and her father had built together. She had drawn extensive pictures of the face of the moon there with the Thorne brothers, back when the true love of their lives was astronomy. And the man she was hopelessly in debt to, the man who frightened and aroused her and made her doubt everything she believed in her life, had destroyed it, and had already done so even before he offered her that first smile and handshake.

She'd had nightmares about the devastation for a long time after she'd discovered what had been done to the place; a place that had no special designation. They had always just called it Bald Hill. It was a bald mountain, really, with slopes covered in Douglas fir. The road wound along its wooded side in hairpin curves. It stopped much farther down the slope before the logging road was built. It had been quite a little hike to get themselves and the telescopes up the hill before sunset. Once there, they'd settle in for a meal of peanut butter sandwiches. They saved the Thermos of hot cocoa Dr. Thorne always furnished them with for later when it got colder and their fingers became uncooperative on the scopes and on their pencils and notebooks. And now that place existed only in her memory. She was vividly reminded of that when she rounded a sharp curve and found herself face to face with devastation she could barely believe. Oh, she'd seen clear-cuts before. Everyone who grew up in the Northwest had, but it had never been personal until this one. The extreme slope had rendered the whole area only slightly less than a mud slide. The logging road that she now stood on disappeared a few yards ahead of her in the washout caused by heavy rains and erosion. Ultimately, the whole slope above was sliding down the hill. Other than the high cut stumps and the remaining limbs and debris left from logging, the slope was bare, even after all this time. Water ran off in muddy rivulets stained reddish brown from the clay soil, which made it look disturbingly as though the slope itself were bleeding.

She thought she had known what to expect. She'd seen pictures. She'd read reports. She'd done all she could to prepare herself. But it wasn't enough to prevent the cry of anguish that tore from her throat. Her stomach rolled with nausea and the devastation burst on her senses like an abscessed wound, driving her to her knees in the mud.

For an eternity, she knelt there in the mire blinking back tears, waiting to vomit, waiting to pass out from the pain of it, from the insult of it, from the mourning for what was lost. But when she didn't retch, when she didn't even weep, she fought her way to her feet and stood looking out over the ruined waste, and it was not the good memories of her childhood that washed over her, but memories of what had brought her to this place, and thoughts of why she had to see it for herself, why she needed to be here.

She stood until she felt as though she was no longer really there. She stood until she felt as though she was simply looking down on her body from a distance, from a place that had nothing to do with her childhood or her early days in New York or what was yet to come. She had waited for it, the separation, the place she had gone so often in those difficult times; the place where Stacie Emerson was untouchable. Being able to separate herself from all the pain, all the chaos, had helped her survive. It had been a long time since she'd needed to be outside herself, but she knew with certainty that she'd need to a lot in the weeks to come.

Calmly, she took her BlackBerry from her pocket and began to snap pictures as fast as she could. She maneuvered herself carefully out onto the remains of the road below the slope, all the while knowing full well that she shouldn't, all the while in the back of her mind noting that the rain had steadily increased, that the muddy flow of water, which had come down in streamlets, was turning into raging torrents around her. She inched her way forward along the incline where the road had been, trying to gauge the size of the devastation. Without the familiar landmarks from her youth, it was hard to even tell where she was.

She practically stepped on something half stuck in the mud. She gave a little yelp of surprise, pulling her foot back just in time and nearly losing her balance in the process. There was little more than a skeleton left, ribs rain-washed and poking sharply from under what remained of a pelt of thick fur too muddied to help in identifying the unfortunate animal. A large rodent of some kind, Stacie guessed. She leaned forward to take closer shots.

As she did so, the piece of wood on which she was balanced gave under her weight and slid sideways. She teetered wildly, clutching at the BlackBerry for dear life. And though she managed to hang on to the device, thus saving the pictures she had taken, the wood snapped and sank farther, sending her tumbling end over end, BlackBerry clasped to her chest with one hand, the other outstretched to stop her slide. A rock poking from the soup of mud and rubble tore her waterproof trousers and took the skin off her knee as she fell. She managed to right herself and force her way to her feet, nearly belly-flopping in the mud again before she got her balance. Quickly, she slipped the BlackBerry into the zippered pocket and caught her breath. Her heart raced in her chest and blood roared in her ears. It took her a second to realize she'd walked much farther into the center of the devastation than she'd thought, and with the tumble and slide she could no longer see where she'd left the remains of the road. But all she had to do was keep the upside of the slope to her right, she told herself, and she'd work her way back to the car. She might not be able to get it unstuck, but she'd be dry and warm inside, and she might even have a Snickers bar or two in the glovebox. She'd be OK. Gingerly, she tested her knee. It was bleeding, but it was only an abrasion, and the knee itself didn't seem damaged. When she was sure her brain hadn't been scrambled and nothing was broken, she began a careful schlep back to the car.

The flat metal daylight was quickly closing in and morphing to something darker and more ominous. She had a flashlight in her backpack, but she couldn't remember the last time she'd checked the batteries. She'd just have to make it back to the car before dark. But no matter how focused her efforts, the going seemed a lot slower on the return journey. The rain had turned cold, and she was tired and sore from the fall.

She kept her head down against the wind that now blew the rain into her face like little pellets of ice. She was almost back to the road when she nearly ran into him, a man shrouded in camouflage, hood drawn tight against the weather, shadowing his face in the swiftly diminishing daylight.

Stacie's insides knotted, and she felt as though her heart would jump from her throat. It wasn't possible. Surely it wasn't possible he'd found out, and even if he had, he wouldn't come for her, but he might send someone, and that would be much worse. Fear clawed up her spine. She looked around frantically. Her only means of escape was across the devastation. She let out a wounded animal yell and turned to run, but the man was on her before she'd managed even a few steps.

With the rain hammering her face, she struggled blindly against his strength, jerking and shoving. But he grabbed her, pulling her to him in a hard embrace.

'Stacie! Stacie, it's me, Harris Walker.' He pulled away from her just enough to look her up and down. 'Jesus, woman, what did you do, roll in it?'

In the overwhelming flood of relief that followed recognition, she would likely have lost her balance and fallen backward if Harris hadn't grabbed her. Embarrassed by her display of panic, she tried to calm herself. The laugh she offered was high-pitched and thin.

'You could say that.' Not wanting him to ask hard questions, she went with the obvious. 'Did you get any pictures?' She nodded at the muddied desolation.

'Not this time. Come on, let's get out of here. This whole slope could go any minute. There are flash flood warnings for the area, but I'm guessing you didn't listen to the weather report.'

'No. I didn't,' she yelled to be heard above the raising wind.

‘We gotta go,’ he said. ‘This is as good as it’s likely to get.’

That was the last they spoke until they slipped and slid their way back to the vehicles. ‘My car’s stuck. Can you pull me out?’ She nodded to the Lexus.

‘I’m serious, Stacie, we’re leaving. We can come back for the Lexus when the weather clears.’

She panicked. ‘No! I can’t leave it. Not here.’

‘Goddamn it, Stacie, this is serious business,’ he said. ‘We need to get out of here.’

‘I know how serious this is, and I’m telling you I don’t want my car left here.’

‘It’s just a lease. It’s not even yours.’ He grabbed her arm and tried to guide her toward the Jeep, but she pulled away.

‘I don’t want my car found here, all right.’ There! She’d said it. More than she wanted him to know, but having her car discovered here was a complication she couldn’t afford.

He shot her a look that felt both questioning and accusing, and then, without a word, threw back his hood and turned to assess the situation. At last he spoke. ‘All right, get in the car and start it.’

She did as he said and rolled down her window for further instructions.

‘You’re not really stuck,’ he said, ‘you’ve just got no traction. Put it in gear, and when I say, gently give it gas, slow and steady.’

‘What are you gonna do?’ she asked.

‘Take my life into my hands,’ he called over his shoulder as he moved to the back of the car to push.

His comment might have made her angry if she hadn’t agreed with him and if the whole situation hadn't been over in less than 30 seconds with the car back in the center of the road.

Once again, he came to her window. 'I'll follow you until we get to the main road, just to make sure you make it OK, then you follow me to my house. You're wet and cold and it's a long way back into your place. Are we clear?'

She nodded.

For a second, he held her gaze. 'I mean it, Stacie. My house. We need to talk.' Then he moved to the Jeep like he was going to a fire.

By the time she had the Lexus on the move, he was following close behind. With the rain and the mist, that was now descending like a thick blanket, she could barely make out his headlights in the dusk. When they were back on the forest service road and almost to the highway, Harris' Jeep passed her, and he took over the lead.

His house really wasn't very far. She had been there before, to attend the cookout Harris had held as an engagement party for Dee and Ellis, but the sight of the split-level log cabin set against the iron-grey mirror of the lake still took her breath away. Even in bad weather, it was beautiful.

She barely managed to shut off the engine before Harris opened her door and half helped, half dragged her out. 'Are you all right?'

'Fine. I'm fine, just wet and muddy. That's all.'

For a second, he stood staring at her, then huffed out a tight breath. 'You scared the hell out of me, you know?' To her surprise, he didn't seem particularly angry, but there was something else in his voice, something equally edgy. Before she could consider what that might be, he continued. 'Come on, let's get out of the weather and find you some dry clothes. How did you know about that place?' he asked as he unlocked the door and ushered her into a screened-in porch.

'I've known about it for a long time, before it was logged.' That was all she dared say for fear of the emotions that the place stirred.

'Listen, I know you said you wanted to watch me work, but that place … Stacie really, that place isn't even safe. It's like hell on earth.'

'I know,' she replied. 'It's not among the places you photographed.'

'No, it's not. For a long time the land was posted and even when it wasn't any more, I just couldn't bring myself to go there.'

'And I forced the issue,' she said. 'I'm sorry.'

For a long moment, he stood with his lips pressed in a tight, thin line as though whatever was on his mind, he was choosing his words carefully. At last he spoke. 'I don't like those kinds of shoots, Stacie. I do them because I think they're important, I think people need to know what's happening to the world. But I don't like them. They're … hard.' Before she could respond, he said, 'Never mind that. You shouldn't have gone out there alone. Even in good weather you should have at least let someone know where you were. That whole hillside could have come down on you and no one would have ever known.' The way he emphasized the word *ever* with a hard slam of the screen door made her consider, for the first time, that he had really been worried about her.

'I did tell someone,' she said. 'I told you.'

‘And if I hadn’t come, what would you have done, spent the night in the Lexus? Assuming it hadn’t gotten washed off the mountain.’

‘Something like that.’ Stacie still couldn’t get her mind around the fact Harris Walker had come to her rescue. ‘I’ve got pictures.’ She pulled the BlackBerry from her pocket and would have dropped it if Harris hadn’t caught it mid-flight and laid it on a low chest next to a forest green bench that sat against the wall.

‘You can show me when you’re warm and dry,’ he said. Then he pushed her hands away, unzipped her Columbia, and slid it off her shoulders. The act felt strangely intimate; and Stacie was surprised by the resulting tremors low in her belly. ‘You’re worn out,’ he said. The irritation rose in his voice. ‘What were you thinking?’ He slid her waterproof trousers down over her hips and eased her back onto the bench.

She knew he wouldn’t like her answer even if she were willing to tell him, so she said nothing, only leaned back against the wall and closed her eyes as he moved to unlace her boots. ‘Well, at least you know how to dress for the great outdoors. Guess you’re not as much of a city girl as I thought.’

‘I wasn’t raised in the city. I’ve been on more than my share of camp-outs and hikes in the mountains, and in conditions way harsher than these, so don’t get snooty with me, Mr. Walker.’

After he’d removed her boots and muddy socks, he eased the waterproofs off over her bare feet, exposing her legs from under her walking shorts. Then he turned his attention to her injured knee.

‘It’s just an abrasion,’ she said, trying to pull away from him. ‘It’s nothing, really. I’m all right.’

But he held her calf in a firm grip, pulling a first aid kit from the drawer of a small chest. 'I'll be the judge of that. It's bleeding still, and if it's a puncture, what with all the tree limbs and debris up there – well, you don't need it to get infected. Plus, it looks like you'll be sporting one helluva bruise.'

His hands were strong and competent. She recalled he was certified in first aid. Using a gauze pad and something from a bottle that stung like hell, Harris cleaned the wound.

She flinched and sucked air between her teeth.

'Hold still, you big baby,' he said. His voice was soft, but she was pretty sure there was a smirk hidden in there somewhere.

Before she could tell him to fuck off, he continued, 'Why were you so anxious to get the Lexus off the mountain? I mean, granted it's a nice car, but if you were concerned about that you wouldn't have taken it up there in the first place.' She felt his hard stare, as though he had temporarily forgotten about her wound. 'Why were you up there to begin with, Stacie? That's definitely not an artsy place.'

'Because I thought it might be a site we could use for a photo shoot if you decide to exhibit with me,' she lied. 'You know, so I can see you work.'

'Jesus, Stacie, first you nearly get us arrested at The Boiling Point and now you want us to risk life and limb in a mud slide. Is this your way of getting even with me for being rude? Because I have to say it's a good one.'

She twisted enough in her seat that she could reach her BlackBerry and, with a flick of her finger, she pulled up the picture of the dead rodent, and shoved the device into his hand. The response was exactly what she had hoped for. She could tell from the look on his face, from the catch in his breath, from the concentration knitting his brow that he was intrigued. And that's exactly how she wanted him. What she didn't want was him giving her the third degree.

'These are gruesome,' he said. She saw the line of his jaw tightening just beneath his closely trimmed beard. 'Seriously, Stacie, this is not a nice place. You shouldn't have been there.'

'It's too late now, isn't it? I have been. So will you allow me to exhibit your work for the opening of New World Gallery West?'

She hadn't intended to be so blunt. She had a reputation for being a patient woman, but there was no denying he would think what she had seen today, what she had done, was done with him in mind, and it was best to use it that way.

He looked at her over the top of her BlackBerry, cocked his head slightly to one side as though he had never seen anything like her before, and simply said, 'Yes. I will. I would have done even without these.' He nodded down to the BlackBerry.

Just like that, after all her thwarted efforts, she had her main exhibitor, with no protest, no conditions, no argument. Just a yes. For a second, the overwhelming sense of relief bled into the exhaustion and the impact of what she had seen, and she closed her eyes and slumped back against the wall. 'Thank you,' she half whispered. 'Thank you, Mr. Walker.'

Laying the device aside, he continued ministering to her knee. 'You're welcome, Ms. Emerson. Look through the images on my website. Tell me which ones you want, and they're yours to use. After I've done an Armageddon Shoot, I don't like to revisit the photos. Once is way more than enough.' Then he offered her a quirk of a smile and a quick sideways glance from under hair that was still damp and curled slightly from the rain, hair that could have used a trim, but Stacie decided he looked better for the lack of it. 'Are police raids and mud slides going to be a regular part of our business association? Because if so, I'd like to plan accordingly.'

'I'm not making any promises,' she replied.

His face darkened. He continued to work on her knee, gently bandaging it with what she was certain was way more care than it demanded – not that she minded. His touch was comforting.

'Stacie, about last night …'

She reached down and touched his hand. 'Harris, it's all right. It was one of those things. Nothing went according to plan for any of us. Let's just forget it and start with a clean slate, OK?'

He glanced up at her, his expression unreadable. For a second, he said nothing, then he nodded slowly. 'You're right, of course. Start with a clean slate.'

Then he went back to binding her knee like a man on a mission.

Chapter Fourteen

Harris woke with a hard-on. Hell, he'd gone to sleep with a hard-on – when he'd finally managed to get to sleep. He hadn't taken care of it because he was a neurotic bastard, he supposed. What the hell? Was he afraid Stacie would hear him jerking off? After all, she was the cause of his uncomfortable state, and he didn't want her to know that, did he? They were going to let bygones be bygones and start again with a clean slate, he reminded himself. A clean slate didn't involve having sex with the woman he'd soon be working with. It didn't! And it irritated the hell out of him that though his brain completely understood all the reasons why sex with Stacie Emerson was a bad idea, his body didn't care, and especially not when the woman was asleep in the next room.

The house was quiet. In fact, everything was quiet. The storm had passed, as had been predicted. For a second, he held his breath and listened, straining to hear any evidence that would suggest his guest might also be awake at this hour. But then he figured even if she were, she'd be trying to keep from waking him.

He had found a pair of Dee's sweats and a T-shirt that she left for the overnighters the Three Musketeers had from time to time, and once Stacie was out of a hot bath and dressed, he had fed her his mother's tomato soup. She always brought it over from the valley, made fresh from her home-grown tomatoes and ready for his freezer. All he had to do was nuke it in the microwave. He'd rummaged in the cupboard for some saltine crackers that weren't past their sell-by date, and the two had eaten at the breakfast bar. Even with all Stacie's contagious enthusiasm for the upcoming exhibition, he could tell she was exhausted and that her experience of the clear-cut had shaken her deeply. He had no doubt it would have shaken anyone, but he couldn't imagine how it must feel for someone who had fond memories of the place before it became another Jamison statistic. Among the green folks in the Northwest, of which there were many, the place had become known as Jamison Hill. He had bought the timber rights and, in a move that was only just barely legal, sold them to a company that had been notorious for particularly ruthless clear-cutting. Before anyone knew what was happening, the place had been turned into a wasteland.

It made Harris extremely nervous being around anything that had Terrance Jamison's stamp on it, and Stacie's refusal to leave the Lexus on the mountain made him even more so. He made a mental note to get Cal over at *Wilderness Vanguard* to do a little more research on the clear-cut just in case there was something he didn't know, something he'd missed.

As much as the exhibition intrigued Harris, he had a shitload of questions that had nothing to do with art or photography. Stacie had done her best to hide it from him, but either she wasn't a very good liar, which he figured was probably the case, or he was pretty intuitive, which was also pretty much the case.

There were things she wasn't telling him. Why the hell had she gone to that awful place on her own? She wasn't stupid. Why would anyone with memories of what the place had been like before want to see it like it was now? Why had she really been so hell-bent on getting her car off the mountain? And why had she reacted like she did when she first saw him? Clearly she was expecting someone else, and whoever it was, she wasn't glad to see them. In fact, it was safe to say she had been flat-out terrified. That certainly wasn't like the Stacie Emerson he knew. If her behavior had anything to do with Jamison, he could completely understand why she was frightened.

Harris tossed between the covers, shoving at the pillow. Thinking about the clear-cut and the danger in which Stacie had put herself definitely took the edge off his arousal. It chilled him to think what could have happened. And that was only what he knew nature could have thrown at her. Add to that whatever Stacie was afraid of, and he shuddered to think. The room felt stuffy and close. Because he seldom spent time inside when he could be out, he kept as many of the windows and doors open as he could when he was home. He'd only closed his bedroom window to keep the deluge from blowing in.

He shoved back the blankets and crawled out of bed, nearly tripping over his discarded jeans. He bit back a curse, then moved to open the window and let some real air in. The sky was clear and the stars now reflected off the obsidian surface of the water. The sliver of the waxing moon looked as though it were floating suspended there. He threw open the window, and, for a second, he stood just breathing in the cool, rain-washed air. He was about to grab the camera he kept handy to take a few night shots, then the hard-on was back with a vengeance.

Below him on the dock, wrapped in a blanket, stood Stacie, looking out over the water. And in spite of his body's overwhelming desire for her, he felt something other than lust stirring, something that had been easing its way into his brain ever since he'd made such a fool of himself the other night at Ellis' place. It was respect. This woman was completely at home in New York City. No one could deny Stacie Emerson was polished to a cosmopolitan sheen. And yet the passing of a storm would draw her outside to see the world without city lights, to listen to the quiet, all the layers of quiet that were practically their own symphony outside on Harris' lake.

Almost before he knew what he was doing, he'd slipped into his jeans and moved quickly on silent feet down the stairs and through the darkened house to where the French doors led to the decked balcony and then down to the dock. But just before he reached her, she dropped the blanket, and he was afforded an exquisite, if all too brief view of Stacie's long legs, rounded buttocks and the slender curve of her back, rendered porcelain-pale in the diminished light. Then she stepped off the dock into the lapping water.

Once again, he reacted without thinking, quickly stepping out of the jeans and leaping off the end of the dock with a splash, which resulted in a squeal of surprise and a mad swirling of the water from Stacie.

'It's me,' he managed before swallowing a good-sized mouthful of the lake as he lunged to touch her arm reassuringly. But her panicked flailing dragged them both beneath the surface. For a second, he felt his own panic rising as he desperately tread water, one of his shins brushing the mooring of the dock. Then they both surfaced, coughing and sputtering. 'Stacie! Stacie, it's me,' he said. She clung to him, shivering. 'Are you all right?' He slipped his arms around her hips for support.

He could feel more than see her nodded response. 'Sorry,' she gasped. 'I didn't mean to drown you. I woke and the storm was finished and the stars were just so beautiful over the lake. I couldn't resist. Sorry I disturbed you.'

His embarrassed laugh forced his belly and other parts of him into her delicious, totally naked, personal space. 'You didn't disturb me. I think if anything it's the other way around. I interrupted your communing with nature, which is almost an unforgiveable sin in my world.'

He felt her breasts pressed hard-nippled against his chest in her own little laugh. 'It isn't necessarily a given that I wouldn't welcome your interruption, that I wouldn't want to share the pleasure with someone who appreciates it as much as I do.' In her efforts to tread water, she kicked him in the thigh, but before she could apologize, he kissed her and felt her breath catch as he trapped her leg, sliding it around his waist.

'Harris,' she breathed his name. 'We can't –' But he stopped her words with another kiss and lifted the other leg so that both her thighs gripped him around his waist, his hands supporting her bottom, his legs treading to keep them both afloat.

'Sh! Stacie,' he whispered against her throat. 'Sh.'

'We talked about a clean slate. We said we'd –'

‘Maybe I don’t want a clean slate.’ He kissed her harder. To his delight, she responded in kind, curling her fingers in his wet hair and eating at his mouth. ‘Maybe I like our slate just the way it is. What do you think of that?’

And then he heaved her up onto the floating dock, causing her to gasp and mumble a protest that ended in a little whimper as he pulled her close to the edge, shoving her legs open until his mouth could find the warm, wet depth of her, open and inviting. His tongue made an ice-cream-lick of a path up the soft, moist valley of her that yielded and tensed and yielded again to his mouth. The flavor of her was honeyed and dark and better than anything he’d ever tasted. He held her, squirming and writhing, him licking and sucking all the way up to the apex of her where he settled a heavy, hungry kiss that ended in a nip to her clit. She bucked against him and trembled all over as she tugged at his hair.

His senses were filled with Stacie, the taste of her, the scent of her, the overwhelming presence of her. It was the play of a cool breeze goosefleshing his back that made him aware her shivering wasn’t entirely due to his sexual prowess. With some reluctance, he pulled himself away from his explorations and heaved himself onto the dock. She did her part to drag him up next to her, then, with both of them shivering in the cool air, she hauled her blanket over them like a tent, with him still scrambling to get another taste of her. But she wriggled and squirmed and twisted, elbowing him in the tender part of the inside of his arm before she settled and shifted so that he could feel her warm breath against his pubic hair just before she cupped his balls and took his erection deep into her mouth.

'Oh God, Stacie,' he managed to gasp before he pillowed his head on her wet thigh and opened her legs to find his way back to her. At his first deep dive into her softness, he felt her moan against his cock, a moan he couldn't keep from imitating against the open, enticing swell of her. The muscles low in her abdomen tensed and jerked and he could feel his belly doing the same. He could feel his thighs tensing. He could feel his buttocks clenching and relaxing as he rocked and shifted his hips with an in and out motion.

Their chilled shivering and the convulsive arousal they were both experiencing made their lovemaking deliciously awkward and lacking in finesse, but way too intriguing for them to possibly consider stopping. The night sounds were overshadowed by their heavy breathing, by their moans and whimpers. Harris, who was accustomed to being quiet in the great outdoors so that he could hear and not be heard was lost in the exquisite sounds of the woman in his arms, and the way his own sounds harmonized with hers. The feel of her was as exquisite as he remembered, but this time it was skin on skin, all skin on skin, textured with gooseflesh that made him crazy to have her still closer, to be inside her.

With an effort that felt like it ripped some part of him in two, he pulled away enough to speak. 'Stacie, I don't have a condom. We need to go inside.'

'Shut up, Harris,' she said against his cock. 'This time we're not going anywhere.' She rose to straddle his body without lessening the pressure of her lips, without losing her rhythm, then settled above him, lowering her hips until the splay of her rested just above his face, just in the perfect position for him to guide her down onto his tongue, onto his mouth, onto his hungry lips.

She gasped against him and moaned. ‘Finish me this way, Harris, then we’ll go back to the house.’ She tightened her lips around his cock and found her rhythm. Her mouth was like a velvet sheath, with her tongue doing things he was pretty sure weren’t even anatomically possible.

‘Stacie,’ he groaned, ‘I can’t hold out that long.’

‘Then don’t.’ With that, she gave his balls a firm kneading with her hand, raked her teeth along the full length of him, and took him still deeper and tighter until he could stand it no longer. He tried to pull away when he felt the inevitable happening, but she gripped him harder and took him, all of him, as he exploded into her mouth. The juddering and jerking of his own body drove his face deeper and tighter into the cleft of her, causing her to lose her own control, and she came trembling and shaking against him.

After the tremors of pleasure eased and they could breathe again, they became fully aware of the chill . As she eased herself off him, her teeth chattering, he rose and pulled her to her feet, wrapping the damp blanket around them both. She bent and grabbed up his jeans, nearly losing her balance but for his grip around her waist, and they both dissolved in a wave of giggles as they stumbled off the dock, back up the stairs and into the house. From there, it was a beeline to the warmth of his bed.

As they snuggled deep beneath the comforter, he pulled her so close that she was practically on top of him, and finally found his ability to speak again.

‘I can make us some cocoa if you’d like.’ Immediately he thought how stupid that sounded at a moment like this. ‘You’re freezing.’

She raised her face to his and settled a soft, open-lipped kiss against his mouth. ‘I love cocoa, Harris, but there are better ways for you to warm me up.’ She took his hand and guided it down between her legs, back to the soft, slick warmth of her center. ‘Or do you need a little time?’

He grunted half a laugh and reciprocated, guiding her hand down to where his cock was stiffening with enthusiasm once more. ‘I’ll manage,’ he said.

For a long time, they kissed. In some ways, the exploration with tongue and lips, accompanied by the gropes and darts of hands under the covers, had the wonderfully naughty feel of teenagers exploring for the first time. That was unbelievably arousing in itself. But they weren’t teenagers, and though Harris hadn’t had a lot of sex, he wasn’t totally lacking in experience, and clearly Stacie knew her way around male anatomy. For a very brief, very uncomfortable moment, he wondered if it had been the Thorne brothers she had learned it with. But when she eased a finger down to stroke his anus, he instantly forgot all about Ellis and Garrett. Everyone had a past, and that didn’t interest him right now. What interested him was the woman in his arms, the woman he’d wanted nothing to do with, the woman who was way more of a mystery than he could have ever imagined.

It didn’t take long for him to be fully erect again. It wasn’t just her alternating caresses of his cock and his anus. It was the fact that her full, round breasts were pressed up tight against him, nipples digging at his bare chest, and that his own fingers were scissoring deep into the slippery, soft cleft of her that gripped at him like a hungry mouth.

'Harris.' Her voice was a stretched whisper. 'I need you to fuck me. Now. I need you inside me.'

Her honesty, her ability to ask for what she wanted without mincing words was outrageously arousing, and he certainly wasn't going to argue with her. He slipped a condom from the drawer of his bedside table, sheathed his cock and slid home. And they both cried out in a sound that was somewhere between pain and pleasure, exquisite and primal. Then there was no more sound other than their ragged breathing, other than the sound of flesh against flesh, straining and pressing, until she convulsed and whimpered beneath him and he emptied himself inside her like he'd not come for ages, even though the taste of him was still fresh on her lips.

Stacie woke up naked with Harris Walker wrapped around her possessively. For a second, she was pretty sure she had to be dreaming. It all felt entirely too good to be true. He held her to him with his face nuzzled at the back of her neck and his hand cupped to her breasts. His breath against her nape was warm and even; the relaxed breathing of sleep. His erection pressed against her bottom, and she felt herself quiver in anticipation of what would happen when he woke up, when they woke up together, him hard with his morning need and her wet and ready for him.

The sky was just greying with dawn as the events of the past evening came rushing back to her. She would have spent the night in the Lexus at the clear-cut if Harris hadn't come to her aid. And she was pretty sure if that had happened, she wouldn't have slept at all. She shivered as she recalled her encounter with Harris, before she knew it was him, when all she could think was that it had to be Terrance Jamison. It made no sense, really. The man couldn't have known she was there.

But the place and the time didn't really matter. Eventually he would come for her, sooner rather than later, she suspected. And when that happened, he wouldn't take no for an answer, and she would have to face the music.

Harris moaned in his sleep and loosened his hold on her slightly, giving her space to wriggle out of his arms. She slid quietly from under the comforter and for a long moment sat naked on the edge of the bed watching the man sleep. His face was relaxed, his eyelids fluttered, evidence that he was dreaming . She couldn't help hoping his dreams were more peaceful than hers had been recently. 'Stacie,' he mumbled; she caught her breath for fear that she had awakened him, but he slept on. Only dreaming, she reminded herself, and calling her name as he did. She hoped desperately that it was a good dream, that it was one he would be happy to linger in. She was pretty sure when everything happened as she knew it would, as she knew it would have to, he wouldn't be having pleasant dreams of her, and as sad as that made her, ultimately she knew there was nothing she could do about it. Things had gone too far now to be undone. There was no way to go but through the thick of it. And she most definitely didn't want to drag Harris Walker though what was to come.

She let out a low sigh and stood carefully, her eyes still locked on the sleeping man. Then, almost as an afterthought, she bent and brushed a soft kiss across his lips, in spite of everything, half hoping he would wake up and pull her back down into the dream with him, but knowing that couldn't happen no matter how much she wanted it to.

In the guest room, she slipped into the borrowed sweats, then gathered her muddied clothes from the porch, along with her BlackBerry and her backpack, and left the house. On the way home, she ran the Lexus through a car wash so that it wouldn't be quite so obvious she'd been using it as an off-road vehicle, then she headed toward her flat just as the sun stained the eastern sky pink.

At home, she showered and dressed for her day at the gallery. She took extra care with her make-up and her choice of clothing. She was pretty sure today was the day she'd have to face Jamison, and she needed to be ready for it. She had deliberately shut off her BlackBerry. She wasn't ready to talk to the man yet, but that wasn't the reason. She was sure he'd never let a little thing like her ignoring him stop him from getting what he wanted. Mostly, she didn't want to talk to Harris just yet. She couldn't picture him being particularly happy about her leaving without saying goodbye. Plus she didn't want to face his questions, questions she knew he would have asked last night if she'd given him space, and questions she was certain would have been on the breakfast menu if she had stayed. It was better, at least for the moment, not to have to face Harris' disappointment. There would be way more than enough disappointment she'd have to face before long. This was just a little reprieve.

Once she was dressed and ready, she hopped in the Lexus and made her way to the gallery, where she'd be meeting with Martin Flannery about installing the security systems. He knew what she wanted, and he was probably one of the few people in the city of Portland who could make it happen, exactly like she wanted it to, before the gallery opened, and certainly he was the only one she trusted with the job. There was plenty to occupy her mind, plenty of things to keep her busy and keep her thoughts from wandering to the man she wished she was still lingering in bed with over a seriously hot morning fuck or the man she knew was about to turn her world upside down again. Yes, she needed to keep her mind occupied.

Chapter Fifteen

Where the hell are you?

Harris punched the message into his BlackBerry, then he deleted it, slammed the device down on the nightstand and headed for the shower. Incredible sex followed by Stacie Emerson doing a runner; this was a habit he didn't need. How could the woman leave without at least waking him up to tell him to fuck off? He thought they were really connecting. He thought they had something good going. He thought he had really found someone who understood … what? Just because she liked the great outdoors didn't mean she wanted anything more than for him to exhibit his work at her gallery. He shoved his way into the shower and cranked the hot water; a cold shower was no longer necessary. Waking to find Stacie gone had pretty much taken care of his hard-on and given his ego one helluva bashing.

Best he didn't dwell on it. Best he just got on with what had to be done. Oh, he'd do her exhibition, just like he said he would. Of course she was right. Of course they should have left things on a nice, friendly, professional level. But then it was already way too late for that, wasn't it? From the first time he kissed her all he could think about was being with her again. Jesus, could he be more stupid? Kendra would give him a serious talking-to for being such an idiot with his heart. It wasn't his heart, he told himself, couldn't possibly be his heart. It was just lust, that was all. Just lust. He'd get over it. Stacie just wasn't his type, he reminded himself for the hundredth time – never had been, never would be. And the fact that she had a history with both Thorne brothers – well, that just made the whole situation strange.

Once he was out of the shower and sitting with a much-needed cup of coffee, he pulled up his email. Several messages from *Wilderness Vanguard* were waiting for him – nothing unexpected in that when they were on a deadline with the latest issue. He could expect a dozen more emails from the assistant editor before the day was over.

In addition, there was a message from the local wildlife photography group he'd agreed to speak to. There was a message from Doug, the naturalist down on the other side of Prineville who had spotted a mountain lion, possibly the same female Harris had photographed two years before along the Crooked River. Doug thought she was nearly ready to mate again. And in spite of Harris' best efforts to distract himself, he couldn't keep from thinking how much he would love to take Stacie along on a shoot of that mountain lion.

There was a message from Ellis asking if he was free for lunch one day next week. No doubt he wanted to know all about the meeting with Stacie. Well he'd be happy to know that Harris had told her yes. Damn, he hoped the word hadn't been passed on via Kendra and Garrett, who were quickly becoming the most efficient grapevine in the Northwest, about what had happened between him and Stacie at the Boiling Point, but no doubt it had. There was no privacy left in the world, he grumbled.

Once he'd had coffee and some toast with peanut butter, he rounded up his new, post-owl backpack, shoved in another peanut butter sandwich, a Thermos of coffee, and headed for a particularly deserted part of the Pacific Crest Trail, which he knew how to access through old logging roads. It was the cure for almost everything that ever ailed him – a good walk and some up close and personal time with wildlife. Surely it would be the cure for Stacie Emerson as well. And now he was committed. He'd have to see her again. Jesus, why did she have to be so intriguing, and why couldn't he have just left well enough alone and continued to send her his *fuck-off, not interested* message? God, he hated complications. He slammed the door behind him and hopped into the Jeep. But before he started it, he checked his BlackBerry one more time for a message from Stacie. There wasn't one. He shut it off and shoved it into his pocket.

Stacie was going over the details for the installation of the bank of security monitors. Martin Flannery had reassured her there'd be no problem installing the switches to control the cameras where she wanted them and making sure that nothing was obvious. The monitors could easily be housed in the large closet next to the bathroom in her office. She was giving the blueprint one last look-over when the landline rang. She picked it up without thinking. That was a big mistake.

'Stacie, returning my little gift has cut me to the core. Surely you don't hold the past against me ...'

Terrance Jamison's voice was as velvety smooth as it always was, like something you wanted to rub up against, like something you wanted to get lost in. Like something in which you did those things at your own risk. She could almost hear him smiling as he spoke.

She grabbed for the edge of the desk and would have missed the chair she was about to drop into if Martin Flannery hadn't saved the day by sliding it beneath her at just the last minute. She forced a smile and gave him the thumbs-up. Security officer, PI, ex-military – he was the best at what he did. The last thing she wanted was for him to be suspicious.

'Sorry, now's not a good time.' She tried to sound matter-of-fact over the phone without raising any red flags with Flannery. 'I'm in the middle of something.'

'Surely it won't last forever, darling. Be a lamb, finish it up now,' Jamison said. 'I'm sending my limo to bring you to my place for lunch, and I won't take no for an answer. I've been very lax in my hospitality, and it's past time that I welcomed you back to Portland properly.' No doubt he heard the reluctance in her silence and somehow he managed to make the hurt in his voice seem nearly tactile. 'It's just lunch, Stacie. I promise I'll be a total gentleman.' He offered a soft chuckle, just barely loud enough for her to hear and yet loud enough to make the fine hair on the back of her neck rise. 'Though God knows you don't always make that easy for me.'

Before she could do more than shudder, he went on. 'I just sent Todd with the limo and, taking into account construction on I-5, I'd say you have about 30 minutes to wrap up whatever business it is you're handling at the moment and make any of those ever-so-perfect excuses you're so good at making to whomever you need to. Oh, I know you're a busy woman, and I'm a busy man, so I promise I'll have you back to the salt mines in plenty of time to toil on. I'll see you soon, darling.'

The line went dead.

'Stacie? Stacie, are you all right?' It was only when Martin Flannery shook her arm gently that she realized she was still sitting with the phone gripped to her ear in a painful fist.

She caught her breath and nodded. 'Fine, Martin. I'm fine. Just an unexpected meeting. Are we finished here?'

'You are. My men have already started working in the basement and they'll be working around the clock to finish up for you, just as you requested. It'll be done in plenty of time.'

'And the money?'

Martin offered her a broad smile. 'Paid in advance is something we seldom get in my line of work, Ms. Emerson, but yes, thank you. The money for the job has already been deposited, just like you said it would be. Now just leave the rest to us, and don't worry.'

And she wouldn't. At least not about the security system. She was sure with Martin and his team on it, it would do exactly what she needed it to. She barely had time to freshen her make-up and check her hair before the limo arrived. She wouldn't go before Jamison alone, for the first time in more than ten years, without looking her absolute best. She needed every edge she could get.

There was no way to hide anything from Martin, and that worried her a bit. Still, there was nothing for it now but to be as upfront as she could. She found him on the ground floor, looking over the schematics with one of his colleagues. 'I have an appointment across town,' she said, trying to act like it was all business as usual. 'I'll be back as soon as I can.'

He offered her a reassuring smile and held her in his sharp blue gaze. 'We'll be here. Don't worry.'

It was the second time he'd told her not to worry. And somehow that reassured her in spite of what was about to happen.

She was thankful that the limo was unmarked and as discreet as a limo could be. Terrance Jamison was a master in the art of discretion when it suited him. But then he wouldn't consider his connection with her something to be discreet about, and this was probably the last time she would be able to hide it. Still, she hoped that no one had seen the limo arrive around back to her private entrance of the gallery.

As she slid onto the leather seat and the driver shut the door, she thought about Harris Walker, thought about their night together, thought about the fact that there were still bright spots in a world that was about to turn very dark. For a painful moment, she wanted desperately to stop the limo, get out and run to Harris, forget everything else and let it all go. With a sudden shiver, she remembered Zoe, remembered finding her like she did, knowing what she knew, and living with the constant niggling doubt, the constant wondering if she might have been able to do something, anything. Surely there must have been something she'd missed, something that, if only she had done it, could have made the difference. But there had been nothing. She had been totally and completely helpless.

When she remembered that night, the night she truly realized just how in over her head she really was, she recalled it with the sounds of sex. Perhaps that was because when she revisited that night in her dreams, she always heard their lovemaking from a long way off – if you could call it lovemaking. It was only much later, too late, that she learned just how cruelly Jamison had used Zoe. In her dreams, she could hear them the moment she entered Zoe's building. She could hear them in the elevator all the 29 floors to the flat as she rode with her heart in her throat, fearing for her friend, wondering why she hadn't shown up for their dinner meeting, or at least called. Zoe hadn't been herself since – well, since Jamison came into the picture as more than the distant presence Zoe spoke about from time to time. In her dreams, she heard their moans and gasps as she exited the elevator and walked the interminable distance to Zoe's front door. In her dreams, the door was always wide open with a view into Zoe's bedroom, with her naked on the bed, with Jamison on top of her.

In reality, she had heard nothing, been aware of nothing, until it was too late. In reality, she feared the worst. So when Zoe had left no messages and not returned her phone calls, when there was no answer at the door, she let herself in with the spare key Zoe had given her. In reality, it was the fact Zoe's bedroom door was closed that had led her to knock softly, call Zoe's name, and push the door open, fearing … She wouldn't have dared name exactly what it was she feared. And looking back, even in dreams, she could never visit that unnamed fear without its true horror being thrust upon her in reality far worse than any of her nightmares. It was the beginning of the end – or at least in her memories that's how it felt. But in reality, the end had begun the moment Zoe had introduced her to Terrance Jamison, with Stacie still flushed from the excitement, from the glitz and the triumph of her second exhibition.

Even after she pushed the bedroom door open it took her a few seconds to make the connection, to figure it all out. At first she saw only a man's back, a man lying face down on Zoe's bed. For a split second, she thought someone was assaulting Zoe. It was then she heard the sounds of sex, as though someone had just turned up the volume, as though a tidal wave of noise and smells and connections had washed over her, threatening to drown her. And then she heard Zoe's yelp of surprise, saw a naked arm shove from under the fully-clothed man, and Zoe called her name.

'Stacie, Jesus, Stacie, I'm so sorry. I'm so sorry. I meant to call. Really I did.'

It was all so disjointed in her mind, even though at the time every second of it felt like a pinprick to cold skin, so vivid, so powerfully focused.

It was then she realized the man was Jamison. He rose from the bed, still wearing that same smile he always wore, as though he owned the world and he were greeting a favorite vassal. She had interrupted their lovemaking and he welcomed her as if he were inviting her to tea at the Ritz. 'I wasn't expecting you, Stacie,' he said. But she knew that he had been. She could see it in his eyes, feel it in the way he looked at her. She was exactly who he was expecting, and it was as though he had forgotten Zoe was even there.

‘I’m … I’m sorry. I was worried. I was worried,’ she managed before turning and fleeing. In the back of her mind she could hear Zoe’s voice, high-pitched and thin with words staccato and clipped, the way she always sounded when she was drunk. But her words sounded like gibberish against the hard hammering of Stacie’s pulse in her ears as she fled, feeling mortified and humiliated and other hot prickly things she didn’t want to think about. Then Jamison yelled something that had silenced Zoe. Stacie heard the bedroom door slam with a loud crack, and then he was calling after her.

‘Stacie! Stacie, wait!’ He caught her by the arm in the hallway by the door, his grip talon-tight. His white shirt was untucked and unbuttoned to show the mat of hair across his chest that glistened with the heat of arousal. He’d made no attempt to do up his fly, and his erection fought against black boxers. He smelled faintly of whiskey. Mostly he smelled of sex and something else, something that prickled along her skin and made her shiver. He had never been anything but pristine, never been anything but under control, and the sight of him like this frightened her, confused her.

‘I’m sorry.’ She forced the words through the desert of her mouth. ‘I’m sorry, I didn’t know.’

And then he pulled her to him with such force that she cried out, and he kissed her. It wasn’t a kiss she had ever dreamed of or hoped for. It was a scorched earth kiss that took no prisoners and left no hope for survivors. As fear rose to the surface over lust and confusion, he crushed her hand to his bare belly, his muscles tightening as though she had punched him. He slid her palm down into the tent of his boxers, down over the prickle of pubic hair, and forced her fingers closed around the obscene heft of his erection, the erection he'd elicited by what he had done to Zoe. Before she could utter a sound, he took her mouth again and shoved her hard against the wall, his hand bruising an irresistible path up under her skirt, over the tops of her stockings and into her panties.

From her bedroom, Zoe was repeating the same gibberish over and over again like a mantra, like a hypnotic spell. And whenever she remembered that night, Stacie felt as though she might well have been hypnotized or drugged or maybe temporarily insane. Or maybe, she'd hoped against hope, maybe she had only dreamed it.

All of it, the noise, the smell, the fevered touch of his body, of his mouth pushing at her until, at some point in an eternity that couldn't possibly have taken more than minutes, Stacie kissed him back. At some point, she curled her fingers in her hair and cried out in frustration, in confusion, in fear, pushing back, clawing and gripping at him where he still held her hand to his cock. And then he shuddered against her and she felt the warm stickiness of his semen erupt over the tight grip of her fingers, and still he held her. Zoe's high-pitched mantra became mere background noise as he stroked feverishly between Stacie's legs and dug thick fingers between her raw folds, grunting to gain his breath, cursing and shoving at her.

'I keep waiting for you and you keep running from me, making excuses,' he gasped against her ear. 'So I'll take what I can get. For now. But I won't wait much longer. I always get what I want. Always. You should know by now, those are the rules.' With a nearly painful rub of his thumb, she came in a trapped animal cry that drowned out the high-pitched rhythm of Zoe's mantra as it clawed its way through her lungs and out of her throat. Then he stepped back, his chest rising and falling spastically, his eyes locked on hers, and that was the first time she ever remembered his eyes joining in the emotions of his face. It was hunger that stared back at her, like he would devour her whole, like she was prey and he had already taken her before she even knew what had happened. He jerked her hand from his boxers and wiped it on the hem of her skirt. With a little kitten cry, she shoved him away and ran out the door.

It was ages before she came back to herself. 'New World Gallery, lady,' the cabbie was saying. 'This is where you wanna go, ain't it?'

She paid him and stumbled up to her flat. Hours later, she woke in the middle of the night, trembling and goose fleshed and, at the same time, aching with arousal. In her dreams she had revisited Zoe's flat and relived the experience. This time, Jamison had fucked her against the wall, bruising her insides with each thrust, raking her raw even as he wrung orgasm after orgasm from her wounded flesh. It was only after she had masturbated, masturbated in great, gasping sobs that felt like they would gut her, that she remembered exactly what Zoe had been saying that night. "Don't hurt her, don't hurt her! Terrance, don't hurt her!" Over and over again she'd said it, begged it, pleaded it. Stacie had not been able to go back to sleep.

Chapter Sixteen

Stacie shook her head as though that would somehow dislodge the memory she didn't want and most definitely didn't need under the circumstances. With Jamison it had never been just hate. That would have been so much easier. Somehow, with Jamison, hate co-existed with all-consuming lust, and he was able to fan the flames of both, a fact that made the agony of those early years in New York more horrendous and more riddled with guilt.

She stared out the window of the limo as they crossed the Willamatte River. Her mind was made up. She wouldn't drag Harris Walker into this mess. And she wouldn't allow him to matter to her any more than any other artist she had ever worked with. She wouldn't. She straightened in her seat and focused, focused all of her energy on meeting Jamison. She couldn't dare go to him unprepared. Not this time.

When the limo pulled up in front of the Hotel Monaco, Stacie got the message. He was meeting her in a hotel, as he would a prostitute. It was one of the subtle ways he would devalue her and demoralize her to remind her of her place in their relationship. She rode the elevator to Jamison's grand suite on the top floor, once again looking down on Stacie Emerson from outside herself, once again distancing herself from what was to come. It didn't matter what he did to her. She would endure what she had to. She knew that going in.

She barely finished knocking before he threw open the door in a grand gesture, as if he was welcoming a long-lost friend. But then he simply planted himself in the doorway, looking her over. She stood with her shoulders squared, allowing the inspection she knew she had no say in, as he took her in with a gaze that felt somehow invasive and yet totally polite. No one who saw them together would ever catch the subtext and yet she did, as he knew she would.

He was like he always was: perfect. He couldn't have been more so if he had showered and dressed only minutes before. His eyes were sparkling blue ice. His white-blond hair was perfectly cut and styled. His charcoal suit accentuated his slender build, hinting at hard-muscled, broad shoulders beneath tailored lines. It was understated enough to say *expensive* without taking any attention from the man who wore it. He was tall enough to look down on her, but not so tall that he stood out in a crowd. He didn't need the extra height to stand out in a crowd. He was stunning. Frighteningly so. He was a master in human behavior, in negotiating strategy, leaving her standing in the hallway under his intense gaze just a second too long for comfort before he took her hand and led her over the threshold, bowing to brush a cool kiss across her knuckles. As the door closed quietly behind them, he captured her other hand as well and stood gazing into her eyes with a look that could almost be mistaken for adoration but for the hard-metal edge to it that she had only learned to recognize after it was too late.

She forced herself to stand still, detached from past nightmares and future hopes, as she looked Terrance Jamison right in the eyes and smiled.

At last he spoke. 'I don't know how it's possible, Stacie, but you look even more stunning than you did the last time we were together in a hotel room.'

She felt as though he had just punched her in the stomach; she felt as though he had found the thread that held her together, the one that would unravel the last ten years of her life and leave her cowering in the corner as he had left her back then. But she was no longer that woman, she told herself. That woman was dead. 'I look much better when I'm not bleeding,' she said.

The look he gave was one of deepest repentance. 'Stacie, have I not tried over and over to apologize for that unfortunate incident? I was provoked. You know that. I never wanted anything but the best for you, my darling, always the very best. I was wounded to the core that you took that little incident so personally.'

That was it. That was the whole of his response. He was provoked – meaning of course, that it was her fault. He was provoked! He was fucking provoked! Good! A little anger in her belly was what she needed right now. As he folded her arm over his, she felt as though molten steel had just replaced her backbone and she could feel it hardening even as it burned like acid.

He led her to the dining table in the sitting room, which was already laid with a feast. 'I hope you don't mind. I took the liberty of ordering us the smoked chicken salad. I seem to recall that was one of your favorites, am I right?'

He knew he was. He never forgot a detail about her, and never missed an opportunity to use those details against her. But that was then.

'I'm not hungry, Terrance,' she said. 'You didn't stay on the line long enough for me to tell you I'd already eaten.'

'And so I didn't.' There wasn't the slightest hint of irritation in his voice. That was never very reassuring once she'd discovered just how quickly his moods could change. 'But then how can you blame me, my darling? I couldn't run the risk of you turning me down, now could I?' Ignoring the beautifully laid table, he nodded to the sofa. 'Come, sit with me then, and let's talk. We have so much catching up to do. Can I at least offer you a coffee? Water, perhaps?' Without waiting for her response, he took a bottle of sparkling water from the fridge and poured them both a glass. Then he sat down next to her on the plush sofa, watching her expectantly.

She decided not to wait for it. She took a sip of her water and began. 'I can't take your money, Terrance, you know that.'

'No, I don't know that. I don't know that at all. I was crushed when you left like you did. Crushed. You never gave me the chance to apologize. You never gave me the chance to make it right, and I would have, Stacie. I would have made it right.'

'Terrance, you make it sound like I walked out on a relationship. I got out of your debt, that's what happened. I got out of your debt on my own power.'

His mouth twitched slightly and he straightened his jacket with a brisk tug. 'I'll be the first to admit it, darling, you've proven yourself over and over again as a businesswoman. I'll give you that. And believe me, no one has been more impressed with the way you've turned New World Gallery around than I have. It's very clear that I underestimated you.'

'Terrance, I –'

He held up a hand and stopped her. 'I know you've been taking money from your savings to finance New World Gallery West, Stacie, and I know that you paid for the art auction from your savings. And really, darling, I've seen the hovel you live in right now. It's embarrassing for a woman of your caliber to be living in such squalor. It's so beneath you.'

'Where I choose to live and how I pay for what belongs to me is none of your business,' she said, with way more conviction that she felt.

'Your savings won't last forever. We both know that. There are so many … unexpected expenses, as I'm sure you've seen. Goodness me, Stacie, a little paint spattered by misbehaving teenagers is a small thing to fix compared to what could happen. I shudder to think. You can't do this without help, and with a vision like yours, it would be such a tragedy for you not be able to bring it all to full fruition.'

'I haven't asked you to worry about my vision and how I bring it to fruition. The responsibility is mine, and I don't want your help.'

He sipped his water and studied her over the top of the cut crystal glass. 'No one else knows what kind of financial trouble you're in, do they?' He looked at her as though he was the parent and she was a child who simply didn't understand. 'Of course not, or they'd be offering you more help than you'd know what to do with. They'd never have let you resort to spending your savings, and all you'd ever have to do is ask. But you didn't, did you? You haven't asked anyone, have you, Stacie?'

'And I haven't asked you either,' she replied. She hadn't realized it until that instant, but all the while she had been easing herself closer and closer to the end of the sofa, farther and farther away from him.

'Ah, but you don't have to ask me, my darling. I know what you need even before you do, just like I always have. I know how to give you all that's best for you. But you just don't know how to accept it and let me help you. That's always been your problem, Stacie. You've never been able to relax and let me help you, let me do what I know's best.' He scooted closer to her on the sofa until she was pressed to the edge with no place to go. Then he ran a cool hand along her cheek, sliding the pad of his thumb across her lips, and she felt everything in her flutter in an impossible mix of desire and horror. This was not unexpected, she reminded herself. This was exactly what she knew would happen, exactly what she had prepared herself for, and still she felt like she was being undone one cell at a time.

He moved closer and brushed a kiss across her lips that, even in its unassuming way, felt as though it demanded everything from her and would settle for nothing less. She laid a hand on his chest to keep him from doing more.

'I don't want your help,' she managed, still feeling his insistent breath against her lips.

He pulled away and folded his hands in his lap almost as though he was about to pray. For a second, he held her in an unreadable gaze, then his lips curled into the slightest hint of a smile, and he threw her by changing the subject.

'What do you think of the Monaco? It's nice, isn't it? Nice rooms. Bed's comfortable. Excellent service. I've never stayed here before. I have little need to, actually. As you know, I have a lovely flat here and a ranch near Redmond if I need a little country fix. But I don't like doing business in my home, especially not certain kinds of business.'

If he was waiting for her to ask, she didn't. 'The hotel's fine, Terrance, but unnecessary for me.'

He pulled her hand into his lap and began to massage her fingers. 'Oh, it's not for you, my darling. I'm just trying it out, really. And I've decided it'll be perfect for my meeting with the lovely Ingrid Watson, the perfect place to tell her about the three exhibitions I've lined up for her.'

Stacie felt the fire in her belly turn to ice as his grip on her hand tightened and he continued. 'Ms. Watson is ever so grateful for my help, Stacie. And she's quite good at showing her gratitude, unlike you were.' Even his soft chuckle hinted at accusation, at disappointment. He ran a nearly painful thumb over the back of her knuckles. 'In fact, if she continues to show her gratitude so exquisitely, I think I could very easily be persuaded to purchase the dear girl her own gallery and studio.'

When Stacie said nothing, he continued. 'Granted she's still very young and not very skilled in pleasing her benefactor, but with a little discipline and a little effort, she can be taught. I rather like the idea of the lovely Ms. Watson being in my debt, Stacie. What do you think of that?'

Stacie should have kept her mouth shut but she couldn't. 'I think you should leave her alone. I think you should let the woman's talent speak for itself; let her make her own way. She's way too gifted for you to –'

'For me to what, Stacie?' he interrupted. 'Does it bother you that I might choose to bestow my kindness on someone other than you? Are you jealous?'

'I want you to leave her alone, Terrance. She doesn't need your help.'

He offered her a pout and held her hand still tighter. 'I doubt she'd agree with you on that point.'

Before Stacie could respond, he continued. 'Never mind Ms. Watson. She's not why I invited you here, and since you're being your usual obstinate self, we'll approach the topic from a different direction, Stacie dear.' His massaging of her hand became solicitous. 'Your dear friends, the Thorne brothers and that old fart, Marston, none of them know about our shared history, do they?' He gave a dismissive shrug. 'Well, Marston may have guessed a little of it, but he thinks the sun rises and sets in you now, doesn't he? He has no idea the depths to which you would sink in order to get what you want, does he?'

She jerked her hand away and stood to leave, fighting back a wave of nausea, but Jamison pulled her back down onto the sofa; not violently, but with a strong enough grip that his message was clear. He hadn't dismissed her yet, and she wasn't free to go until he did. She forced herself to remain calm, forced the panic down with the nausea, careful to hold her head high and shoulders squared. She was prepared for this, she reminded herself. And even with all of her preparation, she had warned herself that it would be worse than she had imagined. And it was. It was.

'I don't want your money,' she repeated when she was once again sure her voice wouldn't shake.

He still held her hand and stroked it as if he was the most adoring of lovers. 'But you'll take it, won't you, Stacie?' He reached inside his jacket and took a folded envelope from the breast pocket of his crisp white shirt, an envelope on which she recognized her own handwriting; the one in which she had returned his check. When he was certain she knew exactly what it was, he stuck it into the pocket of her blazer. 'You'll take it because you won't want your dear friends to know you've bitten off more than you can chew; you don't want them to know you can't afford to open this new gallery; you don't want them to know you can barely afford to keep the doors to the old one open. You'll take it because you don't want them to know what you had to do to keep the first gallery open.

'Oh there, there, darling.' He kissed her forehead and smoothed her hair again, like she was a frightened child. 'It won't be like it was last time. I've waited all these years to make it up to you, to be back in partnership with you once again, and I assure you I won't make the mistakes I made the last time.'

And in those words, the words that should mean repentance and contrition, she heard the clear threat. She knew only too well that, in his eyes, the mistake was letting her find a way out.

'It'll be so much better this time, I promise you. There'll be only the two of us, and no ugly scenes with Zoe. I'll give you carte blanche to do with the gallery whatever you want. After all, with the unlimited funding I can provide, the sky's the limit, Stacie. The sky's the limit. This time we'll do it together. This time you won't leave before we can achieve our dreams. And it'll be something to behold, darling. It'll be something to behold. Something we'll proudly share with the world.' He leaned in, settling another kiss against her lips. 'There. You see how easy that was.'

He stood and helped her to her feet. And that was the end of the discussion. 'Now, I know what a busy woman you are, so I won't keep you from your work. Todd is waiting downstairs with the limo to take you back to the gallery. I'll send for you again soon when we're more at our leisure.'

He escorted her to the door, with Stacie struggling to maintain enough control to walk under her own power. There, he kissed her tenderly, as if totally oblivious to her lack of response. He smiled down at her as though they had just shared the most exquisite experience. 'Don't worry, darling. It'll be so much better than it was before. You'll see.' He heaved a happy sigh and looked around the foyer of his hotel suite. 'Yes, I think the Monaco is the perfect place to bring Ms. Watson. I'm sure it'll delight her.'

In the hall, one of his security men was waiting to escort Stacie down to the lobby.

So already it had begun. Already he wanted her to understand that he controlled her, that he owned her. Well, that too was expected. She remembered little of the walk down to the lobby. All she remembered was the check in her pocket, the weight of which seemed nearly unbearable, the proposition, the subtle threat, the beginning of the end.

She sat like a stone in the back of the limo all the way to the gallery, not thinking, not moving, just barely breathing. If she actually tried to take in what had just happened, she was certain she would be sick, so she held it all at a distance, held it all until she could get to a safe place. But then after today, there were no safe places. Not really.

When she arrived at the gallery, she didn't go in. Once the limo had pulled away, she went straight to the Lexus. She might have doubted if it were safe for her to drive under the circumstances, but she was in the eye of the storm, the calm center that would see her through for a little while longer. Just a little while. She drove to her local bank and deposited the check into the account Dina had set up. She did the whole thing without feeling. She did it as if someone else had momentarily taken up residence in her body, and she was happy for the takeover, knowing with dead certainty that it wouldn't last and that when she came back to herself, the world would be a much darker place.

She carefully pulled the Lexus into her parking space, then made her way up to her flat, let herself in, and locked the door behind her. Once that was done, she dropped her bag on the floor and stripped off her clothes as she stumbled blindly to the bathroom, just managing to turn on the shower before her knees gave and she sat down on the floor beneath the cascade of water and wept. She wept as she hadn't done since that last, horrible night in the hotel room, that night when she had wept to the place way beyond despair, the place of raw, parched emptiness. And when the ambulance had come for her, when Alan Marston sat beside her, holding her hand in the hospital room, when the bruises and the aches and the broken bones had become like dull background noise to the tidal wave of rage that flowed over her, she knew that she would find a way out.

Chapter Seventeen

Harris had just stepped out of the elevator at the Executive Suites of the Pneuma Building when his BlackBerry buzzed. It was an email from Cal, who did research for *Wilderness Vanguard*. The message, in response to his request about the clear-cut Stacie had been investigating, stopped him in his tracks. There was nothing in it he didn't already know, and that meant there was every reason to stay as far away from the horrible place as possible. So, what the hell was Stacie up to? He was still staring at the email when Dee practically threw herself into his arms in a friendly bear hug.

'There you are! Ellis told me you'd be joining him for lunch. Lynn's ordered enough Chinese food for the whole Pneuma Building, so I've invited myself along. Hope you don't mind.'

'You know I don't, Ms. Diva.' He returned the hug and stuffed his BlackBerry in his pocket, struggling to pull his attention away from the message.

'And Harris –' she pulled away slightly '– just so you know, Stacie's going to join us too. She needs to be involved in the planning meetings for Vigilant Trust if she's to be able to represent it to contributors for the gallery opening, whether you exhibit with her or not, and frankly, I think that you –'

'I've agreed to exhibit with her, Dee. It's OK.'

There was another bear hug. 'Great!' Her smile turned to a look of total mischief. 'I'm really glad to hear you didn't let that little mishap at the Boiling Point keep you from doing the right thing. Or maybe that's what convinced you?'

'Jesus, there is no privacy in this world,' Harris growled.

'Nope. None at all.' She threaded her arm through his. 'Now come on. We don't want lunch to get cold, do we? I don't know where Lynn gets it, and she's not telling, but it's the best Chinese takeout ever.'

Harris thought Ellis' office, with its grand view of Mount Hood and its coolest-apartment-ever feel, was the best part of the Pneuma Building. And time spent with Ellis was always good. Dee was an added bonus, but now he wanted to turn and leave. He really didn't want to face Stacie in this company knowing that they all knew about the Boiling Point, knowing that they all knew he'd had sex with her. But they didn't know what happened next, and he didn't know how she'd react. And shit, if that wasn't bad enough, he was concerned about why she'd been at the clear-cut.

Dee knocked softly on the door, then pushed her way in with Harris reluctantly right behind her. Ellis was not at his desk, and the door that separated his office proper from the lounge was closed. Again, Dee knocked and let herself in. Ellis sat on the end of the sofa with Stacie on the love seat next to it, her back to the door.

'Dee! Harris!' Ellis motioned them in. 'You've gotta see this. Stacie's plan for the photographic part of the exhibition is total genius.' Dee sat down next to him, and he gave her an affectionate hug and a light kiss on the lips. He motioned Harris to sit on the love seat next to Stacie.

And God, why did she have to look so damn good? She was dressed in a burgundy power suit with heels he was sure someone like her shouldn't even attempt to walk in unless they had good health insurance. She wore her hair loose around her shoulders, making his fingers tingle with the muscle memory of just how soft it was. Truth was he thought she looked much more stunning dressed for the great outdoors and covered with a little mud and grime, but then when did she *not* look stunning? She offered him a business-as-usual smile, almost as an afterthought, before turning her attention immediately back to the plans she had spread on the coffee table in front of Ellis. She continued as though he were no more than an employee who arrived late for a meeting.

'There'll be flat-screen monitors here, here, and here.' She pointed a well-manicured finger at places on a modified version of a blueprint of the gallery. 'The one on the main floor and the one in the reception area will run on a loop that cycles every ten to fifteen minutes depending on what Carla puts together for me.'

'Carla Flannery?' Harris asked.

'Yep. Lucky for me, she's a freelancer, and this is right up her alley. Harris, I thought you might want to consider a print version of what she'll be putting together to run in *Wilderness Vanguard* the month after the gallery opening.'

'Possibly. What exactly do you have in mind?'

'Well, I want your photography and Kyle's, mixed

in with her story clips and photos from the John Day landfill and archival shots from the Northwest. What I want to do is put together a looped, narrated clip showing how photography as a political and as an environmental statement has made a difference in the quality of life in the Northwest, not only for the natural world, but for humans as well. It's not really an exposé so much as a way of sharing with people how art can make a difference in the world in which we live and how it can be so much more than just pretty images.'

She sat on the edge of her seat. Her voice was animated and she spoke with her hands. Harris could feel the excited energy practically radiating off her, and he grudgingly had to admit that not everything was about him and that Stacie really was amazing at what she did.

'What that means –' she turned slightly to face him '– is that I'll need to record a commentary from you and from Kyle.' Then she added, 'I've looked through your images and chosen the ones I want to use. I'll get a list emailed to you this afternoon. What I'd like to do is have Carla do that commentary in the form of an interview after she's had a chance to study your work. Then the loop will contain a commentary on the photos, what they mean to the photographers, the environmental implications, and so on. It'll all be mixed in with some of the best shots of the success stories of reclamation and humans living in harmony with nature. It won't run so loud that it'll disturb people; in fact, it may very well be subtitled. But there'll also be smaller monitors placed strategically in quiet nooks and crannies where people can turn up the volume and listen in more detail. But the material itself should be eye-catching and well done enough to hold people's attention and hopefully send them scurrying to learn more.' She shrugged slightly and Harris noticed the color in her cheeks that was either a modest blush or just understandable excitement for her vision of the opening exhibition. And though he didn't think it was possible, that slight blush made her even more desirable.

'I know we're a little pressed for time and that's my fault for waiting so long to be persuasive enough to get you on board, but still, it's all very doable without too much pressure. So, what do you think?' Her voice was a little bit breathless, full of energy and enthusiasm. 'Is this something you're OK with?'

It took Harris a second to realize she was talking to him and not to the general audience. 'Yeah, of course. It sounds like a great idea. Just let me know what you need me to do.'

'Perfect.' Instead of the adoring thanks he would have liked, she turned her attention back to Ellis. 'I'd like to have Carla ask you a few questions too, Ellis, since Vigilant Trust is your brainchild – yours and Harris', that is – and since you're a recognized crusader for the cause.'

'Of course.' Ellis nodded enthusiastically. 'You know I'll do anything you need me to do on this.'

'I don't suppose anyone will be terribly surprised to hear that the Ryde Agency is taking care of the PR for this project.' She smiled as though she was thinking of a private joke. 'Pretty much a waltz in the park and easy money for Ryde, but hey, I have friends in high places.'

‘I’m glad to hear that the Ryde Agency is back in business full strength and giving the competition a run for its money,’ Dee said.

Harris nodded his agreement, still amazed that Kendra and Stacie had hit it off so well. But then he shouldn’t be, he supposed. Ellis had been right: give the woman half a chance and she’d win you over. That was the problem. She’d won him over a little too well. And now he was suffering the consequences, even if she wasn’t. Well, he’d just fucking get over it, he told himself. He didn’t believe in going where he wasn’t wanted. He’d just back off, give her space and keep it all professional, just like she wanted. Then he remembered the email he had received just before the meeting, and nerves shivered in his belly. God, what on earth was the woman playing at? Well, he’d have to find out, and he’d have to warn her up front if she didn’t know how dangerous Terrance Jamison was, but he couldn’t imagine she didn’t, and that scared the hell out of him.

Just then both Ellis and Dee’s secretaries arrived toting several large paper bags with twisted twine handles. The smell coming from inside would have made his mouth water if he didn’t have more pressing things on his mind than filling his stomach.

Harris was relieved that even through the meal, the focus was on Vigilant Trust and on the opening exhibition of the gallery. He ate without tasting, not wanting to draw attention to himself by not eating, and he did his best to stay focused on the plan, which was a damn good one. Stacie’s exhibition would be spearheading several major reclamation projects in the Northwest that would dovetail nicely with the photographers' exhibitions and the film she had hired Carla Flannery to produce. The woman's mind was a fascinating place to be pulled into, and yet it had chosen to leave him in the middle of the night without saying goodbye. And it had led her deliberately into an extremely dangerous place. Neither of those facts was ever far from *his* mind through the meal and through Stacie's plan.

They'd just dispensed with the fortune cookies when Ellis' BlackBerry buzzed. 'That'll be Lynn telling me that my 2 o'clock is here.' He raised a hand when people started to shift. 'No need to rush. The meeting's in the library, so just relax and finish your lunch.'

Dee washed down her cookie with a gulp of iced tea and stood to join him. 'I'm seeing Alan Marston for a last minute planning meeting before Jason gets here from Paris and the real fun begins.'

'Al's here?' Stacie said. 'Give the man a bear hug for me.' She looked down at her own watch. 'If he's free for dinner maybe he'd like a little company. I'll give him a call. Anyway, I have to go too.' She began to gather her stuff.

Harris laid a hand on the middle of the blueprint before she could roll it back up. 'We need to talk before you go,' he said. The panicked look that crossed her face was nothing more than a flash, but he caught it. He held her gaze. 'About the clear-cut.' That seemed to relax her just a little bit. At least the thought that he might bring up her leaving his bed without saying goodbye made her nervous. That was something, he supposed.

'Clear-cut? What clear-cut?' Ellis asked, stopping mid-stride. Dce too stopped in her tracks. And Harris realized it might be a good time to have some powerful allies.

He spoke to Ellis, but he held Stacie's gaze. 'The one Stacie nearly got herself killed in last week.'

Ellis dropped back onto the couch and Dee with him. All eyes were on Stacie. 'Stacie?' Ellis' voice was full of warning.

'I was checking it out,' she said, folding her arms defiantly across her chest. 'It's Bald Hill, Ellis. You remember?'

'Of course I remember.' His expression hardened; his jaw tensed. 'You know I remember, but dear God, Stacie, why would you want to go back there now?'

'I wanted to see if there was any way it could be one of the reclamation projects.'

Ellis' gaze softened. 'Stacie, you know it can't be. Believe me, I've thought of that, and there's nothing I'd love more, but you know the damage is too great. There won't be the funds for at least several more years for anything of that magnitude, and that's if we can find a way to stem the erosion. Plus –'

'The Bald Hill clear-cut was the result of a timber rights sell-off that Terrance Jamison orchestrated,' Harris finished Ellis' sentence.

Whatever it was Ellis said under his breath, Harris figured it probably wasn't very nice.

'I know,' Stacie said. 'I know all of that. But I had to see.' She turned her attention back to Harris. 'I wouldn't have been in any danger if the storm hadn't blown in, and that's my fault for not checking the weather before I headed up there.'

'Stacie, stay away from Jamison or anything that involves him.' Ellis' voice held a lethal edge. 'The man's capable of anything.'

Her spine stiffened; the hammering of her pulse was visible against her throat. 'I know what he's capable of.' Then, with a quick intake of breath and a settling of her shoulders, she forced a smile that almost passed for relaxed. 'Believe me, I know what a nasty piece of work he is.'

The tight knot between Harris' shoulder blades convinced him Stacie wasn't being completely above board, but then he had suspected that for a while now.

Ellis still held her in a gaze that would have peeled paint. 'Stacie, I mean it. Stay away from anything that has to do with Jamison. He's bad news.'

'I'm not going to go back up there, so relax, will you? It was a bad idea, that's all.' She started to roll up the plans again and offered a wicked smile. 'Even I have a bad idea every once in a while.'

But Harris didn't believe her for a moment, and he doubted that Ellis did either if the look on his face was any indication.

'Go on.' She shooed Ellis and Dee with a nod of her head. 'You'll be late for your meetings. I've been properly chastised.' She shot Harris a quick glance.

'Stacie, I mean it, this is –'

'Just go, Ellis. I said I'll stay away from the clear-cut, all right? Now go, both of you.'

Ellis and Dee left reluctantly, pulling the door shut behind them and leaving Harris and Stacie alone.

'Oh, stop looking at me that way, Harris,' she said. 'I told you I'm not going back, so problem solved, wouldn't you say?' She shoved the plans in her bag and turned to go, miscalculated the position of the coffee table leg, tripped, and sent herself sprawling across the floor, bag flying in the opposite direction.

Instantly he was on his knees next to her. 'Jesus, Stacie, are you trying to kill yourself?' When he offered her his help up, she pulled away.

'Don't. OK, Harris, just don't. I'm fine. I've been stumbling around my whole life and I'm not dead yet.' For a second, he thought she was going to cry, which was not like Stacie at all.

'Hey, are you all right?' he asked, this time not allowing her to push him away as he helped her to her feet, then guided her back onto the loveseat. 'I'm sorry. Let me look at that.' He cupped her calf in his hand where he could already see the knot swelling in the middle of her left shin. 'I'll bet Ellis has ice in the fridge. Just hold still.' He moved to the bar area where the fridge was and found an ice pack. 'Thought Mr. Thorne would be prepared for the odd bump or bruise,' he said, returning to his position on the floor between her legs. She caught her breath with a sharp hiss as he gently rested the ice pack against the goose egg. 'It's gonna sting a bit until it starts to freeze,' he warned her, resisting the urge to kiss it better. Instead, he stretched to pick up her bag and handed it back to her.

She took it from him, hoisting it onto her shoulder as though she was preparing for a quick getaway. 'This is getting to be a habit,' she said, nodding down at the abrasion on her knee – now nearly healed – from the fall she had taken in the clear-cut.

It was good to hear her sounding more like her old self. He smiled up at her. 'Not that I wish you pain or anything, but your stumbling about does give me a chance to fondle sexy female legs, something I don't get to do very often.' He shrugged. 'Unless you count the female badger I rescued from a trap last spring. But she nearly bit my finger off.'

She smiled down at him. 'I promise I won't bite, Harris. Not unless you ask me to.'

He couldn't keep from smiling back. 'Now there's an intriguing proposition.'

She was instantly serious again. 'I'm sorry, Harris. I should have never dragged you into that mess at the clear-cut. It's just that – well, I never dreamed you'd come after me.'

'I never dreamed you'd go up there alone in such weather. Hell, I wouldn't have wanted to be in that place alone in any weather.'

'Don't worry.' She spoke softly, avoiding his gaze. 'We won't be going back there.'

For a second, they were both silent. The table was still strewn with the remains of their lunch; the sound system still played soft chamber music Harris didn't recognize. It just slipped out. 'Why did you leave?'

She smoothed the hem of her skirt unnecessarily and took a deep breath. 'I got scared, Harris.' She still wouldn't look at him. 'You know when you wake up and wonder what you've just done.'

He lifted her chin so she couldn't avoid his gaze. 'Are you sorry it happened?'

'Of course I'm not sorry. I just don't want you to get hurt. And there are things … Things you don't know.'

Before he knew what he was doing, before he could control himself, he let the ice pack fall away and slid up onto the couch next to her. He pulled her into his arms and took her mouth. She offered only a whimper of surprise before she slipped her arms around his neck and returned the kiss with a ravenous passion that startled him, that delighted him, that frightened him just a little. And then he couldn't get close enough. There was too much clothing between them, too much air, too many unspoken words.

'Are you planning on hurting me?' he asked, when he pulled away breathless.

'Of course not, but there are things … things that you don't –'

'Things that I don't know about. Yes, you told me that, but I don't need to know everything, Stacie. I just need you to stay until we're finished, and we were nowhere near finished when you left. You know that.'

A single tear slid down her cheek and she wiped it aside angrily. 'Harris, please don't make this more difficult.'

He pulled her to him so tightly that he forced the breath from her and he kissed her again, kissed her until she clung to him, kissed her until she yielded. 'I am going to make it difficult, Stacie. I'm going to make it as difficult as I can for you to walk away next time.' He held her face in his hands and forced her to look at him. 'I don't know what the hell's going on, but I do know that it's good when we're together, and I want more and I'm pretty sure you do too.'

She closed her eyes and swallowed a tight breath. 'Harris, you don't know what you're asking.'

'Then suppose you tell me – or at least give me a hint.' She tried to pull away but he held her. 'Does it have anything to do with that clear-cut, with Terrance Jamison?'

This time, the beautiful blush drained from her face and her features were porcelain pale. 'Harris, I –'

The door burst open and one of the cleaning staff

stepped in. When she saw them, she reddened and apologized profusely in a very strong Polish accent. 'I didn't know that anyone was here. I'm so, so sorry. I will come back later.'

'No, it's all right.' Stacie somehow managed to sound like it was business as usual again. 'It's all right, we're finished here, and I was just leaving.' She forced her way up from the sofa, shouldered her bag, and fled, this time without stumbling.

By the time Harris pushed past the embarrassed cleaning lady and made his way to the elevators, Stacie was nowhere in sight. It didn't matter, though. He knew that Stacie hadn't run because she didn't want to be with him. If she was scared, well, he could deal with that. Right now he'd give her a little space to let her nerves settle a bit before he texted her, or maybe he'd just drop by the gallery unexpected. After all, he really should find out just where this amazing exhibition he'd agreed to would be taking place. An artist needed to know these things. Stacie was about to find out that he was at least as tenacious as she was. In spite of her obvious discomfort, in spite of the fact she was clearly hiding something that distressed her, all at once, his day felt a whole lot brighter.

Chapter Eighteen

He didn't kiss her when he opened the hotel room door. He didn't invite her in. He didn't even offer her a smile, in spite of the fact that they hadn't seen each other in two weeks, and in spite of the fact that his regular texts left her hopes soaring. Then there were the gifts – expensive jewelry, clothes, rare art books, something almost every day. She'd been convinced he really did want to be more than just her mentor. She'd been convinced that maybe he really did find her irresistible. The edgy anticipation she'd felt, the elation mixed with a good jangle of nerves that Terrance Jamison had flown her to Oregon to be with him – even flown her first class – dissolved into a knot of dread.

He stood in the doorway just looking her over with that distant look of his, the one that, for some reason, always frightened her a little bit. It somehow made her feel more like an object than a person. But then surely it was just his way. Surely the man didn't get to where he was in the business world without a good poker face. At last he spoke. 'Why aren't you wearing the dress I bought you?'

Instinctively, her hand came to rest against her chest, just above her breasts, and she couldn't fight back the resulting blush. 'Mr. Jamison.' Her voice came out high and thin, not at all the confident purr it had been in her fantasies. 'I couldn't wear it in public. I brought it with me, of course. But I thought it was just for … you know … for us.'

For a second, he said nothing, only held her gaze until she looked away, embarrassed, confused. At last he spoke. 'You have nice breasts, Ingrid.' Jeez, did he have to say it so loud? Anyone could be passing by. Anyone could hear. He continued as if they were simply talking about the weather. 'You shouldn't be ashamed to show them off.' With her still standing in the hall outside his door, he shoved her hands away from her chest and gave each breast a hard grope followed by a look of distaste. 'With those dowdy bras you wear, it's hard to tell what's real, and I like to know what I'm getting. I like to see your tits under your clothing, not all this padding.'

With that, he ran a hand up the lapel of the summer shirt dress she wore and gave it a hard yank. She yelped as buttons went flying. But before she could fold her arms across her now embarrassingly exposed cleavage, before she could even give a quick glance around to make sure no one was watching, he pinned her arms to her side, shoved the dress off her shoulders, and kissed her savagely.

Just when she feared she'd suffocate, just when every muscle in her body warned her to recoil and run away, he pulled her to him and held her close, and his touch became soothing, like the touch she'd seen her father use on a frightened calf. And her fear dissolved into desire that was even more alarming. How could she desire him after what he'd just done?

When at last he pulled away, they still stood in the

open door, and he still hadn't invited her in. 'You need to show me what you've got, Ingrid. You need to show everyone what you've got. That's what you've wanted from the beginning, and I'm happy to see, so don't play coy, don't hide it.'

'But it's my art I want people to see. My art,' she managed. She was near in tears now, standing half-naked in the hall of a very exclusive hotel, being reprimanded instead of welcomed.

He reached behind her and unhooked her bra, then ran his hands beneath the waistband to catch her breasts up in his palms and caress them roughly. She was shockingly aroused in spite of the humiliation. 'You have to learn, as Stacie Emerson had to learn, that you are your art, you are your own emissary, and it's you people will look at, at least as often as they do your sculpture. That's an important lesson, Ms. Watson.' Then he took her hand and led her across the threshold, closing the door behind them. 'Now, get out of that rag, and your bra, and wait over there on the sofa until the bellboy brings up your clothes, then I can dress you properly.'

The words were barely out of his mouth before there was a soft knock on the door. He nodded to the sofa and went to answer. Ingrid did as she was told.

She sat with her heart racing and her arms folded protectively across her chest, knowing at any second the bellboy could crane his neck just right and see her sitting there on the sofa in nothing but her panties.

'Ingrid, take your arms away from your breasts.' She jumped at the sound of Mr. Jamison's voice as he returned. 'And sit up straight. Let me see you.' He studied her just long enough to make her blush hard and long enough to make her squirm against the sofa. Then he sat down next to her, efficiently removed her panties, and pulled her onto his lap as though she was a child. Her balance was awkward until she slipped her arms around his neck, crushing her right breast against the buttons of his jacket, which he opened to better accommodate her.

'I'm sorry to be so harsh with you, darling. But you have to learn.' He shifted her forward slightly and lifted her bottom and, with a start, she realized he was undoing his fly. 'Never mind,' he was saying. 'You've had a long flight, sweetheart. I know you're tired and you need to relax a little. Shall I fuck you and help you relax?' He fingered her open and she quivered at his touch, even as her cheeks burned with shame. 'Goodness, it feels like that's exactly what you need, darling; a good fuck to settle your nerves.' His last word ended in a little grunt and he entered her surprisingly easily this time. She bit her lip and bore down with a little sigh as he began to shift and rock beneath her. 'That's my girl,' he said. 'You'll feel better after you've come.'

And he was right. She did.

It felt like déjà vu, waking up in the middle of the big bed, naked and alone. Ingrid's stomach knotted and then relaxed as she heard his voice from the other room, talking business on the phone probably, even though it was still the middle of the night. But for all she knew, he could be talking with someone in China or Europe. That made her feel proud for a second, then her stomach growled. They had eaten smoked chicken salads last night in a very fine restaurant where everyone else was enjoying steak or seafood. But in the dress he'd bought for her, there wasn't a lot of room for feasting. He said it was tight on purpose. He said someone who expected to be a star needed to constantly be reminded of her weight, needed to constantly be reminded that people were watching her. So she had picked at the salad and only eaten a bit of the passion fruit crème brûlée he had ordered for her.

Back in the room, the lovemaking had been rough and impersonal, though he had made sure she came – even came a lot. But just when she thought it was a sympathy fuck, just when she thought this was the point at which he told her she really wasn't worthy, that he had lost interest in her, he snuggled her close and caressed her gently. He had told her what a jewel she was, what a find, and how excited he was to be able to help her reach her full potential. And she had slept, reassured. And now he was in the lounge on the phone. She shoved her way out of the bed and peeked out the window. It was dark, and it was raining. But she was wide awake. She found the robe hanging in the closet and pulled it on, recalling how unhappy he had been to have her in his shirt.

In the living room, he was pacing in front of the sofa, fully dressed, as though they had never made love at all. He didn't even look slightly rumpled. He offered her a quick glance and pointed to the couch. She sat. And waited. He made no effort to hurry the call, a call that had something to do with some tract of land in Valderia. And was she mistaken, or did he say something about the presidency? The presidency of the country? Surely not. She might have actually dozed again before the brush of his cool lips across her ear woke her.

When her eyes fluttered open, he pulled her onto his lap and held her close, and she wrapped her arms round his neck, feeling strangely vulnerable, strangely near tears. At last he spoke. 'You should be in bed, my darling, sleeping. I have a very busy day planned for you tomorrow. Now come.' He lifted her into his arms as though she were a child and carried her back to the bed. Carefully, gently, he slipped the knot of the robe and eased it off her body, pausing to admire and caress her breasts until she couldn't hold back a tetchy little moan. 'Are you aroused, sweetheart? Is that it?' He ran a hand down over her belly and in between her legs and, as her breath caught in a little shudder, he tut-tutted. 'Goodness, you are a horny little slut, aren't you? Do you want my cock? Is that what you want?'

She was way too embarrassed by his use of such filthy talk to say what she wanted, and even more embarrassed that he had found her so needy, when all she had really hoped for was a little conversation, a little sharing. But he was already opening his fly. He made no effort to take off any of his clothing. She lay there fully exposed as he pushed her legs apart. 'Goodness, look at you, darling. All wet and begging for it. Who knew that a little girl from down on the farm could be such a dirty thing?' Before she could protest, before the heat in her face could dissipate, he positioned her and climbed on top of her. Just a single grunt and a shove, and he was in, and the hard stretch with no foreplay took her breath away and burned up inside her, but only for a minute, only until she got used to the thickness of him again, the depth. The raw rub of his thrusting against her clit was startling and almost too much to take, but it gave way to a deep, rhythmic thrumming that made her slippery and tight and hornier than she would have imagined possible under the circumstances.

‘There now, that’s my girl.’ His voice seemed so relaxed in spite of the hard swell of him and the tight thrust. ‘Let me take care of you and then you can rest. Goodness, you’re so tight, you’ve got me about to come too.’ And then he thrust harder, and she was embarrassed to hear her growls and moans, sounds she wouldn’t have believed herself capable of making during sex. She clawed at the back of his crisp white shirt and bucked against his heavy penis. One last hard thrust and she came, gabbling and mewling like a hungry calf led to the teat, and she felt the tensing of his abdominal muscles as he ejaculated.

Long before she was ready, he pulled away and found a towel. ‘There, now, that feels better, doesn’t it? You can sleep now, darling.’ He wiped her clean and gave her breasts a fondling. ‘And in the morning, my PA will pick you up at nine o’clock sharp.’ He brushed a kiss across her lips before she could protest. ‘I have to work tomorrow, sweetheart, but Terri has a wonderful day planned for you, and I’ll see you in the evening.’

Short of fleeing the very expensive hair salon still clad in the black and gold tunic that shielded her clothes, there was nothing Ingrid Watson could do to keep from becoming a blond. He wanted it that way, the stylist explained in his smarmy French accent, and what Monsieur Jamison wanted, Monsieur Jamison got. But of course she would look much more elegant and sophisticated as a blond, he reassured her. She figured the man would lie out his backside for Monsieur Jamison. And yet who would know better than Terrance Jamison what would make her into the successful artist she wanted to become.

Of course he was right. She was the emissary for her art. She absolutely had to look her best. And, really, how could a farm girl from the middle of nowhere know much about being sophisticated? She had her own style, and it had suited her just fine. But Minnesota wasn't New York City, was it? Her focus had always been on creating her art. She'd spent little time thinking about how to package it, how to sell it, and how to sell herself as a brand. Surely she should listen to Mr. Jamison, and really, it was just the color of her hair. What did it matter? Her father wouldn't like it, but surely even he'd come around when he realized it was good for her career.

So she let Jean Pierre shampoo her and style her and make her into a blond. Then there was a trip to a local spa where she was plucked and waxed and slathered to within an inch of her life before she was dressed in a teal pencil skirt slit high up one side and a white silk blouse that showed way more cleavage than she was used to. That was after she was shoved into expensive panties that were so silky they felt like they might slide right off her butt and a bra that mounded her breasts up until they looked like they could tumble over the top of the blouse any minute. Though she struggled not to be self-conscious, she couldn't say she didn't like it. And Mr. Jamison *had* said she had lovely breasts. So if he wanted her to flaunt her boobs – well, she'd get used to it.

She was told that Mr. Jamison had furnished the clothing for her, but he had requested the spa not do her make-up. And yet, even with no make-up, she felt like a new woman. Standing in front of the mirror with her matching heels and bag, she had to admit her new look was a lot more sophisticated than the old Ingrid Watson. In fact, dressed as she was, with her blond hair and push-up bra, she looked a little like Stacie Emerson.

Now she thought about it, the hairstyle Jean Pierre had given her was almost identical to the one Stacie Emerson wore in some of the photos she'd seen. She could do worse than to emulate a women she admired so much, the women who'd given her the big break. But as the limo arrived to take her to the hotel, she couldn't help wondering if maybe Mr. Jamison had planned it that way. Maybe he wanted her to look like Stacie. Maybe he and Stacie actually had been lovers, and maybe he still had a thing for her. She pushed the thought out of her head and tried to feel good about her new look. It had certainly worked for Stacie Emerson. With any luck, it would work the same magic for her.

At the hotel, she had the suite all to herself. She took a bottle of sparkling water from the bar and paced through the rooms, wondering what time Mr. Jamison would be back. She didn't have long to wait before she heard the electronic lock click, and she turned to find him standing inside the door wearing the biggest smile she'd seen on his face since she first met him. 'My darling Ingrid, you look enchanting! Stunning. Such a transformation. I'm bowled over, completely bowled over.' Before he could do more than pull her hand to his lips and brush it with a kiss, there was a knock on the door. 'That'll be Hilda. She'll do your make-up for the night, and then we'll celebrate. We have so much to celebrate, my dear Ingrid. I've arranged for you to see a gallery that you might possibly like, and I –' he offered a deferential smile '– well, I've just bought myself a president in Valderia. But never mind that. That's nothing with which you need to trouble your thoughts. A private victory. But even I still have to celebrate these things, you know? Now go with Hilda. When she's finished your make-up, I'll dress you myself, and then you'll be perfect. Just perfect.'

Dressed like she was queen of the world, Mr. Jamison had shown her the empty building on the Willamette River in a part of town that had been wonderfully renovated. The place had room for her studio and for the equipment she would need, none of which she could really afford, but he told her not to worry about that. It was spacious and full of light and high ceilings with a lovely wrought iron catwalk. And there was a luxurious space for her apartment. The gallery itself would extend, not only to the main exhibition room, but into what would become a huge sculpture garden overlooking the river. Well, that was his vision for it, and he was so enthusiastic she could almost see it in her own imagination, though having a gallery seemed a bit premature to her. But surely he knew what he was doing.

Afterward, the limo had taken them to a fabulous restaurant. The name now slipped her mind. By then she was already slightly tipsy from the champagne with which he had toasted their successes in the back of the limo on the way. She would ask him to remind her of the name tomorrow so she could tell her father and her friends back home all about it.

And then there had been sex. Wow, had there been sex! They'd barely got back to the limo after dinner before he was all over her, and it was so naughty to do it in the back seat that she came all over herself and all over him.

By the time she fell asleep, in the big bed in their suite, her lovely black dress had been thoroughly ruined, but he promised to buy her another one just like it if she wanted. He had promised to make all of her dreams come true, and as she drifted off to sleep, she couldn't help thinking that her father wouldn't approve. There's no such thing as a free ride, he'd always said. Watch out for the hidden price tags. They're the ones that come back to bite you in the backside. With that thought, she fell into a deep, dream-filled sleep.

Chapter Nineteen

'I'm at the back door with pizza. I'm assuming you're the one burning the midnight oil or else your gallery's haunted, Ms. Emerson.'

Stacie gripped the BlackBerry tight to her ear, and she was sure the smile was about to split her face. She shouldn't be so happy to hear his voice. She should tell him to go away, but she didn't.

'Harris, if the place were haunted, believe me, with the hours I keep, I'd know it. Pizza, did you say?'

'Yep. Canadian bacon and mushroom. I believe that's what Garrett said your favorite is. Now, are you gonna let me in, or do I have to eat it all by myself sitting on the sidewalk looking like a nutcase?'

'Hang on.' When Harris called, she was sitting in the control room Martin and his men had just finished so she pulled up the monitor for the back door. Sure enough, there he stood looking sexy and outdoorsy as usual. She'd been familiarizing herself with the new security monitors and link-ups. 'I'll buzz you in, then just wait in the foyer and I'll be right down.'

She pushed the button and he immediately opened the door and stepped inside. She watched him for a second as he stood there taking in her domain – well, at least as much as he could see from the foyer. She'd had fantasies about proudly showing him around her gallery, fantasies about him being über-impressed. But those fantasies had never taken into account the risk he might be at if their relationship took a turn for the intimate. And still, she couldn't fight down the butterflies of excitement that came from knowing he was waiting for her just downstairs.

As she joined him, he pulled her into a delicious sloppy kiss, carelessly balancing the pizza box on one forearm. His hair was damp from the rain. He looked as though he might have just come from the hide, photographing some fabulously elusive wildlife, and he smelled like the outdoors, which set off little tremors of excitement just below her navel.

'You didn't think I'd agree to an exhibition and not want to see where my work would be displayed, did you?' The twinkle in his grey eyes made her giddy.

'Of course not, and I'm ready for you. If you'd care to come this way, Mr. Walker, I'll be your guide for the New World Gallery West deluxe tour package complete with an exclusive look at the pizza-eating facilities, which are upstairs off the mezzanine.'

She heard the catch of his breath as they made their way into the main exhibition hall. Even lit with only the security lighting and the moon coming in through the skylights, it was impressive. She smiled to herself. She really hoped he would like it.

'Wow!' he said. 'You don't do things by half, do you, Ms. Emerson?'

'No, I do not, Mr. Walker.

'And I see you've already got the monitors up for the film loop. You're really speeding along.'

'Have to. The exhibition will be here before you know it. Carla tells me she's now got the footage and the interviews with both you and Kyle Waters. You see, things are coming together. You know how time flies when you're having fun.'

'Oh, I do indeed,' he said, following her upstairs to the mezzanine. 'In fact, I've been getting more shots of the owls. This time with the BlackBerry turned off.' He gave a shrug to indicate the rucksack on his back. 'Brought the iPad in case you'd like to see them.'

'Of course I would,' she said, feeling extremely privileged that he had brought them to her first.

'I thought about inviting you along for the shoot, but sadly there wouldn't have been room for both of us on the tree branch. Besides I'm not sure I'd have been able to concentrate on the owls if you'd been up there with me.'

'Well I, for one, am very happy that you've taken your safety into account this time. At least partially. I'm sure Dee would be very unhappy with you for being up in that tree instead of in the hide.'

'And you're not?'

The smile slipped a bit. 'I understand the need to take risks to get what you want, Harris.' Before he could respond, she led him into her office, which was now fully decorated and equipped. She had already broken it in properly by spending a couple of nights on the sofa.

'Wow! Your facilities beat the hell out of mine. Well, at least the ones for *Wilderness Vanguard.*' He set the pizza box down on the coffee table next to the sofa, dropped the backpack on the floor, and looked around. 'In all fairness, though, I do most of my own work from home, so that's a pretty great place to work, and even you have to admit my view's better than yours.'

‘Not tonight it isn’t.’ She took his hand and guided him to stand in an area where she had had a small dormer and the accompanying alcove of space turned into a miniature sun room. At the moment, the nearly full moon looked as though it might fall through the glass from the strain of its own weight. Harris let out a low whistle and picked up an open sketchpad from the floor where it lay with several charcoal pencils. On the pad was a detailed drawing of the moon’s face – at least, as detailed as she could make it.

‘I was sketching it earlier,’ she said. ‘Before the first rainstorm.’

He looked up at the sky and smiled. ‘OK, maybe tonight you win. But only for a few minutes. It’s supposed to rain again any time now.’

‘Guess we’d better enjoy it while we can then,’ she said, still looking up at the moon. ‘I’ll get the pizza and we can eat here.’

She turned to go, but he grabbed her hand and pulled her back, pulled her into his arms. ‘Pizza’s not what I’m hungry for at the moment.’ He dropped the sketchpad on the floor and settled a lazy, lingering kiss on her lips with his opportunistic tongue darting into her mouth when she gasped her surprise. ‘Pizza’s not going anywhere, and I have it on good authority that you love it cold.’

‘Mmm.’ She slipped her arms around his neck. ‘Garrett Thorne has a big mouth.’

‘Yes, he does, and I plan to take full advantage of it. If you won’t talk, he seems more than willing.’

‘Oh, I’m sure he is, but don’t believe everything he says. Remember, he is my ex.’

‘I’ll keep that in mind.’ His hand slid over her

bottom and groped for the edge of her skirt, which he shoved up until he could feel the top of her stockings and garter belt. 'If you dress like this before the gallery's even open, I can't wait to see what happens when it's up and running.'

She slid his jacket off to land on the floor with a soft swish and began work on the buttons of his plaid shirt. 'I've had meetings with VIPs all day and haven't had the chance to change yet.' She didn't tell him that now she was always dressed and ready for Jamison. She couldn't afford to give the man the slightest hint of weakness. For a brief second, the tension in her belly was not arousal, but visceral fear, fear for the man in her arms. And just when she was ready to push him away and tell him he had to leave, the moon's veil dance with the clouds sent bright shafts of silver through the glass, highlighting his face, his beautiful face, with its sun-freckled skin and its tight growth of beard, which looked like it fit the wild outdoors he loved. She felt the slight callous of his hand against the tender skin of her bottom. His other hand was wound fist-deep in her hair. In that moment, the heart of the man was laid bare in the clothes he wore, in the boldness of him coming to her just as he was, in his excitement to share with her his passion, excitement for her to be the first to enter his secret world. And she was lost. She could no more turn him away than she could stop breathing.

'I need you now, Stacie.' His voice was coarse with arousal. 'I'm too hyped after tonight; I'm too full of the experience, the experience I wanted to share with you.' He pulled aside the crotch of her panties and stroked the soft humidity he had exposed, his breath catching, no doubt at the feel of how much she needed him too, as she bore down onto his caressing fingers.

She fumbled desperately with his fly. As she freed his erection into her hand, he produced a condom from one of the multiple pockets in his pants. Then, together, they sheathed and maneuvered until he plopped down ass-first on the hard wood floor and she straddled him. He guided her until she sat on his lap, facing him in the flood of moonlight, then, with a slight shifting of his hips, he penetrated her, not gently, but deeply, intensely, urgently, as though he couldn't wait, as though it had to happen now.

'Oh God, Stacie,' he whispered in her ear. 'You feel so damn good.'

She had managed enough buttons of his shirt for the two of them to wrangle it off over his head. He returned the favor, first with her blouse, and then with inpatient pulls and tugs at the straps of her bra until her breasts tumbled free into his hands, and then pressed up tight against his chest. Everything else was subsumed in pushing and thrusting and rocking, the contours of their bodies undulating in the silver and slate of the intense moonlight.

The scent of him rose like the tide on the rocks and washed over her own scent, reshaping and devouring the smell of desire at its peak before they tumbled into orgasm, orgasm that blended more than just their scent, orgasm that somehow blended the driving force of each of their lives and their passions.

'Wow! I don't think I've ever seen such a powerful picture of a great horned owl,' Stacie whispered, almost as though she were afraid her voice might scare the bird away.'

'I know,' Harris said. 'I thought the shots I got last time were good, but these … Wow! It was almost like the bird knew I was there and didn't care. I'm anthropomorphizing, I suppose, but I really did feel a connection.'

'It shows.' Stacie scooted closer for an even better look at the image Harris had pulled up on the iPad. 'I wasn't wrong to choose you for my photography exhibition,' she said. 'Was this your experience when you photographed the mountain lions?'

'No! God, no!' He rubbed his bare arms as though he were cold. 'I wasn't in control in that situation at all. I was damned lucky, really. I was shaking so bad I'm amazed any of the shots turned out, and they tolerated me. They knew I was there. They never let me forget it. And every second felt like a gift, a gift they could take away from me at any moment.'

She leaned in, pressing a kiss against his bicep. 'It must have been the most amazing experience ever.'

'Well, one of them.' He slipped his arms around her and gave her a lingering kiss, then pulled her back down onto the floor beneath the skylight, which was now pockmarked with the soft sizzle of rain. They were both still naked. Stacie was amazed at how comfortable Harris was with nakedness. Why she had thought him to be prudish, she couldn't remember now. After they'd made love, he came out of the post-coital bliss like a ravenous lion, shoving pizza into his mouth and feeding her as though she were one of the begging branchers in the owl family, first from his fingertips, then from his lips in a rough and tumble across the floor that had both of them licking tomato sauce and mushrooms from nipples and napes and thighs.

In the fridge, she found a couple bottles of Mirror Pond she'd stashed for those long overnighters, and they had shared them, him leaning on the wall, with her back up against his chest. That worked well until he deliberately began to miss his mouth and drizzle beer over her nipples and down her belly. That had been an hour ago, and now the room smelled of beer and pizza and sex. She wondered what kind of message that would send visiting dignitaries. She'd have to make sure and pay the cleaners a little extra the next time. Eventually, they'd managed a shower, but even that had taken way longer than it should have. She had planned her office space after Ellis' at the Pneuma Building. She had wanted it to be a living space because it would be, as the New York gallery had been, so much a part of her life. So there was a lovely shower with plenty of room to share.

Harris nuzzled her neck and ran a hand through the tangle of her hair. 'Why do I feel like I should have a camera on you, Stacie, like I should be observing you from the safety of the hide so you won't bolt?'

'Probably because you're a smart man with good instincts, Harris,' she answered, circling his nipples in turn with her index finger.

'Garrett said you knew way more about the great outdoors than either he or Ellis did back when you were growing up together.'

'I did all right for myself.'

He laughed. 'All right for yourself? Mother was a naturalist, father a Russian translator assigned to work with her at Lake Baikal. You were born there, weren't you?'

'Garrett really does have a big mouth,' Stacie said, giving his nipple a pinch that made him flinch then roll to pin her beneath him.

'Lucky for me.'

She studied him against the skylight and felt the knot tighten once more in her stomach, warning her she was making a mistake, reminding her there were very good reasons why she shouldn't let him into her life. 'Harris, there are things about me both Garrett and Ellis could tell you that aren't anywhere nearly as glamorous. And there are things … Things even they don't know …'

He covered her mouth again with his and she could feel his returning erection pressing against the inside of her thigh where he had wriggled his hips so he was poised and ready. He pulled away, breathless. 'You can't scare me away, Stacie Emerson, so stop trying.'

'You're either brave or stupid, Harris Walker,' she managed in between nips and kisses. 'The jury's still out.'

'Either way,' he said. He ran a splayed hand down her belly and eased it over her mons and between her legs. She shifted her hips, opening to him as though to do so were the most natural thing in the world. It was certainly the most desirable. It had been a long time since one man had moved her so powerfully. His mouth followed the trail along her belly, then to the tops of her thighs and made an assault down between to find her open and ready. His kisses were accented with little nips of his lips and his front teeth and alternated with deep, diving, open-mouth gulps of her, from her clit all the way back to her anus. And when she juddered and bucked her first orgasm, he held her tight, mouth still pressed against her opening, the heat of his heavy breath grazing the swell of her clit. She curled her fingers in his wild hair and held on to him until she was a little less sensitive, until she could breathe again. Then she realized that his mouth was on the move, making a delicate feather path up the valley of her toward her clit. A sharp nip sent her tumbling over into orgasm again, just as he rose and pressed into her, this time not waiting for her to calm. This time he rode in hard and deep and mercilessly until they both came together and the room echoed with their cries of pleasure.

Later, much later, he asked her, 'Why won't you tell me what's going on with you and Jamison?'

She pushed away from him and sat up. The sky above was now iron grey with the coming of dawn.

'Was he your lover?' Harris asked, moving to sit next to her, taking her into his arms when he realized she was shivering.

'No. No, he wasn't a lover. He was never a lover.' There was no disguising the venom in her voice, nor did she try. There were times when the amount of hatred she felt for the man couldn't be disguised. 'I need a shower, Harris. The workers will be here in a little while. I've got another appointment with Martin and the security guys, and Carla's coming over to show me the videos of the interviews.' This time she didn't invite him to join her.

Chapter Twenty

The dreams were mostly disconnected images, like flashes on a movie screen, only there for a second and then gone. Images of being gnawed on by something with sharp teeth, something she could never quite see; images of sculpting a piece of white marble while Terrance Jamison told her which bits to chip away next. She wasn't sure it was the images or the sound of voices that woke her. Clearly Mr. Jamison wasn't alone in the suite. It was a male voice she could hear. She wondered what someone was doing there in the middle of the night, but a squint toward the window told her it was after dawn. Still a strange time for a visit.

The conversation was muffled at first, but as she rose from the bed and went to the bathroom to pee, she could hear more clearly. At the mention of Stacie Emerson, she froze in her tracks and held her breath, listening. Could this be another exciting plan Mr. Jamison was hatching to further her career? If it was, certainly Stacie Emerson was the person who could do it. She still felt bad about blowing off the dinner after the art auction in New York – especially since she was the person of honor. It was really rude now that she'd had time to think about it, and surely it wouldn't have hurt Mr. Jamison to wait until the next day to wine her and dine her. But, at the time, none of that mattered. At the time, all that really mattered was that her work had sold for a million dollars and she had caught the attention of someone with the funds and the connections to push her career into high gear.

'I told you not to come here,' Mr. Jamison was saying. His voice was clipped and impatient. 'You've been tailing Stacie Emerson ever since she settled in Portland, and you're just now getting back to me. This had better be good, Baker.'

Tailing Stacie Emerson? Ingrid held her breath and inched her way closer on tiptoes. Why was this man tailing Stacie?

'Oh, I think you'll find it worth your while,' the man responded smugly, which made Ingrid cringe. Jeez! She'd been with Mr. Jamison long enough to know being smug in his presence was never a good idea. The thought made her stomach knot and her palms sweat. Baker continued, 'She's been hanging out with Harris Walker, you know, the –'

'I know who he is,' Jamison interrupted.

'Of course. Anyway, she wants Walker to do an exhibition for the opening of her gallery.'

'I know that too, Baker. Tell me something I don't know.'

'Well, I'll let the pictures do the talking.' Ingrid could hear the rattling of paper. 'These were taken a week and a half ago at Walker's home on his lake. It's clear they're … intimate. I suspected as much when I tailed them at the Boiling Point, but there was a raid and I lost them in the crowd. These – well, these were taken after the woman had been wandering around on the Bald Hill clear-cut. Walker, it seems, came to her rescue.'

The silence prickled along Ingrid's spine, raising the fine hairs on the back of her neck. What in the world was going on, and what difference did it make if Stacie Emerson was boinking someone? She was an adult. She could do what she wanted. Ingrid recalled a mention of Harris Walker in some of the Portland research she'd done. He was a wildlife photographer and apparently a brilliant one. She hadn't paid much attention. It had nothing to do with her.

At last Jamison spoke. 'Is there any indication this is more than a one-off?'

'I've just come from her gallery where he spent the night,' Baker said. 'I suppose they could have been working, but he showed up late with a pizza and left this morning a couple of hours before the work crews got there.'

There was another charged silence, ending in an explosion that sounded like shattered glass. Ingrid jumped and felt every nerve in her body go tense as she clasped a hand tightly over her mouth to keep from yelping in surprise.

'She knows better than this,' Jamison was saying. 'The bitch knows better than this. It'll cost her, and it'll cost him. Why can't she just behave herself? Why does she have to be such a little whore?'

Ingrid felt as if she had been slapped. How could he even say such things about Stacie Emerson, *the* Stacie Emerson? The woman was a goddess in her field. Everyone admired and adored her. She had a high enough profile that if she were sleeping around the gossip rags would have picked up on it, and even if she were, that was her business and her right. It had nothing to do with Jamison. Nothing!

Suddenly it was all she could do to stand on her trembling legs. Quickly, she returned to the bed. She hadn't turned on the light and, for a long moment, she sat there, holding her breath, trying to gauge just what was going on and how long she might have. Mr. Jamison never actually slept with her, once they'd had sex. She wasn't sure where he went or what he did after, but he'd probably leave her on her own until morning. If she kept her head down, he'd never know that she'd overheard. If she just pretended she was asleep, then tomorrow … tomorrow what? She found herself desperate to be safely back on the farm with her father, working in the old barn he'd cleared for her. Her stomach lurched so hard that she feared she'd vomit, and it wasn't the alcohol. If Jamison was going to make this Harris Walker pay for sleeping with Stacie Emerson, then would going home put her father at risk? Dear God, how had she gotten herself into this mess?

From the nightstand next to her bed she grabbed her iPhone, doing her best to be quiet. She emailed Stacie Emerson.

Ms. Emerson, I'm in town with Terrance Jamison. I'd love to see you as soon as possible. I was just wondering, are you all right? Is Mr. Walker all right?

'What are you doing up?' Jamison's voice broke into the silence. She jumped as though she had been shot. But she somehow had the presence of mind to press "send" before he took the phone from her hand.

She offered him a weak smile and a little sob. 'I was having bad dreams. I woke up and decided to email my father. I miss him. I know that sounds strange, but we're close.'

He settled onto the bed next to her, still holding her phone in his hand, and she tried not to stiffen when he touched her to stroke her cheek and push her mussed hair away from her face. 'I'm sorry to hear about your dreams, darling. I was actually afraid I'd woken you. I had some business to attend to and my colleague knocked a vase off the table.' His smile was solicitous, but his eyes were unreadable.

'I … I suppose that might have been what woke me from the dream. I don't know, what with the busy day and the alcohol. Normally I don't drink much. That sort of muddles my brain, you know?'

With no more effort than the caress he'd just been indulging in, his large hand moved down to press hard against either side of her trachea. 'Don't lie to me, Ingrid. Don't ever, ever lie to me. You're not very good at it, and I make my living detecting when people are lying.' Then he leaned in and kissed her ever so gently, all the while his hand threatened to cut off her breath. 'I get very angry when someone lies to me, so don't ever do that. Do you understand?'

She nodded carefully, trying not to increase the pressure of his hand at her throat, trying desperately not to cry. At this point, crying would definitely not help.

'Good girl,' he purred, releasing his grip as though it had been nothing. 'I'm glad we understand each other so that it won't happen again.' Carefully, he laid the iPhone back on her nightstand.

She was so relieved that he hadn't looked at her message, so relieved to have his hand off her throat that she didn't see the first blow coming.

Chapter Twenty-one

It was like déjà vu. Harris found himself wondering how a night that was so hot and so full of promise ended with him fucking it up. Again! The connection between Stacie and Terrance Jamison had all sorts of alarm bells going off in his head loud and clear. He didn't like it, hadn't liked it from the beginning. And, frankly, he was really scared for Stacie. He liked that even less.

He'd left the gallery with little more than a terse thanks for the pizza and "don't let the door hit you in the butt on the way out" in the way of a goodbye. Back home, he'd grabbed a quick shower and now sat in front of the computer with his third cup of coffee. Once more he went over all the details Cal had sent him about the Bald Hill clear-cut and Jamison's connection. He followed as many of the leads back from that direction as he could – all of them dead-ending nowhere close to Stacie Emerson. If Bald Hill was her only reason for hating the man, well, she'd have to take a number.

Thanks to quality time spent with Pneuma Inc.'s tech genius, Wade Crittenden, Harris' computer system was way more than state of the art, and he could access things that were only slightly less than illegal. The Crittenden upgrades had come in very handy in research and work he had done for the *Vanguard*, but it was a far cry from Wade's system.

By the time the sun rose properly over the lake, Harris was researching New World Gallery in New York. Even if there'd been no connection to Jamison, Zoe Hanson's suicide and the fact that Stacie was the one who found her, the one who had to carry on with the gallery after her death, was enough to really mess anyone up. But it was the implication that Jamison had been her lover that had closed Stacie down. Her response had chilled Harris' blood.

Stacie had paid off the tremendous debt single-handedly with the exhibition from the Hermitage, featuring objects that had never been exhibited abroad before. Harris checked through as many write-ups about the big event in as many papers as he could. Accompanying the *New York Times* write-up was a photo of Stacie standing with the Saint Petersburg representatives and several of the major contributors in the States. He recognized Al Marston flanking her and … he squinted hard, then magnified the photo as much as he could on his system. Sure enough, in the background, not looking particularly happy, was Terrance Jamison. Harris felt the skin on the back of his neck crawl. Even with the bad image resolution, it was clear Jamison's unpleasant look was reserved for Stacie.

No matter how hard Harris searched, though, he couldn't find out who the gallery was in debt to. No matter how good his system might be, it just couldn't do what Wade's could. Another cup of coffee, more mounting frustration, and he called Wade.

'What?' came the usual terse answer.

‘Can I use the Dungeon’s computer for a little while? I need to do some techie research.’ That sounded better than questionable research, research that, no doubt, would have made Stacie furious if she knew, and was probably illegal as well.

‘Let yourself in,’ came the distracted reply. ‘Bring lunch. I’m starving.’

Harris looked down at his watch. It would be an early lunch, he thought, but then Wade dined when he felt like it, labeling whatever meal he ate randomly. ‘Anything in particular?’ Harris asked.

‘Don’t care. Gotta go. Busy.’ The line went dead.

An hour later, he arrived at the Dungeon, as Wade’s domain in the Pneuma Building was affectionately known, with burritos and nachos from the only restaurant he could find en route that was serving lunch so early. Wade was definitely not a foodie and could probably digest old tires if it meant he didn’t have to leave his research to eat, so Harris figured he was safe enough in his choice. Wade met him at the door, took the offered brown bag, and nodded to the driver’s seat in his boudoir.

Another hour and two Cokes later, Harris realized Wade was looking over his shoulder. ‘Why are you trying to access New World Gallery’s finances?’ he asked.

‘It’s something that’s bothering me about Stacie Emerson,’ Harris replied.

Wade folded his arms across his chest and offered him the evil eye. ‘Are you stalking her?’ Before he had time to answer, Wade reached over his shoulder and, with a few quick key strokes, pulled up the files and then some.

'Jesus, Wade,' Harris managed around a tightness of nerves in his chest. 'You scare me sometimes.'

'I know,' came the matter of fact reply. Then he pulled up a chair next to Harris and rubbed his hands together. 'What do you want to know?'

'There's no debt,' Harris said. 'There's never even a mention of any debt until Stacie's big media show of paying it off after the opening of the Hermitage exhibition. And look here, even the bank records you pulled up – and I don't want to know how you did that – show that everything was meticulously paid off. Always. There was no debt.'

'Why the sudden interested in Stacie's finances, Walker?' Wade asked.

'I'm not interested in her finances. I'm interested in her connection with Jamison.'

'Probably her connection with Ellis,' Wade said.

'Possibly, but if Jamison were interested in hurting Ellis through the people he loves, it'd be Dee he'd be turning his attention to, don't you think?'

'Hold it.' Wade's evil eye was back in spades. 'You never said anything about Jamison turning his attention to Stacie. What the hell is going on?'

'First she nearly gets herself killed on the Bald Hill clear-cut, out there alone. And every time Jamison's mentioned, the drawbridge comes up and she turns into a fortress and … Whoa, wait a minute! Look at this.' He squinted at the monitor. 'There are colossal expenses here. Major damage to the facility. The basement flooding twice? What are the chances of that? Damage to art, complete electrical overhaul due to unsafe wiring. Three repairs due to vandalism …

What the hell's going on here, Wade? This sounds like major sabotage. And every time it happens there's a big influx of cash from … Omega Trust. Who the hell is Omega Trust?'

It took another hour and a half of searching before the roots of Omega Trust were uncovered, exactly where Harris had feared. It seemed Omega Trust was really Omega Holdings, which became the Omega Group and was swallowed up by Core Invest. 'Fuck!' The two men said at exactly the same time. It was Jamison who had first Zoe Hanson, then Stacie by the short hairs.

All at once Harris felt nauseated. 'But why? Why any of this?' He nodded to the series of expensive repairs that, when pieced together in the puzzle, clearly had to be the result of deliberate damage.

Wade scrolled through the financial record again. 'We were running Pneuma Inc. out of a shoebox at the ass end of Gresham then. Nothing there to interest Jamison. Far as I know, Ellis had no contact with Stacie then, and neither did Garrett.'

'Did it have something to do with Zoe Hanson?' Harris asked.

Wade pulled up what he could find about Zoe, by which time Harris had nearly forgotten how illegal what they were doing was. 'Zoe Hanson. Born to a family of moderate wealth. Only child. Inherited the gallery. Nothing I can see that would draw Jamison's attention. Unless …' Wade pulled up a photo of Zoe two years before her suicide. 'Unless Jamison's a collector of more than just fine art.'

Harris let out a low whistle at the picture of a porcelain-skinned redhead who looked as though she could have come straight out of a Pre-Raphaelite painting. 'You really think it was just that? The way she looked?'

'I'm not a psychologist,' Wade said. 'But rich people have expensive hobbies, and how legal those hobbies are doesn't matter if there's enough money.' He brought up details on Zoe Hanson from who knew where? 'Educated at Harvard, spoke French, German and Italian fluently. Travelled extensively before her father's death from a heart attack forced her to take over the gallery. She was a formidable yachtswoman, which she gave up when she took over the gallery.' Seeing Harris' questioning look, Wade nodded to the monitor. 'There are records here for the sale of a yacht about the time she took on New World Gallery, but no purchase records of another one. She sounds like an interesting diversion for Jamison.'

Harris thought about what he knew of Stacie's background. If Zoe had been an interesting diversion, then Stacie must have been completely enthralling. But that was just a theory, he reminded himself.

Into the tense silence, Wade's BlackBerry buzzed. He cursed and picked it up. 'What? I'm bus … We'll be right up.' He shoved the device back into its holster and tugged at his grey hoodie. 'That was Ellis. There's been a coup in Valderia. All our properties have been nationalized.'

When Wade and Harris arrived at Ellis' office, the meeting had begun. Dee, Ellis, and Alan Marston, who was in town for talks, all sat at the conference table with files spread and laptops open. Lynn, Ellis' secretary, took notes fast and furiously.

Dee gave Harris a tight hug and nodded him to a seat next to Ellis just as Martin Flannery gave a soft knock on the door and let himself in. Harris knew the man was way more than head of security for Pneuma Inc. Flannery was ex-special forces with connections that even God didn't have.

Flannery nodded his greeting, then turned his attention to Ellis. 'We've got most of our people out of Valderia except for the few in the deep interior. They aren't going to be easy.'

'I don't care what you have to do,' Ellis said, 'and I don't care what resources you have to use, Martin. Just get them to safety. That's our number one priority. I want no loss of life. None.'

'Understood.' The man pulled out his BlackBerry and typed furiously for only a few seconds, then put it away. 'I'm pulling in all the favors I can muster.'

'I know you are.' The muscles tightened along Ellis' jaw as he held Flannery's gaze. 'It's Jamison, isn't it?'

Flannery nodded. 'He's made no attempt to cover it up. Says he's protecting Valderian interests.'

'Read into that his interests,' Marston said. 'The fucker has deep pockets.'

'My sources tell me he's already taking bids on the Valderian forest,' Flannery said.

Harris always felt slightly giddy when he recalled the photo shoot he'd done for Ellis in their whirlwind trip to Valderia. They had trekked through the most pristine forest he'd ever seen at what could have only been described as a forced march. As they struggled to assess the situation, Ellis and his team negotiated to buy up all the properties that would allow Jamison access to clear-cut and remove timber from the forest, in essence making it impossible for the man to get to or export the timber he'd purchased. The cost to Pneuma Inc. must have been colossal, yet Ellis never flinched about doing the right thing. It had been a well-coordinated work of total genius between Ellis, Wade and Dee. As proud as Harris was of his own involvement, he still couldn't think about the efforts of his best friend without a sense of extreme pride. Dee had proven her worth a thousand times over during that very tense time. How could Ellis not have fallen head over heels for her? They had all worked hard, way above peak performance, to keep Jamison from selling the virgin forest for clear-cutting. Surely all that work couldn't have been for nothing. And Harris knew, as very few did, that with the team of people around this table, if there was a way they'd find it. If there wasn't, they'd invent one. Yet the very thought of the possible loss still made him feel sick inside.

'Fortunately, my uncle was out of the country when the coup happened,' Dee said. Another surprise, that. Who knew Dee had an uncle in the Valderian government? Well, not a blood uncle, but someone close to her, someone who loved her and respected her enough to willingly pull strings from the inside. 'Most of those in President Vasquez's cabinet have been imprisoned for interrogation, or worse. Uncle Gustavo's working from Paris to call in favors and see what can be done. No one knows at the moment if President Vasquez is alive or dead.'

'Can Jamison really finance an entire coup?' asked Harris.

'He doesn't have to,' Wade chimed in. 'All he has to do is unload his forest to someone sympathetic to the regime change, then he can withdraw whenever it suits him.'

'He's given Alberto Rojas a taste of power,' said Flannery, 'and convinced him it's his for the taking – with Jamison's help, of course. From here on out, the man's putty in Jamison's hands. And Jamison's only interested in getting his money's worth. That, and getting even with Ellis.'

'Fucker's just a glorified drug lord,' Marston said.

'And if he gets too full of himself –' Flannery added '– Jamison can always have him assassinated.'

'Jesus Christ!' Marston looked like he could bite nails. 'So what the hell are we gonna do about it?'

'We can try to circumvent the sale,' Ellis replied. 'Do we know who the prospective buyer is?'

'Not yet, but we'll find out.' Flannery shifted uncomfortably in his seat.

'What is it, Martin? If you've got something we can use,' Ellis said, 'then spit it out.'

'I don't know whether this has anything to do with anything, or even if you knew already, but Stacie Emerson and Jamison have talked.'

'What?' came the nearly unison response.

Flannery tugged at his collar as though it were too tight. 'Keep in mind I'm working for the woman, and if this is considered a breach of confidence, which it damned well could be, then I deserve to be fired on the spot, but it wasn't a good feeling I got.'

'Tell us,' Ellis said. 'If Stacie's in trouble, we need to know.'

It was all Harris could do to stay in his seat.

Flannery leaned forward and placed his hands on the table. He took a deep breath and began. 'She tried to keep it from me, but I overheard the phone call. She didn't look happy about it. One minute she was laughing and joking with me, and we were looking over the plans for her security system, and the next minute, I thought the woman was gonna pass out on me. She looked scared. Almost sick, in fact. Oh, when she hung up, she tried to make light of it. And when he sent the limo, she tried to convince me that it was just business.'

'Jesus,' Harris burst out. 'Stacie went to see him? Why the hell didn't you stop her? She knows what he's like. After what he did to her in New York, why would she go to him?'

Instantly all eyes were on Harris, but before he could say anything, Wade blurted out, 'New World Gallery was in debt to Omega Trust, which, through some barely legal bullshit, is now Core Invest.'

For a second, the room was silent. Harris could swear everyone was holding their breath. At last, Ellis inhaled slowly. 'I had no idea. Jesus! Why didn't she tell anyone? Fuck! It's a wonder she came out of it alive.'

Harris felt a cold prickle rise up his spine. It was all he could do to keep from leaving right this minute to find her, to make sure she was safe. He forced his attention back to what was being said, what he might need to know before he made a quick exit to her.

'All this time I thought Jamison spent the big bucks at her auction just to thumb his nose at me,' Ellis said.

'There's something else you should know.' Flannery had the room's attention again. 'Stacie didn't tell me this, but a couple of the workmen did. New World Gallery West was vandalized a couple of weeks ago.'

'What?' Harris was out of his chair and so was Marston.

Flannery continued, 'The foreman said when she saw it, she didn't look so much angry as scared. Then, apparently, she pulled herself together, refused to call the police, and asked the foreman to bring in extra crews, work extra shifts, whatever it took to get the repairs done.'

The knot in Harris' chest was nearly painful. 'I need to go to her,' he managed.

But Dee laid a hand on his arm and settled him back into the chair. 'You need to know what's going on first.'

'Just like New York,' Wade said. That got the full attention of everyone. Then he and Harris explained what they'd found during their little research session in the Dungeon.

Stunned silence settled over the room again. At last, Ellis offered a strangled whisper. 'I had no idea. None of us did.'

'Fuck!' The look on Alan Marston's face was pure anguish. 'When Zoe Hanson committed suicide and saddled Stacie with all that debt, Jamison owned her. Goddamn it! I'm so stupid. Why in God's name didn't I see it before? I shoulda. It's obvious now.' He tugged on his tie hard enough to strangle himself and continued. 'Like I said, Stacie and I, we go way back. I met her when she started working at New World Gallery. I knew she was a bright young lady even then. I was there. When the shit hit the fan I thought she'd made some bad deal with some loan shark, and when she ended up in the hospital –' Marston's face went beet red and he looked like he could explode. 'It was that motherfucker. Had to be! Had to be!'

'What? He beat her?' Harris felt a mix of panic and raw rage burn in his chest. 'Jamison beat Stacie?'

Marston nodded, now looking a little green around the gills. 'I knew Jamison and Zoe Hanson were thick as thieves, but I had no idea with Stacie. All I knew was that Zoe had left her in a real mess, and I thought she'd turned to some loan shark for help. And Stacie, well, she never asked me for help, never complained, never said a word. Wouldn't take help when I offered, except toward the end for treatment for Zoe, and she paid every cent of that back. I introduced her to Sasha Ivanov from the Hermitage Museum. I thought maybe something could come of it; at least keep the wolves at bay for another month. And damned if she didn't negotiate one of the biggest exhibitions of art from the museum the US has ever had. Enough to get the gallery running in the black. I was there the night she paid it all off. Me and half of New York City's movers and shakers and I don't know how much goddamned news media toasted her.'

'I can't believe Jamison would let her walk away, even if she did pay off the debt,' Ellis said.

'Doubt he would've if she hadn't done it all in such a public way. I reckon that was K. Ryde's doing. She did tell me that she'd hired the Ryde Agency for PR. Back then nobody'd ever heard of them, but fuck if they didn't get the job done.'

Before Harris could let the thought of Kendra having a role in Stacie's very frightening past sink in,

Ellis spoke up.

'I still don't understand why Jamison would be involved with an insignificant gallery, one that was by all appearances a bad investment,' he said, then he turned his attention back to Martin Flannery. 'And I can't believe after what you saw you'd just sit back on your hands and do nothing, Martin.'

Flannery gave a square-shouldered shrug. 'I didn't say I sat back on my hands. The limo took Stacie to the Hotel Monaco. She was there for less than 30 minutes. My man tells me it was Jamison who answered the door. When she came out, Jamison had one of his security thugs escort her to the limo, which delivered her back to the gallery. But she didn't come inside. Instead, she got in the Lexus and went to the bank. After that, she went straight home. What?' he said as if he'd just noticed all eyes were on him. 'She might fire my ass if she finds out. But it was a risk I felt was worth taking.'

Harris' respect for Flannery skyrocketed. Jesus, no wonder his daughter was such a pit bull journalist.

'Oh, one more thing you should know,' Flannery added. 'Jamison's having Stacie tailed. I've seen the guy around outside the gallery a couple of times. Had him checked out. He's a good PI – one of the best, actually. Just not as good as I am.'

'It sounds to me like maybe Jamison hasn't let Stacie go then,' Ellis said.

'While I find Stacie's situation disturbing,' Wade said, 'I don't see how it has anything to do with the coup in Valderia.'

'Maybe it doesn't,' Ellis replied, 'but if Stacie's in danger, then we need to take care of it. We need to make sure she's safe.' He ran a hand through his hair and puffed out a heavy breath. 'Martin, keep your men on her at all times. I don't care if she fires your ass. I'll reimburse you. Just keep her safe.'

'Yes, you just keep that young lady safe,' Marston added. 'That's the main thing.'

For a few seconds, there was silence around the table. Harris felt as though his pulse would explode from his throat. How could he have underestimated Stacie so badly? And she was clearly in danger.

'I'm going to her,' he said. 'If you need me, you know how to reach me.'

He gave Dee a quick hug and was halfway out the door before Ellis called after him.

'Be careful, Harris. This doesn't feel good.'

Chapter Twenty-two

The bouquet was nearly as big as the delivery man, who peeked around it, offering Stacie a broad smile. No doubt he figured she'd be pleased to get such a lovely gift. But even as she tipped him and sent him on his way, she felt a rising sense of dread. She knew the flowers were from Jamison. His bouquet had been by far the largest at Zoe's funeral. Everyone thought he mourned her. Everyone thought he honored her memory.

'Do you like the flowers?' he had whispered as he had scooted in next to her on the pew.

Her response had been a non-committal nod. She hadn't wanted to talk, and especially not to him. The pianist played Bach's *Prelude Number 1 in C Major*. It had been Zoe's favorite. The church was packed. Zoe had lots of friends, most of them now Stacie's friends as well, but no amount of flowers or music could disguise the raw sense of shock and loss.

Disregarding the place and the occasion, he traced the curve of her ear with his finger, and she would have slid away from him, further down the pew, if she hadn't already been at the end. The kiss he planted lingered just a little too long in its humid urgency, making her feel as though he had shoved her against the wall and pinned her there. 'The flowers –' his voice was just loud enough to be heard above the music, just loud enough to make the people in the pew next to them glance over '– they're really for you, Stacie. You're the one who'll suffer Zoe's loss the most.'

Shaking off the memory, she steeled herself and opened the envelope that had come with the flowers. A picture of some woman she didn't recognize fell out onto the floor. She picked it up and offered it a passing glance, then turned her attention to the note, making sure she was seated before she read it. It was a good thing. Inside the envelope was a memorial card from a funeral home.

Stacie shoved a hand against her mouth and swallowed down rising panic. Everything in her went cold with dread. On the front of the card was a stock print of praying hands. Inside was a Bible quote from Ecclesiastes.

To everything there is a season, and a time to every purpose under the heaven:

A time to be born, and a time to die; a time to plant, and a time to pluck up that which is planted.

Relief made her weak all over when she saw there was no name of a deceased on the card, no obituary, no list of close relatives. Instead there was just a note.

My Dearest Stacie,

The beauty of these flowers pales in comparison to your own. But alas so much of beauty is fleeting, isn't it? We both experienced that in the loss of our dear Zoe. One must enjoy every moment to the fullest as you and I so well know. You and I both understand how quickly so much that we value can be taken from us; in an instant, in a heartbeat, almost as though it had never been.

BTW, do you like Ingrid Watson's new look? My goodness, I think the girl has a bit of a crush on you. Hero worship, you know? I think she wants to be just like you, and of course, I can deny her nothing, as I could never, nor shall I ever deny you. I'm delighted at our chance to work together once more, my darling, and I look forward to enjoying your company again very soon.

Yours always,

TJ

She picked up the photo from the desk and studied it. Sure enough, she could now see that it was Ingrid Watson, all blond and primped and looking nothing at all like herself. Looking creepily like Stacie.

She grabbed for her BlackBerry, tried Ingrid's number. There was no answer. She sent a text.

Are you all right, Ingrid?

Not wanting to worry the woman unnecessarily, she added quickly;

I haven't heard from you in a while and I was hoping we could catch up. Would love to chat with you at your convenience.

She had just pulled up email to cover all her bases when she saw the message from Ingrid. It was sent at 6:30 this morning, but for some reason she had only just gotten it. It read,

Ms. Emerson, I'm in town with Terrance Jamison. I'd love to see you as soon as possible. I was just wondering, are you all right? Is Mr. Walker all right?

Panic rolled over her in a wave and the knot of fear

in her chest felt like a fist. The message was sent hours ago! Why the hell hadn't she gotten it? She punched in Harris' number frantically, and cursed out loud when there was no answer.

'Call me. Now,' she half yelled into his voicemail. She dropped her device three times before she managed a text and an email to him. She was just getting ready to call Ellis when Harris bust through the door of her office and scooped her into his arms, into a hug that left her breathless.

'Thank God you're all right.'

'I was so worried.'

They both spoke at the same time, then he took her mouth in a crushing kiss. 'Why the hell didn't you tell me? Jesus, Stacie, did you think I wouldn't understand?' He pulled her still tighter against him. 'I was so worried. We were all so worried.'

'Understand what? What are you talking about?' She'd barely managed to catch a breath before his attention lit on the flowers and the funeral card lying on her desk.

'From Jamison.' It wasn't a question. Before she could do more than nod, he picked up the card and read it. The transformation on his face was a study in hard lines and harsh angles, a place where anger and frustration coexisted in tight knots of muscles and square set of jaw. His breathing, which had never slowed since his arrival, shoved at his chest faster and faster, as though it couldn't wait to escape its confinement.

Willing her hand to remain steady, struggling to control her own upwelling of emotion at his safety, at his presence, she took the card from Harris and laid it back on the desk. 'He … He sent flowers like this, almost identical, to Zoe's funeral.' She looked up into his angry eyes. 'He knew I'd make the connection.'

'The sick fuck,' Harris fumed. He picked up the picture of Ingrid Watson from the floor where it had fallen, and flinched as though he'd been slapped, looking first at her and back at the photo. 'Jesus,' he whispered. 'His doing?'

She nodded. 'Has to be. Ingrid had beautiful dark hair and she was slightly goth-ish. The look fit her.'

'Have you been in touch with her?' He asked.

'I texted. I was about to send an email, then I got this. It just came. I don't know why the delay.' She handed him her BlackBerry.

'Fuck, Stacie! Jesus!' He looked up at her.

'You're gonna want to ignore the message I left with your voicemail. When she mentioned your name, asked how you were, I … was scared. I never did hear back from Ingrid. With any luck she's safely on a flight home to Minnesota by now.' She wanted to believe that desperately. But she didn't. Not really.

'Stacie.' He took her in his arms and held her close. 'Stacie, why's he doing this?'

She wasn't sure what words might have come from her mouth if her BlackBerry hadn't rung. She gave a little yelp of surprise and grabbed it back from Harris' hand. He moved close to her to listen in.

'Who is it?' he whispered. 'Is it him?'

'It's the hospital,' she mouthed. Then she sat down hard in the chair with Harris kneeling next to her, straining to hear. 'I'll be right there. Please tell her I'll be right there,' she managed. Her voice sounded far away, like it belonged to someone else.

‘What is it? Stacie, what’s the matter?’ He shook her gently.

‘It’s Ingrid Watson. She’s in the hospital. She’s been assaulted. She’s asking for me.’ Stacie shoved to her feet and grabbed her bag and keys.

‘I’ll drive,’ Harris said. ‘We can take the Jeep. You don’t need to do this alone.’

For that, Stacie was relieved. Right now, she didn’t want to let Harris out of her sight.

They didn’t speak again until they were in the Jeep and on the road. Then he shot her a sideways glance. ‘You all right?’ He couldn’t help noticing her white-knuckle grip on the arm rest.

‘Fine.’ Her voice was breathless, like she’d been running.

Before she could say more, he continued, ‘Jamison did this to her?’

She only nodded, staring out the windshield at the road in front of them.

He glanced at her again. ‘I know what he did to you with the New York Gallery, Stacie.’

The look she shot him was panic-stricken, wild-eyed. But he didn’t give her time to respond. ‘Why didn’t you tell anyone? Why didn’t you tell me?’

She stiffened. His shoulders tightened in empathy, in fear that he’d said too much. At last, she replied in a voice that was tight with control. ‘I don’t talk about that part of my life because it was horrible, that’s why. And because …’

‘Because why?’

‘Because I don’t want anyone feeling sorry for me. I made it out alive, which is more than I can say for Zoe.’

Harris felt the bottom drop out of his stomach. 'Did he …? Did Jamison …?'

'He might as well have. He badgered her and used her and threatened her until she despaired. Zoe wasn't strong. She never was, and he knew it, and he … He killed her as surely as if he had put the gun in her mouth and pulled the trigger. And now he's after Ingrid for no other reason than to get to me.'

They stopped for a red light and he studied her, rigid and angry as he'd never seen her before. But he was beginning to suspect that he really had never actually seen her before. 'Look, I understand you not wanting to dredge up the past. No one would under the circumstances, and especially not after all you've done to move beyond it. But what's going on now isn't the past. The man's a monster and, for whatever reason, he's made you his target as well as Ellis.'

She jerked against the seatbelt and turned her gaze on him. 'Ellis? What's he got to do with this? What's he done to Ellis?'

'There's been a coup in Valderia. All of Pneuma's access properties have been nationalized. Jamison's financing that coup.'

Whatever she said under her breath, Harris was guessing it wasn't nice. She turned her attention back to the road. 'I didn't know, but it doesn't surprise me, knowing Jamison.'

'Stacie –' he glanced over at her as the light changed '– why's he bothering you now, after all this time?'

For a long moment, she said nothing, as if she were choosing her words carefully. Then she spoke, with the full measure of venom in her voice. 'Because I provoked him.'

'You provoked him? You provoked Jamison? How did you do that? Why would you do that?'

'You've provoked him too by not staying away from me,' came her response. Before he could tell her that was just too damned bad, she continued, 'Harris, please. I don't want to talk about this now. Can we just get to the hospital?'

He released an uneasy breath and focused his attention on the road. 'All right. I can wait. But I want some answers, Stacie, and I'm not the only one.'

As a reminder of the others waiting for answers, his BlackBerry rang. He picked up in spite of his strict no-cell-phones-while-driving policy. He knew it was Ellis.

'She's all right. We're on the way to the hospital. Ingrid Watson's been assaulted.'

He held the device away from his ear as Ellis let loose a string of expletives. 'She's asking for Stacie,' he finally managed. He gave Ellis the name of the hospital, knowing that if some of Flannery's men weren't there by the time he and Stacie arrived, they would be shortly after. He disconnected and stomped on the gas.

He didn't offer to drop her at the entrance of the hospital while he parked the Jeep, and she didn't ask. He got the distinct impression it was a toss-up as to who was the most afraid to let the other out of their sight.

It was a footrace to keep up with her as she made her way to the emergency room reception desk just as Flannery and two of his men showed up to flank them. But the desk was in chaos. There at reception, a harried ER doctor was gesticulating wildly and the nurse behind the desk was calling security.

‘This woman needs medical care. You can’t just swoop in and take her away like this. The police may need to be contacted,’ Harris heard the doctor say.

Suddenly Stacie gave a growl that sent chills up his spine. She broke from his tight grip on her arm and shoved her way past the doctor. It was then that Harris saw the man hovering over a battered-looking woman in a wheelchair. It was Terrance Jamison. And the woman, whose face was swollen and bruised, could have passed for Stacie. Harris felt sick at the sight. He lurched forward and grabbed for Stacie, but she was already kneeling in front of the wheelchair, holding the woman’s hands.

‘Ingrid. I’m here. I came as fast as I could.’ Stacie smoothed the hair away from her swollen face and addressed the ER doctor. ‘Why is this woman being released? She clearly needs medical attention?’

‘I agree, Stacie darling,’ Jamison responded before the doctor could as he reached a solicitous hand out to Stacie. She ignored it and glared at him. He continued as though nothing out of the ordinary was happening. ‘I have access to much better medical treatment than our poor Ingrid will ever get here. I want her where she can receive the best, and I’m the one who can see she gets it, who can best oversee her convalescence. Portland can be such a dangerous place. And really, I feel responsible, since it was I who invited her as my guest.’

When Jamison grabbed for her, Stacie jerked her arm away. ‘She asked for me, Terrance. Not you. And she’ll get what she needs just fine here. Now leave us alone.’ As she spoke, Harris moved to back her up, with Flannery’s men flanking. But Jamison wasn’t alone either. The two Armani-suited men hovering by the reception desk were no doubt his, and Harris suspected the two men loitering by the door were as well.

Jamison took him in with a smirk Harris would have liked to beat off his smug face, then he waved a dismissive hand. 'Really, Stacie, you didn't have to bring your fanboy.'

'You touch her again and you'll see just how much of a fanboy I am,' Harris growled. One of Flannery's men laid a warning hand on Harris' shoulder.

For an instant, Jamison's smirk flattened out to raw, bullet-proof hatred, then softened and brightened again as he turned his attention back to Stacie. 'It's simple. After the nurse called you, Ingrid changed her mind, realizing that I could best see to her medical care and make sure she gets the protection she needs.'

Stacie didn't budge from where she knelt holding the woman's hands. 'Well, you haven't done a very good job of protecting her so far, have you?' Then she turned back to Ingrid. 'Sweetie, you need medical attention, and here's the best place for you to be. Don't worry –' She smoothed Ingrid's newly blond hair again. 'I won't leave you. I won't let anyone hurt you.' She nodded to Flannery's men. 'These men, they know what they're doing. They'll help me keep you safe'

The people crowded in the waiting area were now watching with rapt attention. The ER doctor had nervousness written all over her face, and the hospital security guards now stood by the door, not knowing what to do. 'Look, this is a hospital,' the doctor said. 'This woman needs to be here. We don't know the extent of her injuries, and taking her away without treatment could be detrimental.'

Jamison completely ignored the doctor. His self-indulgent smile rested only on Stacie. 'Well, I'm certainly not going to remove Miss Watson against her will. Why don't we ask her what she wants?' He knelt next to Stacie and patted the woman's arm. Was Harris mistaken, or did she actually flinch? 'Ingrid darling, you can certainly stay if you want to, and perhaps everything will be just fine if you do. You have to understand me not wanting to trust you to anything but the best, sweetheart, and of course I want to be by your side, since I feel responsible for what happened.'

'Ingrid, you don't have to go with him,' Stacie said. Harris could see the woman's white-knuckled grip on both Stacie's hands; he could nearly feel the tension in her shoulders. 'I promise I won't leave you. I'll stay with you and keep you safe.'

'Really, Stacie, you're so dramatic,' Jamison said. 'Without Thorne's beneficence, how on earth are you going to keep her safe, when you can't even pay your own bills?'

Harris saw the color drain from Stacie's face and felt as though he'd been gut-punched himself. Money problems? Stacie? Surely there was some mistake. He found himself moving forward and laying a hand on Stacie's shoulder. 'Stacie's right, Ms. Watson. We'll see that you're safe.'

A single tear slid down the girl's bruised cheek. Harris was pretty sure she was digging her nails into Stacie's hand. At last, she spoke with difficulty. 'No. No, it's OK, really. I did call Mr. Jamison. I want him to take care of me so I can go home to my father all the sooner.'

'You see?' Jamison's smile was all sweetness and light. 'Surely the poor dear must be homesick, and to have had such a terrible experience so far from home, I can hardly imagine. Perhaps I'll have her father flown out to be with her.'

'No!' Ingrid practically came out of the wheelchair before catching her breath in a sharp gasp of pain. 'No, that won't be necessary. Daddy won't be able to get away from the farm right now, and I'm in good hands. Really I am. Besides –' another tear slid down her cheek '– I don't want to worry him.'

Anyone with half a brain could see the woman was terrified. And Harris couldn't keep his mouth shut a moment longer. 'Jamison, why don't you and all your thugs just wait outside for a few minutes, maybe go down to the cafeteria for coffee, and give Ms. Watson here just five minutes to speak for herself without you threatening her.'

Stacie's shoulders tensed. Flannery's men snapped to attention and the ER doctor shot a panicked look at the hospital security men. But Jamison only offered an indulgent smile, the kind he might offer a child who just didn't understand the situation.

'Mr. Walker, this is not your affair, and in the future, I would advise you remember just how much this is not your affair. Now, if you'll excuse us –' He carefully extricated Ingrid's clenched fingers from Stacie's hands and gave them a squeeze. 'I'm taking this poor girl to where she can get exactly what she needs.'

Harris helped Stacie to her feet, afraid she might lunge for Jamison, who, with everyone looking on, took up the position behind the wheelchair and began to push it toward the exit, flanked by his bodyguards.

He stopped and turned back. 'Oh, and Stacie, it would be wise for you not to bite the hand that feeds you.' Then he left, pushing Ingrid Watson's wheelchair as though he was the most attentive, most affectionate man alive.

It was all Harris could do to hold Stacie. 'He did this to her. He did this to her because of me.' Her anguish ripped at him as he felt every muscle in her body straining against him.

'It's not your fault, and you can't help her like this.' Harris spoke softly. 'We'll regroup. We'll find a way to get her back, Stacie.' He lifted her chin until she couldn't look away from him. 'We'll deal with Jamison. We will, and we'll make it right.'

Chapter Twenty-three

The grey light of the hospital room exaggerated the sunken planes of Zoe's cheeks. Even the blanket that covered her couldn't hide the sharp angles and protrusions of a body too thin for itself. Stacie ached at the sight and tried not to think about how her friend had looked only a few months ago when things were better, and she was happy. She knocked softly on the door and stepped inside. Instantly, Zoe's face was transformed into a smile as she reached out her hand to take Stacie's.

'I didn't think you'd come,' she said, her eyes brimming. 'I … would have understood if you hadn't, under the circumstances.'

'Of course I came, Zoe! How can you even think that I wouldn't? I came as soon as I could.' When she'd gotten news of Zoe's overdose, Stacie had been in Boston, meeting with an artist she'd been trying for months to get to agree to an exhibition. The lion's share of the work, by then, was already falling to her, and it was a lot. Zoe tried, but the stress of Jamison's badgering and the unhealthy relationship Stacie knew she was in with the man had only exacerbated the substance abuse problems Zoe had battled all her life.

Stacie sat on the edge of the bed, still holding her friend's hand. 'Zoe, why didn't you tell me things were so bad? We could have gotten you help. We could have seen that you got what you needed.' She hurried on before Zoe could protest about the money. 'We'd have found a way. Don't we always find a way? I can't do this without you, Zo. I need you. You don't get to opt out, do you understand? I thought we were clear on that. We're in this together.'

A blush rose to her friend's ravaged face, and she extricated her hand from Stacie's grasp. 'Stacie, I wouldn't. I mean, I didn't. I swear to you, this wasn't deliberate –the overdose, I mean. Did the doctors tell you that? Because it wasn't. I promise you, I'd never leave you saddled with all this mess.' She worried the edge of the sheet between her slender fingers, holding it nervously to her breasts as though she were naked and trying to cover herself. She shot a nervous glance toward the door. 'Have you talked to Terrance? Did he tell you that I had tried to …?'

'I talked to him briefly in the hall, yes. But I talked to the doctor first, sweetie, and he said that –'

'That the … overdose was deliberate.' She spoke the words in barely more than a whisper. 'Well, he's wrong, Stacie. He's wrong. It wasn't deliberate and, honestly, I don't know how it happened. I swear I don't.'

Stacie grabbed her hand again. 'Then prove it to me by getting some help.'

There was another frightened look toward the door and Zoe swallowed back a sob. 'I can't, Stacie. I can't while he's … while I'm with …'

This time it was Stacie's turn to glance nervously at the door. 'Yes, you can. I can help you. He doesn't have to know. I'll run interference if I have to but we'll get you the help you need.'

'Stacie, you're not running interference.' All at once, Zoe's eyes were hard and clear. 'We both know what that would mean, and I couldn't bear it. I'm the one who got you into this mess, and I couldn't bear it if you … if he …' She reached out to stroke Stacie's cheek. 'I couldn't bear it if he …' Her eyes misted again. 'If he hurt you.'

'What in the world are you talking about, Zoe darling?' Both women jumped when Jamison burst into the room, all smiles and light. 'I'd never hurt our Stacie.' As if to demonstrate, he pulled Stacie to her feet and gave her a kiss that was hard and possessive and overly familiar, one that he made no attempt to hide from Zoe. Then he turned to Zoe and brushed a kiss across the top of her mussed red hair. 'I'd never do anything to hurt either of my girls, now would I? I want you both healthy and strong and working hard to make our gallery a success.' The look he gave Stacie started below her navel and worked its way leisurely up to her face. 'Although, shame on you, Zoe dear. Your carelessness in your nasty habits means that our poor Stacie will have to work twice as hard to take up the slack. But then –' He offered a soft chuckle that made Stacie shiver. 'She's been taking up the slack for a while now, hasn't she, darling?'

He sat on the edge of the bed and slipped an arm around Zoe, pulling her close. Then he spoke next to her ear. 'And that means our poor Stacie has no time for leisure of her own.' Stacie felt naked in his gaze that moved over her again before it came back to her face. 'And I find that very sad; very sad indeed, Zoe.' Even from where she stood, Stacie could see his embrace tighten and morph to something no longer affectionate, something much more threatening, and his voice lost its genial veneer. 'So I would suggest you pull yourself together and do your part for the team effort, darling.'

Then he stood and began to pace. 'Now, as far as getting you the help you need, Zoe, believe me, I do understand that you're ill, and you need treatment. So I've made arrangements to have you moved to a facility that can help you get what you need.'

'No!' Stacie pushed in next to Zoe and took her hand in a tight grip. 'That's not necessary, Terrance. I'll see that Zoe gets the help she needs. I'll see to her.' She stood stiff-backed and square-shouldered, hoping he couldn't see how her knees were shaking. 'I've already got it sorted,' she lied. 'We'll take care of it.'

The man stopped his pacing and stood like a statue in the middle of the room. In her peripheral vision, Stacie could see his hands tighten to fists, and the line along his jawbone was hard. She braced herself, holding tightly to Zoe, who held her back.

But he only offered a little laugh. 'Suit yourselves, ladies,' he said. Then he bent and took Zoe's mouth like he owned it, holding her chin cupped in his hand, his thumb and forefinger tight against her jaw as his tongue snaked into the opening he forced. And it was impossible for Stacie, who observed in rising panic, not to understand the punishment that kiss promised and the rage it made little attempt to hide.

He kissed Zoe until she whimpered and raised a hand in an effort to push him back. He kissed her until Stacie reached for his shoulder to pull him away, then he released her and she fell with a harsh grunt against the pillow. He turned to Stacie so quickly that she feared he'd hit her. Instead, he raked her with another hungry look that twisted into a smirk, then he said, 'Good luck with those rehab plans. I think the first step is to admit you've got a problem, isn't it?' Then he left.

Stacie didn't argue when Ellis convened a meeting at his place. She didn't argue when Harris bundled her into the Jeep and drove her there. She knew the man had a million questions, all questions she'd have to answer, but he had the good grace to leave her alone with her thoughts during the drive over. Though, in all honesty, they weren't thoughts she really wanted to be left alone with. They seldom were when they strayed back to that dark time. And these days they seemed to stray there a lot. Not surprising under the circumstances.

She couldn't keep from wondering if maybe Harris had left her alone with her thoughts because he was too disgusted to talk to her after what Jamison had let slip. It didn't matter. She'd do whatever she had to do to get Ingrid safely out of Jamison's hands. Ingrid was an innocent. Ingrid had done nothing to deserve this. So if Harris now hated her, if he wanted nothing further to do with her – well, good for him. What better way to keep him safe than for him to despise her and not want to see her again.

With her hand clutched tightly in his, Harris led her into the study at Ellis' place, where Harold was pouring coffee, which she declined. She didn't think she could get anything past the tight knot in her chest at the moment. Ellis and Dee sat side by side on the love seat across from Wade and Al Marston, who sat in wing-backed chairs. She and Harris sat on the sofa next to Flannery. It certainly looked like the whole gang had been invited, she thought grimly.

It didn't take long for Ellis and Wade to update her on the Valderian situation. That they feared she might somehow be involved was clear. It didn't take her much longer to reassure them that she wasn't, but it hurt that they thought she might have been.

Harris was way more obliging with information about her funeral flowers and emails from Ingrid than was his place, but then maybe he was afraid she'd balk. She wouldn't have. It was too late for that now.

When everyone had been brought up to date on the incident at the hospital, Martin Flannery cleared his throat and scooted forward on the sofa. 'As you might expect, no one was keen on sharing information at the hospital. So I took some liberties.' He pulled out his BlackBerry and began to scroll down. 'Yes, here it is. The first assessment on Ingrid Watson's condition was that there were no bones broken and no internal bleeding, all pending further examination, of course. Apparently Ms. Watson was assaulted in her room at the Monaco. No one saw anyone go in or come out. She claims it happened in the dark and her assailant woke her out of a sound sleep.

'Bullshit,' Al interrupted. 'I don't believe that for a minute. Jamison did it, and you can take that to the bank. She's not the first woman he's beaten up.' He shot Stacie a quick glance and she felt her cheeks burn with humiliation, even after all this time.'

'She was terrified. That was obvious,' Harris said, tightening his grip on Stacie's hand.

‘She claims to have been alone in the suite, a suite that Jamison rented for her,’ Flannery continued. ‘The notes say she absolutely refused to let the police investigate. Claimed she was too scared and couldn’t go through with it.’

‘Oh, she was scared, all right,’ Al growled.

‘Wait a minute,’ Dee said. ‘Can she even do that under the circumstances?’

‘With Jamison in control of the situation, the law doesn’t apply,’ Ellis answered.

‘I should have made a scene,’ Stacie said. ‘I should have forced the issue, then she’d be safe, then she’d be out of his hands.’

‘You did the best you could,’ Harris said, scooting closer to her. ‘It was the only thing you could do. You stayed safe to fight another day.’

‘And Ingrid’s still with him,’ she replied.

‘What’s really going on, Stacie?’ The sharp edge of Ellis’ voice cut through the tense atmosphere in the room. ‘You need to tell us.’

This was it. The muscles in her throat tightened until she could barely breathe, let alone speak. This was the part she had most dreaded, had even hoped she might be able to avoid. The problem was just her ego, just her pride. In the end, it was only a small thing, but it felt practically insurmountable. She took a deep breath, closed her eyes for a second, feeling the gaze of the whole room on her. Then she squared her shoulders and just said it. ‘I owe him money.’ The room exploded around her with everyone talking at once. It didn’t surprise her when Al Marston’s voice, with its loud southern drawl, cut through the chaos.

‘What the fuck do you mean, you own him money?

You paid that bastard off a long time ago. The gallery's yours free and clear.'

She spoke above the chokehold of nerves. 'The New York gallery is paid off, yes. But this new one – well, this new one's caused me some problems.'

She forced the words out of her mouth, fighting the urge to swallow them back, fighting the urge to say something less damning, something less painful, anything else but what she had to say. Her shoulders ached from her efforts to stay calm, her eyes burned from a night of too little sleep and a day that was shaping up to be as full of nightmares as the night had been. And hardest of all to take was the scorch of Harris' gaze locked on her.

'That's bullshit,' Al spoke up. 'That's bullshit and you know it, Stacie. Now I wanna know just what the hell's going on.'

'Al, please.' Ellis' voice was once again soft and as reasonable as it always was. He turned his attention to her. 'Stacie, why? Why did you go to him? You know you could have come to any of us, and we'd have never batted an eye about helping you. Why?'

The disappointment in his voice cut bone deep, but there was nothing for it now, and really, it wasn't unexpected. 'I've never asked for anything from any of you,' she said. 'And I feel like I've caused enough problems for you and Garrett. I just couldn't. Ever since … everything happened with us, I've managed, I've tried to stay away. Especially in the early days.'

'Jesus, Stacie, this isn't the early days,' Ellis said. 'The early days are long gone. We know what you went through in New York. Al told us. How could you go back to Jamison again after that?'

She felt the humiliation flash hot in her face and she fought it back. She had to do what she had to do, she reminded herself, and really, it was no one's business. 'Al has a big mouth,' she managed before he cut her off at the pass.

'Damn right I have a big mouth, woman, and if it'll get you out of trouble with that bastard I'll sing like a stool pigeon.'

She turned on him. 'You don't know anything about what happened back then, Al. You don't know anything!'

'I know plenty, goddamn it! I'm not totally stupid, and when Wade and Harris did a little research and put two and two together –'

'What?' She felt as though the floor had dropped from under her. 'You checked me out? You had no right! This isn't your business. It's not your problem.'

'The hell it isn't,' Harris growled, holding her gaze. 'You're in danger. That makes it our business.'

Al ranted on. 'What were you thinking, Stacie, pulling a goddamned stupid stunt that has you up to your eyeballs with that sack of shit again? And now with the mess in Valderia, how the fuck could you expect me to keep my mouth shut? I know what he did to you. At least that Watson woman could leave the hospital under her own –'

'Shut up, Al!' Stacie broke. 'What happened in the past doesn't matter. Bringing it up won't change a thing and it won't bring Zoe back.' She caught her breath and struggled to regain control. 'Look, I made a mistake, all right. I didn't actually go to Jamison. He found out about my situation, and he came to me. He caught me at a weak point when I was desperate, and I thought things had changed. Then he sent a check just when I needed it most.'

'Is that after he had your gallery vandalized?' Ellis asked. 'You weren't gonna tell us about that either?'

'I wasn't going to tell any of you about any of it because it's nothing to do with you.'

'You can't possibly be that naïve,' Al said.

'Al, you know I love you to bits and I respect you more than just about anyone I know, but I'm asking you to stay out of it and let me deal with it.' She gave them all a sweeping look. 'I'm asking you to all stay out of it. I got myself into this situation and I'll get myself out. Like I did last time.'

'And last time nearly killed you.' Al's voice was little more than an angry snarl.

Chaos enveloped the room once more, but it was Harris' voice above the din that silenced everyone. It wasn't loud, but it was heavily weighted with a conviction that took her breath away. 'I'm not staying out of this and I'm not leaving, Stacie. Get used to it.'

'Do you think he'll stop at hurting Ingrid? Do you think he'll leave any of you alone now? You read her email, Harris. She emailed because she was afraid for you. She believed Jamison would hurt you.'

'He can try,' Harris said, and the room erupted again.

This time it was Wade's quiet voice that cut through everything. Wade always wielded that sort of unpretentious power. 'I don't believe you. I don't believe any of this, Stacie. I think you're lying. I just don't know why.'

She straightened in her seat and forced herself to remain calm. The one thing she really didn't need was

Wade snooping around. 'It doesn't matter what you believe, Wade. I was weak. I gave in to him. You all know how persuasive he can be. I didn't want any of you to know about my money problems. I figured it would all be over once the exhibition ended and I could pay him back. I can endure anything for a little while, and it'll only be for a little while. I promise.'

'I don't believe that and neither do you,' Ellis said. 'Let me take on the debt. You know that I can.'

'You've got your hands full with the Valderian situation,' she reminded him. 'And even if you didn't, you know he wouldn't let that happen. And that would just give him something else to hold over you. I don't want him having anything to hold over any of you.'

'Then, Stacie, I want to know what you need from me.' Martin Flannery spoke for the first time since he had informed everyone about the hospital situation. His words were tightly controlled and the anger in his voice was barely hidden. When everyone turned their attention to him, he tugged at his tie and, still holding Stacie's gaze, he continued, 'I have a daughter like Mr. Watson does, like Mr. and Mrs. Emerson do, and I would gut anyone with a dull pocket knife who touched a single hair on Carla's head.'

For a long moment, Stacie held his gaze, then she let out a slow breath. 'I need you to finish what you started, and I need you to keep the people I care about safe until this is over.'

He nodded.

'I can't pay you.'

His jaw tightened and he tugged his tie again. 'You've already paid in full for the security system. Was that money from Jamison?'

'No. That money was mine. And when this is over, I'll pay you for the rest.' She shot Al a glance that she hoped he would understand was appreciation of his help and friendship. 'I always pay my debts.'

'Stacie.' Ellis spoke again. His grip on Dee's hand was tight and his eyes flashed fire. 'You have to do what you have to do, but you need to know you're not alone this time and we, none of us, are prepared to sit back and do nothing if … if he tries to hurt you. If that happens, all bets are off.'

She swallowed back the emotions that threatened her control, once again aware of Harris' hand holding hers. 'All I ask is that you let me get on with it. I'll pay him back. I promise you that. I'll pay him back.' The last words felt like bile rising in her throat.

'Then, I'll reiterate Martin's question,' Ellis said. 'What do you want us to do?' Everyone in the room nodded and all eyes were on her again.

She felt as if exhaustion reached up and grabbed at her heart and squeezed. 'I need …' Tears threatened, but she forced them back. 'I need to make sure Ingrid and her father are safe.'

All eyes were again on Flannery, who was typing something onto his BlackBerry. He spoke without looking up. 'Ingrid has just been returned to her room at the Monaco, accompanied by Jamison's personal physician. Her father's fine and thinks his daughter is having a great time in Portland.' He glanced up at everyone. 'He's likely to stay that way as long as Ingrid cooperates.'

'There has to be a way,' Stacie said. 'It's all my fault that she's in this horrible mess.'

'It's not your fault,' Al said. 'It's that bastard,

Jamison's fault, and don't you forget it, missy! You tried to get her away from him in New York. You tried to get her to come with the rest of the artists. I was there, so don't give me that all my fault bullshit.'

'She's pretty safe for the moment,' Flannery said. 'If experience is any indicator, Jamison will treat her like royalty until she's recovered. He'll be gentle and loving and the epitome of kindness. He'll act like he's so sorry for what he's done; even make her think that once she's healed, she's free to go with no strings attached. That'll make the jerking her back all the more devastating, to her and to you.' He offered Stacie an apologetic smile. 'But for now, she's as safe as she can be. That gives us time to make a plan.'

Harris slipped an arm around Stacie's shoulders. 'Then if there's nothing else we can do right now, I'm taking Stacie back to my place for the night. I don't want her by herself.'

She bristled, but before she could say anything there was a nod of agreement around the room and Flannery was back on his BlackBerry. 'My men'll be there to make sure you two stay safe.' He leveled a look at Harris. 'They'll check out your house before you go in.'

'I figured as much,' Harris said. As he stood and helped her to her feet, it was all she could do to keep her mouth shut. It was all she could do to just leave it like this. She knew Jamison would muddy the water. She knew he'd never let it be easy. But she had gone too far down the path to undo what had been done. She nodded her meek thanks to everyone, feeling like Typhoid Mary, once again bringing suffering to those she cared about. Then Harris led her downstairs and outside into waning sunshine that she barely noticed as he helped her into the Jeep for the ride to his place.

During the drive to his house, Stacie said nothing, just sat staring out the window. He didn't attempt to make conversation. All the anger he had felt, all the upset for all that she hadn't told him and for all that he was sure she still wasn't telling him, had been replaced by the feeling that she had been somehow violated by the confrontation at Ellis'. There were parts of his own life he would never want dragged out for the world to see, and all of his dark secrets paled in comparison to what Stacie had experienced, and to the humiliation dredging it all up again must have put her though.

He had gone where he wasn't invited. He had seen what should have been hers to share at the right time, when she was ready, at a time when she trusted him more fully. That had never been his intention, and yet he felt as though he had run roughshod over her privacy. Well, so be it, damn it! If that's what it took to keep her safe, then so be it. Yet none of what she had said made sense. None of it rang true. His gut told him that, even as poor Ingrid Watson was proof of what Stacie had said. And yet it made no sense.

When they pulled into the drive next to his cabin, she only sat there as he turned off the engine. He went around the Jeep and helped her out, then led her upstairs where she stood looking listlessly out the big picture window over the lake. Then he had an idea.

'I'm hungry. You must be too. When was the last time you ate?' He saw her half-attempt at a shrug as he began to rattle around in the kitchen. 'I don't cook,' he told her. 'I ate the last of my mom's tomato soup last night, and we're too far from any place that delivers.' He opened the freezer and peered inside. 'I've got frozen pizza, couple of lasagna ready meals. Some fish sticks – oh, and a package of Tater Tots.' He turned to find her standing next to him, just as he'd hoped.

'How old are these eggs?' she asked, inspecting the pathetic contents of his refrigerator.

'Oh, they're fresh. Eggs, bacon, toast; that sort of thing I can cook. In fact, it's a staple.'

'Boring too,' she said. 'Don't suppose you have any flour?

'There might be some in the pantry,' he said. 'Back from when Kendra and Dee decided to surprise me with a homemade birthday cake.'

'And how was it?' She pulled the flour from the pantry.

'The surprise was great,' he said. 'The cake, not so much. We ended up at Dairy Queen eating banana splits instead.'

'That's not so bad then, as far as birthdays go.' She dug around until she found a bowl that would pass for mixing and the pan he used for eggs.

'It was a great birthday, actually. My birthday's in November. It's usually not warm, but it was then. We went canoeing. Had a picnic. Watched the sun set over the lake.'

'I like your friends,' she called over her shoulder. 'Even if they can't bake a cake.' Then she added. 'Do you like pancakes?'

'Hell yes, I like pancakes. Pretty much I like anything I don't have to cook.'

She laughed softly, and the sound of it made him

happier than he'd have thought possible. 'Pancakes it is, then. And you can fry up some bacon.'

He opened two bottles of Mirror Pond Ale, handed one to her, and they worked in comfortable silence preparing the meal. He liked the feel of her in his space. He liked it a lot. They settled in to feast at the breakfast bar just as the sun was turning the lake golden.

Flannery's men were already there when they'd arrived, a very subtle intrusion for which Harris was grateful. He knew Stacie was worried about him, but all he could really think about was Ingrid Watson's battered face and Marston saying that Jamison had done much worse to Stacie. He'd never had thoughts of hurting anyone and certainly not of killing anyone, but the thought of Jamison laying a hand on Stacie did things to him, things that were startling and not fit for civilized conversation.

She nodded to the painting of a mountain lion above his mantle. 'You've already got it hung.'

'Of course I do,' he said. 'I had that place in mind when Lynn bought it for me at the auction.'

'Vargas is a good artist. She really captures the feel of the outdoors. I'd like to do an exhibition of her work at some point.'

'If the mountain lion's any indication, then I'd be inclined to agree,' Harris replied around a mouthful of pancake.'

She turned her attention back to him. 'Tell me about the mountain lions you photographed.'

Her request surprised him, but not in an unpleasant way. He loved it that his photographs of the mountain lions mattered enough for her to ask about them. He washed down the last of his pancakes with the cocoa she'd made to go with their meal. 'I came upon them by accident. I mean, I knew they were there. I'd seen scat and there'd been sightings by a naturalist friend of mine. I came upon a female with three kittens – really young, still nursing. I'd never seen kittens that young.' He smiled at the memory. 'I'd never seen kittens at all. I'd only ever seen adult lions twice and that was just their backside as they disappeared.'

She leaned forward over her plate, closer to him, and sighed. 'Wow. It must have been amazing. I get goosebumps just thinking about it.'

He gave a grunt. 'I got more than just goosebumps. I nearly pissed myself. The first dozen shots I took, I was shaking so bad you could barely tell what they were. And then – then the female saw me. Jesus, I thought I was in trouble. I froze and she let out one of those hair-curling screams.' He chafed his arms. 'The sound of a mountain lion isn't a roar. They can't roar. They don't have the vocal chords for it. It's a scream, and it's the most terrifying sound I've ever heard. Anyway, she just stood there for what felt like ages, just stood there staring me down. And then she huffed out a little groan, nuzzled her kittens, and settled onto the rocks. After that, I swear it was like she and the kittens were posing for me.'

Stacie sat with hands wrapped around her cocoa cup, her eyes bright in amazement. He wished he could keep her that way. He wished he could keep her mind off of everything.

'I don't know how long she let me take pictures of her little family, but I ended up with several hundred shots – some you've seen, were amazing. Then, for no reason I could see, she stood and sauntered off with the kittens nipping at her tail.'

'Wow! I wish I'd been there. I wish I'd seen the cats. I wish I'd seen you there, shooting like crazy in spite of being scared. I'd love to have seen you in your element in that amazing situation.' She nodded again to the painting above the fireplace. 'Why not one of your photos there instead? They're wonderful. Any of the ones on your website would look amazing there.'

He glanced over at the painting. 'I don't know; it seemed too personal. I suppose that sounds silly, but they feel almost like intimate moments, pictures I want to look at all the time, but still sort of keep them private. I mean, they've been in magazines and in exhibitions, it's true, but still, here at home, they feel too intimate to go up over the fireplace for everyone to see. I have a couple in my study and one in my bedroom, but then you probably didn't notice it the last time …'

She smiled a smile that looked a little sad around the edges. 'I had other things on my mind last time I was in your bedroom.'

He curled his fingers around her hand where it lay on the counter next to her empty plate. 'I'm surprised you didn't notice, actually, considering how keen you were on getting me in your exhibition.' Immediately, he wished he'd not brought up the subject.

She pulled away from him and began clearing the dishes. 'Harris, I shouldn't even be here.' She spoke without looking at him. 'I left that night because I didn't want to involve you in this mess, and if anything, it's even more dangerous for you now.'

'You're not getting rid of me, so stop trying.'

She dropped the plate in the sink with a hard clatter and jumped back with a gasp. There she stood with her back to him, spine stiff, shoulders tight.

'Stacie, talk to me. You don't need to keep this all to yourself.' He reached for her, but she pulled away and wiped her wet hands on her skirt.

'I need a shower, Harris. It's been a long day. Do you mind?'

He watched miserably as she mounted the stairs like she was off to a fire. He ached inside for her, even as he raged. Then he had an idea. He picked up his BlackBerry from the counter and called Flannery, who said he'd take care of the rest.

Chapter Twenty-four

Harris dug through the guest room drawers until he found a pair of Kendra's yoga pants and a T-shirt. Stacie was curvier than Kendra, but yoga pants were stretchy, and OK, he was a guy. If they were a little tight on Stacie's excellent curves, well, he could live with that if she could. It was either that or scrounge something from his closet. Not that the idea of having Stacie's naked body swaddled in his clothing didn't do something for him, but he figured she'd be more comfortable in the yoga pants.

He was still thinking about the plan Flannery was helping him put together when he realized Stacie had left the bathroom door ajar, and instantly his mind was completely focused on the woman in the shower. He knocked softly and stepped into the humid room. 'Stacie? I brought you some clothes.' His voice sounded breathless, as though he'd been running. 'Are you all right?'

He set the clothes down on the shelf near the shower and, really, he hadn't planned it, but his hands had a mind of their own, and they were removing clothing – his clothing. And once the process had begun, it avalanched until he stood on the tiles in front of the shower buck naked. Then he took a deep breath and stepped into the steam.

She gave a little yelp of surprise as he moved in next to her, but the sound she made when he took her into his arms was more of a deep-chested purr. Encouraged by her enthusiastic welcome, he went to work on her mouth with his, feeling his erection expand and press upward against her belly in the tight space between them as he anticipated the warm, tight depth of her.

'You all right?' he asked again, pulling away just enough to speak.

'Better now,' she said, giving his cock a stroke as he reached for the shower gel and began soaping her breasts, his mouth watering as he thumbed and stroked the nipples to taut peaks.

He flinched and sucked breath between his lips when she fisted a hand against his cock and began to stroke. 'Easy,' he said, placing his palm on hers to slow her progress. 'You keep that up and I won't last long enough to get you really clean.' He forced her against the wall and lifted her arms around his neck.

'I don't want to hurt you, Harris,' she whispered. 'I never wanted to hurt you.'

'Then don't,' he said.

'Harris, I –'

He stopped her words with his mouth again. His tongue moved deep, stroking and lapping as though he could devour the words that he was pretty sure he didn't want to hear, as though he could, with his own tongue, with his own breath, give her the right words, the words that would cause them to wake up and find that Terrance Jamison was nothing more than a bad dream. 'Right now, I need you, Stacie,' he said at last, trailing kisses down her throat and onto her sternum, cupping her breast to his face. 'We need each other, and don't say we don't because you know we do. I won't let you go through this alone, so stop thinking I will.'

It stunned him to realize just how much he really did need her and how much he wanted her in his life. And how terribly much he'd underestimated her. There were secrets she was still keeping. He knew that, and he'd find a way to get her to open up, he'd find a way to win her trust. She made soft little grunts and groans and arched into his touch as he laved each erect nipple with his ravenous tongue before dropping to his knees and pulling her to him, resting his cheek against the rapid rise and fall of her belly. He ran a hand through her tight curls, feeling her breath catch and her hips tense and shift toward him as he slid two fingers into her. Only a few hours ago he had been desperate to talk to her, desperate to hear what she was hiding. Yes, he still wanted to know, but now it mattered less. It mattered much less than the woman in his arms.

'Harris, I need you,' she said. 'Harris, I need you.' Over and over again she said it in tight little breaths as he opened her with a scissoring of his fingers, opened her where she thickened and swelled against his touch, where the soft glide and slip of her invited him deeper. And God, he wanted to go deeper, way deeper than her body would allow, way deeper than he could ever go just holding her in his arms.

Kendra told him his problem was that he was too intense, that he wasn't ever willing to keep it simple with women, to keep it uncomplicated. Jesus, she was so right! And the very thought of what Stacie kept hidden from him made him ache, not because she kept secrets – everyone had secrets – but because he could see they hurt her. He could see what she kept hidden wounded her deeply and yet she kept it, held it, locked it away.

He lifted her right foot to rest on his shoulder, forcing her to lean back on the tiles and open still further. Even over the scent of shower gel, even in the rising steam, he could smell her scent, he could smell her desire. He buried his face in the warm wet of her and she gave a little jerk and a sigh before curling fingers in his hair.

She let out a little cry. 'Harris, oh God, that's …' Her words trailed off and the curl of her fist tightened next to his scalp as he bore down on the rise of her clit, alternately sucking and kissing, then licking a path around her hardness with the press of his tongue. He felt the tension tighten her whole body around him. Her grip in his hair was nearly painful. Her body went rigid and her back arched against the wall as she convulsed against his mouth. And, in the spasms that racked her, her foot slid off his shoulder and she slipped to the floor next to him, pushing and shoving him back until he sat flat on the shower floor with his spine resting on the decorative glass blocks of the wall, and he was thankful it was a big shower.

That was his last coherent thought that didn't involve Stacie's deep, expressive mouth wrapped around his cock. She did things with her tongue … while she cupped and stroked his balls, she did things with her tongue, opening her throat until he was deep inside and then pressing all of her tongue up against the length of him, flat and slick and tight, tighter than he could have believed possible. Then, somehow, she moved it, shivered it, and lapped at the whole of his length. And God, the sensation made him insane. He ground his ass against the floor of the shower and pushed her hair to one side so he could watch, so he could see Stacie Emerson sucking his cock. Jesus! Stacie Emerson was sucking his cock! And it was the hottest thing he had ever seen. And she was getting him there in a big way, in a big hurry.

He tried to pull away. He tried to suggest they go back to the bedroom so he could get a condom, but she only tightened her grip around him, and fuck, he realized she was playing with herself, stroking the flat of her hand between her legs in that amazing place where his tongue had just been, where his face had been only minutes ago. And that did nothing to slow progress.

'Stacie, I can't … I need to …' But she sucked harder and lifted her bottom until he could make out the movement of her fingers snaking in and out of her and circling over her clit, and there was no way he could hold back any longer.

He came hard, crying out something strangled, something incoherent followed by her name as he jerked and banged his already addled head against the wall. Not that he noticed anything but how Stacie took him, shivering out another orgasm against her fingers. She took him, all of him, swallowing down everything; she took him until he was completely spent. It was only then that he realized the shaking of her shoulders had nothing to do with sexual release; that she wept in great, wracking sobs. He scooped her onto his lap, into his arms, and held her, feeling miserably helpless in spite of their lovemaking. He held her until she relaxed, until he relaxed. And they clung to each other until the pelting water of the shower turned tepid. At last she breathed a shaky sigh and stood, offering him her hand.

'Come on,' she said. All at once her voice was neutral, as though nothing had happened. 'We'll catch a cold.'

She had just reached for the towel, standing there in the harsh light of the bathroom all goosefleshed, nipples and areolas impossibly swollen, and Harris couldn't stand it. It wasn't enough. Jesus, it was never enough. He scooped her into the towel, and lifted her into his arms, still drenched and dripping and leaving wet tracks on the wood floor in the hallway as he carried her to his bed.

Ignoring her protests, he wrestled her into the mattress, making a halfhearted attempt to dry her, but there were places he wanted to leave wet, very wet. It was when she kicked and writhed in a ticklish shudder that the towel fell away, and he grabbed her ankle and ran his tongue up the instep of her foot, settling his lips around her big toe.

This time the shudder was followed by a tight gasp and a moan, and her legs fell open to offer him exquisite views of what lay between, what he could never get enough of. His cock tightened and jerked and stretched toward her in spite of the fact that he'd come only minutes ago, and he felt full all over again. He made his way to suckle and lick each of her toes in turn, with her lying there unselfconscious in her vulnerability, in her exposure, grinding her bottom against the mattress and arching her back in turn. The gasps and groans had made way for soft purrs and delicious mewling sounds that pushed his cock beyond half-mast to full wood. As he began the torturously delicious tongue-bath up her ankle and onto her calf, she slid her fingers down, first to cup her pubis, then to tweak her clit and dip into her swollen depths. But he pushed her hand away.

'That's mine,' he managed, nipping at the sinuous muscle of her calf. 'Don't touch it. This time it's totally mine.'

'Oh God, Harris,' she moaned, reaching to rake grasping fingers through his hair in an effort to pull him up to her. 'Then hurry up. I can't stand it. I need you in me.'

He shoved her hand away and continued his ascent up the inside of her knee and onto her thigh. The ocean heat scent of her made him feel like he would burst if he didn't enter her soon.

'Harris, pleeese,' she gasped, practically bouncing off the bed when his still-damp hair grazed the splay of her. And then, always the proactive type, she arched and stretched and writhed her way up the bed, the hand not still trying to find purchase in his hair, fumbling for the drawer of the bedside table. She wriggled and bucked until she could almost sit up, with him moving to grasp her hips as he licked and kissed and nipped ever closer to her wet, slick heat.

He heard the rattle of the condom wrapper. And then she shoved it at him. 'Put it on, Harris,' she hissed sucking a tight breath as he nipped her clit. 'Put it on now and fuck me. Now!'

He was desperate to be inside her. His ascent of her body was at least as torturous for him as it was for her. The agony was like a sweet, tensed fist cupping and squeezing the weight of his need, and his erection ached with the fullness that tightened every muscle of his body, that made breathing an unbelievable effort. He sheathed his cock a little more slowly than he would have liked, arousal making him awkward and uncoordinated.

'Hurry,' she moaned. 'Please hurry, Harris. I need you!'

There it was again. Stacie Emerson needed him. It did things to him when she said that. The condom in place, he obliged her, moving in between her thighs, giving her delicious slickness one last long slurp with his tongue before rising above her and sinking into her velvety, warm depths.

She rose up to meet him, her legs sliding into place around his waist, slipping against the water droplets that still sheened his hips and back from the shower. Only a couple of hard thrusts and she came again, hands fisted against his upper back, face buried against the curve of his neck. This time her shudders were ones of pleasure and they belonged to him. Because he'd just come so recently, he was able to slow his pace, revel in the tensing and straining of her body, suss out just what he could do to make her come again and again. Her grip around the length of him was a deep, suckling pull that tightened and tugged with each thrust. Even when he held still to kiss and caress her breasts, to thumb the demanding rise of her clit, even when he held her still, pinned beneath his weight, unable to thrust, the tight grip and release, grip and release of her strong inner muscles had him on the edge again.

With each of her orgasms building on the one before, each causing her spasms against his cock to clench still tighter, it wasn't long. It wasn't long until a particularly hard thrust sent them both over, gasping and convulsing and spilling into each other, grasping at each other as though their very existence depended on it. And even though he didn't want to think about it, even though at the moment he wanted to chase all of the nightmares Stacie had endured away from her and leave her with only good dreams and good realities, he knew that Jamison wasn't going to go away and Stacie would never be safe as long as he was in the picture. He pulled her to him with such force that she groaned. He'd keep her safe. He wouldn't let what happened to her in New York happen again. Ever. He'd keep her safe here with him.

Neither of them spoke. Instead, they shoved and pushed their way under the blankets and slept the sleep of exhaustion.

Chapter Twenty-five

'Stacie, wake up.' Harris kissed her ear, and her hand moved to her face as though she were swatting away a fly. If circumstances were different he'd have loved nothing so much as to watch her sleep, but this was a special day. He'd woken to the email he'd hoped for from Doug, over on the Crooked River, so watching her sleep would have to wait for another time, and he absolutely planned to make sure it happened.

He kissed her again and pulled back the covers, a mistake on his part because seeing her naked in his bed made his cock stir and tighten in his walking trousers. But thoughts of what he'd like to do to her there in his bed would also have to wait.

'Hey, sleepyhead. Get up if you want to see the mountain lions.'

'Wha …?' She fought her way from the tangle of sheets to sit naked on the edge of the bed. 'Mountain lions? Really?'

'Doug's emailed to say he's spotted the female on her territory, and just yesterday he spotted a big male. Love's in the air. Come on. We don't want to miss our window of opportunity.' Before she could ask he said, 'I hope you don't mind but I had Flannery send someone to your flat to pack up something suitable for you to wear.' He nodded to the bag he'd just brought upstairs. 'Now, get a move on. I'm making some sandwiches and coffee, and we're off.'

In spite of the short notice, Stacie was downstairs and ready to go in less than ten minutes. She stopped in her tracks at the sight of the blond sitting at the breakfast bar, sipping coffee opposite Flannery.

'Stacie, meet Dianna. She works for me,' Flannery said. 'She'll be you today and tomorrow if need be. Kenny over there, who you've already met –' the man drinking coffee and gazing out the picture window gave a nod and a wave '– he's all set to be Walker while you two are off cougar-spotting.'

Harris filled the Thermos and shoved it in the side of the backpack. 'We're officially not leaving the cabin today. Now hurry up, we have a long drive.'

Stacie took it all in with very little effort as though the plan made perfect sense to her. Outside, he shook his head as she started to climb into the Jeep. He nodded to one of Flannery's black SUVs instead, and she let out a wicked chuckle. 'Harris Walker, you're a deliciously devious man.'

'Anything for mountain lions,' he said, opening the door on the passenger side and motioning her in.

It was still dark outside when they pulled onto Highway 26 heading toward Central Oregon. In fact, it would be dark for several more hours. Harris loved that Stacie seemed as bright-eyed and excited as he was about the chance to see the lions. He shot her a glance from behind the wheel. 'You know there are no guarantees. Cats can be really elusive. We may end up having nothing more than a long drive and a hard hike.'

'It's all right,' she said, offering him a cup of coffee from the flask. 'I'm up for a road trip and a hike. In fact, that's exactly what I need. I've already emailed Jenny to let her know I won't be in. What has to be done at the gallery today she can take care of with the help of the two interns. They're working on the Japanese exhibit. Carla's interviewing Ellis this afternoon for the film loop. After that, she can begin the final edits. Oh, there's lots to be done and we're getting down to the wire, but I'm pretty anal, so we'll be ready.'

He sipped his coffee and nearly burnt his tongue. 'Then you're OK with this?'

'I'm better than OK, Harris. I told you I wanted to watch you work.'

'This is not an Armageddon shoot,' he said. 'It's not like the photos you'll be displaying.'

'That's even more important,' she replied. 'I told you I wanted the good things, the hopeful future, the treasures that are worth protecting, to be a part of the exhibition as well. You and Kyle and the photos you take are the conscience of the Northwest. You're able to show people what's at stake in a way no one else could. That's what you did for Ellis in Valderia, and that's what you do in every issue of *Wilderness Vanguard* and in every photo you take.'

Harris felt himself smiling in the darkness. It delighted him that his efforts to take her mind off the Jamison situation had worked so well. It delighted him even more that she understood his passion so much better than he could have ever imagined. 'I take the pictures for my own pleasure,' he said. 'Well, at least that's how I started out. The oil slicks, the clear-cuts, they came from just feeling that people needed to know. Those I don't enjoy. Those make me sick.'

'They should make everyone sick. Why haven't you ever exhibited any of them before?' she asked. 'OK, I know you didn't want to work with me, and I understand why, but I've studied all your exhibitions to date, and there've been a few. Why none of the Armageddon photos?'

His grip on the steering wheel turned painful, and he handed her back the coffee cup, not wanting any more. He found it difficult to speak. 'I told you, Stacie, they make me sick.'

For a long moment, she studied him. He could feel her gaze more than see it in the dim light of the dashboard. 'What? You mean those shoots literally make you ill?'

'Sometimes I get headaches, sometimes I throw up. I always have nightmares.' He felt cold, and the coffee felt like acid in the pit of his stomach.

Stacie reached her hand across the seat and laid it gently on his leg. 'Harris, I'm sorry. I didn't know.'

His hand closed around hers in a tight grip. 'I wasn't really … looking forward to talking to Carla Flannery about my work, and I really didn't want you to see me … like that.'

'And yet you went through with it,' she said softly.

He nodded, not knowing if she could see him or not. 'It's a good idea, what you're doing. It's a brilliant idea, and the reason you're doing it's a good thing.' He glanced over at her. 'But for me, it won't ever be an easy thing.'

Again he felt her gaze on him. 'For you, Harris, for a man of your passion and your love for nature, how could it ever be easy?'

For a long time after that they rode in silence, each lost in their thoughts. Harris watched the road unwind in front of him as they made their way off the flank of Mount Hood, thick with conifers and rhododendrons, and descended into the dryer woodlands that dropped them down onto the Warm Springs Reservation. At some point, Stacie drifted off to sleep, her head resting against the window, her breathing even and relaxed. Harris hoped her dreams were pleasant ones that had nothing to do with the nightmares of her past or the situation she now faced. But when she uttered a startled cry and convulsed hard against the seatbelt before fighting her way up into the waking world, he figured that wasn't the case. 'You all right?' he asked.

'Yes! Fine!' Her rapid, panicked breathing told him otherwise, but he let it go. 'Where are we?'

'Just passed through Prineville.'

They ate the first of the peanut butter sandwiches before they parked the SUV and headed up a dry canyon on foot, leaving the whisper of the Crooked River below them in the greying dawn. The packs were heavy. Most of the weight was water, since there were no sources beyond the river. The ascent ahead of them was strenuous, and the day, though still chilled with the desert pre-dawn, could turn warm.

'My cat has several daybeds up here,' Harris said. 'Doug knows her haunts pretty well by now. You won't see any footprints, though; cougars are light-footed, and this canyon is mostly rock. It was nearly two years ago I took the photos, and mountain lions breed only every other year, so if Doug's right, then we might see the male too. The pair'll stay together anywhere from three to ten days if mating. Otherwise, they're solitary, except for females with kittens.'

They'd been walking at a steady ascent for nearly an hour when they heard the first scream. Stacie gasped and let out a little yelp. She was nearly on top of Harris when the second scream erupted and echoed through the canyon.

'That's the male?' she whispered, the beat of her pulse metering her voice.

He shook his head, slipping a hand in hers to give it a reassuring squeeze. 'That's the female calling the male. She's ready to mate. Terrifying sound, isn't it?'

She nodded as it came again. 'I've heard about it, but I never imagined …' Her voice drifted off.

'Come on.' Harris motioned up the trail, easing open his camera case. 'If Doug's right, this route should put us up above the daybed with a good view.'

As the cry came again, Stacie didn't hesitate, but nodded toward the sound and followed Harris up the trail.

The sun was just staining the sky pink when they topped the rise that overlooked an outcropping of rocks opposite them on the other side of a narrow canyon. And there on a ledge were the two mountain lions. Harris could feel the tensing of Stacie's body in the excitement he knew she felt because he felt it too. From the looks of the situation the female had been calling for a mate, and the male, who crouched on the outcropping just above her, had just arrived. Harris breathed deeply and slowly to steady his hands as he aimed the camera. He was so engrossed in the cats that it took him a second to realize Stacie had her own camera, and he couldn't help feeling a swell of pride at just how calm she was, already shooting next to him. But then he reminded himself she'd grown up in the Russian wilderness. Beneath the big city veneer, she was made of stern stuff. He leaned close to her. 'This is my cat all right. See the little notch in her left ear, some old injury.' His voice was less than a whisper, but she nodded that she understood.

And then the action began as the two cats went about the business of getting acquainted. The female stretched long and lean across the rock before the male, not unlike Harris had seen Dee's two tabbies do when they found a particularly nice place to sunbathe. In the crisp quiet of the morning, they could hear the rumble of the purr emanating from the female's throat. It was a feline act through and through as the two made little grunts and growls at each other and the male sniffed the female's readiness. It didn't take long until the female rolled back onto her belly and positioned herself, flicking her tail to one side and lifting her bottom.

Being privy to such an intimate act of nature, such an intensely wild and primordial act, made Harris' pulse thunder against his throat. Seeing the two cats together like this was an unparalleled privilege, but to share it with Stacie made him feel as though he had somehow offered it to up her, as though he'd had something to do with the cats' presence here. It felt right on a level that he had no words for. If he were ever to share such an experience, it should be with her. It couldn't be with anyone else.

At some point he realized she was taking pictures of him as well as the cats. He could see the rapid rise and fall of her chest through the dark green fleece she wore. He could almost feel her intense concentration and her delight at sharing the experience, at watching the cats as they got on with the business of creating the next generation. He loved that she'd made no nervous twitters, no off-handed remarks about the cats' mating. Most people would have. Most people would've been uncomfortable with seeing something so raw, so blatantly and unashamedly sexual.

The sky had gone from pink to blue and the monochromatic world had brightened to subtle desert shades of tan and mauve and khaki, bathing the cats in golden light as they stretched and preened. Then Stacie and Harris watched as they moved on silent feet single file off the ledge, and disappeared into the canyon.

They stood and watched long after the cats were gone, as though to move or to speak would somehow destroy the moment. Harris understood. He'd sat for nearly an hour after photographing the female with her kittens, unable to move, unable to do anything but try to take in what he'd just witnessed.

It was Stacie sniffling that brought him back to reality. He turned to find tears streaming unabated down her cheeks. She offered an embarrassed smile and wiped at her eyes with the backs of her hands.

'Amazing,' she managed. 'They were amazing, so beautiful and powerful and …' She looked up into his eyes. 'Thank you for bringing me here.'

'It was a pleasure.' Harris resisted the urge to take her into his arms. What she was feeling right now had nothing to do with him, and he didn't want to take away from it.

‘I’d love to come back and try to find her after the kittens are born,’ she said.

It encouraged him that she was thinking in terms of the future, a future without Terrance Jamison. ‘I’m sure Doug’ll let us know when that happens. It’ll be three months, maybe a little more, before they’ll be born.’

‘In the dead of winter? That’s a harsh time to bring kittens into the world.’

‘Don’t worry. She’s up for it. Doug told me she’s successfully raised at least two litters before the one I saw. She knows what she’s doing.’

Stacie looked after the cats again, and Harris couldn’t resist. He lifted his camera and took a couple of shots of her. When she flipped him off and then offered her usual teasing smile, he only shrugged and said, ‘Just returning the favor.’

The blush that crawled up her throat made her look even more beautiful, if that were possible. ‘Yes, but you look outdoorsy and ruggedly handsome. I look all swollen-eyed and under-slept.’

He kept shooting. ‘To me you look beautiful. You belong here almost as much as those cats do.’

She sat down against the cliff face; and the smile slipped from her lips. His chest tightened, and he wondered if he’d said something wrong, but he was comfortable behind the camera. It had always been his safe place, with mountain lions and great horned owls and, at the moment, it felt like the safest place to be with Stacie Emerson, so he kept shooting.

At last she spoke, looking out over the canyon. ‘I nearly died.’

He felt his heart stop then start again in his chest,

but he kept shooting. Somehow it felt safer for both of them.

'He owned me outright, Jamison did. At least that's the way he saw it. And no matter how hard I tried, I couldn't get free of the debt; of him. It didn't matter that the situation was illegal, he was Terrance Jamison, and he could do what he wanted. His abuse, his humiliation, I could handle. When Zoe died, I knew what I was in for, and I was determined to work off the debt, to do whatever it took, for Zoe, and for me, I suppose. The gallery was something of my own, something I'd earned. But then he wanted me to do things –' she pulled her knees up to her chest and wrapped her arms around them '– things with other men. He said that the debt had to be paid and my body was just currency. Oh he … had me whenever he wanted, mostly to humiliate me, to remind me of my place. I was resigned to that after Zoe died. It was her … relationship with him, her sacrifice, that kept me safe, so it wasn't unexpected. But this – this was different. My reputation was all I had, Harris. My name was associated with the gallery, and I'd made it matter. I'd made the gallery mine. And it was all I had left of Zoe. You asked me if he was my lover. But I promise you no lover would have ever done the things he did.'

Harris lowered the camera. What he'd waited for, the honesty he'd hoped for, was exploding onto him, and he was no longer sure he really wanted it. He was certainly sure he didn't want her to have to relive it for his benefit. 'Stacie, you don't have to –'

She continued. 'When I couldn't take it any more, when I wouldn't … do what he asked me, then he …'

Her breathing was rapid, ragged. Harris moved closer, fearing she'd hyperventilate. But she took a couple of deep breaths and hugged herself still tighter. 'He hit me. And … he kept hitting me. I tried to fight back, but I was no match for him. And when he was done, when I couldn't … respond any more, he left me.' She pulled a couple more tight breaths and shifted so that her back pressed up hard against the stone. Amazingly, her eyes were dry. 'I don't know how, but somehow I managed to call Al Marston before I lost consciousness. I woke up in the hospital.'

The knot of rage Harris felt growing at his center threatened to rip him apart. He wanted to do things to Jamison; he wanted the man to suffer like he'd made Stacie suffer. The sound of her voice, soft, sure, neutral in spite of what she shared with him, drew him back, held him tight there in the present where she was with him.

'When I finally came to, I could understand Zoe's despair. I could understand why she … why anyone would contemplate … a way out. But Al wouldn't let me despair. I owe the man so much for standing by me. When I was well again, he introduced me to Sasha from the Hermitage in Saint Petersburg. We hit it off right away. It didn't hurt that I speak Russian and that I know how to hold my vodka. Sasha was a powerful player, with questionable connections of his own, so Jamison backed down on using me as a whore, and for those few months leading up to the exhibition he gave me a little more space to work. I suppose I was effectively under Sasha's *krysha*, his protection, during that time. But even with such a major exhibition, I knew I'd need help, I'd need a plan. That's when I found K. Ryde. I was one of the agency's first clients, and it was Ryde's PR genius as much as my own desperation that helped me force Jamison's hand, to make him take the money and leave me alone.'

Harris didn't know what to say. There were no words for what he felt, for what Stacie had been through or for what he wanted to do to Jamison. For a long time he said nothing, only sat next to her, looking out over the dry canyon as though somehow by avoiding her gaze he could give her a little space, a little privacy for her vulnerabilities, for how she had lain herself bare before him. It was only when he realized she was shivering that he settled closer and pulled her to him. At last, he gathered his thoughts from the maelstrom enough to speak. 'Why did you go back to him? I mean this time?'

She pulled away and chafed her arms. 'I told you I was desperate.'

'You don't really expect me or anyone else to believe that, do you?'

'It doesn't matter what you believe.' Her reply was cool, distant. 'What matters is that I'll pay my debts. I promise I will. Then all of this'll be over with.'

She stood to put her pack back on, and he came to his feet and caught her by the shoulder, not wanting it to end like this, not wanting her to leave until they were good again. When she tried to push him away, he pressed her between his body and the stone of the cliff face. 'You can't just shut us all out, Stacie.'

'I never wanted you involved in the first place. I never wanted any of you involved but you couldn't leave it alone.' She jerked back against him but there was no place to go. 'You couldn't just let it go.'

He moved in closer until his body pressed up to hers, holding her tightly against the stone. 'No, I couldn't, and I can't, and neither can anyone else who cares about you and neither would you if the situation were reversed. So whether you like it or not, I'm here to stay. We've already discussed this, so get used to it.' He punctuated his point with a harsh kiss that couldn't have been very pleasant for her, but then he was angry, worried, scared for her.

Instead of shoving at him as he'd expected her to do, she curled a hard fist in his hair and ravaged his mouth with every bit as much ferocity as he had given her, pulling him still closer, rubbing her body against his, making him instantly and startlingly erect.

She snaked a hand down between them, savaging his fly until he feared for what lay beneath, until her fingers wriggled and dug their way into his walking trousers to possess his cock with a tight grip, as though it was a weapon, one she was about to use to do serious damage.

He fumbled to return the favor, with her ripping at her own fly to make room for him, to guide his fingers down over her mons. Her eyes locked his in a devastating gaze that felt as though she could see right through him.

'I need you to touch me there.' Her voice was a breathless whisper. 'Where I'm wet, where I'm open, where I'm always hungry for you.' Her breath caught; her eyelids fluttered and she sucked her bottom lip as he found her cleft, wet and open as she'd promised. 'You can't tell me you don't want to be like those cats.' She guided his hand still further, manipulating it until first two, then three fingers pressed up into her. 'You can't tell me that when I present myself to you all hot and ready and begging for it, you don't want to service my need. You can't tell me you don't want to get a little primal with that cock of yours.' She gave him a hard squeeze and drove her hand up and down his length, thumbing the already abundant precome over and around the tip until he gritted his teeth and held his breath while his hips bucked hard against her efforts.

He scissored her deep with three fingers and raked the silky slickness of her up and over her clitoris, and the sounds coming from the back of her throat easily resembled the sounds the female cougar made when the male mounted her. Wildly, madly, they fucked each other's hands. The wind had risen and, even on the clear morning, the chill left no doubt about lingering for more than the quickest of releases. Then she shifted, pressed her back hard against the stone, and rested both of her hands on his shoulders. Before he could protest the removal of her fingers from his cock, she wrapped her legs around his waist, her still clothed crotch rubbing tight and insanely hot against his exposed cock as she began to rock and gyrate, and it was all happening way too fast.

'Stacie, I –'

'Shut up, Harris.' She spoke between chattering teeth. 'I need to come, and so do you. You can fuck me properly when we get back to the SUV. It's too damn cold to linger.' With each sentence she ground against him, bearing down with the extra leverage the cliff at her back afforded. Almost before the words were out of her mouth, she convulsed. Her spine stiffened and her shivers had nothing to do with the cold. Harris could stand no more. He felt the eruption deep in his groin. It might have been embarrassing had the circumstances been different, but as he tried to cover himself, tried to hide the results of Stacie's hard ride, she shoved his hand away, pushed him back, and practically fell into the space between them positioning herself so that she caught his release, all of it in her mouth. What could he say to that? What could he do but hold her there, helplessly grunting the weight of his need into the back of her throat? It was an act as intimate and as primal as the cougars mating on the rocks minutes ago. And sex, any kind of sex, with Stacie Emerson was worlds apart from any other sexual experiences he'd ever had.

As she stood and wiped her mouth on the back of her hand, the look of hunger in her eyes, the promise of more sex to come in the SUV before the trip home couldn't help but lighten the mood. As they straightened and tucked and donned their packs, he wondered if that was why she did it. Whatever her reason, it definitely worked for him in ways he was still trying to get his head around.

The walk back to the SUV was at speed. They had seen the mountain lions and the wind had risen to a howl, bringing with it fast-moving nimbus clouds that, this time of year, could easily enough drop their load on the Cascades in the form of snow.

Back at the vehicle, Harris shook his head when Stacie started to get in on the passenger side. 'Into the back seat, woman. You promised me a fuck and I intend to collect with interest.' She offered him a salacious smile, then tossed her bag into the back.

Even before she was seated, she'd pulled off her fleece and sweater. Harris nearly split the seam of his trousers when she unhooked her bra and shrugged it off, then pulled the door to behind her as she slid into the seat totally topless, nipples hardened by the cold and, he hoped, by thoughts of what he intended to do to her. She held his gaze with a look that was only slightly this side of filthy as she undid her trousers and slid them down along with the lace underwear that matched her bra. Her bare bottom, which, no doubt, was still slippery from their cliffside romp, rested against the pristine black leather and the flutter of her eyelids told him she appreciated the contrast of the cold seat against her hot nether parts.

Harris nearly tore his zipper out to free himself as she shifted in the seat and opened her legs wide, shoving until the walking trousers were down around her shins. Then, as though he wasn't even there, she began to stroke herself, one hand resting low on her belly, almost as though she was attempting to hold everything in tight so she could watch the other hand dipping and swirling and sliding between her thighs. The SUV smelled of dense, sweet heat. As Harris released himself, his own hot scent added to the thickening pheromonal cocktail of arousal.

She moved a hand to pinch and tweak her nipples, watching as he released himself from the bind of clothing, then she turned just enough that he could see what she was doing between her legs, even hobbled as she was with her trousers and boots. 'So, are you gonna make me do this alone or are you gonna saddle up?'

It took him two seconds to slide into the condom and then they scooted and maneuvered until she was directly in front of him, her delectable bare bottom nearly in his face. He shoved the driver's seat all the way forward so they had leg room and, with her leaning up so he could finger her open, he hunched in for a quick taste that made her quiver all over. Then he eased her back, enjoying the exquisite view of her sheathing him, slowly, deliciously, all the way until she sat down onto his lap, her back to his front. Then she began to rock in tight little circles onto his erection. He reacquainted one hand with the weighty swell of her breasts and the urgent press of her nipples while the other stroked her clit with slick little thrusts between his index and middle fingers.

The road wasn't much travelled, but still anyone could have seen them – or at least anyone could have seen them before they steamed over the windows with their heat. The SUV rocked and bounced beneath them as their efforts grew more urgent, as their need for release grew more intense. Stacie grabbed onto the back of the driver's seat and bore down hard. Harris braced his feet against the floorboard and returned the favor, feeling the wet rush of her arousal like liquid silk against his probing fingers, and the hard nub of her clit like granite against the pinch and stroke, pinch and stroke of his hand.

'I need to come, Stacie,' Harris gasped against her bare back. 'I feel like I'm gonna explode.'

'I want you to come,' she managed. 'I want you to come and I'll come with you, hard, just like the cats.'

And with that, she gave a little grunt and a shift followed by a tight squeeze, and they both climaxed hard and deep and wrenching. It could never have been otherwise after the day they'd had.

There was no easy way to snuggle in the back seat, but they managed a modified spoon position, feet and ankles still bound with trousers and boots and Harris still cock-deep inside Stacie's delicious body. As their breathing slowed and he felt himself softening inside her, he nuzzled her neck, and she offered a slow, lazy laugh. 'I haven't done it in the back seat since high school.'

He nibbled at her nape. 'I've never done it in the back seat. OK, in the back of a pick-up once but that's hardly the same, is it? Nearly froze my ass off.'

'Speaking of which,' she said, 'it's not getting any warmer in here and I'm starving. You have any more of those gourmet peanut butter sandwiches you made this morning?'

'I just happen to have a couple,' he said, pulling out of her. 'I'll give you the recipe if you'd like.'

In a few minutes they were dressed and headed back to Portland, polishing off the rest of the food Harris had packed and the last of the coffee as they drove.

Chapter Twenty-six

'Nothing left in the freezer but a couple of frozen lasagna dinners and some Tater Tots,' Dianna yelled down the stairs.

Kenny looked up from channel surfing in the middle of the couch in Harris Walker's TV room. 'Jesus, I didn't think they'd be gone this long or I'd have laid in supplies. Did you think they'd be gone this long?'

Dianna came down the stairs and leaned against the wall with her arms folded across her chest. 'Well, they were looking for mountain lions, and Flannery did say they might spend the night. Plus they're fucking each other so I'm not surprised, no.'

'Then why didn't you bring supplies if that's what you suspected? Did you know that the place is too far out for deliveries?' he asked, turning off the TV.

She gave a non-committal shrug. 'I can call Bud and have him get us something if you want. He's always up for it.'

Kenny grunted, tossing the remote onto the coffee table. 'It isn't that. Fuck, I'm just going stir crazy. All that lovely outdoors just beyond our window and we can't even take advantage.'

'It's dark,' Dianna said. 'What are you gonna take advantage of?'

‘How ’bout a breath of fresh air? Hmmm? How ’bout just not being caged up all day and night.’

She shrugged again. ‘I can forgo fresh air and the great outdoors for what I’m being paid, thank you very much. I’ll heat up the lasagna.’

‘Wait,’ he called after her as she turned to the stairs. ‘How ’bout I go bring back something?’ He reached for a hooded sweatshirt hanging on a hook next to the stairs. ‘I could wear this, pull the hood up, you know. I’m already dressed like Walker.’ He slipped into the jacket and pulled the hood up.

His partner shook her head. ‘Dressed like that you’ll have any respectable takeout place thinking you’re there to rob them. Anyway, I’m fine. I don’t mind whatever’s in the freezer.’

‘Eat like a bird, do you, Di?’ he asked.

She flipped him off.

‘Well, I’m not fine. I’m starving and I want … I don’t know. At least I want a really good pizza, or there’s that Chinese takeout we passed to get here, you know the one I’m talking about?

‘Yeah, the one in the all-night Chevron station.’

‘That’s the one. Strange combination, but how bad can it be? What do you say? At least it’ll be different. You up for it, Di?’ He looked around the room, still wearing Harris Walker’s sweatshirt. Here, I’ll wear this.’ He found a battered canvas hat he imagined the man wore for outdoorsy sort of things and put it on. ‘What do you think? I look just like him, don’t you think?’

Di stood once again with her arms folded across her chest, looking him up and down. ‘Flannery won’t like it.’

‘Flannery doesn’t have to know. I’ll just take the Jeep. I mean, Walker left me the keys and I’ll be back before you even know I’m gone. What do you think?’

She gave him a bored look. ‘You bring it, I’ll eat it,’ she said. ‘But it’s your ass if Flannery finds out.’

‘Fair enough.’

In less than five minutes, Kenny was rattling along the sorry excuse for a road that led to Walker’s cabin. You’d think with a house like that on a lake like that the man would at least have some work done on his road, but who knew how these environmentalist types thought. Anyway, the Jeep was a nice one, fully loaded, and, in all honesty, Kenny had driven a whole lot worse. He’d love to take it off road and put it through its paces. But, sadly, for tonight, a sweet and sour chicken run was the only pace the Jeep would get put through.

He had a suspicious mind, Kenny did. But in his business that was definitely a job requirement, so when an SUV pulled out behind him from the next road up, he kept one eye on it and the other eye on the road. Just in case. He couldn’t really imagine anyone following him on this no-brainer of a job, but it was his training. There was always the little niggle that something might not be right. That niggle passed when he signaled and pulled into the turning lane to the Chevron station and the SUV signaled too, but turned into the street just beyond. There, no worries, he reassured himself and turned his attention back to Chinese food.

When he finally arrived at the Chevron, it was completely deserted and the dumpsters had been pushed to the side of the building for the morning trash pick-up. If he didn’t know that the place was open 24 hours, he'd have driven on by thinking it was closed. He parked by the scrub of rhodies out of the way of the gas pumps, though it wasn't like there was a crowd. Oregon had no self-service pumps, so if he'd parked by the pumps, the attendant would come out. Having moved up from Texas, he still couldn't quite get used to someone else pumping his gas.

Inside, his order hadn't taken long, since it was the only order. The chef, who looked like he could use a nice long sleep, offered Kenny a tired smile as he handed over the takeout bags. Kenny wondered how such a place stayed open, but he figured in tourist season they made up for the slow times. He walked longingly past the cooler proudly sporting some of the area's best micro-brews. Sadly, he was working, so he picked up a couple of two-liter bottles of Coke, then thought better of it and made one of them diet. He grabbed a handful of any kind of candy bar that might pass the time more interestingly and a couple bags of chips. He was contemplating getting some brownie bites when the cook ran toward the door shouting "fire".

Kenny shoved his stash on the counter, nearly upsetting one of the takeout bags, and ran after the clerk, who followed the cook yelling something about damned kids having no respect any more and something really rude about what should be done to their parents.

It was then Kenny saw the blaze in the dumpster. As he ran to help put it out, what he didn't see was the man sneaking from the shadows beyond the rhododendron thicket, the man who squatted, then slid flat on his back beneath Harris Walker's Jeep.

*　　　*　　　*

Harris hadn't really planned to get them back home so late. But he discovered, after their adventure with the mountain lions and the incredible lovemaking that followed, he wasn't willing to give up having Stacie all to himself just yet. He couldn't think of a safer place, nor a more exciting place than the Painted Hills unit of the John Day Fossil Beds to keep her mind off of everything for a few more hours. They'd feasted on a picnic they'd bought in Mitchell. They found a place in the protection of several of the multi-colored hills where the biting breeze couldn't get to them and the autumn sun could. Then they'd driven the extra miles over slow winding roads through the exquisite emptiness of the high desert with its intriguing play of color splashed liberally across distance, color that was barely green and barely blue, yet always guaranteed to mesmerize. On the narrow twists and turns of the high roads there could be no speeding even if they had wanted to, and they didn't. They arrived in time to catch glimpses of the palisades of the Clarno Unit of the fossil beds just before the sunset. They'd had the remains of their picnic on the long drive back to Portland, after which Stacie dozed in the passenger seat – seemingly dream-free this time. For that Harris was relieved. He knew she had to be exhausted and way beyond stressed out. If she could rest, that was the best thing for her.

He found himself driving slower and slower the closer they got to his house. There had never been a time when he wasn't happy to return to the cabin on the Water Hole. It was home, and he had loved the place since he was a little boy when it still belonged to his grandfather. But this was different. He had managed to keep Stacie away from thoughts of Jamison and all that they had to return to. It had felt good to be able to ease her burden for just a little while, though he had to confess it was a burden he still didn't fully understand – other than the trouble that Ingrid Watson was now in with Jamison. But even Marston had said that Ingrid had walked into that herself.

Stacie was a fortress of secrets, and with every little bit she did share, he found himself feeling more and more fearful of what she still kept hidden. He let her doze, though he noticed from time to time that she wasn't dozing at all, that she was staring out the window, lost in her thoughts. He pretended not to notice. It had been hard enough for her, what she'd had to reveal these past few days. He wouldn't make it harder by prying.

They were about to turn down the road toward his house when his cell phone rang, and they both jumped. He nodded to Stacie, who picked it up.

'It's Flannery,' she said, putting it on speaker phone without asking.

'Walker.' The man's voice sounded strained. 'Are you and Stacie all right?'

'Yes, we're fine. We're almost home.' Harris felt the hair on his arms prickle. 'Why?'

'Listen very carefully. I need you to turn around, wherever you are, and go to the Pneuma Building to the private entrance. Wade'll meet you there. Don't go home first. Under no circumstances are you to go home first. Do you understand?'

'OK. I'm on my way.' Harris was already off the road and turning around. 'What's going on?'

‘I’ll explain when you get there. Just do it, OK?’

‘On my way,’ Harris repeated, shooting Stacie a questioning look.

It was after 2 a.m. when they arrived at the Pneuma Building. Wade was at the private entrance waiting for them. He gave Stacie an uncharacteristic hug and offered Harris a nod.

‘You wanna tell us what’s going on?’ Harris said.

Just then, Flannery’s SUV pulled up beside them, and he got out looking tired and frayed. But when he saw Stacie and Harris, he spoke without greeting.

‘It’s Kenny.’

‘What, you mean Kenny out at Harris’?’ Stacie asked, her grip on Harris’ arm tightened.

‘He’s dead.’

Stacie gave a little gasp and Harris felt her knees give as she braced herself against him. ‘Dead? What happened?’ he asked.

‘Look, I’ll tell you everything, but I think it’s better if we do this inside.’

No one spoke again until they were in Wade’s Dungeon. Ellis, Dee, and Marston were waiting there already. There was a whirlwind of hugs and someone thrust coffee cups at each of them as they all settled on the sofa and in the chairs Wade had pulled into his lounge area. He took point in a ratty recliner that was always his favorite.

‘What happened?’ Stacie asked again, setting her coffee cup on the end table untouched.

‘It was an explosion,’ Flannery told them. His face looked ashen and the lines of his mouth were hard. ‘Your Jeep, Harris. The man decided he wanted some takeout Chinese, so he took your Jeep, wore your jacket and hat just in case.'

Stacie blinked twice, as though she was in bright light, then shoved her way off the sofa and made a run for the door. She might have made it if she hadn't tripped over Harris' foot and practically fallen in his lap, struggling to get away as he closed his arms around her. 'This is all my fault, my fault. This is all my fault,' she said over and over again, her voice breathless. 'I have to leave. I have to get out of here. He did this, Jamison did this, and it's all my fault.'

'It's not your fault, Stacie. If it's anyone's fault it's mine for thinking up such a scheme.' Harris held her tight, taking a knee to the inside of his thigh before he settled her down onto the sofa next to him, still holding her.

'It damn well isn't your fault. Either of you,' Marston said. 'The sonovabitch has crossed the line this time. He can't get away with this.'

'Yes he can.' Flannery spoke quietly. 'They caught the man who did it. I did a little background check. He claimed to work for some obscure group called the Valderian Liberation League. Claimed his efforts were all due to some bullshit he's been told about Walker helping Ellis take jobs away from honest, hardworking Valderians.'

'That's hogwash. There's no such movement,' said Wade. 'If there were, we'd know, and there's certainly no one in Valderia who would welcome what Jamison would bring.'

'Of course it's hogwash,' Flannery said. 'But it'll pass to get Jamison off the hook, and anyway, it doesn't matter. One of the policemen who caught him got a little bit too handy with his gun, so he's dead. No one can cross-examine him that way. More people in Jamison's pockets, I suppose.'

'The point is,' Harris said, 'it was supposed to be me.' He felt strangely calm about that fact. He could hardly feel happy when someone had died in his place. All he was really happy about at the moment was that Stacie was safe next to him, and he wasn't about to let her out of his sight.

'That's exactly the point,' Flannery agreed. 'And though you may not believe it, the fact that it was supposed to be you gives us a little bit of a grace period.' Instantly the man had everyone's attention. 'Maybe for at least a little while we can let Jamison and his thugs believe they accomplished what was intended, that it was Harris Walker killed in the explosion.'

Stacie gripped Harris' arm and shivered.

Flannery continued, 'That means, at least for the moment, Walker's safe.'

Stacie's grip got even tighter on Harris, and he couldn't say he didn't like it.

'What about notifying next of kin, that sort of thing?' Wade said. 'I don't mean to be morbid, and I certainly wouldn't want to cause unnecessary trauma, but if we want to keep up the ruse, that'll have to happen.'

'Believe it or not,' Harris said, 'my parents are trekking in the Andes. I won't hear from them for the next week at least. That's one less thing for us to worry about.' He turned his attention to Stacie. 'By the time they get back to civilization the exhibition will be over and we'll have dealt with Jamison.'

‘Good, that’s good,’ Wade said. ‘Until they can get in touch with Harris’ parents, the cops will keep the identity of the deceased confidential. I’ve seen to that already.’

‘You need to let me go,’ Stacie said in a voice that was barely more than a whisper. ‘That’s the best way to deal with Jamison right now. You need to leave me alone, all of you, and let me do what I have to.’

‘Not gonna happen,’ Harris said. ‘I’ve already told you.

‘Stacie.’ Flannery spoke to her as though she were the only person in the room, the way he always did when every word he said mattered. Harris had noticed that about him. ‘If we’re going to take advantage of this bit of luck –’

‘Bit of luck,’ Stacie interrupted. ‘How can you call it a bit of luck when a man’s dead?’

Flannery flinched as though she had punched him, though his gaze never left hers. ‘Kenny is dead because he broke the rules. He left his post. He knew better. He knew that if he wanted anything all he had to do was ask. In my line of work, a man doesn’t leave his post. And certainly not for takeout Chinese.’ He said the last two words like they were a curse. His chest heaved. He straightened until his back was ramrod stiff in the chair. ‘So, if we’re going to take advantage of this bit of luck, I need you to do what Stacie Emerson would do if it hadn’t been Kenny Hearn in that Jeep. I need you to do what Stacie Emerson would do if it had been Harris Walker in that Jeep.’ The alarm registered in her eyes, but before she could speak, Flannery went on, ‘Look, you’ve told us that you know what you’re doing.

You've told us that you'll pay your debts, that it'll all be over after this exhibition, and I have to say, I'm greatly suspending my disbelief to see how the hell you can make that happen, Stacie. But I trust you. I have from the beginning. And if all hell breaks loose, if there are … other unforeseen events Jamison throws our way, then I want to be ready. So can you do as I asked?'

Stacie mirrored Flannery's posture and the panic that seemed about to consume her vanished. She nodded slowly. 'When Zoe died … I just got on with it. It was a week before a big exhibition. Like now. Things were insane. There was way more to do than there was time to do it, and that was good. That's what I did. Everything, anything.'

'Good. Then I'm sure this situation will be the same, and Jamison's an observant man,' Flannery said. 'He'll think you're acting out of grief.'

'He'll approach me. He'll probably text me. He'll be very apologetic that I forced him to do this … thing.' She shoved her hair back from her face and continued. 'I can ignore the texts for a while. That's what I would do. That's what I did because I was … helpless to do anything else. I was helpless to do what I really wanted to do. If this time is the same, eventually he'll send for me or he'll come to me.'

'That's not going to happen,' Harris said. 'I'm not going to let that happen.'

'You have no choice, Walker,' Flannery told him. 'You're dead, remember? You have to stay invisible, at least for the grace period we have, which more than likely won't be long.'

'There's no way!' Harris pulled Stacie so tightly to

him that she gave a little gasp. 'There's no way I'm gonna hide out back here and do nothing while Stacie's exposed to that piece of shit.'

'Harris, Harris!' Stacie extricated herself from his tight grip and took his hands in hers, this time more gently, this time more in control. 'Harris, he's not going to hurt me, at least not physically, and if you're not in the picture, then he can't hurt me by hurting you.'

'Fuck!' He felt more helpless than he could ever remember. 'I can't just sit back and do nothing.'

'Oh, you won't be doing nothing,' Wade said. 'I promise you that. You'll be helping me here in the Dungeon. Trust me, we can do more good getting to the bottom of this situation here and finding a way to keep Stacie safe than we could any place else.'

'You don't understand,' Stacie said, her voice dead calm. 'I am safe. I'm completely safe. Jamison knows the very best way to hurt me is to hurt the people I care about, so if you want to help me, Wade, than keep Harris safe, keep everyone else in this room safe, and Kendra and Garrett and Ingrid Watson.'

'Look, you're both exhausted,' Ellis said. 'We all are. This has been a helluva week, and we've all done everything we can do tonight. Right now, we all need rest, and we can start again fresh in the morning. Wade?'

Wade nodded. 'I've got the guest room all ready.'

'You have a guest room?' Harris asked.

'Of course I have a guest room,' the man said. 'Upon the insistence of Beverly Neuman back in the early days. And just to be sure I got it right, she had her decorator make it nice.' He offered a wisp of a smile. 'It's not the Ritz, but after Beverly's decorator got through with it, it damn near could be.'

'Does anyone really know just what down here in the Dungeon?' Harris asked.

'Nope,' Ellis replied. 'I'm not even sure Wade does any more. And frankly, I'm not sure I'd be brave enough to find out.' He stood and helped Dee to her feet. 'Get some rest, both of you. Wade'll be a good host. Tomorrow, Stacie goes into work as the grieving lover, and we get to work on finding out how to bring that fucker down.'

Harris was taken aback by Ellis' easy use of the word "lover". Everyone but Stacie seemed to be comfortable with the idea of him being her lover. And with her, he was constantly afraid he'd get too close and she'd make a run for it.

Stacie knew that she was dreaming, but she couldn't stop it. The dream would play out to the end, as it always did. The end was always the same and always horrible. She knew what would happen next, and knowing made her skin prickle, knowing made her stomach knot until it hurt. There were stairs, endless stairs, and she never knew why she hadn't taken the elevator instead. Surely if she had, she'd have been able to save Zoe. If she'd only taken the elevator instead. But she climbed flight after flight after flight, racing across landings and panting and sweating and forcing her aching thighs to press on. She should be there by now. Surely she should be there by now, and Zoe, dear God, Zoe had suffered enough. Every time Zoe was late, every time she seemed unhappy, every time she was in a room where there was alcohol,

Stacie worried about her. But she was doing better. It had been almost a month since she'd touched a drink or anything else. The group meetings seemed to be helping, and Stacie had done something she promised she'd never do. She'd borrowed money from Alan Marston to help pay for at least a few sessions with a psychiatrist and get any meds Zoe needed. If Jamison found out there'd be hell to pay, but he wouldn't. She'd make sure he didn't. They were doing all right. They were managing. Surely Zoe was OK. Surely she had just forgotten the time. And fuck, how many more flights could it be? She must be almost there. Surely she had to be almost there. Why hadn't she taken the elevator? But at last she threw open the door to the landing and raced down the hall to Zoe's flat, the key already clutched in her sweating hand.

Almost there, almost there!

She shoved the key home, and the gunshot went off, louder than a cannon, louder than a sonic boom, louder than anything, drowning out the scream that tore from Stacie's throat as she threw open the door and raced into Zoe's study.

But it was too late. It was far too late. This time there was no mistaking Zoe's intentions. This time death painted itself in garish crimson splatters all over the white curtains and the butterscotch wall, and the room smelled of hot blood and cordite, and there was no making it better. No making it better ever again. How could she have been mistaken? She'd been sure Zoe was getting better. How could she have not known? How?

Then he was there, next to her, whispering in her ear. 'Too bad, really. We'll miss poor old Zoe. And now you'll just have to take up the slack.'

Stacie burst into the waking world with a jerk, as though she had been falling. Next to her, Harris slept soundly. She eased herself onto the edge of the bed, not wanting to wake him. The man was exhausted and he blamed himself for what had happened to Kenny. She reckoned he'd have to take a number where blame was concerned. Right now, what mattered was that he was alive. Dear God, he was alive, and it could have so easily been him instead of Kenny Hearn. It would have been him if not for the mountain lions. For the moment, he was safe. But Jamison would find out, and when he did, she'd have to act fast.

Careful not to wake Harris, she slipped into a robe that hung in the closet of Wade's guestroom. He wasn't kidding when he said it felt like the Ritz. She found her way to the study and to the laptop on the desk. From the refrigerator, she rummaged a bottle of sparkling water and settled in to write an email to K. Ryde. It was not an email she would send tonight, but one she figured she'd probably have to send in a hurry when the time came, so best do it now while her mind was clear and she had the time to give it some thought.

Chapter Twenty-seven

After the second night in Wade's Dungeon, Stacie woke from a sound sleep to find Harris gone. She knew he was an early riser – even earlier than she was – so she figured he was working with Wade, who almost never slept. It was good for him to be busy. He was going stir crazy in the confined quarters. The man belonged outdoors in the sunshine and fresh air, and even though he was fascinated with all Wade's inventions and technology, and probably understood them better than anyone else but Wade, he was miserable.

Last night, Wade had grumped over the dinner that he'd ordered in for them from his favorite Italian restaurant that Harris wasn't very good at playing dead. It was true. Stacie had never met a man who was more fully alive than Harris was, and during their confinement in the Dungeon, he had channeled a good bit of his pent-up frustration into totally sizzling sex, lots of it. Even though she benefited greatly from that sexual energy, she would have still preferred him to be able to get out and do what Harris Walker did best and loved most. Between their sexual feasting and Wade's engaging him in new ways to try and find out all they could about Jamison's Achilles heel, Harris was hanging on, but barely. Still, she didn't care if they had to tie him to the bed and sedate him in the end; if that's what would keep him safe, she was willing. At this point, every minute that Jamison didn't know Harris was still alive was a gift.

So far, Jamison had made no contact. That worried her. She figured he'd be more than anxious to gloat about Harris' supposed demise. She went to the gallery every day and did what needed to be done. As it had been when Zoe died, there was so much to do that it kept her from dwelling on what would happen, what she knew must happen, after this grace period. Marston had flown back to New York, but planned to return for the exhibition and, as always, Dee and Ellis were insanely busy, though she knew her problems and the coup in Valderia were taking the lion's share of their time. She wished she'd been able to keep her situation with Jamison from them. That had certainly been her plan. No one was to know and no one was to get hurt. But it hadn't happened that way. She hadn't counted on Harris Walker taking the castle by storm. So now she could only move forward, hoping and praying for just a little more time with Harris before Jamison turned everything upside down again.

She was standing in front of the big mirror in the bedroom, putting the final touches on her make-up, when she heard the door open. 'Morning,' she called over her shoulder, an effort that ended with her poking the mascara wand in the corner of her eye. She hunted blindly for tissue and Q-tips to clean up her panda face. When she was once again able to see clearly, he was behind her, leaning against the door frame, watching her like she was breakfast.

'Wade's gone bowling,' he said. 'And I decided to

seek out a little entertainment of my own.'

She could have guessed that by the way his jeans were stretched tight and bulging at the fly. She offered him an innocent smile through the mirror. 'Knowing Wade, I figure he's got every computer in the place fully loaded for just about any game you'd want to play.'

'I figured as much, but I'm looking for something a little more interactive. 'He slid a hand down to rest against his cock. And she smiled into the mirror.

'I see you brought your own joystick. Do they still use joysticks any more in gaming? I've lost track.'

'I still use mine on a regular basis,' he said. Then he moved into the room and embraced her from behind, rubbing his fully clothed erection against her bottom until she could feel her skirt ruck up. 'Would you like a demonstration? If you're good, I might even let you play with it.'

He slipped a hand up under her skirt and ran it around her thigh, over the tops of her stockings, before sliding it into her panties, causing her to gasp and wriggle her bottom against him. 'You'll make me late for work,' she managed, bearing down on the fingers he pushed up into her.

'You're the boss,' he said. She could feel him fumbling with his fly. 'Surely you won't get fired for being a few minutes late.' He stroked her clit with a wet finger, and the look on his face told her he knew exactly what to do to detain her long enough to get what he wanted and to make her want it too.

'Undo your blouse for me,' he whispered against her neck. 'I love being able to see you while I make love to you. I love being able to watch your face and to see how you look when I'm inside you.'

She did as he asked, and eased open the blouse to offer teasing views. Then, as he gave her clit another hard stroke, she undid the clasps at the front of her bra and lifted her breasts free of the lace cups. She held his gaze in the mirror as she caressed and kneaded herself, feeling heavy and swollen in her hands – a feeling that tightened her grip against his fingers and made him catch his breath and moan. She could feel the smooth, engorged heat of his cock against her upper thigh as he freed himself with a soft curse that hissed between his teeth. 'Jesus, Stacie, I can't get enough of you.' He shoved her skirt up until her bottom, in its black thong, was bare, then she waited in impatient arousal as he stretched the crotch to one side and examined her with wet fingers. She shifted her hips and he pushed her forward over the vanity toward the mirror, then knelt and buried his face between her buttocks to run his tongue along the length of her cleft, making delicious shivers climb her spine, making it harder and harder for her to hold still. Then he reached around her and, with a tight laugh, pulled a condom from the drawer of the vanity. 'I swear Wade has condoms stashed everywhere. Who the hell are his guests anyway?'

'Apparently some very horny folks,' she said, with a little gasp as he pushed into her and began to thrust. 'Can you imagine?' Her last word ended in a little yelp as she turned her ankle in one of her pumps and would have lost her balance if Harris hadn't grabbed her around the waist and practically lifted her off her feet. From the mirror, she watched the glorious look of concentration, of pleasure, of abandon on his face.

That she was the source of his pleasure made her feel things, things she hadn't felt in a really long time, maybe things she'd never actually felt before. She was glad she hadn't missed the chance to be with Harris Walker. Waking up with him, laughing with him, knowing that she could come home to him – she wished like hell it could last. Her insides ached with that wish and yet mostly, right now she just wanted to keep him safe. Keeping him safe. Yes, that was all that really mattered. And then the urgency of their lovemaking forced her into the moment, into the tight present that was just now, just here, and just her and Harris. His grip on her grew tighter and tighter, and she relished the feel of him so close to coming, so close to taking his pleasure from her, and that was enough to send her over, with him tumbling after a second later.

He mantled her against the vanity table, breathing like his chest would explode, burying his face against her neck, nuzzling and nipping and gasping. 'Stacie Emerson, where have you been all my life?' he sighed into her nape.

She felt her eyes well and her chest tighten as she reached over her shoulder to caress his head. 'Too far from you, Harris Walker. I've been way too far from you.'

For a long time they stood like that, wrapped around each other, until at last he pulled out. 'I have to go,' she said, glancing down at her watch. 'It's a busy day today even if I am the boss.'

'You're not gonna shower?' he asked.

As he pulled off the condom, she took hold of his softening cock and cupped it in her palm. Then, while he watched, she ran her hand down her sternum, spreading his essence onto her breasts. 'Not today, Harris. I want to go with your scent still on me.'

He offered her a broad smile, then took her mouth in a lingering kiss. When he pulled away, he held her very close and whispered against her ear, softly, but not so softly that she couldn't hear it. 'I love you, Stacie Emerson. Hurry back, OK?'

She drove through the morning traffic with Harris' scent between her breasts and his goodbye words doing strange things to the beat of her heart and the pit of her stomach. He loved her. There were never words she wanted to hear more or dreaded to hear so much. It was now he loved her, now, when they were in the eye of the storm, but how could he possibly love her if he knew what was really in her heart, if he knew what she would do when the time came, when she had to? But, for the moment, Harris Walker loved her and she would bask in that thought for as long as she possibly could.

She had just settled in behind her desk in her office with a freshly brewed cup of coffee when the text came. The chill that passed through her felt colder than winter, colder than death.

You must be so relieved that Mr. Walker escaped the dreadful death intended for him. Terrorists are such a horrid lot. They'll stop at nothing to get what they want.

Yours always,

TJ

She stared at the text until the words became meaningless symbols on the screen of her

BlackBerry. The chill she felt was bone deep, and the world around her went quiet and dark. For a long time, it was only breathing in and out that she could manage. There was somehow comfort in that, somehow a place at the center where, at least for the moment, she was in control. And then the light came back into the world, light that had been there all along. And she heard the bird song, smelled the coffee, heard Jenny talking with the workmen downstairs. This wasn't New York, she remembered. This was now, not then. She could, and she would do what she had to. She sent back a text.

Perhaps these terrorists would be willing to negotiate if given the right incentive.

The response was almost immediate.

Perhaps they would. Given the right incentive.

A second later, her phone rang. It was Jamison, just as she knew it would be. Ten minutes later, she hung up. With hands that were amazingly steady under the circumstances, she pulled up the email she had written to K. Ryde, gave it the final touches, and sent it.

It was early afternoon when Kendra arrived. Jenny ushered her upstairs and left the two women with Kendra pulling Stacie into a tight bearhug.

'Have you had lunch?' she asked.

'Not yet,' Stacie said. 'But I really don't have time for it today. I can have Jenny order us a takeout if you'd like.'

Kendra was wearing jeans and a red sweater and, if she hadn't already expected it, something in her no-nonsense stance told Stacie that this was not a lunch date she could get out of.

‘You need to take a meeting with K. Ryde,’ Kendra said. ‘Do you really want to do it here?’

‘I thought K. Ryde didn’t take meetings in person,’ Stacie said, trying to make light of a situation of which there really was no light to be made.

‘He’s making an exception.’

Stacie released a long breath and glanced down at her watch. ‘All right, then let’s take the Lexus and go to see Portlandia. But I can’t go anywhere without my bodyguard. Flannery’s insisting. Stan’ll ride in the back seat and sit out of earshot at the coffee shop. Are you all right with that?’

‘I think having a bodyguard along for the ride is a fantastic idea. Good for Flannery,’ Kendra said. ‘Just two friends having coffee and catching up. Stan’ll be none the wiser.’

‘We don’t really have to do this,’ Stacie said. ‘I know what you’re going to say and it won’t change my mind.’

‘I don’t care,’ Kendra said. ‘We do have to do this. It matters to me, and K. Ryde can be damned persuasive at times.’

Not this time, Stacie thought, but she rolled her shoulders in a vain attempt to release tension, then grabbed her bag and her keys. She told Jenny to close up shop at the end of the day. They’d finish the last details in the Samurai Room in the morning.

There hadn’t been much traffic, and it wasn’t long before they settled at a table with their lattes and paninis and a good view of Portlandia reaching down to them. Safely out of earshot, Stan was ensconced in the corner near the door, reading his paper. Wasting no time, Kendra spoke. ‘I don’t like this, and I don’t want you to do it.’

Stacie picked at the panini she knew she couldn’t eat, not needing this encounter right now, but certain it was inevitable. ‘I know you don’t like it, but it’s the only way.’ Before Kendra could protest, she went on, ‘If you … If K. Ryde doesn’t want to do what I’m asking, I understand. I’ll manage without the Ryde Agency. I’ve always known it might come down to that, and now Garrett’s in the picture and all, I can’t make you choose over your friends. I can certainly understand –’

‘For fuck sake, Stacie, I didn’t just suddenly get soft because Garrett’s in the picture, and my friends are not K. Ryde’s business. I didn’t say I wouldn’t do it. I’m sure as hell not letting you go through this alone. My part’s easy. My part’s nearly done, but I would be doing you, as my client, and as my friend, a huge disservice if I didn’t tell you that I don’t want you to do this, if I didn’t urge you to reconsider.’

‘You think I have a choice?’ Stacie snapped, then ran a trembling hand through her hair. ‘I’ve gone way too far down this path to have a choice in the matter, if there ever really was a choice, but then we’ll never know about that, will we?’

Kendra watched her from the cool distance that Stacie knew was still K. Ryde, though at the moment, she figured there was a bit of a power struggle going on. ‘You look like hell.’

She nodded. ‘I’m not feeling great at the moment. I always get a little nauseated when we talk about … this.’

Another long silence ensued while Kendra studied

Stacie unabashedly and Stacie let her. What choice did she have? If she were going to pull this off, especially sitting across the table from K. Ryde, she would have to act carefully and be really convincing.

'Look –' Kendra leaned over her latte so close that Stacie could feel the heat of her breath as it came out in a little hiss. 'There has to be another way. Harris is in the Dungeon. That's probably the safest place on the planet, and you have Ellis and Wade and K. Ryde and Flannery. You have a shitload of top-notched people. They can help you. They can protect you. They can keep you safe until they can find a way to bring the bastard down.'

This time it was Stacie's turn to study Kendra. 'You want me to hide away like a coward? You want me to give up what's mine and run? Is that K. Ryde's advice? Because if it is, then I want my money back.'

Kendra flinched against her seat, and for a tight moment, she said nothing. Stacie was pretty sure she was thinking about the horrid time in her life when she'd had to run away. It hadn't been her intention to remind Kendra of that awful experience, but if the shoe fit. At last, Kendra took a deep breath and spoke. 'No. I don't recommend running away from what's yours. I tried it once. It didn't work. I just … I can't bear the thought of you going through this alone.'

'I'm … I'll be all right. It's just Harris. He won't understand, and I … I don't want him thinking badly of me.' These were not words Stacie had intended to share with anyone, but they were out before she could stop them, and out in the hearing of one of Harris' best friends.

'Do you love him?'

The question took Stacie's breath away. It was not a question K. Ryde would ask. Yet it was a question that, at the moment, seemed the most relevant of all questions. And the answer that only a few days ago would have come as a big surprise now seemed obvious. She nodded slowly, feeling the wonder of it flood her, feeling it reach out to her like the powerful arm of Portlandia reaching down to them in the sunlight.

'I do. I love him, and I can't stand the thought of hurting him, and I can't stand the thought of him thinking less of me for what I'm about to do.'

Kendra offered her a knowing smile. 'Well, you may love him, but you don't know him very well or you'd know that if he's made love to you, shared his bed with you, shared his mountain lions with you, then he knows your heart. And he'll be angry and scared for you and he'll rage and he'll be hurt, but he'll never, ever think less of you for doing what you have to do.'

In an upwelling of emotion that nearly took her breath away, Stacie grabbed Kendra's hand. 'I need you to tell him for me. I need you to tell him that I love him. Because …' She wiped angrily at tears threatening.

'Stacie, now you're just scaring me. You need to tell him yourself. You need to make sure he knows that … Stacie? Are you all right?'

'I'm not feeling well,' Stacie shoved back the chair and fled to the bathroom, leaving Kendra and Stan looking on.

Chapter Twenty-eight

The drive to the Monaco took almost no time, and now that it was all beginning, she was impatient to get to the end of it, one way or another. The worst part was knowing Harris was back at the Dungeon waiting for her, knowing how upset he'd be, how disappointed when she wasn't there to share his bed tonight, knowing how angry and hurt he would be that she might very well be sharing Jamison's. The thought made her stomach churn. But she pushed it back. She had known that was always a possibility, and if she had to, if that's what it took, then she'd do it, as she had before. As she made her way through the light afternoon traffic, she remembered.

Jamison had slid into the limo next to her as they left Zoe's funeral service for the drive to the cemetery. She didn't even let her heart skip a beat when he reached forward to shut the privacy window, thought better of it, and left it open so the driver could hear her humiliation, could see it in the review mirror. She shed no tears, nor did she struggle when Jamison shoved a hand under her skirt and yanked aside her panties with such force that she heard the fabric rip. 'Lift it,' he commanded.

She obeyed. From now on, she'd have to choose

her battles very carefully, and this wasn't one worth fighting.

'You made it harder on yourself by not coming to me when I wanted you,' he said as he undid his fly. 'And I'm not stupid, darling. I know you wanted me too. You made me wait, Stacie, and that made me angry. It was a foolish thing to do when you know I always get what I want in the end.' He kneed her legs apart and shoved into her, hard. Somewhere in the back of her mind, she felt the pain of him entering her unready, and her eyes watered from the burn of flesh forced to accommodate, but it didn't matter now. She wouldn't fight him. Not now when she couldn't win. He held her there for a moment, impaled like a piece of meat on a spit, his breath warm and sweet against her face, his eyes colder than the winter outside the limo. 'I'll fuck you now, Stacie,' he said as he began to thrust. 'And you'll stand by Zoe's grave with my come marking you as mine. Oh yes. I'll fuck you now. And from now on, I'll fuck you whenever I please, and I promise you, you'll be surprised at just how many ways I'm going to fuck you.'

She let the memory slip over her like armor, as she had when it had happened, as she had when she'd prepared herself for life without Zoe, for life that Jamison controlled. She had gotten through it then. She would get through it now.

At the Monaco, one of Jamison's bodyguards escorted her up to the room. It was the same room where he had met her before. The man showed her into the lounge, where she waited to a soundtrack of rough sex from the master bedroom. There was nothing for her to do but wait. And listen.

She knew the game. He wanted to humiliate her. He wanted her to understand that she was nothing to him and that she was completely at his mercy. He wanted her to understand that even his sexual dalliances took priority over her fear for the man she loved and for a young woman who was innocent of anything deserving his ill-treatment of her. But none of what she knew, none of what she understood, mattered. What mattered was that if she pushed the issue, it would be those she loved who suffered. What mattered was that, even as he fucked some expensive hooker, she still had a few cards left to play. So she waited, trying to filter out the grunts and whimpers that came from just behind the closed door; trying to remind herself this was a game she knew. This was nothing she hadn't expected.

Finally, she heard the shower running. Of course he wouldn't come to her smelling of sex. He would always come to her from a position of power. He would always come to her like a god above it all, a god toying with her as though she were an insect. Again she waited. Whoever it was he'd been with didn't leave the room, but then that would also be beneath him. He would have paid her well to wait and stay quiet until after he was ready for her to leave. He'd called Stacie a whore once. That was the first time she thought about killing him.

'There you are, my darling.' He swept into the room, offering an expansive smile as though she were his oldest, dearest friend. He sat down next to her and pulled her hand to his lips. 'I'm so sorry to keep you waiting, but –' he nodded toward the closed bedroom door '– Ingrid Watson is a horny little cunt. Way more demanding that you ever were, but then perhaps that's just the artist in her.'

In spite of the somersaulting of her stomach and the rage threatening to burst her chest at the thought of Ingrid Watson in bed with the bastard after being so badly beaten by him, she kept her voice neutral. 'Is she ready to go? I have a cab waiting for her.'

He looked disappointed. 'Oh come now, Stacie, why such a hurry to whisk the poor girl away from such rich surroundings, and to where – your drab little flat? Her father's smelly cow farm? She'll be so disappointed not to have another fuck before she goes. The girl is such a slut. She reminds me a lot of you, back in the day.' He brushed a kiss against Stacie's lips and she struggled hard not to flinch. 'Of course you played the hard to get card. Perhaps it's a sign of the times. Our dear little Ingrid didn't even bother. She spread for me like warm butter, and all the while there's me trying to be a gentleman. Never mind that, darling. Though she might be willing to do what you weren't, in spite of her voracious libido, the dear girl is so young, so naïve. She hasn't yet learned, as you and I have, how harsh life can sometimes be.'

'You told me you'd have her ready for me. You told me I could escort her downstairs personally. You promised.'

He gave her a pout. 'Oh all right. Ingrid, darling –' he called over his shoulder '– do get dressed and come out here.'

He turned his attention back to Stacie. 'My, dear, you look pale, even a little thin. Are you sleeping? Are you eating all right? I know you must be under so much stress right now, with the gala exhibition just around the corner and always so much to do, so much responsibility. And everything is so terribly expensive these days. But really, darling, there's no need to worry. I'll make sure your debts are well covered and anything you want, anything you need for the gallery, I'll make certain you have it. Now, let me order you something to eat.'

'I'm not hungry, Terrance.'

He held her in a tight gaze. 'I insist.'

She found herself once again choosing her battles. 'All right. If you want to order something, you know what I like. And I'll eat as soon as I see Ingrid safely to the cab.'

He offered a gracious dip of his head, that effort at being modest and humble that now seemed nearly obscene, knowing him as she did. 'As you wish.'

It was the look in his eyes that made her aware they were no longer alone. Stacie couldn't have explained it if someone had asked, but in the shiver that chilled her, she thought of the bully boys in grade school who took pleasure in pulling wings off flies and torturing small helpless things. She turned to see that his eyes were on Ingrid.

'My goodness, Ingrid, couldn't you fix yourself up a bit? We have company, girl, and you look like a ragamuffin.'

Even between the bruises that were now fading to a sickening shade of green, Stacie could see the crawl of a blush. In truth, the poor girl had made an effort. The dress she was wearing was clearly new and clearly expensive. Her nails had been done and she had made an attempt at applying make-up; all things

Jamison would have demanded of her. But Stacie didn't contradict him. She remembered only too well the cost of a throwaway statement. Instead, she stood and nodded toward the bedroom door. 'Get your bag, sweetie. I have a cab waiting outside for you.'

Once Stacie had escorted Ingrid to the taxi, she found one of Jamison's bodyguards waiting for her at the elevator bank. He escorted her to a different suite, one considerably more upmarket than even Ingrid's had been. Jamison was waiting for her there, and room service had already arrived. The table was set, and a pear-poached chicken breast on a bed of seasonal vegetables was served for her. He pulled the chair out and settled her into the meal she didn't want.

He smiled happily at her as she forced the first bite down her tight throat, then he opened his arms wide. 'I hope you like the suite, my darling. I couldn't bear the thought of you being in the suite I'd fucked Ms. Watson in. That did seem a bit unchivalrous of me.'

'It's very nice, Terrance,' she said, still careful to say just the right things, but nothing more. When she figured she had eaten enough to meet his approval, she wiped her mouth with the linen napkin and spoke. 'Thank you for releasing Ingrid.'

His magnanimous smile drooped to a pout. 'My darling, you make it sound like the dear girl was my prisoner. I'm really quite amazed you could get her to leave, actually. But then again, I did insist that she go. And to be honest, I was getting rather bored with her.'

'And what about –?'

'And what about your Mr. Walker,' he interrupted before she could finish. 'You want to know whether

Mr. Walker will be safe.' The hard lines of his strong jawbones tightened. He toyed with his tie, and something in the way he held her gaze sent ice up her spine. 'Stacie darling, in the business world, we fuck our competitors all the time. It's just a part of the job. But your fucking Mr. Walker, aside from being very unprofessional, has nothing whatsoever to do with business. Surely you know that won't do. As long as you're spending my money, every breath you breathe is of interest to me. Surely you haven't forgotten the rules, Stacie.' He offered a consenting nod. 'Granted it's been a while since you and I have been in … business together, but I would have thought I had impressed upon you back then the importance of following those rules.'

'That was a part of our deal, a part of my agreeing to come to you, to stay with you – that you'd leave Harris Walker alone.'

'And I'll keep my word, Stacie, my love. I'll leave him alone if you leave him alone.'

'I told you that I would, but …' She toyed with the remains of her chicken, then laid the fork down. 'Harris Walker is one of my key exhibitors, and that makes him your investment too. And it means I may have to see him.'

He nodded slowly, still holding her gaze. 'I'm aware of that fact, Stacie. But I would very strongly advise you to limit your interactions with Mr. Walker to professional only. There are –' he paused to smooth away a nonexistent wrinkle from the leg of his trousers '– circumstances in which sacrifices have to be made, even in the business world, and you know me well enough, darling, to know that I can make sacrifices ruthlessly when the need arises.' He raised a hand before she could protest. 'Mr. Walker is the right choice for your exhibit, of course, and it would be a pity if you should have to find someone else. Therefore, I would suggest you keep that in mind. I understand your assistant – what's her name, Jenny? I understand that she's very competent. I see no reason, now that we're down to the wire, why any interaction that remains to be done with Mr. Walker couldn't be left in her quite capable hands. In fact, I must insist upon it. If you follow those simple rules, my dear, Mr. Walker has nothing whatsoever to fear from … terrorists.'

In spite of the gut wrench of not being able to see Harris, she felt an upwelling of relief at Jamison's words that made her weak all over. But he gave her no time to linger in that relief.

'While you're keeping your new, less personal relationship with Mr. Walker in mind, it seems like a good time to establish some ground rules for our renewed relationship, darling.'

Again he raised his hand before she could speak. 'Stacie, I really do want to keep our association civil and amenable, but you have to do your part. Surely you understood that going in?'

She braced herself. 'I'm here, aren't I?'

'Of course you're here, darling, but I'm not so naïve as to believe that being here is your first choice. I have no problem with that. I don't care about your choices, what I care about is your behavior. What I care about is you keeping the rules.'

She made no response.

'I don't like where you're living,' he said. 'Oh,

believe me, I understand and admire your efforts to save money. It's just good business sense. But it's beneath you, Stacie, way beneath you.'

'I got that,' she said. 'That's why I'm here. My bag's in the trunk of the Lexus.'

'Good. That's good, because as you know, the impressions other people have of us are not limited to what we do during business hours. Therefore it's essential you give a good impression in where you live, the way you dress.' He waved a hand at her clothing. 'Oh, there's nothing wrong with the way you dress, my darling. That you've always managed to make yourself as enticing as the art you exhibit is one of your gifts. But where you live just won't do. And money is no longer an issue for you. That being the case, I've rented you this suite in the Monaco, as befits your status and your position in the community. I specifically chose it for you, darling, because it's next to mine so that I can be with you whenever I choose.'

She barely had time to shiver from the thought of him being with her whenever he chose before he continued, 'Oh, the suite is a temporary fix. It's only until I can find an apartment that's suitable for you. There's no need arguing; it's a done deal. I've sent someone for the rest of your clothes. Though I hope you don't mind, I've taken the liberty of picking up a few things for you just to tide you over until you're settled in.' He nodded to the bedroom. 'You'll find your closet is stocked with all you'll need until your things arrive and you can make yourself at home. Of course, I understand you won't have much time to think about such things until after the exhibition, so with that in mind, I did take a few liberties, as I said.'

It demanded every ounce of self-discipline to sit still and endure it, to sit still and allow him to take everything away from her and take full control of her life. But it was no surprise. She had expected it and, in the end, it didn't matter. None of it mattered as long as Harris and her friends were all safe.

She sat feeling as though someone had just opened her vein and let all the life bleed out of her, let all that mattered drain away into nothing. But this was always the way it would be. She had known it, and she had walked into it deliberately.

She forced her attention back to Jamison, who was saying, 'I've already had the bellboy bring your bag to your suite. You can keep the Lexus, as I believe it'll make things a bit easier for you until after the exhibition, but after that, you won't be needing it any more. Also, as of tomorrow morning, I'll be replacing Martin Flannery's security team with a team of my most trusted men to keep an eye on you and on our investment. You may call Mr. Flannery and let him know, or he may be in for a rather rude awakening in the morning.'

'I've already done that,' she said.

'Good girl.' He leaned in to brush a whisper of a kiss against her lips. 'I was afraid that maybe you'd grown so wild since our last business partnership that I'd have to … reacquaint you with my expectations.' He ran a thumb across her bottom lip. 'I'm glad to see you're already beginning to anticipate me.' He sighed happily. 'It's such a lovely arrangement when one business partner can anticipate the needs of the other.'

He looked down at his watch and then stood. 'Finish your meal, darling. I've booked reservations for a celebratory dinner tonight in honor of our renewed relationship, and since I doubted you'd come prepared for such an occasion, I've taken the liberty of seeing you're provided with appropriate clothing. You'll find them in the bedroom. I'll pick you up at 7:30. And now, I have some business to take care of in Valderia. Since I'm sure your assistant can handle anything you've not sorted for the day at the gallery, I would suggest you get some rest when you've eaten.' He lifted her chin and held her face so that he could inspect her. 'You look exhausted, my darling, and I can't bear to see you so tired. So I insist that you take advantage of the bed, which I'm sure you'll find very comfortable. I'm sure you'll agree that you'll need to be rested for what we have ahead of us. Oh Stacie, I'm so excited that we're together again. Tonight we celebrate; then tomorrow we can pick up where we left off.' He kissed her again. 'You and I have unfinished business, Stacie Emerson.'

Without warning, he pulled her to her feet, nearly tipping over her chair. He pulled her close with such force that she gave an involuntary gasp. He curled his fingers in her hair and held her so she couldn't look away from his fiercely cold eyes. His breath came in accelerated bursts against her face and there was no ignoring the press of his hard-on against her. He forced a hoarse laugh that barely escaped the tight press of his chest. This time when he took her mouth it was with bruising brutality, causing fear to spike in her chest until the crush of him against her felt suffocating, felt as though he stole her very breath, her very life force from between her lips. She curled a tight fist against the back of his jacket, feeling her nails dig into her palm. At last, he pulled away, breathing hard. He wiped his mouth on the back of his hand. 'Yes, we have unfinished business, Stacie, and this time I have every intention of finishing what I started.'

'What do you mean she gave you the slip?' Harris catapulted from the sofa, sloshing the array of drinks and water on the coffee table in the process. 'How the hell could she give you the slip? How the hell could she give *both* of you the slip?'

'Harris, sit down and shut up. Let me talk, and I'll explain everything,' Kendra said. She took a huge drink of the Diet Pepsi Wade had offered her and continued, 'I thought, both Stan and I thought, she'd gone to the bathroom to throw up. She said she was sick, and she ran off like she was. I mean, no woman wants company while she pukes, so of course we gave her a little privacy. Turns out she wasn't sick at all. Turns out she climbed out the back window of the bathroom, and believe me that was no small feat. But by the time we figured it out, she was long gone.'

'Do you know where she went?' Ellis asked.

'To the Monaco. That's where she planned to meet Jamison.' Kendra nodded down to her BlackBerry. 'She's not trying to hide anything. She sent the message not long after we figured out she was gone.'

'Why?' Harris felt like he'd just been gutted. 'Why the hell would she do that?'

Kendra looked at him as though he was a moron. 'Because she wanted to keep you –' she opened her arms to include everyone in the room '– and the rest of us safe, that's why. She got a threatening email from Jamison this morning right after she got to the gallery, confirming that he knows you're alive. Not long after that, K. Ryde got an email explaining what Stacie was going to do and what she wanted from Ryde. That's when I broke my number one rule and went to see her at the gallery. I thought it would be good to get her away from there. I stupidly thought that Jamison was coming for her there. And really, she did lead me to believe that.'

'So how long has K. Ryde been involved in this mess?' Harris asked, sounding a lot more belligerent than he intended, but then he was pretty damned angry that his best friend had just sold the woman he loved up the creek.

'Stacie Emerson and New World Gallery have been clients of K. Ryde from the start. Though in all honesty, it was against both our better judgments when we agreed to keep working together after we became friends. But there was no one else who could do what Ryde could.'

'And just what the fuck could Ryde do?' Harris asked.

Dee laid a hand on his arm. 'You know that's confidential, Harris.'

He jerked away. 'I don't give a fuck. If that bastard harms one hair on her head, one hair …'

'Ryde is trying to make sure that doesn't happen,' Kendra said. 'You know that, Harris. And even if I could tell you exactly where Stacie is at the moment, your life would be in danger if you went to her, assuming that you could get to her at all. And whether I'm K. Ryde or Kendra Davis, there's no fucking way I'm putting you in danger. Now, will you shut the hell up and let me do my job?'

Harris settled back on the couch with his arms folded across his chest glaring at her. 'Go ahead, then. Do your job.'

Kendra glared right back. Then she looked down at her BlackBerry. 'This was the email she sent me this morning.' Kendra scrolled down her screen and began to read.

There are things that none of you know, that I have good reasons for keeping from you. For that, I'm truly sorry, but if you've ever trusted me, I'm asking you to trust me now. I'm asking you to let me do what I have to.

I've asked K. Ryde to deliver this message because I trust K. Ryde, as I have long before I knew most of you, long before breaches were healed and I got my friends back.

At the moment, I'm safe. Please believe that I am. I'll continue to work at the gallery every day. The exhibition, the grand opening, the gala for Vigilant Trust will all go on according to plan – everything exactly according to plan, and I'll see you all there to toast new beginnings. I promise you that.

In the meantime, please don't try to see me. That's essential. I won't ever be alone, and Jamison has replaced Flannery's men with his own. Martin, I can't thank you enough for all you've done and for all your efforts to keep us all safe. You're a good friend.

If you need me or if you need to talk to me, send a message through K. Ryde at an address Ryde will pass on to you shortly. If you come to the gallery I won't be able to speak with you, but my associate, Jenny, will be happy to welcome you there.

Please believe that all I've done, I've done of my own free will, and that every debt will be paid in full as soon as I'm able. It was never my intention to drag any of you into this, nor to involve you in any way. I deeply, deeply regret that, and I'll do all that's in my power to make it up to you.

In the meantime, please, for your safety and mine, honor my requests.

SE

The room was silent. Harris couldn't breathe. He felt like he'd been slapped. He felt like his heart had been ripped out and stomped on, and all there was of the woman whose arms he'd slept in, the woman whose body he'd been inside only hours ago, was this distant, impersonal email sent through someone who didn't even exist.

He stood. Wade's Dungeon felt almost unbearably claustrophobic.

'Harris, what are you doing?' Dee's voice came from a long way off. 'Harris?'

'I'm getting the hell out of here. I assume as long as Stacie agrees to be Jamison's pet, I'm no longer under a death threat. If she's the price, then it's too damned high.'

The room erupted in chaos. Ellis grabbed him by the arm. 'Let me go, damn it!' He jerked away.

'Stop being a jackass, then.' Ellis looked like he could breathe fire. 'Sit down, shut up, and let's see what we can do to help Stacie.'

'Nothing!' Harris growled, balling his fist, ready to fight his way out if he had to. 'Didn't you hear the fucking email? We can't do a goddamned thing, and I'm sick and tired of sitting around playing dead. I'll find her and drag her away if I have to.'

Then everyone was talking at once, and Harris and Ellis might have come to blows if there hadn't been a loud knock at the door, and Ellis' secretary stuck her head in.

'Excuse me, but a taxi just dropped off an Ingrid Watson. She's been with Stacie Emerson, and she insists that she be brought directly to you or K. Ryde.'

The room was instantly silent as Lynn opened the door and stepped out of the way for a woman Harris had only seen once and, sadly, recognized by the bruises on her face that looked as if she had hastily tried to cover them with make-up. Even the smart designer clothes she wore couldn't cover the battered, haunted look about the woman, who appeared to be barely more than a girl. Her gaze settled on Harris, and her eyes welled. It took him a second to realize that he was probably the only one in the room she recognized.

'Ingrid?' He spoke softly. 'I'm Harris Walker, you remember me?'

She nodded and her lip quivered.

He moved forward, and slipped an arm around her shoulders, which seemed incredibly fragile. Ingrid flinched then relaxed. He guided her to sit on the couch next to him. Wade brought her a bottle of chilled water and she drank it down thirstily.

'I ordered Chinese,' Ellis' secretary said. 'Poor girl looks like she's starving. 'You hungry, sweetie?'

Ingrid nodded.

'It should be here shortly,' Lynn told her. 'I asked Chang to hurry it along.'

After Lynn left, Wade, who was a surprisingly

attentive host, brought the girl a cup of cocoa.

'What?' he said when he saw they were all staring. 'Everyone knows cocoa's the cure for trauma.'

She took it gratefully and sipped.

'What happened?' Ellis asked her. 'How did you get here?'

'Stacie Emerson came for me. He made her wait while he ...while we ...' She swallowed back a sob and slopped the cocoa onto her hands and onto the bright yellow skirt.

Harris took the cup from her and offered her a couple of tissues from the box on the table.

'When he was ... finished with me, he left. I heard them talking. She asked for me. She said she had a cab waiting.' She wiped her eyes on one of the tissues Harris had given her and left a smudge of mascara. 'At first I thought it was only another one of his games, but then he told me to get dressed and come out. And she was there. And she did. She took me downstairs all the way to a taxi that was waiting for me. She told the driver to bring me here and not to leave until he knew I was safe. I didn't want to be alone. I was scared. I wanted her to come with me, but she said she had to stay.'

Harris felt sick. It wasn't just what Ingrid Watson had been through, but that Stacie now willingly submitted herself to Jamison to guarantee the girl's safe return as well as his own safety. The thought was almost more than he could stand.

'Is K. Ryde here?' the girl asked. 'Stacie told me that K. Ryde could tell me about my father.'

'I represent K. Ryde,' Kendra said. 'And your father's safe. He's taking that long holiday abroad he always dreamed of, and if you'd like to join him, K. Ryde can arrange it.'

The girl wept openly, making no effort to still the sobs that ripped at her. 'I'd like that. How soon can I go?'

Kendra looked at Ellis, and Ellis nodded. 'If K. Ryde will just let my pilot know where he's flying to, I'll have the jet on standby for when Ms. Watson's ready.'

'Thank you,' Ingrid managed. 'It can't be soon enough.' She blew her nose and worried the tissue between nervous hands. 'I'm sorry, I don't want to be a bother, but is there someplace I can have a shower?' She tugged at the blouse as though it fit too snugly. It was Dee who stood and motioned her back into the area where the guest suite was, but as Ingrid stood to go, she stopped. 'Oh, I almost forgot. Stacie asked me to give this to you.' She handed Harris a folded piece of paper.

The note was short and handwritten.

I'm sorry that I ran, Harris. You can't know just how sorry I am, how much I wanted to stay there with you. Please, please trust me in my decision and let me do what I have to. And Harris, thank you for the mountain lions.

Love,

Stacie

Kendra, who had now moved to his side, slid an arm around him and spoke softly. 'She asked me to tell you something, Harris. She wanted me to tell you that she loves you. I told her to tell you herself, but then you know I've got a big mouth. I'm sure it'll be much better, though, when you hear it from her.'

If the note and Kendra's words eased his misery, it did nothing to ease the fear and dread he felt for Stacie. As Harris watched Ingrid Watson disappear into the bowels of the Dungeon, leaning heavily on Dee, he loved Stacie more than he ever dreamed he could love. Fighting the sudden tightness in his chest, he turned back to Ellis.

'Can you get a doctor for Ingrid? Seems to me that after what she's been through, she should probably have a check-up before she flies, then –' he turned to Kendra '– maybe K. Ryde can make sure she gets any medical attention she needs wherever she's going.'

'K. Ryde's already done that at Stacie's request,' Kendra replied.

Chapter Twenty-nine

Stacie had done her best to provide good arm candy and stimulating conversation for Jamison. If she had to endure being with him, then she would try to make it tolerable, not because she cared about his pleasure, but because she recalled only too well what happened the last time she was uncooperative. And really, with the exhibition just days away, it was the perfect topic of conversation that was of interest to both of them. Focusing on the optimism she had for the exhibition and for the money it was already raising for the Vigilant Trust, even before it opened, helped keep her mind off Harris and how much she missed him.

She had received a cryptic text from K. Ryde saying *The package is safely sent. The photographer is fine –tho not happy abt situ.* That was a positive to focus on, and that made what she'd had to do seem worth it. The one thing that she didn't want was for Jamison to have any reason to be angry at her, nor to turn that anger on any of the people she loved.

Terrance Jamison was as she remembered him, completely capable of being charming and intriguing. That was what had drawn her to him in New York. It was stunning that a man who came across as such a charmer could be such a monster underneath. But for the evening, he was attentive and considerate. She did her best to focus on that, to focus on how pleasant it was at the moment. It helped take her mind off what he really was and what he was capable of doing. And she had done a fair job of placating him until they were back in her hotel suite together and the grab of nerves in her stomach was nearly painful. She knew that he had no intention of ending their evening with dinner. There was never any thought that it would be otherwise. She had always known he would expect sex from her, and she had always believed she could do it, as she had done in New York. But that was before Harris Walker pushed and shoved his way into her life. It didn't matter, though. She'd do what she had to.

There was champagne chilling in a bucket on the table; he poured them both a flute while she opened the curtains, desperate not to feel quite so shut in, not to feel quite so much the prisoner she knew she really was.

'To new beginnings, my darling,' he said, handing her the glass and raising his in a toast. 'To us.'

She raised hers and sipped the tiniest bit. Jamison offered her a teasing smile. 'Come now, sweetheart, I seem to remember you love good champagne.'

'Oh I do.' She managed another small sip. 'But I don't drink much before a big exhibition. I find my system's very sensitive and not very tolerant of a lot of things I normally have no problems with. You know, the stress of it all?'

The look of concern on his face would have surprised her if she hadn't known him so well. He smoothed her hair away from her cheek and pulled her into his arms. 'Of course, my poor darling. And this has been a very stressful time for you what with the money situation and all, hasn't it?'

She nodded against his chest. With a solicitous hand, he stroked the middle of her back where it was exposed by the dress. 'I'm so terribly sorry you've had to go through such a time, and I'm so glad that I can now be here for you to ease the burden.' His hand slid to her hip, and the he pulled away enough to meet her gaze. 'You do feel a bit thin, Stacie. Oh, not as thin as you were in New York, but you were working yourself to death there, never willing to let me take some of the weight of it, never willing to let me make it easier.'

Her stomach lurched and burned with the rage of it, the insult that he could even bring up her efforts in New York, as if there had ever been any choice. But she pushed it down deeper, saving it all, saving it for the time when it could do her some good. For the moment, he didn't have to know the quiver of her lip was anger and not the threat of tears at the memory of how she had turned away his help. For now, he could see the emotions on her face and think what he wanted.

'And you're so pale, darling. But all of that'll change now you're with me. I'll make sure you eat well and rest, and you know that whatever you need is yours for the asking, my darling, even before the asking. So you see; there's no need to stress.'

She offered a weak smile that she hoped would pass as gratitude, but then surely he had to know that she was only playing the game with him, only doing what she had to in order to get what she wanted.

His hand moved from her hip up along the outside of her breast and to the bodice of the dress that showed more cleavage than she would have preferred. 'Your curves, Stacie, your lovely womanly curves; it wouldn't do for you to lose them, now would it? He ran the slight cup of his palm over each of her breasts in turn, catching his breath at the feel of her nipples responding to his warmth.

'Oh my dear, you have no idea how exquisite you are, do you? You never have. That's a part of what's always made you the most intriguing woman I've ever known.' He kissed her collarbone, then slid one strap away from her shoulders. His cool lips nibbled an arc of kisses along the rounded muscle of her shoulder. 'You were the work of art I most wanted to possess that first night we met in New York. I could see nothing else, think of nothing else, dream of nothing else.'

He reached behind her and, with a slow, practiced hand, unzipped her dress.

And she held herself. She didn't flinch, she didn't stiffen. She held everything inside. This was not unexpected. This was a part of the price, the price she was willing to pay. She ignored the rise of bile in her throat and swallowed it back. She could do this. She had to do this. And she would.

With a flick of his thumbs, he slipped the dress off her shoulders. As it slid down her body to pool around her feet, he caught his breath. 'Dear God, Stacie Emerson, how you have haunted me all these years, and tonight –' He cupped her cheek and took her mouth in a lingering kiss. 'Tonight I'll have you again at last.' He took her hand and steadied her as she stepped out of the dress, standing before him in nothing but stockings and garter belt and dangerously high heels. His gaze felt as physical as his touch had been as he studied her body the way he would a piece of art. Then he took her hand and led her to the bedroom.

And Stacie Emerson did what she had to do.

Jenny knocked softly on the open door to Stacie's office and stuck her head around it, looking slightly nervous. 'Um, Harris Walker's downstairs. What do you want me to do?'

Stacie nearly dropped the sandwich she'd been nibbling while going over the schedule of events, and everything in her tensed and ached with yearning. She was about to tell Jenny to send him away, but then she remembered he hadn't yet seen the finished film loop.

'Good. Jenny, take Mr. Walker into the small guest lounge and put the film loop on for him to watch. Tell him it's important that I get his final approval while there's still time for Carla to edit it.' There wasn't time for Carla to edit it. It was a done deal now, but that didn't matter.

She listened, with her heart in her throat, to Harris' protests as Jenny escorted him into the small guest lounge. She could hear Jenny explaining what Stacie wanted him to do, and then, at last, there was silence. She waited another minute, until she could stand it no longer, and then she slipped into the control room for the security cameras and pulled up the monitor for the small lounge, keeping the door open just in case any of Jamison's men got suspicious. Sure enough, Harris was there. She made a grab for the chair and nearly missed it, she was trembling so badly. She could see his impatient face waiting for the film loop to begin and no doubt planning to storm the ramparts the very second it was done. A quick search of the other security monitors showed two of Jamison's men at either end the main exhibition hall, seated as though they were docents at a museum, looking rather bored. A third stood at the main entrance and a fourth was at the private rear entrance. A look around the parking lot showed no sign of any vehicles she didn't recognize. She didn't know how Harris had managed to sneak in, but it didn't matter. No rules had been broken. If any of the security team entered the lounge or her office, what they'd see was Stacie checking out the security system and one of her key exhibitors downstairs in the lounge, watching the film loop that he starred in. With a trembling hand, she flipped the switch. Harris nearly jumped out of his seat when, rather than the film loop, the image of her, finger pressed to her lips to shush him, came onto his screen.

'You're not supposed to be here,' she said.

'No, I'm just not supposed to be here with you.' He offered her that wry smile of his that she'd love to kiss off his face and, in happier times, she would have. 'I couldn't stay away, surely you know that. I had to know you were all right.'

'I'm fine, Harris. He didn't hurt me, and anyway, once Ingrid was away and I knew you were safe I was a good girl, and did what I was told.'

His face darkened; the look of pain made her ache to touch him, to hold him and reassure him. For a second, he struggled to find his voice, and when he spoke, the words were tight, as though something horrible might happen if he lost control. 'I slept at home last night, and I … I couldn't stop thinking … and I wanted to rip his throat out and –'

'Harris,' she interrupted. 'I didn't have sex with him.'

She heard his groan of relief, and he scrubbed a hand over his face. 'How? Surely he wanted you? I mean, how could he not want you?'

'Oh, he wanted me all right.'

'Then what happened?'

'I threw up on him,' she said, as matter-of-factly as if she'd been telling him the weather.

Harris shoved his hand over his mouth to fight back a sob of laughter. 'Seriously? On purpose?'

She nodded. 'It wasn't that hard to do under the circumstances.' For a second, they only sat smiling at each other, and then she felt her smile slip. 'Harris, my convenient little stomach bug is just a temporary fix. You know that. In the end, I'll do what I have to. I need you to understand that.'

'No! I don't understand. I don't understand at all. And, Stacie, when this is over and we get you out of this mess. He'll pay. He'll pay dearly for everything he's done to you. I promise.'

'Harris, I don't want to talk about him, OK?' She leaned closer to the control panel, a poor substitute for the intimacy she craved with the man whose face on the monitor looked so pained. We only have a few minutes. Tell me something good. Tell me something that I can hold on to.'

'Doug saw our mountain lion again yesterday. He says she's looking pretty pleased with herself.'

Stacie closed her eyes for a second, letting his words sink in. Then she smiled back at him. 'There'll be kittens in a few months.'

He nodded. 'I'll take you to see them when Doug gives the OK.'

'I'm counting on it,' she replied, not daring to think that far ahead, but wanting to so badly. 'What else?'

'Wade's working on some promising technology that will help prevent erosion and reclaim damaged land that's already suffered from erosion.'

'That's good news.'

'I went for a swim this morning in the waterhole. Water's just freezing, and not nearly as much fun without you.' He pressed his hand to the screen. 'Stacie, I love you.'

But before she could respond, in the background she could hear male voices heading toward the small lounge. With an urgent gasp, she flipped the switch. The film clip continued, and Harris' face was gone. His last words settled around her with an impossible mix of pain and hope.

Chapter Thirty

'This is getting to be a goddamned habit,' Al Marston said. The big man had just arrived from New York for meetings with Dee and for the opening exhibition at New World Gallery West tomorrow night. 'Wade, if you're planning on taking up entertaining, you really ought to see if you could hire Beverly's decorator back. The place is a dump.'

Wade ignored him, settling into his ratty recliner as though he were about to hold court. Dee, Ellis, Flannery, and Kendra were already there as Marston settled onto the sofa next to Harris with a grunt. 'What the hell's going on? How's Stacie?'

'Stacie's fine,' Wade said. 'She's just fine. But the one thing Stacie Emerson is not is broke.'

There was a collective intake of breath, and then the room went silent. 'It took some serious doing to track down the woman's resources. Whoever set up this scheme for her was a bloody genius.'

All eyes were on Kendra. She shook her head. 'She's K. Ryde's client, so don't ask. What you've found, you've found, but don't ask.'

Harris exploded. 'Goddamn it, Kendra, this is Stacie we're talking about!'

'I fucking know who we're talking about, Harris. So let me do my job, for Stacie's sake.'

Wade only looked from one of them to the other as though they bored him, and then he said, 'It doesn't matter who did it. So far I've traced down enough liquidity to buy the gallery outright several times over and still take half of Portland out for big party after the exhibition.'

That got everyone's full attention. He continued, 'I don't know what the woman's playing at, but she sure as hell doesn't need Jamison's money. She doesn't need anything from him.'

'It doesn't matter what she needs from him,' Ellis said. 'If he harasses Stacie through threatening her friends and through vandalizing her gallery, the odds are in his favor, and he knows it.'

'But why?' Flannery asked. 'Why would he do it? Ellis, do you think it could have something to do with you? I know you say not, but I can't think of any other reason.'

'That little lady got the best of him.' Marston shook a thick finger at everyone. 'And she did it in front of the whole goddamned world, including the press and his rich associates. Ya'll know Jamison has an ego bigger that the whole fucking state of Texas. Don't you see? He can't let that slide, even if it takes him, say, ten years.'

Wade nodded slowly. 'That may well be, but that doesn't explain why all of Stacie's money has been hidden away over the past five years until it looks like she's living off her dwindling savings. Jamison had nothing to do with that. Jamison doesn't know that or he wouldn't be pumping money into an account Stacie just recently set up, now would he?'

'All I know for certain,' Ellis said, 'is that Ingrid

Watson was, for all practical purposes, kidnapped, beaten, and probably raped, and Kenny Hearn is dead because of this man's obsession with Stacie. Now whether the woman says she's safe or not, she's not.'

'I want her out of there.' Harris had been listening quietly to all the facts, the knot in his stomach getting tighter and tighter each second and the urge to storm the gallery and take Stacie by force growing stronger and stronger. 'I don't care how we have to do it. I don't care what we have to do. I don't want that bastard laying another hand on her.'

'I'm with Harris,' Flannery said.

'Hear, hear!' Marston added. 'We have to get her out and get her away from that sack of shit.'

'Then we're talking kidnapping,' Kendra said. She raised her hands as though to deflect the multiple glares of the people around her. 'Stacie Emerson's not Ingrid Watson. She'll have to be taken by force. You'll be taking her away from her gallery, from her home, from her friends.'

'I don't care,' Harris said. 'I'll go with her. We can find a way to keep the gallery open, or hell, buy her another one, I just want her safe! I just want her safe.'

'If we can get her away to someplace safe just for a little while, perhaps we can build a case against Jamison,' Dee said. 'I mean, there has to be a way.'

'We can try,' Wade responded. 'But it'll take time, and we've got to deal with Valderia or there'll be the biggest clear-cut of virgin forest in history.'

'First we get Stacie to safety,' Harris said. 'Then I'll do whatever you need me to do where Valderia's concerned.'

'The exhibition would be the ideal time to take

her,' Flannery said. 'My people set up one hell of an impressive security system for the gallery, so I know it inside-out. We can get her out right after her closing speech. The festivities'll go on for a while, and it'll be easy to get her away. I'll have a plan ready in a few hours, if you want me to go with it.'

Everyone was staring at Kendra again. She forced a huge sigh and said, 'Speaking strictly for Kendra Davis, I want her out of there.'

'We all agree then,' Ellis said. 'We need to get her to safety. There's no doubt.' He turned his attention to Flannery. 'Martin, do what you have to and let us know what you need us to do.'

Harris said nothing. His mind was already made up, regardless of anyone else's consent. He had no intention of leaving Stacie in Jamison's hands one second longer than necessary. That everyone was now in agreement, that powerful forces were in on the plan, made him feel marginally better. But ultimately, he knew he wouldn't really feel right until he had Stacie away from Jamison and safe back in his arms.

As she always did on the night of a big exhibition, Stacie had taken extra time to get ready. And if anything, in this case, she had taken even more time. Jamison had wanted to buy her a new gown for the evening, but she already had one of her own choosing and she had bought it with just this event in mind. This was a big night and she would not preside over it looking anything less than perfect.

She was nearly ready when Jamison came into her room without knocking. He never knocked and that took some getting used to. But it was a small thing, really. Not worth her notice when there were so many bigger things pressing. As he stood in the doorway, admiring her in the black sheath, which hugged her curves and caressed her breasts in a shimmer of silk, for a moment she was struck by how stunning he was in his tux and black tie. She never saw him that way any more. After New York, for her, the outside charm and good looks could never again be enough to disguise what lie beneath. She was just settling Al's pearls into place around her neck when he stepped in close behind her and took them off.

'Pearls aren't worthy to rest around your lovely throat, my darling.' He pulled a padded box from his breast pocket and took from it an elegant choker heavily set with diamonds and rubies. 'These stones are exquisite, each one hand-chosen for this necklace, each one perfect. And you, my beautiful Stacie, outshine them all.' She watched in the mirror as he hooked the choker around her throat. 'Do you like it?'

'It's beautiful, Terrance.' It was all she could do to keep from gritting her teeth. She didn't want his gifts, she didn't want his blatant show of ownership. She wanted Al Marston's string of pearls and what they represented for her. But she said nothing.

'I'm so glad you like it.' He didn't move from behind her, but continued to look her over through the mirror. All the while, he stroked the nape of her neck just below her left earlobe with the back of his index finger. 'And I have another surprise for you darling.' He didn't wait for her to ask. 'After the exhibition's over tonight, I have the jet on standby to take us back to New York. I find Portland so provincial and a little too claustrophobic for my taste. And really, Stacie, I think the best way to keep you out of trouble is to remove you from the temptation.' He offered her a conspiratorial smile. 'Oh come now, I'm not a fool. I know that as long as you're here, and Mr. Walker's here, you'll be tempted, so you see, I'm doing this as much for his safety as I am to protect what's mine. Jenny seems competent enough. I'm sure she can run the gallery here for you, and it'll be in very good hands. So I've taken the liberty of having a bag packed for you, darling, and I've arranged to have my usual suite at the Plaza. You'll love it. And once we're there, we can celebrate your triumph together.'

He continued to gaze at her in the mirror, standing so close that she could feel the press of the dressing table up against her thighs. She made no attempt to move, but allowed him to admire his acquisition. She knew that's how he saw her.

'My goodness, you are exquisite,' He ran a hand up over her belly to cup her breast. His eyelids grew heavy, and his breath caught as he raked her nipple with his thumb. 'So very exquisite.' He brushed a kiss against her nape, then another below it, on her shoulder. Then he sighed and smiled up at her in the mirror. 'Oh, and one more thing, Stacie. When we get to New York and when we're comfortably ensconced in my suite at the Plaza, I'll expect my reward. Your misfortunate illness the other night may have bought you a night or two's reprieve, but after tonight, you'll have no excuses, nothing stressing you, nothing upsetting your … delicate system. And I promise you this time I will fuck you even if I have to do it while you're bent over the toilet retching. Now hurry along, sweetheart. The limo'll be arriving shortly.'

Once he'd left the room, she grabbed Al's pearls from the dressing table and stuffed them into her bag for luck and for courage. Tonight she would need all she could get of both.

Chapter Thirty-one

'Damn, Stacie Emerson really knows how to throw a party,' Kyle Waters said, moving to Harris' side and lifting his champagne glass in salute. 'And she knows how to make her exhibitors feel like they own the world, I'll say that for her.' He looked back over his shoulder at the woman in a tiny gold cocktail dress he'd just been chatting up and smiled.

'Have you seen the Japanese exhibit?' His eyes took in the woman's backside when she turned and sauntered off toward the main exhibition hall. 'I felt like I was transported right back into the time of the Shoguns. And from the looks of the Japanese contingent, and Mr. Fukuda's little speech, I'd say they're pretty pleased too.'

He nodded his head to a woman in blue who was talking to Dee and Ellis. 'That's the reporter from the *New York Times*. Has she spoken to you yet? And over there, the guy who looks like his tux has been too heavily starched, he's from *Time* Magazine. It's a regular who's who of the biggies in here. How the hell does she do it?'

Harris shot a glance at Kendra, who was dressed in red satin, her arm laced through Garrett's. 'She has a good PR firm,' he said. Though he couldn't see Stacie at the moment, he knew she was in the small lounge speaking to the Japanese reporters. He could see Jamison hovering near the door, making sure Stacie didn't escape him. The desire to do the man serious bodily harm washed over Harris like a wave of nausea, and he barely heard what Waters was saying about the reporter from *The Oregonian.*

Harris had already spoken to the press, and the evening had been a torture chamber of handshakes and making nicey-nice that he might have otherwise enjoyed had he not been constantly aware of Stacie's every move and the fact that Jamison never let her out of his sight. She looked breathtakingly beautiful, and he desperately wanted to tell her that, to tell her what an amazing evening she had put together in spite of the horrible situation in which she found herself. But instead he ignored her, waiting on edge for the right moment when she could be snatched away to safety. Ellis' pilot had the plane on standby to take her to a destination even Harris didn't yet know, though he would be by her side wherever it was. In a few short hours, she would be safely away from Jamison, and probably mad as hell, but he could live with that. In a few short hours, nothing would delight him more than to throw himself at the mercy of Stacie's anger. All that mattered was getting her to safety.

As she came out of the small lounge and Jamison latched onto her arm, it hit Harris: he had never seen Stacie truly angry. The women in his life had always been comfortable with anger, and he'd survived more than a few run-ins with both Kendra and Dee's anger. His stomach clenched almost as hard as his fists when Jamison leaned in and kissed Stacie's ear. Stacie made no sign one way or another how she felt about his unwanted affection.

Harris glanced down at his watch. Where the hell was Flannery? He was supposed to have been here when they arrived. His name was on the guest list by virtue of his friendship with both Stacie and Ellis. If their plan was to work, they needed Flannery, and if Flannery didn't show up – well, Harris would take Stacie by force if he had to, but he'd get her away from Jamison one way or another.

Waters had moved back to chatting up the woman in the gold cocktail dress, plying her with expensive champagne he hadn't paid for, and Stacie was talking to several of the Japanese contingent, when Marston came to his side, looking pale. His face was pinched into a tight frown.

'Damn it. Where the hell is Flannery?' he asked. 'I need him. I need all y'all for a word.' He nodded his head toward the small lounge, now deserted. Harris could see Ellis, Dee, and Wade heading that way. Kendra kissed Garrett on the cheek and left him to keep an eye on Stacie.

Stacie and Jamison had just disappeared into the Samurai Room with Garrett trailing discreetly behind, so neither of them saw the small party who now gathered around the computer screen as though they were totally fascinated by the film loop, which played for the hundredth time.

'She's planning to kill the bastard,' Marston hissed without preamble, glancing over his shoulder as if he expected Stacie and Jamison to be listening in. 'I think she may be planning to kill him,' he repeated.

'What?' Harris and Kendra said at the same time.

Not giving anyone else time to comment, Marston

continued. 'I don't know why I didn't think about it, why I didn't make the connection early, but that night in New York when he beat her –' Marston's face reddened; it was hard to tell if he was embarrassed at having to bring up such a time in Stacie's life or if he was angry at Jamison. 'That night, I rode with her in the ambulance. She was sedated and, well, she must have been delirious. She kept saying over and over again that he'd killed Zoe Hanson and that she'd see he paid for it. Mind you, she never said who *he* was. She just kept saying she'd make him pay for what he'd done. Course, I thought she was talking loan sharks or Mafia, something like that. As I said, I never made the connection.'

'Al, the woman had just been beaten half to death,' Kendra said. 'What would you expect her to say? That doesn't mean she'd actually … That doesn't mean she'd …' Her voice drifted off, not sounding too sure any more. 'And besides, Zoe Hanson's death was a suicide.'

'Hell, I know that,' Marston said. 'But you can understand why Stacie would blame Jamison for it. And think about it. Think about the set-up here: the fact that Stacie suddenly and very convincingly is pretending to be broke; the fact that she turns to Jamison, a man she has more reason to hate than any of us do. It's almost like she's baited the trap for the man with the one thing she knew he couldn't refuse. Jamison's a sore loser, we all know that. And he lost Stacie outright in New York when she got the gallery out of debt in such a public way. It was like she thumbed her nose at him in front of the whole damn world. Come on, Ellis, you know the asshole better than I do. Does it make sense to you that he'd let an insult like that stand?'

'It wasn't an insult,' Kendra said. 'It was a woman getting her life back.'

'Course it was,' Marston replied, 'but to Jamison it was an insult.' He glanced around again. 'Where the hell's Flannery?'

'Even if what you say's true –' Ellis said, and he looked like he might almost believe it '– we can't do anything until after the big speech, and she certainly won't ruin the event.'

'She wouldn't do that,' Harris said. 'Stacie would never do such a thing.'

'I know for a fact she has a gun,' Al said. 'She told me so.'

'Lots of people have guns, Marston, but that doesn't make them killers,' Harris responded.

'Goddamn it!' Marston's patience snapped. 'I'm not saying she's a killer. I'm saying that's the only explanation for this whole set-up, the money and all.'

'The question is –' Wade spoke for the first time '– if that's what she plans, is she up for the task?'

'Jesus, Wade,' Harris said. 'I can't believe we're even talking about this.'

'No, listen to me. If that's Stacie's plan –' Wade raised a negating hand to the protests. 'I'm not saying that it is, but if that's what she has in mind, then if she pulls it off, she'd be looking at a long prison sentence. But if it's her plan, and she can't pull it off, then she's in even more danger. We already know Jamison's capable of anything, and she's at his mercy.'

'This is ridiculous, Marston,' Kendra said. 'If she really wanted to kill him, she's way too smart to do it in so public a place.'

'She kept saying it would all be over tonight,' Marston said. 'I thought she planned to somehow pay him back. She did keep saying she'd pay her debts; she'd pay him back in full. What the hell else could it mean when she doesn't even owe him anything?'

'It means we have to get her out of here and away from him,' Ellis said, 'with or without Flannery.' He looked down at his watch. 'As soon as the closing speech is over, I'll confront Jamison about Valderia. That's a valid excuse for me to engage him, and then, Harris, you take Stacie's arm and walk away with her. Jamison won't want to make a scene. We just do it. Then anything else is a moot point.'

'Jamison's never gonna let it be that simple,' Kendra said. 'He has his guards all over the place.'

The sharp tinkling of a bell announced the closing remarks, and Jenny's voice came over the mic, calling everyone to gather in the main exhibition room.

'I'll get her away,' Harris said, as they all moved toward the main hall. 'I'll get her away, no matter what it takes.'

By the time they moved into the hall, Jenny was just introducing Stacie, who came to the podium as if she was above it all, as if Jamison standing nearby with his eagle eyes locked on her and his two guards standing at the main entrance had nothing whatsoever to do with her. She was glorious in a dress that looked like the black silk caressed her each time she moved. She wore her hair up, and the only jewelry was a string of pearls. Any goddess would have felt the urge to do homage, and Harris was pretty sure it wasn't his imagination that the whole room felt that exact sense of awe as she smiled out over them, and silence fell.

'This gallery, this particular exhibition, has been my dream for a long time,' she said. 'Learning the ropes of running a gallery from my dear friend Zoe Hanson back in New York filled me with dreams of having a gallery here in Portland, in my home town, having a gallery that reflected the art and the beauty and the life of the Northwest. Ever since those early days, those lean days, I've dreamed of coming home, of finishing what I started in New York.'

Was Harris mistaken or did she just glance down at Jamison?

She continued, 'But everyone who's here tonight knows the real reason for this exhibition. It's my attempt to give something back to the place I love and the home that I may have left for a while, but that never left me. The Vigilant Trust is all about giving something back. It's about restoring, reclaiming, and returning to nature what we've taken, what we've destroyed. Tonight, you've seen an exhibition of photos that you might not consider art, but I believe that in many ways is art at its most advanced level.

'Art represents the consciousness of a culture and reflects it back. In many ways, art is the *conscience* of the culture that creates it, a constant reminder of what's good, what's bad, what inspires us, what horrifies us, what we are in our darkest moments and what we're capable of becoming at our very best. That's what we've seen tonight, what we are in our darkest moments.'

All at once, the pictures flashing on the big screens around the room were no longer Harris' photos nor were they Kyle Waters'. They were the photos Stacie had taken at the Bald Hill clear-cut the day of the storm. 'When I was a little girl, just moved back to the States with my family, I used to play in this place, watch the stars in this place, pick huckleberries in this place.'

As she continued to speak, the deluging streams, looking bloody in the run-off from the deforested hillside, flashed on the screen. The scars and gouges and the remains of high stumps, looking like specters ready to attack and devour, flashed on the screen. 'You wouldn't know it now to look at the devastation. No one would want their child to even see this place, let alone play there.'

The mammal carcass, so badly decomposed even Harris couldn't tell what it was, flashed on the screen. 'The cost of reversing such damage, of healing the wounds, is enormous, but not insurmountable.'

The logging road, buried by the mudslide, flashed on the screens. 'And yet, for 12 years it's been easier to turn a blind eye than to look at a place that can only cry out to us, that can only convict us.' This time she most definitely looked at Jamison. 'A place that can only demand that we don't look away, that we acknowledge the things we've done, that we make restitution.'

Over the ocean-like roar in his ears, Harris could barely hear Stacie's words, spoken in the silence of a room that held its breath. Knowing that Jamison was responsible for the Bald Hill clear-cut, knowing that he was being publically accused, sent another shot of fear-charged adrenaline through Harris' body. Dear God, please let this have nothing to do with Marston's fears. Stacie wouldn't kill Jamison. She just wouldn't.

It was only by the tight gripping of Jamison's fists

at his side that Harris could gauge his response to what he clearly had not expected. And that made Harris all the more nervous.

Stacie continued, ‘What we are in the darkest of our cultural consciousness, the most greedy, the most destructive, the most brutal parts of us, must be mirrored back at us so that we can see, so that we can understand and move beyond and heal what we’ve so badly damaged.’

The pictures she had taken of the mountain lions and of Harris photographing them flashed on the screen. ‘These shots are my own reflections on what art can do for us, how it can move us, inspire us, drive us to be more than we are. They were taken up on the Crooked River where I went with Harris Walker to watch him photographing one of the millions of reasons why organizations like the Vigilant Trust are so important. If you’ve not had the chance to speak to him and to Ellison Thorne about their conception of Vigilant Trust and about their exciting plans for the future, please make sure you do. And when you’ve talked to them, I’m sure you’ll be as convinced as I am that there’s never been a more worthy cause, and that you’ll be convinced to dig deep and help create a future where humans are a part of nature rather than the cause for its destruction. Thank you.’

There was a huge round of applause, and the film loop began again, but almost before Stacie could clear the podium, Jamison grabbed her arm and steered her sharply away from her clearly adoring audience. Even before Harris fully realized what had happened, two of Jamison’s thugs ran interference to keep him and Ellis from Stacie. While Jamison hurried her out of the room, Flannery showed up, looking the worse for the wear.

'My people are on the door,' he said breathlessly, nodding to where Jamison and Stacie had vanished. 'They won't leave without us knowing.'

'Jesus,' Harris blurted. 'Where the hell have you been? What happened?'

Flannery raised a neatly folded white handkerchief to a swollen lip to check for bleeding. 'Let's just say someone didn't want me at this little soiree.'

Chapter Thirty-two

The Rubicon had been crossed; Stacie knew it by Jamison's bruising grip on her arm and by the way his breath came in angry little puffs against the back of her neck as he half escorted, half dragged her upstairs to her office. He practically shoved her through the door, shut it hard behind him and locked it. Then he offered her a smile that was tight with patience she knew he didn't have.

'What? Did you think your friends would rescue you? Is that why you pulled such a ridiculous stunt? What an incredible amount of confidence you have in your tree-hugging boyfriend and Thorne and his lackeys, you stupid woman. Surely you didn't think just because you were here now instead of New York that the troops would rally, did you?

Keeping her eyes on his clenched fists, she backed slowly away from him until she felt her desk pressing comfortingly against the backs of her thighs. Then carefully, willing her hands to be steady, she felt her way along the desktop until her fingers traced the recessed grip of the middle drawer.

'I don't give a fuck about the Bald Hill clear-cut,' he was saying while Stacie struggled to pull the drawer open, shielding it as much as she could with her body, hoping against hope he wouldn't notice until she found what she was looking for. 'I didn't give a fuck when it happened, and I don't give a fuck now. I've stood with a smile on my face while people with far more power than you'll ever have tried to point an accusing finger at me, and you know what, Stacie, every single time I walked away unscathed.'

Slowly, cautiously, she inserted her hand into the breach and felt for it. All she needed was just to get to it. She knew exactly where it was, and all she had to do was keep him ranting until she could find it. But now it was real, everything was way more difficult than it had been in her head when she planned it. When she planned it, she hadn't been pumped with fear and adrenaline.

'After your little display here, darling, I'm going to take special pleasure in the clear-cutting of the forest in Valderia, down to the very last tree. In fact, I'm going to do my best to expedite a speedy deal and see that logging begins ASAP. Your boyfriend and your ex-boyfriend will have you to thank for that.' And, just like that, he changed the subject. 'Where's the necklace?'

'It's in the safe,' she managed, amazed that her voice sounded so calm. 'The pearls have sentimental value, and I wanted to wear them for the closing speech.' And then it happened: her wriggling finger touched it, practically jammed up against it, and the solid feel of it was so welcome that she wanted to weep with relief.

In a heartbeat, he was on her, his hand twisting the pearls around her neck. 'I don't give a damn how much sentimental value they have.' He tightened and twisted them until they cut into her neck, until she couldn't breathe. 'I asked you to wear my necklace. Perhaps you didn't understand –' He tightened the pearls again. Bright spots of color exploded before her eyes, and she fought to stay conscious. 'It wasn't meant to be a request, Stacie. It was a demand, and you were to obey. Surely you remember the rules.' Then he gave the pearls a hard yank and the necklace broke and bounced and scattered in a flurry of bright white across the desk and the floor by the window. Stacie caught her breath with a rasping cough as he slid his hand onto her throat and rested it there at the ready, twitchy and heavy. She did her best to brace herself, breathing hard, trying to get as much oxygen as she could just in case.

He laughed, then kissed her roughly and bit her lip. 'Here's the reason I wanted you to wear the choker, sweetheart; it's an exquisite cover-up for bruises.'

'You think I don't remember?' The venom in her voice felt almost as strangling as the necklace had been. 'An expensive necklace isn't nearly enough to cover the damage you leave.' It wasn't that she didn't expect the slap. It was just such an insult to her body, and her body hadn't tolerated such insults in a long time. It felt as though he'd broken her neck with the harsh snap-back of the impact, and she tasted blood where she'd bitten the inside of her mouth. She blinked hard, her eyes now watering from the sting. She straightened her shoulders and faced him.

He kissed her again, this time almost tenderly, and he very gently ran his hand over the red mark on her cheek. 'Darling, you know you shouldn't provoke me. Back in New York, the first time we were together, I had only Zoe to use as leverage against you, and her death left me with no other choice but to … use force. But things change, Stacie sweetheart, things change. Now you have so many friends, so many people you care about. Now I have all kinds of leverage. I'll hardly have to lay a hand on you when Harris Walker is never more than a phone call away.' His soft laugh was humorless and cold. He kissed her as though they were simply two lovers having a bit of pillow talk. His hand even strayed to stroke her breast. 'I'm delighted, really. Look how badly you suffered for poor Ingrid Watson, and I barely had a chance to play with her. Then, when Hearn was stupid enough to get himself blown up in Harris Walker's place, honestly, I don't know what was the most moving – how you ran straight to plead for Walker's life or how you suffered such guilt over Hearn's misfortune.'

'My men tell me Jamison had the place well-guarded, but nothing they can't handle,' Flannery said. 'I've already turned off the remaining alarm sensors just in case. Harris, you and I and Daniels here –' he nodded to one of his men, dressed in a black tux '– will wait upstairs at the office door. We'll detain Jamison while you take Stacie, and no one gets hurt.'

Harris was about to say that if Jamison got hurt, he was more than OK with that, when there was a gasp and a shudder among the crowd. All eyes were riveted to the big screens. Everyone looked up just in time to see Terrance Jamison yank the string of pearls he'd been choking Stacie Emerson with until they broke.

'Fuck,' Flannery whispered. 'I didn't see that one coming. Now I understand why Stacie wanted such an elaborate security system. Turn it up,' he shouted to Jenny, who was looking on in horror. Then he turned his attention back to Harris and the others. 'Jamison is about to hang himself with his own rope. Turn up the volume. Now!' he shouted at Jenny again. She did as he asked, just in time for the startled crowd to see Jamison slap Stacy brutally.

With a guttural growl, Harris exploded into action, racing for the stairs, racing to get to Stacie, racing to get her to safety.

On the sound system, everyone Jamison say, 'I can take any of them out in a heartbeat, and you would do well to remember that. I can take any of them out just like I did Zoe.'

The spike of fear and adrenaline and unadulterated hatred for Jamison drove Harris onward. Two of Jamison's men cut him off before he could mount the stairs. They were immediately distracted by two of Flannery's men and the scuffle was on, but Harris didn't have time to wait for the showdown to finish. He needed to get to Stacie now.

Looking around desperately, he headed into the small lounge, where a knot of people were huddled in horror in front of the computer monitor, listening as Jamison said, 'It's all about acquisitions. You've been to my penthouse in Manhattan. You know that I love to collect beautiful things, Stacie, and you know that I always get what I want. I wanted you for my own from the first time I saw you, all enthusiastic and full of innovative ideas for that washed-up gallery, ideas that, by God, you made work. I wanted to break you like I did Zoe. And you should have been easy, but you weren't. And that made me want you all the more. You were smart, you were untamed, you were outrageously talented and you thought you were above it all. I rose to the challenge, and believe me, in my business there aren't that many challenges to rise to any more. And now – well, you see for yourself I can bring down a country and place whoever I want in the seat of control. But, like most powerful men, I need entertainment. I need a diversion. Everyone does, Stacie, everyone does.'

With Terrance Jamison's voice still mesmerizing and horrifying everyone in the gallery, Harris slipped through the patio doors outside the small lounge, which no one was guarding at the moment. He didn't know how long that would last, since things were in chaos and getting worse. He thrust himself up onto a trellis, which was draped in a good-size wisteria, and began to climb. He caught a glimpse in his peripheral vision of several men he recognized as working for Flannery. Somewhere far off, he heard a siren wail. He hoped that help was on its way. Jesus, the woman was fucking brilliant! The amount of patience and scheming that had gone into her plan was amazing, and it would work too, if it didn't get her killed first. He wasn't about to let that happen.

When the trellis ran out, leaving him with a good bit of climbing yet to do before he reached the dormer she had renovated to a sunroom, he was happy he had a few basic climbing skills, skills that had served him well when photographing certain birds of prey. He raised himself onto his toes and managed to reach the window ledge above him. The window was barred, which prevented his entrance, but helped him get the grip he needed to swing himself up. From there, it was an easy reach to the guttering where he could shinny onto the roof and edge his way along to the dormer. He was glad that Flannery had managed to turn off the rest of the alarm sensors. He was sure Stacie would have had the windows on the dormer wired. What she hadn't done was replace the antique glass windows at the front of the dormer with modern safety glass, which meant that, with any luck, Harris could break his way in and come out in the sunroom of the lounge next to Stacie's office. When he reached the dormer, to his surprise the window was unlocked. Had she somehow known that he would come for her? He liked that thought, and it spurred him on.

'Now, get your handbag, Stacie. We've got a plane to catch to New York. You lucked out this time; I'm in a forgiving mood.' He grabbed her hand and pulled her toward the door, but she jerked away.

'For how long, Terrance? Until you get bored with me and kill me like you did Zoe? I know you killed her. I've always known it.'

His lips curled into a snarl of a smile. 'I suspected you knew. And really, darling, I wasn't trying to hide it, at least not from you. You and I were probably the only two people who knew that Zoe would never commit suicide. But you know, Stacie, she was weak, and I was bored with her. It wasn't hard to make her do it with a little … help.

She closed her eyes and felt her knees go weak. She had waited ten long years to hear his confession. Ten long years of nightmares, of anger, of second-guessing herself, of wondering what she might have done differently. It was as though he read her mind.

'You couldn't have saved her, darling. She came

between you and me. And that I couldn't have. So there's nothing you could have done. There. You're absolved. Is that what you were waiting for? Is that what you needed, Stacie, absolution? Now come on, let's go.'

Before she could respond, before she could tell him she wasn't going, he lunged and yanked the desk drawer open. She cried out as Jamison shoved her aside and rummaged through the drawer. 'Is this what you were looking for, you duplicitous little bitch?' In his hand, he held the Glock. With one eye on her, he checked the gun for ammo and laughed as though it were funniest thing ever. 'And it's loaded too. Tell me, were you going to use it on me? Because you know what, I don't think you could do it.' He waved the gun around wildly. 'No matter how badly you hate me, I don't think you've got the balls to pull the trigger.' He laughed again. 'That's what separates the men from the boys, Stacie, how willing they are to do what has to be done. And I don't think you can do it.'

Before she could take another breath, he pulled her to him, her back against his front, holding her around the waist, putting pressure on her fingers until she was sure he would break them. As she opened her mouth to cry out, he forced the gun between her lips until the end of the barrel pressed hard against the roof of her mouth. And dear God, it was her fingers, her own fingers curled around the trigger. Terror tightened around her in a suffocating squeeze. She stopped breathing, she stopped moving. If she could have, she would have willed her heart to stop beating, to hold still, as she held everything else still, forcing herself to stay calm, forcing herself to think.

His laugh burned against her ear. 'You wanted to know how I did it. You've always wanted to know how I did it. Well, this is it, Stacie, this is the magic formula.' He kissed her ear in a gesture that was beyond obscene under the circumstances. 'Zoe's own little hand did the work. Zoe's fingerprints were on the gun. No one else's. Just like yours are now.'

She closed her eyes and took a deep breath. The taste of metal receded and she relaxed. If she died, she died, but at least this time everyone would know, and Zoe would be vindicated. And Jamison wouldn't hurt anyone else. And Harris – dear God, she wished that she'd told him how much she loved him. In fact, until this very second, she hadn't even realized just how much. It would have been good with the two of them. It would have been so good.

'Zoe was too weak to fight back,' Jamison said against her ear. 'Therefore it looked very real. In fact, no one even questioned except you. But then you were the one who found her, and only seconds after her heart-breaking suicide. Only seconds after, and me there with her. Just as anxious as you were to get there before our dear friend did something foolish.' He kissed her temple, then pulled the gun out of her mouth, and Stacie fell to her knees, a sob ripping its way through her throat.

'Come now, darling. Don't cry. I would never end your life that way. I've looked forward to enjoying your company for a long time. Now be a good girl and get your handbag. The plane's waiting.'

Downstairs, the horrified guests literally screamed at the surround-sound vision of what was going on in

Stacie's office. Flannery's men had managed to subdue Jamison's and the police were on their way. Flannery, along with Wade and Ellis, who wouldn't be denied, stormed the stairs to Stacie's office.

'The place is a fucking fortress,' Ellis hissed as Flannery picked the lock on the second set of fire doors.

'It's just a gallery, and an upscale one,' Flannery hissed back. 'But the woman insisted that it be air-tight and all-seeing.' He gave an off-handed nod to the security camera above them. 'Not only can she see from the monitors what's going on anyplace in the gallery – even the crappers if she's so inclined – but she can turn the tables so the monitors downstairs can also tap into the security cameras, any of them. Even the ones in her office.'

Wade let out a low whistle. 'Impressive.'

'Bloody genius,' Flannery said, shoving the door open. 'And there's me thinking all the time that it was overkill. The woman knew exactly what she was doing. If she'd have let me in on the plan, I'd have told her she was totally insane.'

'You'd have been right,' Ellis said as they dashed down the hall toward the office.

Harris' heart started beating again when Jamison took the gun from Stacie's mouth and shoved her onto the hardwood floor. Now there was something he could do. Now he was no longer helpless. He crept around the open door of the security booth until he was directly behind Jamison. Every muscle in his body ached to tackle the man, to pound him to a bloody pulp, to make him eat the gun he held and every bullet in it. But he did hold the gun, and though it wasn't exactly aimed at Stacie, it wasn't far enough from her to suit Harris, so he waited. And listened.

'Get up.' Jamison's voice was soft, but lethal. 'And make yourself presentable. We're leaving, and I don't want a bawling, cringing, frump on my arm.'

The room, which already felt tight to the breaking point, crackled with anger and rage that made the hair on the back of Harris' neck rise. None of that anger, none of that rage belonged to Jamison. Stacie pushed herself to her feet, to her full height, shoulders thrown back, hands hanging in loose fists at her side. 'I'm not going anywhere with you, Terrance. I'm staying right here.'

'It looks like I'm going to have to teach you the difference between a request and an order, Stacie.' He drew back to hit her with the gun, but this time she raised her arm and his efforts deflected off her forearm with a bruising thud.

And in that moment, Harris pounced with a growl that burned through his chest like fire, and all the anger, all the fury he had been holding, storing up for Jamison, joined the maelstrom of rage. He wrestled the man to the floor, grappling to pin him, one hand wrapped tight around Jamison's wrist, his fingers digging into sinew to get him to drop the gun.

A well-aimed kick by Stacie caught the man in the ribs and narrowly missed Harris' thigh. It was a glancing blow, but it was enough of one that the gun fell from Jamison's hand and skittered across the floor. Then Harris dragged him to his feet.

In spite of the situation in which he now found himself, Jamison was laughing. 'You'll both live to regret this,' he said, his gaze locked on Stacie, who picked up the gun. 'Well, at least one of you will live to regret this, and then end up behind bars for a long, long time.' He took in the room and the situation. 'Who knew that Stacie Emerson held such a grudge against me? But it was confirmed downstairs with that closing speech, flashing pictures of the Bald Hill clear-cut all over, letting it be known just how special that place used to be to her. And I'm sure if it was investigated far enough she'll turn out to have long-running connections with eco-terrorists. Oh, I can make it all happen, Stacie. You know I can. And here I am, showing up innocent and unaware that Stacie Emerson has a hidden agenda. Oh, it doesn't really matter what all of your cohorts say, you have no proof of anything I've just said, and I've been giving you money. In your financial situation, who knows what you might try to pull?'

Calmly, almost regally, in complete control once again, Stacie went to her laptop and, with a few keystrokes, brought up what the cameras in her office were recording.

He shrugged. 'What? Are you going to tweet about how much fun you had at your little exhibition? Would you like me to smile pretty for the camera?'

'What you're seeing right now, Terrance –' she spat his name as though it were something vile '– is what everyone in the gallery has been seeing for the past 15 minutes.' She nodded down to the still open drawer of the desk and to the little button along the side. 'I wasn't reaching for the gun. That was only for just in case. I was making sure everyone in the gallery heard every word you said and saw every move you made.' She walked to him and stood nearly nose to nose with him. 'And all of it, every single bit of it was paid for with my money. I don't need a penny from you. I never did. But I do believe in payback.' She nodded to their image on the security monitor. 'No one believes in payback more than I do. And now, for the first time in ten years, I've paid you back, in full, Terrance Jamison. In full! Just like I promised.'

As the color drained from Jamison's face and he looked desperately for a way out, the door burst open and Flannery shoved his way in, his gun already drawn and leveled at Jamison. Ellis and Wade were right behind him. Then, with a grace and poise that completely belied the horrid situation she'd just been in, Stacie turned and walked back to Harris, kissed him hard on the mouth, and took his hand in hers.

Astonishingly, Jamison was laughing again. 'Do you think you've won, Stacie? Do you really think I'd let you? I promise your victory'll be short-lived and empty.'

Harris didn't see from where Jamison pulled the gun. He hadn't even considered that the man might have a concealed weapon. He saw a flash of metal as Jamison leveled it at him. Then Stacie yelled like a banshee and launched herself at him, shoving him out of the way just as the gun went off. They tumbled in a heap to the floor and rolled until Harris felt the edge of the sofa at his back. 'Are you all right? Are you all right?' They were both yelling at once, each trying to reassure the other. It all happened so fast and, even as Flannery made a dive for Jamison, the gun went off again and there was an explosion of red, lurid and thick from the back of Jamison's head. Then he fell to the floor, gun still clenched in a reflexive grip, the corners of his mouth fixed in what could have passed for the grotesque remains of a smile from a joke that was on him. And in between, his lips were parted to swallow the barrel of the weapon back at the perfect angle, an angle he'd have known from experience.

Then the police burst through the door and everyone was talking at once. Harris scrambled to his feet and helped Stacie up. Before he could do more than steady her, before he could pull her back, she moved to Jamison's body. For a second, she stood looking down at him, her chest rising and falling like she'd just run a marathon. Then she said softly, 'I paid you back, you sonovabitch. I paid you back just like I said I would. For Zoe!'

There was a collective gasp of surprise as she drew back her leg and kicked his corpse hard. 'For Ingrid!' This time her voice was more like a loud growl as she kicked him again, a growl that got louder with each kick. Her eyes were chillingly dry and the fire in them was nothing less than pure hatred. Everyone looked on, but no one made an effort to stop her. 'For Kenny Hearn!' She kicked him again and again. 'And for all you stole from all of us, for everyone you hurt! I paid you back. I paid you back. I paid you back!' The final kick was with such force that she nearly lost her balance, but for Harris wrapping his arms around her and guiding her away.

The police officer in charge nodded toward the door. 'Don't go far, but it might be wise if you get her out of here.'

She said nothing as Harris guided her down the stairs, his arm still wrapped protectively around her.

She neither trembled nor did she cry. But she moved in a state of calm that chilled him. As they passed through the main exhibition hall, where once again the film loop was playing mindlessly, the stunned crowd parted for them to walk through. A few people began to clap softly, and then a few more and a few more until the whole hall echoed with applause. But Stacie only stared straight in front of her. Jenny handed Harris a bottle of water and stroked Stacie's arm briefly as they passed.

Outside, the night air was fresh and unusually warm for autumn and Venus hung lazily just above the treeline. Harris guided her around to the small sculpture garden and settled her down on a marble bench. Once she was seated, he opened the water and handed it to her. She sipped, and handed it back, but he refused.

'Drink more,' he said, taking off his jacket and draping it over her shoulders. You're in shock.'

'I'm fine,' she said, trying to push the bottle back at him. 'I'm fine now.'

'Are you trained in first aid? I don't think so, now drink the damned water and sit still while I check you out.' How could she be so calm when she had been through such a nightmare, when she'd practically gotten herself killed? He sure as hell wasn't calm. He figured psychotherapy was imminent, but he'd cross that bridge when he came to it. At the moment, all that mattered was that Stacie was safe here with him.

She sipped the water, then grabbed his hand and pulled him down next to her. 'I think maybe you're in shock, Mr. Walker, and you'll feel better if you just hold me.'

He couldn't argue with that logic. He took her into his arms and heard the little grunt of air he'd forced from her lungs in his enthusiasm to get close to her, to reassure himself that she was alive and well and free of Jamison for good. 'I think you might be right,' he said. 'I feel better already. Sure you don't have some first aid training?'

'Just good instincts,' she said as she offered him the bottle of water.

He took a long pull, then handed it back. 'You're gonna have one helluva a black eye,' he said, pushing the hair away from her face and examining it gently.

She ignored his comment and pulled away just enough to look up into his gaze. 'I love you,' she said with no preamble. 'I have to tell you that. I wanted to tell you for a while, but I couldn't, and after what happened … I was afraid I'd never get to tell you. I was afraid …' Her voice drifted off. and she nuzzled back into his arms. This time she was trembling. 'I love you,' she whispered against his shoulder.

Harris closed his eyes and rested his chin against the top of her head. 'I've waited a long time to hear you say that.'

'I plan to say it a lot now that … things are settled. I hope you don't mind.'

'Can't think of any words I'd rather hear, Stacie, and I plan to say them right back, often and with great enthusiasm. I love you, Stacie Emerson, and now that you're safe, I don't plan to let you out of my sight, oh, for maybe the next 50 years or so.'

'Just try and get rid of me, Harris Walker. Just try.'

That's how Kendra and Garrett found them, sitting on the bench, wrapped in each other's arms. They were followed almost immediately by Dee and Ellis, and Marston and Wade, with Flannery bringing up the rear, an ice bag pressed to his swollen face. Then the ambulance came and the police asked questions and reporters were anxious for statements. Though even without interviews, they had way more of a story than they ever bargained for.

What felt like years later, they returned to Harris' cabin, but instead of going inside, Stacie grabbed his hand and led him to the dock. 'I don't want to go in just yet,' she said. Before he really registered what was happening, she unzipped her dress and stepped out of it. She'd lost the shoes hours ago. 'I want to wash the past few days away before we go inside so I can start fresh in the place I love with the man I love.'

'Sounds like a perfect idea,' he said, kicking out of his shoes and shoving and peeling off the remains of the tux way faster than he'd put it on. He caught a delicious glimpse of Stacie's backside followed by a heavy splash of water as she executed a cannonball that would have made any ten-year-old boy jealous. He followed suit and came up spitting water before pulling her naked and giggling against him. He kissed her throat, and ran his hands down to cup her bottom and lift her legs around his waist. 'You sure you're all right?' he asked.

'I am. I'm just so relieved it's all over.' She gave him a hard hug, and he held her tight, wrapped around him like she belonged there, like she was a part of him. At last she spoke. 'I had nightmares that I'd be too afraid, that I'd be a coward when the time came, that I wouldn't be able to do what I had to when he …

When he took me again.'

Harris pulled her still closer and stroked her hair. 'In the end Jamison was the coward, Stacie. In the end, he couldn't take responsibility for his actions.'

'I don't want to talk about him, Harris. I don't want to talk at all.' She punctuated her words with a bite of a kiss that was possessive and demanding, and Harris responded in kind. In the passionate tangle of tongues and lips, Harris forgot to tread water and they both went under to surface again sputtering and laughing. She reached down between them, took his erection into her hand, and he caught his breath in a tight groan. 'I need you to make love to me, Harris.' She was practically climbing his body as he fumbled between her legs to find her open and receptive, slickened with arousal in spite of the cold water. 'Now I'm free. Now we really can make love with nothing hanging over us.' She sucked her bottom lip with a sigh as he positioned himself and eased up inside of her, feeling the perfect fit of her like a glove, like a second skin, like his second skin.

The water made their lovemaking awkward, and thrusting was a challenge, but her grip on him was tight and pulsing, and he found that by moving his legs in a scissoring fashion each time his efforts to tread water forced him upward, he pressed deeper inside her and each time he pressed up, she grasped hard onto him. The water was cold, and they'd been separated too long not to be needy for each other. All of the adrenaline of the evening translated itself into raw, impatient sex. They came quickly, both sputtering and spitting and struggling to stay above the glassy calm of the lake as they convulsed in each other's arms.

The shed party clothes got left on the dock as they made a mad shivering dash for the house and for the warmth of the shower and more lovemaking, and then the bed.

The sky was just greying with dawn when Harris woke to find himself alone beneath the comforter. Icy panic gripped his stomach as he threw back the covers and stumbled naked to the top of the stairs. It was then that he smelled bacon cooking. Stacie stood wrapped in his plaid shirt with a spatula in her hand. She smiled up at him, raking him with a lusty gaze. 'I'm starving. You want some bacon and eggs?'

'Hell yes,' he said. He slid into a pair of sweats and joined her just as she scooped the food onto two plates and served up the coffee. As Harris settled in next to her at the breakfast bar with a sloppy kiss and a grope of her nearly exposed cleavage, he was pretty sure he could get used to this. He knew one thing for damned sure. He had every intention of making sure that Stacie Emerson got good and used to it, because he wasn't about to let her slip away now that he had her right where he wanted her.

Epilogue

Four Months Later

It was a hideous place, the place of nightmares, not the place for a park, not the place for a picnic, but nevertheless there was a gathering of people, there was laughter and chatter. There was the snapping of cameras and maneuvering of microphones by the press. Perhaps it was her imagination, perhaps it was only what she could see in her mind's eye, but Stacie could swear there was a very slight haze of green now growing over the ruinous wastes of the Bald Hill clear-cut.

There was spontaneous applause as she stepped forward to the portable podium and looked out over the sea of people dressed for the great outdoors. The rain had stopped in the night and the mud under foot wasn't nearly as bad as it could have been. She was extremely pleased by the turnout.

'Thank you all so much for coming,' she said, smiling out over the crowd. Then she turned to take in the surroundings. 'I know it looks like something out of Dante's *Inferno* at the moment, but you're no longer looking at a desolate place. You're looking at a place full of hope and promise. I was up here just last week helping to place erosion barriers, and if I'm not mistaken, I saw some of you up here doing the same.

When I used to come here as a girl, the slopes were covered with lodge pole and ponderosa pine, Pacific silver fir, and Douglas fir. I used to pick huckleberries on these slopes with Ellis and Garrett Thorne. And over there –' she pointed '– the rhodies, when they were in bloom, were so bright that you almost needed sunglasses to see them.' She paused, looking around her again. 'It's a beginning; placing the erosion barriers is a beginning. And though the process will take time, when our children's children are ready to pick huckleberries and hike these slopes so they can watch the stars from the rocky top, they'll be able to enjoy what I did, what Ellis and Garrett did, what so many others did. This is what Vigilant Trust is all about. And though it was conceived by two men I adore, one who's my dear friend and another who's my husband –'

She had to pause once more as the crowd erupted in a spontaneous cheer, and she glanced down at the wedding ring Harris Walker had placed on her finger just two days ago. She wouldn't have thought it could happen so soon, and a few months ago, she never thought she'd say yes to anyone, but it was right. It was as it should be, and if anything, the past few months had reminded her that there are no guarantees and no promises of tomorrow. You can't put a price on the present nor on the privilege of being the keeper of someone else's heart. She shot Harris a quick smile, and he smiled back.

When the crowd was quiet again, she continued. 'Though Vigilant Trust was conceived by two men I adore, it's people like you, every one of you, who make it a reality. Vigilant Trust is everyone out there who wants to leave a legacy to future generations that's rich in biodiversity, that's as endlessly beautiful and fascinating for our grandchildren and for their grandchildren as it was for me and for Ellis and Garrett Thorne. And, most importantly, we'll leave those generations a legacy of living in harmony with the natural world so that all of us, feathered, furred, scaled or human, can benefit.'

She paused again, feeling the tightening around her heart she'd known this moment would bring, feeling the sense of laying to rest something that had ached inside her for so long she'd forgotten what it was like to be free of that ache. Everyone waited politely until she gathered herself. She looked up and smiled broadly. 'Right now, you're all standing on the edge of Zoe's Woods. The trailhead will be where Wade Crittenden is standing over there with the red ribbon.' She nodded to Wade and everyone turned to look. 'Use your imagination if you would. Right now, you're standing in what will become a field of natural grasses and wildflowers, just like it was before the erosion from clear-cut destroyed it. There'll be a picnic table or two, and the rest will be left for nature to reclaim, with a little bit of coaxing from us, and from Vigilant Trust.'

Again there was applause, more prolonged this time. Then Stacie took the scissors offered to her by Ellis, who kissed her warmly on the cheek. She walked down to where Wade stood and cut the red ribbon that was staked symbolically across the place where the trailhead would be. There was another round of applause, and the crowd began to disperse, with those who had come to volunteer for the day's efforts going to the edge of the logging road where several people in park ranger uniforms waited to show them what their jobs would be.

Wade was the first to offer an uncharacteristic hug. 'Good news on all fronts,' he told her. 'Sportwide Extreme Adventures has booked their first eco-tours to Valderia and they're employing an all-Valderian staff. Looks like the failed coup has been a kick in President Vasquez's ass to protect the country's wilderness and push through some serious reforms.'

'Al sends congratulations,' Dee said, giving Stacie a bear hug. 'He says he'd do anything for you, but not tromp around in the gawddamned mud, and I quote.' She was just off the plane from Atlanta, where she'd been observing the reopening of the first of Al's refitted paper mills.

Stacie laughed at Dee's poor imitation of Al's accent, knowing full well that Al wouldn't have missed the dedication if he'd been busy reopening his mill to be the first of its kind to use the Trouvères eco-friendly technology, another win-win deal from Pneuma Inc.

'Oh, and he asked me to give you this.' Dee dug in her daypack and pulled out a padded jewelry box, completely incongruous with the place.

Stacie opened it with her heart in her throat. Sure enough, it was the restrung pearls, and displayed in the box next to them was a matching bracelet. Stacie wiped her eyes on the back of her hand, unable to hold back a tear or two that the pearls were once again ready to wear.

'He said he'd planned to give you the bracelet at the exhibition,' Dee said. 'But he thought under the circumstances the dedication of Zoe's Woods was the perfect time to give them to you.'

As Stacie carefully closed the box and placed it in her bag, Kendra and Garrett group-hugged her, nearly smothering her in their congratulatory enthusiasm. K. Ryde was already hard at work on a PR program for Vigilant Trust that was nothing short of genius. But, of course, K. Ryde didn't attend the dedication.

From where he stood talking to his daughter, who was there with the press, Martin Flannery gave her two thumbs up. And was Stacie mistaken or was Wade giving Carla Flannery the eye? OK, so she was a bit of a romantic these days, but stranger things had been known to happen.

Yes, stranger things had been known to happen, she thought as her gaze sought out Harris, and the butterfly dance in her stomach erupted at the sight of him. Her husband; he was now officially her husband. She still could hardly get her head round the thought. He stood a little bit away from the knot of friendly faces talking on his BlackBerry. He offered her that dry smile that always made her smile back, then he shoved the BlackBerry back in his pocket and came to her side, his eyes sparkling in a way that told her something was up.

'That was Doug,' Harris said as he gathered her to him in a deliciously possessive hug. 'He's seen our mountain lion. She has three kittens and he thinks if we're lucky and we behave ourselves she might be up for receiving a visit from old friends. What do you say to that, wife?'

'I say pack up the Jeep and let's go, husband. Ingrid Watson won't be coming here till next week to discuss her exhibition, and until then, there's nothing that Jenny can't do without me.'

She lifted her arms around his neck and he took her mouth in a long and lingering kiss.

'Get a room, you two!' Garrett Thorne teased.

Harris flipped him the finger with one hand while the other gave Stacie's backside a solicitous grope.

'Galina's cooked up a feast back home,' Ellis said. 'It'd be a shame to let it get cold.' He nodded toward the road and slid an arm around Dee's waist as the procession headed in that direction. 'Besides,' he said, offering one of his winning smiles to Stacie and Harris, 'you haven't really had a chance to celebrate your nuptials with your friends yet. You caught us all by surprise.'

It had been a surprise, Stacie thought, but it was right. And when Harris had asked her to marry him after a picture-perfect Central Oregon day kayaking on the Deschutes River – well, neither of them could really think of any reason to wait. Stacie looked around at the small knot of friends, the people she had come to love. She would never have imagined a few short months ago that she could be this happy, that her life could ever be so full again. She sometimes wondered if it were only a dream. But then the man walking beside her with his arm around her waist leaned in close, gave her ear a humid kiss, and said, 'I love you, Stacie Emerson-Walker. God, I like the sound of that, don't you?'

And she did. She truly did. It was the most beautiful sound she had ever heard.

The Executive Decision Trilogy
By Grace Marshall

Lightning Source UK Ltd.
Milton Keynes UK
UKOW03f1643040614

232826UK00001B/3/P

9 781908 917843